The Last Train to London

ALSO BY MEG WAITE CLAYTON

Beautiful Exiles

The Race for Paris

The Wednesday Sisters

The Four Ms. Bradwells

The Language of Light

The Wednesday Daughters

THE
LAST TRAIN
TO LONDON

A NOVEL

Meg Waite Clayton

HARPER

An Imprint of HarperCollins*Publishers*

THE LAST TRAIN TO LONDON. Copyright © 2019 by Meg Waite Clayton, LLC. All rights reserved. Printed in the United States of America. No part of this book may be used or reproduced in any manner whatsoever without written permission except in the case of brief quotations embodied in critical articles and reviews. For information, address HarperCollins Publishers, 195 Broadway, New York, NY 10007.

HarperCollins books may be purchased for educational, business, or sales promotional use. For information, please email the Special Markets Department at SPsales@harpercollins.com.

FIRST EDITION

Designed by Bonni Leon-Berman

Library of Congress Cataloging-in-Publication Data has been applied for.
ISBN 978-0-06-294693-5

19 20 21 22 23   LSC   10 9 8 7 6 5 4

FOR NICK

and in memory of

Michael Litfin

(1945–2008),

who carried the stories of the

Kindertransport to my son,

who carried them home to me,

and

Truus Wijsmuller-Meijer

(1896–1978)

and the children she saved

I remember: it happened yesterday, or eternities ago. . . .
And now that very boy is turning to me. "Tell me," he says,
"what have you done with my years, what have you done
with your life?" . . . One person of integrity, of courage, can
make a difference, a difference of life and death.

*—Elie Wiesel, from his Nobel Peace Prize acceptance speech,
delivered in Oslo on December 10, 1986*

AUTHOR'S NOTE

Following Germany's annexation of the independent country of Austria in March 1938 and the violence of Kristallnacht that November, an extraordinary attempt to bring ten thousand children to safety in Britain began. Although fiction, this novel is based on the real Vienna Kindertransport effort led by Geertruida Wijsmuller-Meijer of Amsterdam, who had begun rescuing smaller groups of children as early as 1933. She was, to the children, Tante Truus.

Part I

THE

TIME BEFORE

AT THE BORDER

Stout flakes softened the view out the train window: a snow-covered castle on a snow-covered hill ghosting up through the snowy air, the conductor calling, "Bad Bentheim; this is Bad Bentheim, Germany. Passengers continuing to the Netherlands must provide documents." Geertruida Wijsmuller—a Dutchwoman with a strong chin and nose and brow, a wide mouth, cashmere-gray eyes—kissed the baby on her lap. She kissed him a second time, her lips lingering on his smooth forehead. She handed him to his sister then, and pulled the skullcap off their toddler brother. "Es ist in Ordnung. Es wird nicht lange dauern. Dein Gott wird dir dieses eine Mal vergeben," Truus responded to the children's objections, in their own language. *It's all right. It will be only for a few moments. Your God will forgive us this once.*

As the train heaved to a stop, the little boy leapt to the window, shouting, "Mama!"

Truus gentled his hair as she followed his gaze out the snow-dirty glass to see Germans in orderly lines on the platform despite the storm, a porter with a loaded luggage cart, a stooped man in a sandwich board, advertising a tailor. Yes, there was the woman the child saw—a slim woman in a dark coat and scarf standing at a sausage vendor, her back to the train as the boy again called to her, "Maaa-maaa!"

The woman turned, idly taking a greasy bite of sausage as she gazed up at the split-flap board. The boy crumpled. Not his mother, of course.

Truus pulled the child to her, whispering, "There there, there there," unable to make promises that could not be kept.

The carriage doors opened with a startling clatter and hiss. A Nazi border guard on the platform reached up to help a debarking passenger, a pregnant German who accepted his help with a gloved hand. Truus unfastened the pearl buttons on her own yellow leather day gloves and loosened the scalloped cuffs with their delicate black accents. She pulled the gloves off, the leather catching on a ruby solitaire nestled with two other rings as, with hands just beginning to freckle and crepe, she wiped away the boy's tears.

She tidied the children's hair and clothes, addressing each again by name but working quickly, keeping an eye on the dwindling line of passengers.

"All right now," she said, wiping the drool from the baby's mouth as the last passengers disembarked. "Go wash your hands, just as we practiced."

Already the Nazi border guard was mounting the stairs.

"Go on, go quickly now, but take your time washing up," Truus said calmly. To the girl she said, "Keep your brothers in the lavatory, sweetheart."

"Until you put back on your gloves, Tante Truus," the girl said.

It was necessary that Truus not seem to be hiding the children, yet nor did she want them too close for this negotiation. *So we fix our eyes not on what is seen, but on what is unseen*, she thought, unconsciously putting the ruby to her lips, like a kiss.

She opened her pocketbook, a more delicate thing than she would have carried had she known she'd be returning to Amsterdam with three children in tow. She fumbled inside it, removing her rings as the children, now behind her, traipsed away down the aisle.

Ahead, the border guard appeared. He was a young man, but not so young that he might not be married, might not have children of his own.

"Visas? You have visas to leave Germany?" he demanded of Truus, the sole adult remaining in the carriage.

Truus continued rooting in her bag as if to extract the required papers. "Children can be such a handful, can't they?" she replied warmly as she fingered her single Dutch passport, still in the handbag. "You have children, Officer?"

The guard offered an unsanctioned hint of a smile. "My wife, she's expecting our first child, perhaps on Christmas Day."

"How fortunate for you!" Truus said, smiling at her own good fortune as the guard glanced toward the sounds of water running in a sink, the children chattering as sweetly as bramble finches. She let the thought sit with him: he would soon have a baby not unlike little Alexi, who would grow into a child like Israel or dear, dear Sara.

Truus fingered the ruby—sparkling and warm—on the lone ring she now wore. "You have something special for your wife, to mark the occasion, I'm sure."

"Something special?" the Nazi repeated, returning his attention to her.

"Something beautiful to wear every day, to remember a most special moment." She removed the ring, saying, "My father gave this to my mother the day I was born."

Her pale, steady fingers offered the ruby ring, along with her single passport.

He eyed the ring skeptically, then took the passport alone, examined it, and glanced again to the back of the carriage. "These are your children?"

Dutch children could be included on their parents' passports, but hers listed none.

She turned the ruby to catch the light, saying, "They're more precious than anything, children."

BOY MEETS GIRL

Stephan burst out the doors and down the snow-covered steps, his satchel thwacking at his school blazer as he sprinted for the Burgtheater. At the stationery store, he pulled up short: The typewriter was still there, in the window display. He pushed his glasses up on his nose, put his fingers to the window glass, and pretended to type.

He ran on, weaving his way through the Christkindlmarkt crowds, the smells of sweet mulled glühwein and gingerbread, saying "Sorry. Sorry! Sorry," and keeping his cap low to avoid recognition. They were fine people, his family: their wealth came from their own chocolate business established with their own capital, and they kept their accounts always on the credit side at the Rothschild bank. If it got back to his father that he'd knocked down another old lady on the street, that typewriter would remain nearer the light-strung pine tree here in the Rathausplatz than the one in the winter gallery at home.

He waved to the old man tending the newsstand. "Good afternoon, Herr Kline!"

"Where is your overcoat, Master Stephan?" the old man called after him.

Stephan glanced down—he'd left his coat at school again—but he slowed only when he reached the Ringstrasse, where a Nazi pop-up protest blocked the way. He ducked into a poster-plastered kiosk and clanged down the metal stairs into the darkness of the Vienna underworld, to emerge on the Burgtheater side of the street. He bolted through the theater doors and took the stairs by twos down to the basement barbershop.

"Master Neuman, what a great surprise!" Herr Perger said, raising white eyebrows over spectacles as round and black as Stephan's, if less snow-splattered. The barber was bent low, sweeping the last of the day's hair clippings into a dustpan. "But didn't I—"

"Just a quick clip. It's been a few weeks."

Herr Perger straightened his back and discarded the hair into a trash bin, then set the broom and dustpan next to a cello leaning against the wall. "Ah well, memory doesn't fit as readily into an old mind as into a young one, I suppose," he offered warmly, nodding to the barber chair. "Or perhaps it doesn't fit as well into that of a young man with money to spare?"

Stephan dropped his satchel, a few pages of his new play spilling out onto the floor, but what did it matter, Herr Perger knew he wrote plays. He shucked his blazer, settled in the chair, and removed his glasses. The world went fuzzy, the cello and the broom now a couple waltzing in the corner, his face in the mirror above his tie anyone's face. He shivered as Herr Perger draped the cape around him; Stephan despised haircuts.

"I heard they might be starting rehearsals for a new play," he said. "Is it a Stefan Zweig?"

"Ah, yes, you are such a fan of Herr Zweig. How could I have forgotten?" Otto Perger said, mocking Stephan somehow, but kindly, and anyway Herr Perger knew every secret there was to know about the playwrights and the stars and the theater. Stephan's friends had no idea where Stephan got his inside scoops; they thought he knew someone important.

"Herr Zweig's mother still lives here in Vienna," Stephan said.

"Yet rarely does he advertise his visits from London. Well, at the risk of causing disappointment, Stephan, this new play is a Csokor, *3. November 1918*, about the end of the Austro-Hungarian Empire. There has been quite a lot of whispering and intrigue as to whether it will even be performed. I'm afraid Herr Csokor must live with his suitcase packed. But I'm told it *is* going forward, albeit with the publicity to include a disclaimer that the playwright means no offense to any nation of the former German empire. A little of this, a little of that, whatever it takes to survive."

Stephan's father would have objected that this was Austria, not Germany; the Nazi coup here had been put down years ago. But Stephan didn't care about politics. Stephan only wanted to know who would play the lead.

"Perhaps you would like to guess?" Herr Perger suggested as he turned Stephan toward him in the chair. "You are quite clever at that, as I recall."

Stephan kept his eyes closed, involuntarily shivering again even though, mercifully, no bits of hair landed on his face. "Werner Krauss?" he guessed.

"Well, there you are!" Herr Perger said with surprising enthusiasm.

Herr Perger turned the chair back to the mirror, leaving Stephan startled to see—blurrily, without his glasses—that the barber was not applauding his guess but rather addressing a girl emerging like a surrealist sunflower sprouting from a heating grate in the wall below Stephan's reflection. She stood right in front of him, all smudged glasses and blond braids and budding breasts.

"Ach, Žofie-Helene, your mama will be scrubbing that dress all night," Herr Perger said.

"That wasn't really a fair question, Grandpapa Otto—there are *two* male leads," the girl said brightly, her voice catching somewhere inside Stephan, like the first high B-flat of Schubert's "Ave Maria," her voice and the lyrical sound of her name, Žofie-Helene, and the nearness of her breasts.

"It's a lemniscate of Bernoulli," she said, fingering a gold pendant necklace. "Analytically the zero set of the polynomial X squared plus Y squared minus the product of X squared minus Y squared times two A squared."

"I . . . ," Stephan stammered through the blush of shame at being caught staring at her breasts, even if she didn't realize he had been.

"My papa gave it to me," she said. "He liked mathematics too."

Herr Perger unfastened the cape, handed Stephan his glasses, and waved away the cupronickel Stephan offered, saying there was no charge this time. Stephan stuffed the script pages back into his satchel, not wanting this girl to see his play, or that he had a play, that he imagined he might write anything worth reading. He paused, puzzled: *The floor was completely clean?*

"Stephan, this is my granddaughter," Otto Perger said, the scissors still in hand and the broom and dustpan beside the cello untouched. "Žofie, Stephan here may be at least as interested in the theater as you are, if somewhat more inclined toward tidy hair."

"Very nice to meet you, Stephan," the girl said. "But why did you come for a haircut you didn't need?"

"*Žofie-Helene*," Herr Perger scolded.

"I was sleuthing through the grate. You didn't need a haircut, so Grandpapa Otto only pretended to cut it. But wait, don't tell me! Let me deduce." She looked about the room, at the cello and the coatrack and her grandfather and, again, Stephan himself. Her gaze settled on his satchel. "You're an actor! And Grandpapa knows everything about this theater."

Otto Perger said, "I believe you will find, *Engelchen*, that Stephan is a writer. And you must know that the greatest writers do the strangest things simply for the experience."

Žofie-Helene peered at Stephan with new interest. "Are you really?"

"I . . . I'm getting a typewriter for Christmas," Stephan said. "I hope I am."

"Do they make special ones?"

"Special?"

"Does it feel queer to be left-handed?"

Stephan considered his hands, confused, as she reopened the grate from which she'd emerged and climbed on hands and knees back into the wall. A moment later, she poked her head out again. "Do come on then, Stephan; rehearsals are nearly over," she said. "You won't mind a little dirt on your ink-stained sleeve, will you? For the experience?"

RUBIES OR PASTE

A pearl button popped off Truus's scalloped glove cuff as, with the baby in one hand, she reached out to catch the boy; he was so fascinated by the massive cast-iron dome ceiling of the Amsterdam station that he nearly tumbled from the train.

"Truus," her husband called up to her as he took the toddler in hand and set him on the platform. He helped the girl too, and Truus and the baby.

On the platform, Truus accepted her husband's embrace, a rare public thing.

"Geertruida," he said, "couldn't Frau Freier—"

"Please don't fuss at me now, Joop. What's done is done, and I'm sure the wife of that nice young guard who saw us across the border has more need of my mother's ruby than we do. Where *is* your Christmas spirit?"

"Good God, don't tell me you risked bribing a Nazi with paste?"

She kissed him on the cheek. "As you can't tell the difference yourself, darling, I don't imagine either of you will soon know."

Joop laughed despite himself, and he took the baby, holding him awkwardly but cooing—a man who loved children but had none, despite their years of trying. Truus stuck her hands, no longer warmed by the baby, into her pockets, fingering the matchbox she'd all but forgotten. Such an odd sort, the doctor in the train carriage who'd given it to her. "You were sent by God, no doubt," he'd said with a fond glance at the children. He always carried a lucky stone, he'd said, and he wanted her to have it. "To keep you and the children safe," he insisted, opening the little box to show her a flat gravelly old stone that really could have no purpose if it weren't lucky. "At Jewish funerals, one doesn't give flowers but rather stones," he said, which made the thing somehow impossible to turn down. He would collect it from her when he needed his luck back, he assured her. Then he'd debarked at Bad Bentheim, before the train crossed from Germany into the Netherlands, and now Truus was in Amsterdam with the children, thinking there might be some truth to his claim about the ugly little stone's luck-bringing charms.

"Now, little man," Joop said to the baby, "you must grow up to do some extraordinary thing, to make my foolish bride's risk of her life worthwhile." If he was troubled by this unplanned rescue, he wasn't going to object any more than he did when her trips to bring children out of Germany were planned. He kissed the baby's cheek. "I have a taxi waiting," he said.

"A taxi? Were you given a raise at the bank while I was away?" A gentle joke; Joop was a banker's banker, frugal to the core, albeit one who still called his wife of two decades his bride.

"It would be a sturdy walk to their uncle's place from the tram stop even without this snow," he said, "and Dr. Groenveld doesn't want his friend's niece and nephews to arrive with frostbite."

Dr. Groenveld's friend. That did explain it, Truus thought as they walked out into the snow-lace of tree branches, the dirt-stomp of paths, the hard white frost of canal. It was the way so much of the help of the Committee for Special Jewish Interests was doled out: nieces and nephews of Dutch citizens; friends of friends; the children of friends of business partners. So often, accidental relationships determined fate.

THE VIENNA INDEPENDENT

HITLER'S BIRTH HOME NOW A MUSEUM

Relations between Austria and Germany remain strained despite the summer accord

BY KÄTHE PERGER

BRAUNAU-AM-INN, AUSTRIA, December 20, 1936 — The owner of Adolf Hitler's birth home here has opened two of its rooms as a museum. The Austrian authorities in Linz have permitted the public display on the condition that only German visitors, and not Austrians, be allowed. In the event Austrians are found to be given entry to the museum or it becomes a demonstration site for Nazis, the museum will be closed.

The museum is made possible as a result of the Austro-German Agreement of July 11 to return our nations to "relations of a normal and friendly character." Under the agreement, Germany recognized Austria's full sovereignty and agreed to regard our political order as an internal concern upon which it will exercise no influence—a concession by Hitler, who objects to the imprisonment by our government of members of the Austrian Nazi Party.

CANDLES AT SUNRISE

Žofie-Helene approached the snow-dusted hedges and the high iron gate of the Ringstrasse palais with trepidation. She put a hand to the pink plaid scarf Grandmère had given her for Christmas, as soft as her mother's touch. This house was bigger than her entire apartment building, and far more ornate. Four tall columned stories—the bottom floor with arched doors and windows, the upper ones with high, rectangular French windows opening onto stone-railed balconies—were topped with a more modestly sized fifth floor decorated with statuary that seemed to be holding up the slate roof, or guarding the servants who must live up there. This couldn't be anyone's real house, much less Stephan's. But before she could turn back, a doorman in greatcoat and top hat emerged from a guardhouse to open the gate for her, and the carved front doors were flying open, Stephan running down steps as clear of snow as if it were summertime.

"Look! I've written a new play!" he said, thrusting a manuscript out to her. "I typed it on the typewriter I got for Christmas!"

The doorman smiled warmly. "Master Stephan, you might like to invite your guest inside?"

THE MANSION'S INTERIOR was even more daunting, with chandeliers and intricately geometric marble floors, an imperial staircase, and everywhere the most extraordinary art: birch trunks in fall with the perspective all wrong; a seaside village climbing a hill, improbably flat and cheerful; a bizarre portrait of a lady who looked very like Stephan, with his same sultry eyes and his long straight nose, his red lips and almost imperceptible chin cleft. The painted woman's hair was pulled up from her face, and her cheeks were scratched bright red in a way that was both disturbing and elegant, more beauty and blush than wound, although Žofie couldn't help but think of the latter. Bach's Cello Suite no. 1 spilled from a large salon where guests chatted beside a piano, its graceful gold-leaf top propped open to reveal a dramatic white bird with a trumpet in his claws painted even there, on its underside.

"No one else has read it yet," Stephan said in a low voice. "Not a word."

Žofie eyed the manuscript he again thrust to her. Did he really mean for her to read it now?

The doorman—Rolf, Stephan called him—prompted, "I trust your friend had a happy Christmas, Master Stephan?"

Stephan, ignoring the nudge, said to Žofie, "I've been waiting forever for you to get home."

"Yes, Stephan, my grandmère is well, and I had a lovely Christmas in Czechoslovakia, thank you for asking," Žofie-Helene said, words rewarded by an approving smile from Rolf as he took her coat and her new scarf.

She read quickly, just the opening page.

"It begins wonderfully, Stephan," she said.

"Do you think so?"

"I'll read the whole thing tonight, I promise, but if you really insist that I meet your family, I can't carry a manuscript about with me."

Stephan looked into the music salon, then took the manuscript and bounded up the stairs. His hand skirted a statue at each turn as he continued up past the second floor, where doors to a library stood open to more books than Žofie had ever imagined anyone might own.

A fashionably flat-chested woman in the salon was saying, ". . . Hitler burning books—all the interesting ones, I might add." The woman looked very like Stephan, and like the scratched-cheek portrait too, although her dark hair was parted in the middle and hung in loose curls. "The vile little man calls Picasso and Van Gogh incompetents and cheats." She fingered a pearl necklace that looped once around her neck, like Žofie's mother's did, but then looped a second time all the way down to her waist, spheres so perfect that surely if the strand ever broke, they would roll true. "'It is not the mission of art to wallow in filth for filth's sake,' he says—as if he has any idea what the mission of art is. Yet *I'm* the hysterical one?"

"Not 'hysterical,'" a man answered. "That's your word, Lisl."

Lisl. That would be Stephan's aunt, then. Stephan adored his aunt Lisl, and her husband, his uncle Michael, too.

"Freud's, actually, sweetheart," Lisl replied lightly.

"It's only the modernists who set Hitler off," Stephan's uncle Michael said. "Kokoschka—"

"Who of course got the place at the Academy of Fine Arts that Hitler imagines ought to have been his," Lisl interrupted. Hitler's drawings had been judged so poor that he wasn't even allowed to sit for the formal exam, she told them. He was left to sleep in a men's shelter, eat in a soup kitchen, sell his paintings to stores needing something to fill empty picture frames.

As the little circle laughed at her recounting, a door slid open at the far end of the entry hall. An elevator! A boy not much more than a toddler hopped down from a chair inside—a beautiful wheelchair (not his, obviously) with elaborately scrolled arms and a cane seat and back, the annuli of its wonderfully concentric brass handles and wheels perfectly proportioned. The boy wandered into the entry hall, dragging a stuffed rabbit on the floor behind him.

"Well, hello. You must be Walter," Žofie said. "And who is your rabbit friend?"

"This is Peter," Stephan's brother said.

Peter Rabbit. Žofie wished she hadn't already spent her Christmas money; she might have bought a Peter in a little blue coat like this for her sister, Jojo.

"That's my papa by my piano," the little boy said.

"Your piano?" Žofie asked. "Do you play?"

"Not terribly well," the boy said.

"But on *that* piano?"

The boy looked to the piano. "Yes, of course."

Stephan loped back downstairs, empty-handed, just as Žofie noticed the birthday cake in the salon, ablaze with tapers lit at sunrise and left burning all day, an inch an hour, in the Austrian custom. Beside it sat the most glorious tray of chocolates she had ever seen, some milk chocolate and others dark, and all different shapes, but each one decorated with Stephan's name.

"Stephan, it's your birthday?" Sixteen candles for his birthday and one for luck. "Why didn't you tell me?"

Stephan ruffled Walter's hair as the cello piece wound to a stop.

Walter exclaimed, "Me! I want to do it!" and shot off toward their father, who pulled a stool up to the Victrola.

". . . and now Zweig has fled to England and Strauss composes for the führer," their aunt Lisl was saying—words that drew Stephan's attention. Žofie-Helene did not believe in heroes, but she allowed Stephan to pull her into the salon, to better hear about his.

"You must be Žofie-Helene!" Stephan's aunt Lisl said. "Stephan, you neglected to tell me how beautiful your little friend is." She pulled a few pins from Žofie's bun, and Žofie's hair cascaded down. "Yes, that's better. If I had hair like yours, I wouldn't cut it either, never mind what's fashionable. I'm sorry Stephan's mother isn't up to greeting you, but I've promised to tell her all about you, so you must tell me everything."

"It's very nice to meet you, Frau Wirth," Žofie said. "But do continue your conversation about Herr Zweig, or Stephan will never forgive me."

Lisl Wirth laughed, a warm, tinkling ellipse, with her chin tilted slightly toward the impossibly high ceiling. "This is Käthe Perger's daughter, everyone. The editor of the *Vienna Independent*?" She turned to Žofie, saying, "Žofie-Helene, this is Berta Zuckerkandl, a journalist like your mother." Then, to the others, "Her mother who, I must say, has more courage than Zweig or Strauss."

"Really, Lisl," her husband objected, "you speak as if Hitler were on our border. You speak as if Zweig lives in exile, when he's in town this very minute."

"Stefan Zweig is here?" Stephan asked.

"He was at the Café Central not thirty minutes ago, holding forth," his uncle Michael said.

LISL WATCHED HER nephew and his little friend shoot off toward the front doors as Michael asked why Zweig had abandoned Austria, anyway.

"He isn't even a Jew," Michael said. "Not a practicing one."

"Says my gentile husband," Lisl chided gently.

"Married to the most beautiful Jew in all of Vienna," he said.

Lisl watched as Rolf stopped Stephan to hand him the girl's tired coat. Žofie-Helene looked so surprised when Stephan held it for her that Lisl nearly laughed aloud. Stephan surreptitiously breathed in the scent of the girl's hair when her back was turned, leaving Lisl to wonder if Michael had ever snuck a whiff of her hair like that when they were courting. She'd been only a year older than Stephan was now.

"Isn't young love glorious?" she said to her husband.

"She's in love with your nephew?" Michael answered. "I don't know that I'd encourage him to take up with the daughter of a rabble-rousing journalist."

"Which of her parents do you suspect of inciting mobs, darling?" Lisl asked. "Her father, who we're told committed suicide in a Berlin hotel in June of '34, just coincidentally the same night that so many of Hitler's opposition died? Or her mother, who, as a pregnant widow, took over her husband's work?"

She watched as Stephan and Žofie disappeared through the doorway, poor Rolf hurrying after them, waving the girl's forgotten scarf—an improbably beautiful pink plaid.

"Well, I couldn't say whether that girl is in love with Stephan," Lisl said, "but he's certainly smitten with her."

SEARCHING FOR STEFAN ZWEIG

Ah, *mein Engelchen* with her admirers: the playwright and the fool!" Otto Perger said to his customer. He hadn't seen his granddaughter since before Christmas, but they could hear her coming down the stairs at the far end of the hallway now, chattering with young Stephan Neuman and another boy.

"I do hope she prefers the fool," the man replied, tipping Otto generously, as always. "We writers are no good at all in love."

"I'm afraid she *is* a little sweet on the writer," Otto said, "although I'm not sure she realizes it herself." He paused, wanting to delay his client long enough to introduce him to Stephan, but the man had a driver waiting and the children's progress had stalled, as children's progress does. "Well, I'm glad you enjoyed your visit with your mother," he said.

The man hurried off, passing the children in the hallway. He was halfway up the stairs when he looked back and asked, "Which of you is the writer?"

Stephan, laughing at something Žofie was saying, didn't seem even to hear, but the other boy pointed to Stephan.

"Good luck, son. We need talented writers now more than ever."

He was gone, then, and the children were spilling into the barbershop, Žofie announcing that it was Stephan's birthday.

"All good for birth day to you, Master Neuman!" Otto said as he hugged his granddaughter, this child so like her father that Otto could hear his son in the rush of her voice; he could see Christof in her obliviousness to her smudged lenses. Even the smell of her was the same—almonds and milk and sunshine.

"That was Herr Zweig," their friend said.

"Where, Dieter?" Stephan asked.

Otto said, "Master Stephan, what have you been up to while our Žofie was away?"

Dieter said, "He was sitting right by us at the Café Central before Stephan got there too—Zweig was. With Paula Wesseley and Liane Haid, who looks very old."

Otto hesitated, oddly reluctant to admit that this big lug of a boy was right. "I'm afraid Herr Zweig was running for an aeroplane, Stephan."

"That *was* him?" Stephan's dark eyes were so full of disappointment that, with his hair on end at the crown despite all Otto's best efforts, he looked like a toddler. Otto would have liked to assure him he'd have another chance to meet his hero, but it seemed unlikely. All they'd talked about—or all Zweig had talked about, while Otto listened—was whether even London would prove far enough away from Hitler. Herr Zweig knew how Otto's Christof had died; he knew Otto understood what a flimsy thing a border was.

"I do hope you'll heed Herr Zweig's words for you, Stephan," Otto said. "He said we need talented writers like you now more than ever." Which was something, anyway: the great writer encouraging Stephan, even if the boy hadn't heard.

THE MAN IN THE SHADOW

Adolf Eichmann showed his fat new boss, Obersturmführer Wisliceny, around the Sicherheitsdienst Jewish Department, ending at his own desk, beside which sat Tier, the most beautiful slope-backed German shepherd in all of Berlin.

"Good God, he's so still he might be stuffed," Wisliceny said.

"Tier is properly trained," Eichmann responded. "We would be rid of the Jews and on to more important matters if the rest of Germany were half as disciplined."

"Trained by whom?" Wisliceny asked, taking Eichmann's own chair, asserting his superior rank.

Eichmann took the visitor's chair and snapped his fingers once, quietly, calling Tier to his side. He had assured Wisliceny that "the ropes" of SD Department II/112 were quite tidy, but they were in fact as thin and frayed as any rope Tier might have chewed. They operated out of three small rooms at the Hohenzollern Palace while the Gestapo, with its own Jewish office and far more resources, took pleasure in undermining them. Eichmann had learned the hard way, though, that complaints reflected most negatively on the complainer.

Wisliceny said, "Your paper on 'The Jewish Problem,' Eichmann—it's interesting, this idea that Jews can be provoked to leave Germany only if we dismantle their economic footing here in the Reich. But why force them to emigrate to Africa or South America rather than to other European nations? Why do we care where they go, so long as we're rid of them?"

Eichmann answered politely, "We'd not like to have their expertise in the hands of more developed countries that could benefit to our detriment, I shouldn't think."

Wisliceny narrowed his little Prussian eyes. "You imagine we Germans can't do better than foreigners aided by Jews we wish to be rid of?"

"No. No," Eichmann protested, setting a hand on Tier's head. "That isn't what I meant at all."

"And Palestine, which you include as a 'backward' country, is a British territory."

Eichmann, seeing this would only go more poorly, asked Wisliceny for his opinion on the matter, subjecting himself to an overlong bit of wind and bluster backed by an utter absence of knowledge. He listened as he forever did, storing away bits for future use and keeping to himself his own advantages. This was his job, to listen and nod while others talked, and he was very good at it. He routinely shucked his uniform for street clothes in order to infiltrate and more closely observe Berlin's Zionist groups. He'd developed a cadre of informers. He gathered information from the Jewish press. Reported on Agudath Israel. Quietly kept denunciation files. Directed arrests. Helped with Gestapo interrogations. He'd even tried to learn Hebrew to better do his job, although that had gone to rot and now everyone in all of Berlin had heard of his folly—proposing to pay a rabbi three reichsmarks per hour to teach him when he might simply have arrested the Jew and kept him imprisoned for free tutoring.

Vera was sure that blunder was the reason this know-nothing Prussian had been given the place as head of the Jewish Department that ought to have been Eichmann's, leaving him only the sop of promotion to technical sergeant and the same old tasks now to be done with a leaner staff, thanks to the party purge. But Eichmann knew that wasn't the reason he'd been denied the promotion. Who would have imagined that becoming a specialist in Zionist matters would make him too valuable as an expert to be "distracted" by administrative responsibilities?

Better to be a pug dog of a Prussian with a theology degree, a hideous laugh, and expertise at precisely nothing if you wanted to climb the Nazi ranks.

ONLY AFTER WISLICENY left for the day and Eichmann had tidied his desk did he allow Tier to move. "You are such a good boy," he said, stroking the dog's pointed ears, lingering on the velvety pink insides. "Shall we have some fun now? We're deserving of a bit of fun after that charade, aren't we?"

Tier shook his ears, then cocked his pointy snout, as expectant as Vera just before sex. Vera. Today was their second wedding anniversary. She would be waiting at their little apartment on Onkel-Herse-Strasse with their son, whose birth Eichmann had had to report to the SS Rasse und Siedlungshauptamt just as he'd had to report his marriage, after first proving Vera was of impeccable Aryan stock. He ought to go straight home to Vera's big eyes and lovely brows and round, sturdy face, her voluptuous body that was so much more inviting than the sharp-edged women now in fashion.

But he walked the long way, with Tier at perfect heel. He crossed the river and wandered the Jewish ghetto, slowly up one street and down another, just to delight at how, despite Tier's perfect behavior, children scattered at the sight of them.

A LITTLE BREAKFAST
CHOCOLATE

Truus lowered the newspaper and looked across the narrow break-fast table. "Alice Salomon has been exiled from Germany," she said, the words escaping with the shock of the news. "How can the Nazis do this? An internationally acclaimed pioneer in public health who is no threat to anyone? She's old and she's ill, and she isn't even political."

Joop set his *hagelslag* on his plate, a sprinkle of chocolate falling from the bread to the plate while another sat unnoticed at the edge of his mouth. "She's Jewish?"

Truus looked out the third-floor window, over the flowerpots on the sill to the Nassaukade and the canal, the bridge, the Raampoort. Dr. Salomon was Christian. Devotedly so, probably from a family like Truus's, affluent Christians who appreciated God's gifts to them, who'd shared those gifts by taking in Belgian children during the Great War. But telling Joop the Germans had exiled a Christian would only alarm him, and Truus didn't want to give him any reason to inquire about her plans for the day. She had hoped to go into Germany to meet with Recha Freier about what more might be done to help Berlin's Jewish children, now barred from public schools, but her message had elic-ited no response. She'd already arranged to borrow Mrs. Kramarsky's sedan, though. She could at least make another run over the border to the Weber farm.

"Some Jewish ancestry, apparently," she said, which had the advan-tage of being true, but still her gaze slid to the flowered wallpaper and the curtains that needed cleaning in this room they'd breakfasted in ever since they married. She doubted that Alice Salomon's ancestry explained her being stripped of her homeland.

"Geertruida," Joop began, and Truus braced herself. Her name had always seemed so solid and unremarkable before she'd met Joop— Geertruida or Truus, either one—but in his voice it sounded rather lovely, really. Still, he rarely called her by her full name.

That which makes a marriage work is to be guarded carefully, her mother had told her the morning of her wedding, and who was Truus to defy her mother's advice by letting on that this little tic of Joop's— using her full name when he meant to persuade her to step off a chosen course—put her on alert?

She took her napkin and reached across to wipe the chocolate sprinkle from Joop's mouth. There now: restored to the properly unsprinkled chief cashier and principal at De Javasche Bank he'd been when they'd first become engaged.

"I'll make you a *broodje kroket* for breakfast tomorrow," she said before Joop could launch into questioning how she meant to spend her day. The deep-fried meat ragout croquette on a soft bun was his favorite; just the mention of it could lift his mood, and distract him.

CHALK ON HER SHOES

Stephan watched at the door as Žofie wiped away half of a mathematics proof that covered an entire chalkboard.

Her professor, alarmed, said, "Kurt—"

The younger man with them just slid his hands casually into the pockets of his white linen suit pants and nodded at Žofie. Stephan felt a little like the doctor in *Amok*, the Zweig character who becomes so obsessed with a woman who won't have sex with him that he stalks her. But Stephan wasn't stalking Žofie. She had *suggested* he pick her up at the university, never mind that it was summer and no one was in class.

Žofie dropped the eraser and, oblivious to the chalk on her shoe, began refilling the board with symbols. Stephan pulled a journal from his satchel and noted: *Drops eraser on her shoe and doesn't even notice.*

Only after Žofie-Helene had finished her equation did she catch a glimpse of him. She smiled—like the woman in *Amok* smiling across the ballroom in her yellow gown.

"Does that make sense?" Žofie said to the older man. Then to the younger one, "I'll explain it tomorrow if it doesn't, Professor Gödel."

Žofie handed the chalk to Gödel and joined Stephan, oblivious now to the two men, the older one saying, "Extraordinary. And she's how old?" and the other, Gödel, answering, "Just fifteen."

THE LIAR'S PARADOX

Stephan ducked from the rain into the Neuman's Chocolates building at No. 2 Schulhof, with Žofie in tow. He led her down a steep wooden stairway into the basement cavern, their wet shoes leaving prints unseen in the cool-stone darkness as the chatter of the chocolatiers upstairs faded.

"Mmmmmm . . . chocolate," she said, not the least bit afraid.

How had he ever imagined anyone as smart as Žofie might fear anything, that he might have that excuse to take her hand the way Dieter did every time they rehearsed his new play? The chalk had washed from Žofie's shoe in the run over through the rain, but still Stephan couldn't shake all those symbols she'd written on the chalkboard, mathematics for which he didn't have even the alphabet.

He pulled a chain to a ceiling light. Crate-stacked pallets leapt into shadow cubes and angles on the cavern's uneven stone walls. Just being here made words tumble in his mind, although he rarely wrote here anymore now that he had a typewriter at home. He opened a crate with the crowbar from the hook on the bottom stair post and untied one of the jute sacks inside: cocoa beans smelling so familiar that he was often left wanting anything but chocolate, the way a boy whose father wrote books might grow weary of reading, impossible as that seemed to him.

Žofie-Helene said, "You *are* going to offer me a bite."

"Of the beans? You can't eat them, Žofie. Well, maybe if you were starving."

She looked so disappointed that he bit back the words with which he'd meant to impress her, about how tempering chocolate is like coordinating a ballet, melting and cooling and stirring so that all the crystals align to leave the tongue in ecstasy. Ecstasy. He didn't suppose he could use the word with Žofie anyway, unless he put it into a play.

He ran upstairs to grab a handful of truffles, and returned to find Žofie gone.

"Žofie?"

Her voice echoed up from underneath the stairs, "You should keep the beans down here. Temperature is more constant in deeper caves, not because of the geothermal gradient at these depths but because of the insulating effect of the rock."

He glanced at his nice clothes—meant to impress her—but grabbed the flashlight from the peg and ducked underneath the stairs and down the rungs to the lower cavern. Still no Žofie. He crawled into the low, gritty tunnel on the cavern's far side, the flashlight beam illuminating the bottoms of Žofie's shoes, her bent-kneed legs, her derriere under her skirt. She stood at the tunnel's end, her dress hiking with the motion so that for the briefest moment before she pulled the fabric down, he could see the pale skin of the backs of her knees and thighs.

She leaned down into the tunnel again, her face now in the circle of light. "It's a new term, geothermal gradient," she said. "It's okay if you don't know it. Most people don't."

"The upper chamber is drier, which is better for the cocoa," he said as he reached her. "Also easier to get things in and out of."

The passageway here was naturally formed, unlike the cement one under the Ringstrasse by the Burgtheater. It appeared to end at a pile of stones several yards away, but didn't. It was the way of this underworld, the labyrinth of ancient passageways and chambers underrunning Vienna: there was usually a way forward if you searched long enough. The low humidity in this part of the underground was the reason his great-grandfather had bought the Neuman's Chocolates building. He'd come to Vienna with nothing when he was sixteen, Stephan's age now, to live in the attic of a walk-up in the slums of Leopoldstadt. He started the chocolate business at twenty-three and bought this building to expand it while he still lived in that attic, before he built the Ring-strasse palais where Stephan's family now lived.

Stephan said, "I could have waited while you explained that equation to those professors."

"The proof? Professor Gödel doesn't need it explained. He established the incompleteness theorems that transformed the fields of logic and mathematics when he was barely older than we are, Stephan—without even using numbers or symbolic formalisms. You would love his proofs. He used Russell's paradox and the liar's paradox to show that in any formal system adequate for number theory, there is a formula that is unprovable, and its negation is too."

Stephan extracted his journal from his satchel and wrote: *The Liar's Paradox*.

"This very sentence is false," she said. "The sentence has to be true or false, right? But if it's true, then, as it says itself, it's false. But if it's false, then it's true. So it has to be both true and false. Russell's paradox is even more interesting: is the set of all sets that aren't members of themselves a member of itself or not? See?"

Stephan turned off the flashlight to mask how very little he did see. Maybe Papa had a mathematics volume that would explain whatever Žofie was saying; maybe that would help.

"I can't even see where you are now!" Žofie said.

He knew where she was, though. He knew from her voice that her face was perhaps an arm's length from him, that if he just leaned forward he might put his lips to hers.

"Stephan, are you still there?" she asked with just a hint of the fear he too sometimes felt in this dark underworld, where one might become lost and never be heard from again.

She said, "I can still smell the chocolate, even here."

He fingered the truffles in his pocket and took one out. "Open your mouth and put your tongue out, and you can taste it," he suggested.

"You cannot."

"You can."

He heard the licking of her lips, smelled the freshness of her breath. He put one hand to her arm, to have his bearings, or maybe to kiss her.

She giggled, a little dove sound that wasn't like her at all.

"Keep your mouth open," he said gently, and he fumbled his hand slowly forward until he could feel the warmth of her breath on his fingers, and he set the truffle on her tongue.

"Just let it sit in your mouth," he whispered. "Just leave it there, make it last, taste every moment of it."

He wanted to take her hand, but how could you take the hand of someone who had so quickly become your best friend without risking the friendship? He stuck his hands in his pockets, where they brushed against the other truffles. He fingered them, then took one out and put it to his own tongue, not wanting the chocolate itself but wanting the shared experience—the darkness around them and the trickle of water up ahead, rain falling through a grate and flowing lower, headed to the canal and the river and the sea as the slow melt of chocolate warmed their tongues.

"It's both true and not true that I can taste it," she said. "The chocolate paradox!"

He leaned forward, thinking he might risk it, he might kiss her, and if she balked he could pretend he'd just bumped into her in the dark. But a critter of some sort (almost certainly a rat) scampered by, and he clicked on the flashlight, a reflex.

"Don't tell anyone I brought you here," he said. "If I'm found out again, I'll be confined to my room for the rest of my life, on account of the thugs and the collapsing. Isn't it great, though? Some of these tunnels are just storm drains, which you have to avoid in heavy rain, and some are sewers, which I always avoid. But there are whole rooms down here. Crypts full of old bones. Columns that could be, I don't know, from the Romans, even. It's an underground network that's been used by everyone from spies and murderers to neighbors and nuns. It's my secret place. I don't even bring friends here."

"We aren't friends?" Žofie-Helene said.

"We aren't . . . what?"

"You don't show it to your friends, but you're showing me, so logically I'm not your friend."

Stephan laughed warmly. "I never met anyone who could be so technically brilliant and so abysmally wrong. Anyway, I didn't show you, you found it yourself."

"So we are friends, then, because you didn't show me?"

"Of course we're friends, you idiot."

The friendship paradox. She was both his friend and not.

"Do these tunnels go to the Burgtheater?" she asked. "We could surprise Grandpapa. Or, I know! Can we get to Mama's office? It's near St. Rupert's, and our apartment too. Do the tunnels go that far?"

Stephan tended to travel the same paths down here so he wouldn't get lost, but he did know the way to St. Rupert's and her apartment. He'd found a few different ways in the weeks since school was out, actually, not that he was like the doctor in *Amok*, not that he was stalking her. He could take her the long way, past the crypts under St. Stephen's Cathedral and through the three levels, impossibly deep, that were once a convent. He could take her under the Judenplatz, the remains of an underground Talmud school from centuries ago. He might even take her through the old stables. Would she be horrified by the old horse skulls? But, knowing Žofie, she'd be fascinated. Well, he might save the stables for himself, anyway, for now at least.

"All right," he said. "This way, then."

"The game is afoot!" she said.

"I meant to tell you I finished *The Sign of the Four*," he said. "I'll bring it tomorrow."

"But I haven't finished *Kaleidoscope*."

"You don't have to give it back. You can keep it. Forever, I mean." Registering reluctance in her hesitation, he said, "I have another copy," although he didn't; he just rather liked the idea of knowing one half of his two-volume set would be in Žofie's hands, or even just on her shelf as she read in bed at night. "I had a copy already when Aunt Lisl gave me one for my birthday," he lied. "I'd like you to have it."

"I don't have an extra *Sign of the Four*."

He laughed. "I'll give it back, I promise."

He skirted the rubble pile, beyond which was a man-made metal stairway circling up into the passageway's ceiling, at the top of which was an octagonal manhole cover of eight metal triangles whose tips met in the center, which you could push up from down here or pull open from the street. He led her on past the stairway for a few minutes, then clambered down some metal rungs to a wide, arched passage made of smoothly stacked blocks. A river ran alongside a railed walk here, illuminated by a caged work light fastened to the ceiling, which threw their oversize shadows onto the wall.

"This part is from when they rerouted the river into the underground, to expand the city," he said as he clicked off the flashlight. "It helped prevent the cholera too."

The passageway ended abruptly, the water flowing on through a smaller archway like the one by the Burgtheater, where you would have to swim through mucky water to carry on. Here, though, there were stairs to a metal walkway over the water, with a coil of rope and a life preserver hanging from the rail just in case. They crossed, descended, and backtracked on the other side to duck into another narrower, drier tunnel. Stephan clicked on the flashlight again, illuminating a rubble pile.

"That's just another place where some of the tunnel caved in, maybe during the war, like by the little tunnel to our cocoa cellar," he said, and he guided her through a narrow gap between the collapsed stone and the tunnel wall. Just past it, he shone the light on a locked gate. Beyond it, in a jumble: coffins, and human bones that seemed to be organized by body part, and one carefully stacked pile that was nothing but skulls.

THE MOST MASSIVE
TYPEWRITER EVER

Stephan had been leading Žofie-Helene through the underground for perhaps a quarter of an hour when they reached a circular stairway to another octagonal manhole cover near her mother's office. There was a closer exit, right on the street outside her apartment, but it was only metal rungs up to an open-grid drain grate too heavy for him to lift. He climbed onto the street and gave her a hand up, letting go only reluctantly. He kicked the triangles closed and followed her around the corner into her mother's newspaper office, where a man operated the most massive typewriter ever.

"It's a Linotype," Žofie explained. "It's automatic, sort of like a Rube Goldberg contraption. It sets the type for a newspaper run."

"Is it hard to learn?" Stephan asked the typesetter, imagining setting a play on it. To make copies now, he used carbon paper and banged hard on the keys, but as you couldn't make more than a few copies that way, he had to write for small casts or type a script out multiple times. "I already know how to type."

"It's impressive that you know so much, Stephan," Žofie-Helene said.

"That *I* know so much?"

"About the underground. Making chocolate. The theater and typing. You just say it too. When I talk, people look at me like I'm some weird creature. But you're sort of like Professor Gödel. He sometimes says I'm wrong about things too."

"Did I say you were wrong about something?"

"About eating cocoa beans. And the cavern," she said. "Sometimes I say things wrong just to see who will notice. Mostly nobody does."

IN THE EDITOR IN CHIEF'S office, a girl even younger than Walter colored at a table while a woman who had to be Žofie's mother spoke on the telephone.

"Jojojojojojo, have you colored me something splendid?" Žofie asked, lifting her sister and twirling her around in a burst of giggles that left Stephan wanting to be twirling too, although he didn't much like to dance.

Her mother indicated with a finger that her call was almost finished, while saying into the receiver, "Yes, obviously Hitler won't be thrilled, but then *I'm* not thrilled about his efforts to force Schuschnigg to lift the ban on the Austrian Nazi Party. And as my opinion doesn't stop him from his efforts, I'm quite sure I oughtn't let his stop us from running the piece." She finished the call and set the receiver in its cradle, already saying, "Oh, Žofie, your dress! Not again."

"Mama, this is my friend, Stephan Neuman," Žofie said. "We found our way here all the way from his father's chocolate factory through—"

Stephan shot her a look.

"His father makes the best chocolates," Žofie said.

"Ah, you're *that* Neuman?" Käthe Perger said. "I do hope you've brought us some of those chocolates!"

Stephan wiped his hands on his shirttail, then pulled the last two truffles from his pocket and held them out. Oh crud, there was pocket lint stuck to them.

"Heavens, I was only joking!" Käthe Perger said, taking one before he could pull them back, and popping it in her mouth.

Stephan picked the lint off the other and offered it to Žofie's sister.

"Žofie-Helene," Käthe Perger said, "I believe you've outdone yourself in cleverness, choosing a friend who not only travels with chocolates in his pockets, but apparently enjoys doing laundry as much as you do."

Stephan looked down at his filthy clothes. His father was going to kill him.

AFTER STEPHAN LEFT, Žofie said to her mother, "He's only one friend, but one is always greater than zero, even if zero is more mathematically interesting."

Her little sister handed Žofie a book, and Žofie sat and pulled her into her lap. She turned to the first page and read, "'To Sherlock Holmes, she is always *the* woman.'"

Mama said, "I'm not sure Johanna is quite ready for 'A Scandal in Bohemia.'"

Žofie loved the story, especially the bit where the king says it's a pity that Irene Adler is not on his level and Holmes agrees that she's on a very different level than the king, except the king means Miss Adler is beneath him, and Sherlock Holmes means she's far superior. Žofie liked the ending too, where Irene bests them all, and Sherlock Holmes won't take the emerald snake ring the king offers him, but does want the photo of Miss Adler, for the reminder of how he was beaten by a woman's wit.

"He's left-handed," Žofie said. "Stephan is. Do you suppose that feels queer? I asked him once, but he didn't say."

Mama laughed, a bubble of sound like the beautiful zero at the center of a line that went to infinity in both directions, positive and negative. "I don't know, Žofie-Helene," she said. "Does it feel queer to you to be so good at maths?"

Žofie-Helene considered this. "Not exactly."

Mama said, "It might seem different to others, but it's just who you are, who you always have been. I expect it's the same for your friend."

Žofie kissed the top of Jojo's head. "Shall we sing, Jojo?" she asked. And she began to sing, with Jojo joining her, and Mama too, "The moon has risen; the golden stars shine in the sky bright and clear."

THE VIENNA INDEPENDENT

NAZI LAWS AGAINST JEWS "NOT FROM HATRED"

Commissioner for Justice: Laws arise from love for German people

BY KÄTHE PERGER

WÜRZBURG, GERMANY, June 26, 1937 — German Commissioner for Justice Hans Frank, speaking at a gathering of National Socialists here today, insisted that the Nuremberg laws were created "for the protection of our race, not because we hate the Jews but because we love the German people."

"The world criticizes our attitude toward the Jews and declares it too harsh," Frank said. "But the world has never worried how many honest Germans have been chased from home and hearth by Jews in the past."

The laws, instituted on September 15, 1935, revoke German citizenship for Jews and prohibit them from marrying persons of "German or related blood." A "Jew" is defined as anyone with three or four Jewish grandparents.

Thousands of German converts to other religions, including Roman Catholic priests and nuns, are considered Jews.

With the passage of the Nuremberg laws, German Jews were denied treatment at municipal hospitals, Jewish officers were expelled from the army, and university students were prohibited from sitting for doctoral exams. The restrictions were loosened in preparation for the Olympic Games last year, in Garmisch-Partenkirchen in the winter and in the summer in Berlin. But the Reich has since stepped up its "Aryanization" efforts, dismissing Jewish workers and transferring Jewish-owned businesses into non-Jewish hands at bargain prices or with no compensation at all . . .

SEEKING

The yellow pot was there, upright on the Webers' frost-covered porch. Still, Truus approached the gate slowly in Mrs. Kramarsky's Mercedes, making sure as she always did that the pot hadn't been tipped over in warning only to be righted by a helpful Nazi. They were old, the Webers had told her when she'd first met them; their own futures were short, but with their help the children's futures might be long. Truus opened the gate, drove through, and closed it behind her, glad for her winter coat and long skirt. She shifted into low gear and drove across the field, to the path into the woods.

It was well past noon before she saw the first telling flicker of movement, a rustle that might have been a deer but became, when she stopped the car, a fleeing child zigzagging through the trees. Truus couldn't fathom it even still, how children survived in these woods and on the moors for days and nights with nothing more in their pockets than spent railway tickets, a few reichsmarks if they were lucky, and bits of bread packed by mothers so desperate that they would put their children on trains to the edge of Germany without a breath of real hope—children who survived often only to be arrested by the Germans or sent back by Dutch border patrol.

"It's okay. I'm here to help," Truus called gently, watching to see where the child hid. She moved slowly, offering, "I'm Tante Truus and I'm here to help you get to the Netherlands, like your mother told you to do."

Truus wasn't exactly sure why the children ever trusted her, or even if they did. She sometimes thought they allowed her to approach only out of sheer exhaustion.

"I'm Tante Truus," she repeated. "What's your name?"

The girl, perhaps fifteen, studied her.

"Would you like me to help you get over the border?" Truus offered gently.

A slightly younger boy poked a head out from the brush, then another. The three didn't look like siblings, but one couldn't always tell.

The girl turned from the others back to Truus. "Can you take us all?"

"Yes, of course."

When the other two returned the girl's gaze without objection, the girl whistled loudly. Another child peeked out from hiding. And another. Good heavens, there were eleven children, one of them no more than a baby, for heaven's sake. Well, it would be a full car. Truus had no idea how the ladies would find beds tonight for eleven children, but she would leave that for God to provide.

TRUUS BUMPED THROUGH the forest, headed back toward the Weber farm with the children all sitting on each other or on the floorboards. They were so silent, so unnaturally quiet for children of any age, much less the young teens most of these children were. Silent and unsmiling, like the children Truus's family had taken in during the war.

Truus had been just eighteen, the war arriving on their doorstep in Duivendrecht just as she ought to have been greeting suitors there. The Netherlands had remained neutral, but still a state of siege had been declared and the army mobilized, the boys all sent to protect areas essential to the national defense, which did not include Truus's front porch. Truus was left at home to read to the little refugees, who'd arrived so weak and hungry that she had wanted to hand them her own plate, and yet wanted as well to eat every bite herself lest she ever be so thin. They had infuriated Truus and saddened her in equal measure, those children whose reticence left Mummy so sad. Those children who thrust Truus herself into mothering too, if she were to be honest, and left her wondering how she might pull her own mother out from under the stifling blanket of the children's silent sorrow. Then the morning of the first snow that winter, heavy and early, Truus had woken to the snow-laden trees, the snow-softened rails on the snow-softened bridges, the pristine white paths such a contrast to the still, dark waters of the canal. She quietly woke the children and showed them the view, and dressed them, thankful on that morning for the hush of their voices even when they did speak. They slipped outside, and in the light of the winter moon reflecting on the snow, they built a snowman. That was all. Just a snowman, three dirty-white snow boulders stacked one atop the other, with stones for eyes and twigs for arms and no mouth at all, as if the children meant to make the creature in their own silent image. Mummy, with her morning tea in hand, had looked out the window just as they finished. It was what she did each morning—her way to see what the Lord had in store for her, she liked to say. That morning, though, she was surprised and delighted to see the children outside, even if they weren't smiling, even if they weren't making any noise. Truus pointed up to her, urging the children to wave. Just as she was doing so, one of the boys threw a snowball at the window, splattering the glass and somehow cracking the silence. The children laughed and laughed as Mummy's startled face gave way to laughter too. It was, to this day, the most beautiful sound Truus had ever heard, even as it had left her so ashamed. How could she ever have wanted anything but the laughter of these children? How could she ever have wanted anything for herself?

Truus pulled Mrs. Kramarsky's sedan to a sudden stop. On the ground below the Webers' porch, the yellow pot lay tipped on its side, spilling dirt onto the path. She backed the car slowly and began to search for an exit over the border through the woods, saying again the prayer she always did, thanking God for the Webers and all they'd done for the children of Germany, and asking Him to keep the courageous old couple safe.

KLARA VAN LANGE

At the Groenveld house on Jan Luijkenstraat, Truus—exhausted from the hours spent searching the woods for an exit, only to cross the Weber farm in the middle of the night with the car lights off and the gas tank near empty—turned the eleven children over to the volunteers. Klara van Lange, sitting at the telephone table in one of those ghastly new calf-baring skirts, covered the receiver with her hand and whispered to Truus, "The Jewish hospital on the Nieuwe Keizersgracht." She said into the receiver, "Yes, we know eleven children is a lot, but it's just for a night or two until we can find families to— Have they *bathed*?" She glanced nervously at Truus. "Lice? No, of course they don't have lice!"

Truus quickly checked the children's hair and set the oldest boy aside. "You have a lice comb, Mrs. Groenveld?" she whispered. "But of course you do. Your husband is a doctor."

"Yes, we can send someone to help care for the baby," Klara said into the receiver. She mouthed to Truus, "I can go."

Well, as much as Truus might like to go with the children herself, she oughtn't leave Joop alone for the night; she should be grateful for the offer.

"All right, who would like a nice warm bath?" Truus asked the children. Then to the ladies, "Mrs. Groenveld, can you and Miss Hackman take the younger girls?" To the oldest girl, she said, "If we draw you a bath, can you manage yourself?"

The girl answered, "I can help with Benjamin's lice, Tante Truus."

Truus, with a gentle hand to the girl's cheek, said, "If I could choose a daughter, dear, she would be a girl just as sweet as you are. Now, you are going to have a nice warm bath all to yourself, and I'm going to find you some bath salts too." To Klara, who had just hung up the telephone, she said, "Mrs. Van Lange, can you put together some cheese sandwiches?"

"Yes, I did persuade the Jewish hospital to take them even though the children have no papers; you're welcome, Mrs. Wijsmuller," Klara responded wryly, reminding Truus of herself as a young woman, although far more beautiful. Klara van Lange did not need to bare her calves in this inexplicable new fashion in order to have men's attentions. Heavens, if she didn't seat herself carefully, her knees would show.

"Of course you persuaded them, Klara," Truus said. "How could even the prime minister say no to you?" Thinking perhaps they ought to try Klara's fashionable skirts and her powers of persuasion on Prime Minister Colijn before, as the rumor mill expected, the Dutch government made it impossible for foreigners to establish themselves here, not literally closing the border but alerting Germans fleeing the Reich without independent means that the Netherlands might be a land of passage, but not a final destination.

THROUGH A WINDOW
GLASS, DARKLY

Eichmann set aside the report he was drafting, for which Hagen, his newest boss, would take the credit if there was any to take—yet another pretender skating on the solid pond of Eichmann's expertise. He opened the train window and breathed deeply of the autumn air as they rocked through the pass from Italy into Austria, his stomach emptied so completely while crossing the Mediterranean from the Middle East to Brindisi on the *Palestina* that the sick-bay doctor had tried to put him off at Rhodes. The whole trip was an absolute bust: an entire month of travel only to have the British allow them a mere twenty-four hours in Haifa, and the Cairo authorities deny them visas for Palestine. Twelve long days in Egypt, that was all they'd gotten for their trouble.

Hagen said, "The Jews swindle each other, that's the root of Palestine's financial chaos."

"It might be more effective if we lay out specifics, sir," Eichmann responded. "Forty Jewish bankers in Jerusalem."

"Forty swindling Jew bankers," Hagen agreed. "Sure, another fifty thousand Jews would emigrate annually with the haul Polkes thinks we ought to allow them."

The Jew Polkes, the only real connection they'd made on the trip, had suggested that if Germany really wanted to get rid of its Jews, it ought to allow them to take a thousand British pounds with them to emigrate to Palestine. That's how he'd phrased it, "a thousand British pounds," as if Germany's own reichsmarks were unspeakable.

Eichmann scribbled into the report: *It is not our aim to have Jewish capital transferred from the Reich, but rather to induce Jews* without *means to emigrate.*

His pencil snapped, unable to stand the pressure of his quick thoughts. He pulled out his pocketknife, thinking of his cold, frugal stepmother, whose family in Vienna had married wealthy Jews of the sort that would be unwilling to leave anyplace without their ill-gotten riches.

"I grew up here, in Linz," Eichmann said to Hagen as the train topped a long climb and the view opened from the woods to all of Austria. This cold on his face now was the cold of running with his friend Mischa Sebba through woods much like these, this emptiness that of his own hands as his parents linked fingers with his younger siblings crossing the platform at the Linz station, when the family had reunited here after that year apart. He had been eight, then, and ten when his mother's gentle voice gave way to his stepmother reading from the Bible in the crowded apartment at No. 3 Bischof Strasse. It had been four years since he'd been home, four years since he'd visited his mother's grave.

"I spent whole days riding across countryside like this," he told Hagen. He'd ridden mostly with Mischa, who'd taught him how to spot deer tracks, how to make all sorts of bird sounds, how to put on a condom long before Eichmann thought the idea of putting his penis inside a girl anything but preposterous. He could still call up the scorn in Mischa's voice at the name of Eichmann's Wandervögel scout pack: *Griffon? It's a bird species that died out before our grandfathers were born, a vulture that lived off the flesh of the dead.* Mischa had been jealous, of course—unable to join the older boys for whole weekends hiking in their uniforms and carrying flags, because he was Jewish.

Eichmann began to put a new point to the pencil. "I'm a keen horseman," he said. "I learned to shoot in woods like those with my best friend, Friedrich von Schmidt. His mother was a countess, his father a war hero."

Friedrich had invited him to join the German-Austrian Young Veterans' Association, and they'd attended its paramilitary training together. But Mischa had remained the better friend even after Eichmann joined the Party—April 1, 1932; member 899,895. He'd remained close if increasingly argumentative with Mischa until Austria closed its Nazi Brown Houses, and the Vacuum Oil Company fired him for no reason but his politics. He'd had to pack his uniform and his boots, then, and cross the border from Austria into Germany, to safety in Passau.

Hagen said, "We're not funding Palestine with German capital, not even German Jew capital."

Eichmann turned from the view back to his report and wrote: *As the aforementioned emigration of 50,000 Jews annually would in the main strengthen Judaism in Palestine, this plan cannot be a subject for discussion.*

SELF-PORTRAIT

Žofie-Helene, with Stephan and his aunt Lisl, stood at the first painting in the Secession Building exhibit room, *Self-Portrait of a Degenerate Artist*. It left her uneasy, the painting and its title.

"What do you think of it, Žofie-Helene?" Lisl Wirth asked.

Žofie said, "I don't know anything about painting."

"You don't have to know about art to have a feeling about it," Lisl assured her. "Just tell us what you see."

"Well, his face is weird—so many colors, although they're beautiful and they all do sort of blend together to seem like skin," Žofie said uncertainly. "His nose is big and his chin is awfully long, like he's painting his reflection from a distorted mirror."

Lisl said, "So many painters have become almost analytic in their abstraction. Picasso. Mondrian. Kokoschka is more emotional, more intuitive."

"Why does he call himself degenerate?"

"It's ironic, Žofe," Stephan said. "It's what Hitler calls artists like him."

Žofe, not Žofie. She rather liked when Stephan called her that, like her sister calling her ŽoŽo.

They moved on to a portrait of a woman whose face and black hair formed nearly a perfect triangle. The woman's eyes were different sizes, her face was blotched with red and black, and the way she held her hands was frightening.

"She's rather ugly, and yet somehow beautiful as well," Žofie said.

"She is, isn't she?" Lisl said.

"This one is like the portrait in your entry, Stephan," Žofie-Helene said. "The woman with the scratched cheeks."

"Yes, that's a Kokoschka too," Lisl said.

"But that one is of you," Žofie-Helene said. "And it's more beautiful."

Lisl laughed her warm, tinkling ellipse of a laugh, and she set a hand on Žofie's shoulder. Papa used to put his hand on her shoulder like that sometimes. Žofie stood there, longing for that touch to last forever, and wishing she had a portrait of Papa by this Oskar Kokoschka. She had photographs, but photos were somehow less true than these paintings, even though they were more real.

BARE FEET IN SNOW

Truus and Klara van Lange sat across a cluttered desk in Mr. Tenkink's office in The Hague, with Mr. Van Vliet from the Ministry of Justice as well. Tenkink had on his desk an authorization to allow the children from the Webers' woods to stay in the Netherlands—one Truus had drawn up, which wanted only Mr. Tenkink's signature. She'd found that the more easily you could arrange for a thing to be swallowed, the more likely it was to get down the throat.

"Jewish children?" Tenkink was saying.

"We have homes in which to place them," Truus responded, ignoring the look from Klara van Lange. Klara had a higher regard for the absolute truth than Truus did, but then she was awfully young, and not long married.

"It's a tough situation, I see that, Mrs. Wijsmuller," Tenkink said. "But half the Dutch now sympathize with the Nazis, and most of the rest of us simply don't want us to be a dumping ground for Jews."

Mr. Van Vliet started, "The government wants to appease Hitler—"

"Yes," Tenkink interrupted, "and stealing a country's children is not exactly the neighborly thing to do."

Truus touched Van Vliet's shoulder; Tenkink was a man who responded more positively to women. So many men were that way, even good ones. She wished now that she had brought the children along—so much harder to deny dark curls and hopeful eyes than to deny the idea of a child, or eleven. But it seemed cruel to drag the poor exhausted dears out of bed and off for the long train ride from Amsterdam to The Hague just to trot them out for a man who ought to be able to make the right decision, who always had been able to be persuaded to do so.

Truus said to Tenkink, "Queen Wilhelmina is sympathetic to the plight of the Germans who wish to free themselves from Hitler's fury."

Tenkink said, "Even the royal family . . . You must understand the magnitude of this Jewish problem. If Hitler makes good on his threat to annex Austria—"

"Chancellor Schuschnigg has Austria's Nazi leaders behind bars, Mr. Tenkink," Truus said, "and there isn't a city in the world more dependent on its Jews for prosperity than Vienna. Most of its doctors, lawyers, and financiers and half its journalists are Jewish by birth if not by practice. Can you honestly imagine a coup succeeding against Austria's money *and* its press?"

"Mrs. Wijsmuller, I'm not saying no," Tenkink replied. "I'm simply suggesting that it would be easier if the children were Christian."

Klara said, "I'm sure Mrs. Wijsmuller will remember that the next time she spirits children out of a country that has already made their parents disappear."

Truus suppressed a smile as she reached for a framed photo propped amid the piles on Mr. Tenkink's desk: a younger Tenkink with a soft wife, two sons, and a chubby-cheeked baby girl. Klara's surprisingly quick tongue was part of the reason Truus had requested her company for this visit.

"What a lovely family," Truus said.

She sat back in her chair, trying not to show her hand as she indulged Mr. Tenkink in the proud fatherly soliloquy she had, after all, invited. Patience was one of the few virtues she could claim.

She handed the photo back to Tenkink, who smiled affectionately.

"One of the German children is a baby, even younger than your daughter is in your photo, Mr. Tenkink," Truus said, using "German" rather than "Jewish," shifting the focus away from the characteristic that most troubled the man and moving to make the point while he still held the photo of his own child. "Surely even the coldest of hearts might warm to a baby?"

Tenkink looked from the photo to the authorization on his desk, then to Truus. "A boy or a girl?"

"Which would you prefer, Mr. Tenkink? One can never tell with babies when they're all wrapped up for the press to admire."

Tenkink, shaking his head, signed the authorization, saying, "Mrs. Wijsmuller, when the Nazis invade the Netherlands, I hope you'll vouch for me. It appears you can talk anyone into anything."

"The good Lord forbid it," Truus said. "But in that event, He will surely vouch for you. Thank you. There are so many children who need our help."

"Well, then," Mr. Tenkink said, "if that's it—"

"I understand that it's impossible," Truus interrupted, "but I have news from the German Alps of thirty orphans forced from their beds into the road in their pajamas by a gang of SS."

"Mrs. Wijsmuller—"

"Thirty children standing in their pajamas in bare feet, and in a thick layer of snow, while the SS set fire to their orphanage."

Tenkink sighed. "What happened to 'only eleven'?" With a glance at his family photo, he said, "And these thirty are all Jewish too, I suppose? Do you mean to save every Jew in the Reich?"

"They're being housed in Germany by non-Jews," Truus said. "I don't have to tell you what the Nazis do even to Christians who defy their prohibitions against helping Jews."

"With all due respect, Mrs. Wijsmuller, the Nazi prohibition against helping Jews does not have an exception for Dutchwomen crossing the border to—"

Truus glanced meaningfully at his family photo.

"Even if I could help," Tenkink said, "word is, we'll pass this law closing our border within weeks, or perhaps even days. Without the information in hand already, I don't see how—"

Truus handed him a brown file tied with green straps, all the information he would want already collected and packaged, an easier swallow.

Tenkink, shaking his head, said, "All right. All right. I'll see if I can arrange to accept them on a temporary basis. Only until homes outside the Netherlands can be found for them. Is that clear? They have families elsewhere, in England or in the United States?"

"Yes, of course, Mr. Tenkink," Truus answered. "That's why they find themselves standing in bare feet in the snow outside a burning Jewish orphanage."

EXHIBITION OF SHAME

Lisl Wirth stood beside her husband at the *Entartete Kunst* exhibit at the German Institute of Archeology in Munich, cubist and futurist and expressionist works purged from Germany's museums for failing to meet the führer's artistic "standards" displayed and priced here in a way meant to provoke visitors to mock. Anyone with any art sense could see that the other exhibit here in Munich, the Great German Art Exhibition at Hitler's squat new Haus der Deutschen Kunst, was all incompetent landscapes and boring nudes by comparison. Really, how could anyone make nudes so dull as that "great" German art? And *this* was the "degenerate art"? This Paul Klee was gorgeous in its simplicity—the jaggy lines of the angler's face, the graceful reclining S-curve of his arms, the charming extension of a fishing pole over a blue as varied and evocative as the sea. It made her think of Stephan, although she couldn't say why. She didn't suppose her nephew had ever fished.

"Do you like it?" she asked Michael, surprising herself with the question. Until the past few weeks, she would have been sure he would love it, if only because she did. "The Klee, *The Angler*," she said, having to identify which one, exactly, because the paintings were all jumbled together, a disrespect made blatant by the words ringing them on the walls: *Madness becomes method.*

In the face of Michael's silence, Lisl focused on the words.

Laughter burst out behind her, the small-minded conforming to expectation.

She lowered her voice and said to Michael, "I thought Goebbels was a fan of the modernists."

Michael glanced about uneasily. "That was before Hitler gave his little speech on degenerate art undermining the German culture, Lis. Before he promoted Wolfgang Willrich and Walter Hansen."

Two denouncers—failed artists, but accomplished denouncers—in charge of which art was to be applauded and which vilified.

Michael said, "This exhibit was Goebbels's idea, and a politically smart one."

Lisl turned from the Klee and from Michael. When had he become someone who valued political cunning over artistic expression?

Even Gustav and Therese Bloch-Bauer were blasé about the Nazi assault on culture, though, everyone too wrapped up in their own families and their own lives to see the politically darkened clouds piling up on the border between Germany and Austria. Everyone thought Hitler was a passing German fad, that it couldn't happen to Austria, that Austria had weathered the assassination of Chancellor Dollfuss and the attempted Nazi coup three years ago, and they would weather this, and anyway people had businesses to run and children to raise, parties to attend and portraits to sit for, art to buy.

Lisl pretended interest in another painting, another sculpture, until she was in an entirely different room from her husband, admiring a Van Gogh self-portrait, Chagalls and Picassos and Gauguins, an entire wall devoted, unflatteringly, to the Dadaists. It was only when she reached the room she would come to think of as "the Jewish room" that she felt her own precarious position. "Revelation of the Jewish racial soul" was written on one wall. Lisl thought the paintings extraordinary; she hoped whatever it was they revealed reflected something about her own soul.

But she was a Jewish woman wandering alone among an unfriendly gathering in Germany.

It was ridiculous, this sudden fear. Munich was barely across the border. In little more than an hour she could be back in Austria.

Still, she went in search of Michael again.

She caught sight of him standing before an Otto Dix of a pregnant woman, her belly and breasts so distorted that it left Lisl almost relieved that she could not bear a child. Michael's face as he considered it, though, was full of longing. He'd always said he didn't need an heir, that Walter could take over her family's chocolate business and Stephan his family's bank—a bank that had only survived thanks to her family money anyway, not that Lisl would ever say so. Michael was a proud man from a proud family that had fallen on hard times, as had so many after the financial markets crashed, and Lisl would never do anything to jeopardize her husband's pride, any more than he would hers. Stephan was a son to Michael, her husband always said, and Walter too. But even before this moment, this revelation in his expression, Lisl had sensed something gone amiss, Michael less and less enamored of the university education and intellectual charms he'd always said were the reason he'd fallen in love with her.

She asked a question of a stranger so that Michael might hear her voice and have time to compose himself. When he had, she rejoined him, taking his arm and saying, "We might buy that Klee," just to have something to say. But they wouldn't buy it, not here or anywhere else, and not just because it was so outrageously overpriced.

ALONG THE QUAY

The overcast sky threatened more snow, a welcome freshening for the filthy crust of the walkways and the canals dulled with scraped ice. Truus, walking with Joop, passed three boats iced into a Herengracht already frozen so solidly that Amsterdam buzzed with speculation that the Elfstedentocht might be skated for the first time since 1933. Near the bridge across to their apartment, a small group of adults visited in the center of the canal, children skating around them, or simply sliding in their little boots. This was Truus's favorite part of the day—she and Joop walking home together the way they had when Joop first courted her, when she was a newly minted graduate of the School of Commerce and had just begun a job at the bank where he worked.

"I'm not saying no, Truus," Joop was saying now. "I'm not forbidding it. You know I would never forbid you something that was important to you."

Truus settled her gloved hands more deeply into her coat pockets. Joop didn't mean to be picking a fight or demeaning her; it was just the casual way even good men like him inadvertently spoke, men who'd come of age at a time when women hadn't yet even gained the right to vote—when, indeed, only men of wealth had that right.

They watched as a toddler boy, new to skating, nearly took down his sister.

Truus said, "Nor would I forbid you something that was important to you, Joop."

He laughed warmly, put his own gloved hands on her elbows, and slid them down to ease her hands out of her pockets and take them in his.

"All right, I deserve that," he said. "It ought to have been in our wedding vows: love, honor, and don't even think about trying to forbid you anything, whether it's important or not."

"You don't think saving thirty orphans left by the Nazis to stand in the snow in their pajamas is important?"

"I didn't mean that, either," he said gently. "You know I didn't mean that. But do think about it. The situation in Germany seems to me to be escalating, and I worry about you."

Truus stood beside him, watching the skaters, the sister now helping her brother up from the ice.

"Well, if you mean to go," Joop said, "I wish you would get it over with before things get any worse."

"I'm just waiting for Mr. Tenkink to arrange the entrance visas, Joop. Now, you said you had something you wanted to tell me?"

"Yes, I received the oddest call at my office this afternoon. Mr. Vander Waal—you know him—one of his clients is quite certain that you have something of value that belongs to him. Something you brought for him from Germany?"

"Something *I* brought? Why would I have brought anything across the border for an absolute stranger?" She frowned, something nudging at her as she looked out at the skaters, the little boy's and girl's father joining them, taking the boy's hand. "I limit my precious cargo to children; I promise you that."

"That's what I said," Joop said. "I assured him you wouldn't have had anything to do with it."

Out on the ice, the sister took her brother's other hand. He said something that made the little family laugh, and the three skated off toward the bridge and under it, the father calling back to the other adults that he would see them soon. Truus looked away then, through the bare trees to the barren sky. How many times had she watched as a group of parents visited together, coming to know each other as their children swirled around them? Never with Joop, though. It was the one bit of herself she'd tucked away even from her husband. After her third miscarriage, she and Joop had pivoted silently, Truus turning to the efforts of the Association for Women's Interests and Equal Citizenship and to social work, to helping children like those her parents had taken in.

A train whistle sounded. Truus just kept looking across the frozen canal, her hands in the anchor of Joop's, wondering if he ever came alone to watch these families. She knew he longed for a child as surely as she did, or more. But she had so carefully tucked away her pain, and he had as well, so as not to bring it fresh to the other in an unguarded moment. And now, after years of avoiding the subject of their childlessness, it was habit, impossible to break. Truus, much as she might long to do so, could not simply reach up and touch Joop's face and say, "Do you ever come here and watch the children, Joop? Do you watch the parents? Do you ever think we might try one more time, before it's too late?" So she stood silently beside him, watching as the skaters cut the ice and the parents chatted and the canal boats, frozen in place, suggested a future that was still a long winter away.

DIAMONDS, NOT PASTE

Truus, after Joop left for the office the next morning, dug into her dresser and pulled out the matchbox the man on the train had given her—had it really been a year ago? She opened it over the table and took out the ugly disk of gravel wedged into the box. She rubbed at it with her thumb until bits of gravel broke free.

She took the bits into the kitchen, set them carefully in a bowl, and filled it with water. She rubbed at the submerged pieces with her bare fingers, the water growing cloudy. She pulled them up from the water and set them on her wet palm.

It was true after all: we are never more easily deceived than when we are ourselves in the act of deception.

She telephoned Mr. Vander Waal's office. "Mr. Vander Waal," she said, "it appears some apologies are in order. My husband was mistaken, it turns out. I *do* have something of your Dr. Brisker's."

There were perhaps a dozen diamonds in the "lucky stone"—value enough to begin a new life. This Dr. Brisker had consciously put the risk of carrying his secret treasure across the border on her, couching it in meaning enough to keep her from pitching it into a waste bin. He'd jeopardized the lives of three children just to get some of his wealth out of Germany. And she had been an absolute fool.

MOTORSTURMFÜHRER

The SD-hosted daylong Judentagung in Berlin was Eichmann's triumph. Dannecker and Hagen spoke first, Dannecker on the need for constant surveillance of the Jews, and Hagen of the complications of an independent Palestine that might seek rights for them. As Eichmann took the podium, he felt as free as he had as a young man racing through Austria on his motorbike, he and his friends defending visiting Nazi speakers against crowds throwing beer bottles and rotten food—and themselves leaving the forums smashed to the last beer glass and mirror. The Palestine trip, though a bust, had helped establish his expertise on the Jewish problem. Now he was one of the speakers, and the Judentagung crowd was roaring support for him.

"The true spirit of Germany resides in the Volk, in the peasants and the landscape, the blood and soil of our unsullied homeland," he told them. "We now face the threat of a Jewish conspiracy I alone know how to countermand."

The crowd exploded in agreement as he warned of the weapons and air power the Palestinian Haganah had amassed, of foreign Jews masquerading as staff for international organizations smuggling out information to be used against the Reich, of a vast anti-German conspiracy led by the Alliance Israélite Universelle, for which a Unilever margarine factory here acted as a front.

"The way to solve the Jewish problem is not through laws restricting the activity of Jews in Germany, or even street-level brutality," he shouted over the thundering crowd. "What is needed is to identify Reich Jews to a person. Put names on lists. Identify opportunities to allow their emigration from Germany to lesser countries. And—most importantly—strip them of assets so that, given a choice to stay in utter poverty or to leave, the Jews will *choose* to go."

CHOICES

It was still the dark of a winter morning beyond the sash window as Truus sat down to breakfast with Joop. She took up the front section of the newspaper with her first bite of *uitsmijter*, the egg and ham and cheese toast still hot.

"Good Lord, they've done it, Joop," she said.

Joop smiled mischievously across the narrow table. "They've raised the hemlines even higher? I know you favor the longer skirts, but you do have the most adorable knees in all of Amsterdam."

She tossed a bit of bread at him. He caught it and popped it into his generous mouth, then returned his attention to his own plate, savoring his breakfast in a way that Truus admired but never could muster even when the news was good.

She said, "Our government have passed this new law banning immigration from the Reich."

Joop set his *uitsmijter* down, giving her his full attention. "You knew they were going to, Truus. It's been what, a year since the government 'protected' just about any profession a foreigner might have been able to support himself in."

"I thought we were better than this. To close our border absolutely?"

Joop took the front page and read the piece, leaving Truus to her self-chastising thoughts. She ought to have tried harder to hurry Mr. Tenkink on behalf of the thirty orphans. Thirty. Too many for her to pass as her own on a passport that listed no children, but she ought to have tried.

"We can still give refuge to those in danger," Joop said, handing the paper back to her.

"To those who can *prove* they're in *physical* danger. What Jew in Germany isn't in danger? But what proof of physical danger does anyone have until the Nazis seize them and haul them away, and it's too late?"

Truus readdressed the newspaper, her mind already on the train schedule to get to The Hague. This was not something she could change, what their government would do, but perhaps Tenkink could be persuaded to bend the rules.

"Geertruida . . . ," Joop said.

Geertruida. Yes, she did lower her newspaper again then. She looked to Joop's hair, graying at the temples, his sturdy chin, his left ear slightly larger than his right, or perhaps it simply stuck out farther; even after all these years, Truus couldn't decide which it was.

"Geertruida," Joop repeated, marshaling his conviction, "have you ever thought about taking in a few of these children, like your family did in the Great War?"

"To live with us?" she asked cautiously.

He nodded.

"But they're orphans, Joop. They don't have parents to be returned to."

Joop nodded again, holding her gaze. She saw in the slight squint of his pale eyes, that brief attempt to hide his feelings, that he too *did* stop along the canal to watch the children play, to watch the parents.

She reached across the table and took his hand, trying to hold on to an overwhelming sense of hope. Joop was so uncomfortable when she became emotional.

She said, "We have the extra bedroom."

He pressed his lips together, accentuating his sturdy chin. "I've been thinking we ought to move to a bigger place in any event."

Truus looked down to the newspaper, the headline about the new immigration law.

"A bigger apartment?" she said.

"We could afford a house."

In the squeeze of his hand, she knew this was what she wanted, and what he wanted too. A different kind of family. A family one chose rather than one God gave you. Children you chose to love.

Truus said, "It would be difficult for you to manage when I'm away."

Joop sat back a little, his grip on her hand loosening, his fingers tracing the rings she wore: the gold band that marked their marriage; the ruby that was real, not one of the paste copies she'd had made for bribes not long after she'd begun bringing children across the border; the intertwined bands he'd given her the first time she'd been pregnant, to mark the beginning of the family they thought they would have.

"No," Joop said. "No, it would be impossible to manage children if you weren't here, Truus, but with this new law there will be no more bringing anyone out of Germany anyway."

Truus looked to the Nassaukade and the canal, the bridge, the Raampoort, all still dark. Across the canal, in another lighted third-floor window, a father bent low to a child still sitting in bed. Amsterdam was just waking. It was empty now, but would soon fill with children carrying schoolbooks, with men like Joop going off to work, with women like herself setting out for the market, or pushing baby strollers, walking in pairs or little groups as they visited together, even on a cold morning like this.

THE MATHEMATICS OF SONG

W hat are we doing here?" Žofie-Helene whispered to Stephan. They'd just emerged from an incense-tinged hallway into a line of well-dressed adults descending from a stairway, waiting to enter the Hofburgkapelle. Žofie had done exactly as Stephan directed even though he refused to explain why: she wore good clothes and met him at the Hercules statue in the Heldenplatz.

Stephan said, "We're lining up for communion with the people coming down from the upper boxes."

"But I'm not Catholic."

"Neither am I."

Žofie followed him into the chapel, which was surprisingly narrow and plain, as royal palace chapels went—a room that went up and up in a Gothic way, circled by balconies from which an orchestra played and a choir sang, but all of it a single white. Even the window glass behind the altar was colored only at the top, terribly unbalanced.

She accepted a dreadful bit of bread and a sip of sour wine, whispering as she followed Stephan back from the altar, "That was quite unpalatable."

Stephan smiled. "They serve Sacher torte at your church, I suppose?"

The people they'd joined in line headed back up the stairs, but Stephan took up an awkward place standing at the edge of the chapel, and Žofie waited beside him. When communion ended, he led her to two open seats at the back. As they sat waiting for the mass to end, he noted in his journal: *Communion = quite unpalatable.*

For no reason Žofie could fathom, they continued sitting even after the mass was over. Most everyone remained although the priest had left. She returned her attention to the ceiling, the unfrescoed rib vault in which the weight of the barrels was carried on the piers at the intersections and the thrust transmitted to the outer walls. If she had been with anyone other than Stephan, she would never have tolerated sitting in a chapel doing absolutely nothing, but Stephan always did have a point.

"Know why this ceiling doesn't collapse?" she whispered.

Stephan put a hand to her mouth, then removed her glasses, cleaned them on her scarf, and replaced them on her face. He smiled and touched her infinity-symbol necklace.

"It wasn't actually a gift from Papa," she whispered. "It was a tie tack he won in school. Grandpapa had it made into a necklace for me after Papa died."

Lines of young boys in blue-and-white sailor uniforms began filing in, lining up in front of the altar. After a hushed moment, a single beautiful voice sang from the choir loft, the first high note of Schubert's "Ave Maria" from a boy left behind. In the abandoned boy's pure voice, the notes trickled rhythmically down and up and down again, settling back to the opening note and resting, just resting in some place inside Žofie that she hadn't even known was there. The boy's voice was answered then by the entire choir of beautiful boy voices soaring even further upward, echoing from the plain white stone of the vaulted ceiling, surrounding her from every direction, mingling in her mind with an equation she'd spent much of the week mulling, as if they were of the same heaven. She sat, just letting the music fill the empty spaces between the numbers and symbols inside her, and then she sat in the hush of the others leaving, until only she and Stephan sat side by side in the empty chapel, the fullest place she had ever been.

KIPFERL AND VIENNESE HOT CHOCOLATE

In the Michaelerplatz outside the Hofburgkapelle and the palace, it was clear and bright and cold, and everywhere leaflets and posters scattered from trucks proclaimed "Ja!" and "With Schuschnigg for a free Austria!" or "Vote YES" in the plebiscite Chancellor Schuschnigg had called to determine whether Austria should remain independent from Germany. Crosses of the Austrian Fatherland Front—the chancellor's party—were painted in white on the walls of buildings and pavements. Crowds in the streets and youth groups chanted "Heil Schuschnigg!" "Heil liberty!" and "Red-White-Red until Death!" while others chanted "Heil Hitler!"

Žofie tried to ignore them all. She tried to hold on to the music and the mathematics still mingling inside her as she headed with Stephan down the Herrengasse toward the Café Central. If the chanting crowds bothered Stephan, he didn't say so, but then he hadn't said anything since the music began in the chapel. Žofie supposed it had taken him into his world of words, just as it had taken her into her world of numbers and symbols. She supposed that was why they had grown to be such friends even though Stephan had known the others far longer than he'd known Žofie—because his writing was like her mathematics in some way they both understood, even if it really did make no sense.

They were pushing through the glass doors of the Café Central when Stephan finally spoke, his eyes dry now although they had been moist in the chapel, which she supposed would have embarrassed him in front of the coffee-house gang.

"Imagine, Žofe, if I could write something like that," he said.

Beyond the pastry case, at the far end of the café, their friends sat around two tables pulled together near the newspaper racks, already gathered and waiting for Stephan.

"But you write plays, not music," Žofie said.

He pushed her lightly at the shoulder, the way he'd taken to doing lately, just being playful, Žofie knew, but still she loved his touch.

"So abominably brilliant, so technically correct—and so abysmally wrong," he said. "Not the music itself, you idiot. A play that would move people the way it does."

"But—"

But you can, Stephan.

Žofie couldn't say why she stopped herself from saying the words aloud, any more than she could say why she'd stopped herself from taking Stephan's hand in the chapel. Maybe she could have said it there, in the silence after the music, like she'd told him about the necklace. Or maybe not. It was daunting, to realize you knew someone you thought might make magic like that someday if he just kept stringing words together, creating stories and helping everyone else see how to make them real. It was daunting to think that his plays might someday be performed at the Burgtheater, his words spoken to an audience laughing and crying and, when it was over, standing and applauding, as audiences did only for the best of plays, those that lifted you from one world and set you down in another that, improbably, didn't even really exist. Or it did exist, but only in the imaginations of those watching, only for those few hours in the dark. The theater paradox: both real and not.

STEPHAN WANTED TO ask Dieter to move up to the end seat so he could sit next to Žofie, to stay close to her and the choir music and the feeling, the hope that sharing the music with her had somehow brought. If she hadn't been coming with him for the read-through of his script, he would have taken his journal and gone directly from the chapel to Café Landtmann, or even better the Griensteidl, where no one would interrupt him; he would have sunk his fingers into words, to make one of his plays better or start a new one. But Dieter popped up to hold the chair for Žofie, and it was Stephan's play they were meeting about; everyone needed to be able to hear him over the din—the table on one side in a heated discussion over a copy of the *Neue Freie Presse* Aunt Lisl sometimes read, the chess players on the other side arguing too, the entire café seemingly abuzz with speculation about whether Austria would go to war with Germany, or when. So Stephan sat in his usual seat and ordered *kaffee mit schlag* and apple strudel, then quietly asked the waiter to bring Žofie—who'd said she wasn't hungry—a *kipferl* and Viennese chocolate, an extravagance for her that it wasn't for Stephan and the rest of his friends.

A FUMBLED CODE

Trolleys sat as empty as the train tracks below the bridge to the Hamburg station, as empty as the German station itself at this early hour. On the walk over from the inn, Truus and Klara van Lange had passed only a single soldier, a young sergeant who turned for a second look at Klara. It was a difficulty, Truus knew, that Klara would forever draw attention, that she was so memorable. But even great difficulties could be turned to advantage. And there were thirty orphans to collect, far more children than Truus could manage alone.

"You will be wonderful at this, I promise," Truus assured Klara as they entered under the huge swastika pasted on the station's ugly facade. Was that glass at the top? It was so filthy, it was hard to tell.

They descended dirty stairs to a dirty platform, brushed a bench with a handkerchief, and set their overnight bags beside them rather than on the even dirtier ground.

Truus said, "Now, here is what I would like you to do: The soldier who will be overseeing the boarding of our carriage? Show him your ticket, and ask him in Dutch if this is where you belong. Perhaps you can express confusion that you are not in first class? But not too much confusion. We don't want him to move you to a better carriage and leave me to tend thirty children alone. If he doesn't know Dutch, pretend a poor knowledge of German, but enough to make him feel attractive. Do you understand?"

Klara looked doubtful. "We don't have papers for the children?"

"We do, but it would be better if fewer questions were asked."

The Dutch entry visas were real, thanks to Mr. Tenkink. The German exit visas might or might not be. Truus preferred to believe they were.

"As I said, you are going to be quite good at this," Truus assured her, "but it will be easier this first time to do it in your own language."

This first time, which might well be the last; Tenkink had somehow managed these entrance visas, but with the new law—the border now closed—there would be no more. Perhaps Joop was right. Perhaps the thing to do now was to take in some of the children, to provide them a home.

She said to Klara, "Fear does funny things even to the best of minds."

After a time, a station agent approached. The man stopped before them, an older man with a disconcerting face, round and pasty white and lumpy. Klara's fear was palpable in her perfect stillness, an animal instinct to blend in, but that was all right. Everyone in Germany was afraid these days.

"You are awaiting a package?" the attendant asked.

Truus answered softly, "A delivery, yes."

"The train is delayed for perhaps an hour," the attendant said.

Truus thanked him for letting them know, and promised to wait.

Klara whispered as the man left, with the smallest of smiles, "Mr. Snowman."

Truus blinked back the image of her parents back in Duivendrecht, her mother's face in the window as the splat of the refugee boy's snowball slid down the glass, her mother laughing at the children laughing out by the snowman Truus had helped them build. Mr. Snowman. The attendant did look rather snowmanly, and the nickname seemed to bode well. It said a lot, too, about Klara van Lange. She was scared enough, but not so scared as to be unable to use humor to cope.

"Perhaps you'd like to shake off the collywobbles by answering the attendant the next time he comes, Klara?" Truus asked. "He'll ask if we're awaiting a package, and we are to respond, 'A delivery, yes.'"

"A delivery, yes," Klara repeated.

After a time, an agent approached again. Truus waited for him to be close enough that she could make out his face under the cap. Not Mr. Snowman.

"You are awaiting a package?" he asked.

Truus, with a brief, unconscious touch to the ruby underneath her glove, nodded to Klara.

"A package, yes," Klara answered.

Truus said, "A *delivery*, yes."

The man's gaze darted nervously about the station, but his posture remained unchanged. It would be hard for anyone who might be observing from a distance to detect his alarm.

"A *delivery*, yes," Truus repeated.

Truus might have said a silent prayer, but she couldn't afford the distraction.

The bells of Hamburg began to ring six.

"I'm afraid the chaos in Austria has made the delivery of packages impossible this morning," the attendant said finally, into the ringing.

"Impossible. I see," Truus said.

Was he calling the transport off on account of Klara's blunder with the code, or was he telling the truth?

Truus waited patiently as he looked again at Klara, who smiled prettily. His face lightened slightly.

"We'll come back tomorrow then," Truus said, not quite a question—she didn't want to invite a direct no—but with a small uptick of her voice at the end, admission that she understood his predicament, that a fumbled code *ought* to leave him as uncertain as he was. "My friend here has never been to Hamburg," she said. "I can show her the city, and return tomorrow."

As Truus and Klara approached the steps to exit the station, someone took Klara's bag, saying, "Let me help you with that," startling them both. He took Truus's bag as well, whispering, "The man to the right at the top of the stairs followed you from the inn. You'd best go left out of the station and around the block." He handed their bags back at the top of the stairs and hurried off to the right. Truus watched him pass a man who did seem familiar, a man from the inn who'd approached her about smuggling gold coins to the Netherlands— a Gestapo trap she knew to avoid. Still, she checked her pockets, remembering Dr. Brisker, who'd given her his "lucky rock." He too had claimed to be helping her.

TYPING BETWEEN THE LINES

Stephan spread Mutti's blanket over her on the chaise by the fireplace as Aunt Lisl, who'd joined them early that morning without Uncle Michael, again adjusted the volume on the radio. The drapes were drawn, leaving a dim cast to the shelves of books that stretched up to the high ceiling of the third story, interrupted by little other than the railing circling the library's upper level, the ladders and the brass rails that Stephan had loved to climb even before he could read. He supposed it was the closed drapes that were so unsettling, as if there were something sinister about listening to the radio with all of Vienna on a bright winter morning.

He tried to read "Incident on Lake Geneva" again, a Stefan Zweig story about a Russian soldier found naked on a raft by an Italian fisherman, a story Papa said was about the extinction of human values under men like Hitler. It was hard to concentrate with the radio on, though, the news of the plebiscite for an "Independent Christian Austria" scheduled for two days later but Hitler already calling it a fraud Germany wouldn't recognize. "Lügenpresse," Hitler called the Austrian press who reported anything else. *Lying press.*

"As if that madman isn't the liar himself," Papa said to the radio as Helga, just entering with breakfast, caught a foot on Mutti's empty wheelchair and nearly dumped the silver tray. "How has Hitler convinced all of Germany that his lies are the truth and the truth is a lie?"

"Here, sir, on the desk?" Helga asked Papa uncertainly.

"Peter," Walter whispered to his rabbit, "we get to have breakfast in the library!"

Breakfast in the library, more unsettling even than the closed drapes.

His mother often had a tray brought to her bedroom on her bad days, but *all* of them being served here? And only black bread and jam and boiled eggs, with no sausages or goose liver or even a choice of *kornspitz* or *semmel* bread, much less a proper morning pastry.

Stephan took a piece of bread and slathered it with butter and jam to hide the rye taste. When he'd stomached all he could, to make Mutti happy, he said, "Well, I might take my typewriter to—"

"You can type here in the library," Papa said.

"But the desk is crowded with the breakfast—"

"You can use the rolltop in the alcove."

It was impossible to write except when he was alone even under normal circumstances, and eating in the library to the tune of Hitler threatening their country was nothing close to normal. In Germany, Goebbels was claiming that all of Austria was rioting and the Austrians were calling for the Germans to intervene, to restore order. But the streets outside their drawn drapes in the middle of Vienna were quiet. A quiet riot, Stephan thought. Žofie-Helene would have some clever paradox label for that.

He was supposed to meet her outside the Burgtheater that evening; she had a surprise for him. Surely by then he would be released. Even his father said there was no rioting anywhere in Vienna, that that was a lie Hitler made up to justify sending soldiers into a country in which they didn't belong.

Breakfast gave way to luncheon, again a tray in the library. Everyone but Walter leaned toward the radio as if that might stem the deluge of bad news. Walter, expressing the boredom Stephan shared, spun their father's globe faster and faster. No one reprimanded him.

Stephan opened the rolltop in the alcove and set his typewriter on it. He fed a blank piece of paper into the carriage, imagining a scene like the one reflected in the mirror above the desk: a roaring fire in a two-level library, with books and railings and ladders, but with open drapes. He put a young girl with smudged glasses at the top of one of the ladders, searching for a book by Sherlock Holmes. He began to type a title page—THE LIAR'S—

"Not now, sweetheart," Mutti said. "We can't hear."

He continued, typing PARADOX, hoping the reprimand was for Walter and the globe.

"Stephan," Papa said. "You too, Walter."

Stephan reluctantly abandoned the typewriter and selected a book from the children's shelf, then pulled Walter into his lap. He read *The Incredible Adventures of Professor Branestawm* in a low voice, the funny misadventures of an absentminded professor who invents burglar catchers and pancake-making machines. But Walter was squirming and Stephan quickly tired of reading in English. That was why Aunt Lisl had brought this book from her last trip to London, because Papa wanted Walter and him to improve their English.

"I could take Walter to the park," he offered, but Papa shushed him.

STEPHAN GLANCED AT the clock as Helga brought a light supper into the library. He ought to call Žofie-Helene to say he wasn't going to be able to meet her, but there was still a little time. He wolfed down a few bites—to news that Hitler was demanding Chancellor Schuschnigg hand over all power to the Austrian Nazis or face invasion—then sat at his typewriter again. He could write as they were eating. He could capture the scene: a girl with smudged glasses now collecting a plate of food from the dishes on the desk and settling in by the fire, like Aunt Lisl was; his father gathering a plate for his mother before serving himself. He would have the drapes in the room closed, after all.

Tap, tap, tap. He tried to type quietly—*by Stephan Neuman*—but the little bell of the carriage return dinged into the voices from the radio.

"Stephan," Mutti said.

"Just let him take the damned thing to another room, Ruchele!"

his father said, startling Stephan, who was sure he'd never heard Papa speak sternly to Mutti in his whole life.

"Herman!" Aunt Lisl said.

Mutti said gently, "I believe you have been the one insisting the boys stay in the library, Herman."

When had those jowls appeared on his father's face? And the lines at his eyes and mouth, the deep gouges on his brow? Mutti had been unwell for as long as Stephan could remember, but the deterioration in his father was new, and alarming.

Papa said, "Stephan, you can use my study. But stay in the house. Save your mother from adding worry about you to the rest. And take Walter with you."

"Peter and I want to stay with Mutti," Walter whined.

"Hell," Papa said, another shock; Papa was a gentleman, and gentlemen didn't talk like that.

Walter climbed up onto the chaise and snuggled with Mutti.

Papa said, "Go ahead, Stephan. Go ahead."

Stephan picked up his heavy typewriter and hurried past his mother's wheelchair before Papa could change his mind. He set the typewriter up in his father's study beside the library and set to work again, realizing only as he pulled out the title page that he hadn't brought more paper. He looked out the French windows for a minute, the same view as from his bedroom on the floor above, through the tree to the street. He rolled the sheet back into the carriage and typed on the back side. He didn't want to risk being stuck in the library again.

When he reached the bottom of the page, he rolled it back up and began typing in the spaces between the lines, listening now to the voices in the library. Yes, his parents and Aunt Lisl were caught up in earnest conversation.

He quietly opened the window, slipped out onto the balcony, pulled the window closed behind him, and climbed out onto a tree branch. Instead of scaling up the tree to the roof as he usually did—late at night, for the view of Vienna in moonlight—he scaled down, dropping from a bottom branch to the ground, near the guardhouse and the front doors. He paused. Where was Rolf? Was no one minding the door? But it didn't matter. There would be no visitors tonight.

Still, he stopped to peer into the window of the little room in the gatehouse that was Rolf's. It was too dark to see if anyone was home. The street was eerily quiet too, his own shadow in the golden glow from the cast-iron streetlights oddly unsettling as he hurried down the block.

CHAOS THEORY

Stephan watched nervously as Žofie-Helene unlocked the Burg-theater's side door with the key she'd pinched from her grandfather's coat pocket.

"We shouldn't be here," Dieter said.

"Stephan will get to see scenes from his own play performed on a real stage," Žofie-Helene insisted, leading them down the hall and into the theater itself. "Just like his hero Stefan Zweig."

"We'll be in so much trouble if we're caught," Dieter insisted.

Žofie-Helene said, "I thought you *liked* trouble, Dieter."

She tossed her coat and scarf on a seat in the theater's back row, then disappeared out into the lobby without explanation.

Stephan whispered to his friend, "'I thought you liked trouble, Dieter.'"

"Only trouble with girls."

"You haven't gotten into any trouble with girls, Dieterrotzni."

"Haven't I? If you want to kiss a girl, you just do it, Stephan. And *you're* the snot nose."

A stage light blinked on, startling Stephan. He lowered his voice further, saying, "You can't just kiss a girl."

"They want you to. They want a man who is in charge. They want you to compliment them and kiss them."

Žofie-Helene appeared on the stage. How had she gotten there?

"'The question now is about hemoglobin,'" she said, reciting a line from his new play. "'No doubt you see the significance of this discovery of mine?'"

When Stephan and Dieter just stood in the aisle, looking up at her, she said, "Come on, Deet. Haven't you memorized your lines?"

Dieter hesitated, but shrugged off his coat, headed down the aisle, and climbed onto the stage. He recited, "'It's interesting no doubt, but—'"

"'It's interesting, *chemically*, no doubt,' Deet," Stephan corrected. "Can't you remember a simple line?" His nervousness was leaking out at Dieter, although he might really be mad at Žofie. But how could he be mad at a girl who wanted to give him the gift of seeing his work performed on the Burgtheater stage?

Dieter said, "It means the same thing."

"It's an homage to Sherlock Holmes, Deet," Žofie-Helene told him. "It doesn't work as an homage if you don't say the words exactly."

Stephan came down the aisle, supposing he ought to take a seat near the stage. Wasn't that what directors did?

"Sherlock Holmes is a man," Dieter said. "I still don't understand how a girl sleuth honors him."

Žofie-Helene said, "It's more interesting with a female sleuth because it's unexpected. And anyway, I've read all the Sherlock Holmes stories, and you haven't read even one."

Dieter reached out and touched her cheek. "That's because you're so much smarter than Stephan and me, and prettier too, my little *mause-bär*," he said, using the nickname from Stephan's own first act.

Stephan expected Žofie-Helene to laugh at Dieter, but she only blushed and looked to Stephan, then down at the stage boards. He ought not to have given Dieter the Selig role to Žofie-Helene's Zelda, but Dieter was the only one with the arrogance to pull it off. Stephan had tried to mix a Sherlock Holmes–type sleuth, the female Zelda, with a character sort of like the doctor in Zweig's *Amok*, a boy obsessed with a girl who wasn't interested in him. He didn't exactly understand *Amok*, though, and when he'd asked Papa why the woman thought the doctor could help her with the baby she didn't want, his father answered gruffly, "You're a man of character, Stephan. You won't ever be in the position of having a baby you ought not to have."

Dieter tipped Žofie's chin up and kissed her lips. She received the kiss awkwardly, but then she sort of melted into Dieter.

Stephan turned his back to them, pretending to care which seat he chose and muttering, "This is a mystery, not a love story, you clod."

He took a seat and looked up at them. Mercifully they were no longer kissing, although Žofie's cheeks were flushed. "Žofe," he said, "start with the line about what a dolt Dieter is."

"What a dolt Selig is?" Žofie asked.

"Isn't that what I just said? If everyone is going to repeat everything I say, we'll never get through the script."

THEY HAD BEEN rehearsing for two scenes and the clocks of Vienna had just struck seven when Žofie heard something. Car horns? Cheering outside the theater? That's what it sounded like: the muffled sounds of crowds cheering, horns honking. She looked from the stage down to Stephan. Yes, he heard it too.

The three of them grabbed their coats and hurried to the theater's front doors, the ruckus growing ever louder. When they pushed the doors open from inside, the noise overwhelmed. Vienna swarmed with weapon-carrying brownshirts, men in swastika armbands, young men hanging off trucks painted with swastikas rushing down the Ringstrasse, past the university and city hall, right past them there at the theater. No one was rioting, though. They were joyous. Everywhere they shouted "Ein Volk, Ein Reich, Ein Führer!" and "Heil Hitler, Sieg Heil!" and "Juden verrecken!" *Death to the Jews.*

Žofie scanned the crowd for Mama as the three of them slipped back into the shadowed darkness of the theater entrance. This must be why Grandpapa had come to stay with Jojo and her tonight while Mama went out, but what was it? Where could this all have come from? The painted trucks. The swastikas being plastered on lampposts. The armbands. The crowds. They couldn't have materialized out of nowhere. Zero plus zero plus zero out into infinity was still zero.

Some boys down the street began painting a shop window with swastikas, skull and crossbones, and "Juden."

"Look, Stephan," Dieter said, "it's Helmut and Frank from school! Let's go!"

Stephan said, "We should get Žofie-Helene home, Deet."

Dieter looked at Žofie expectantly, the excitement in his eyes very like that time Jojo had spiked such a high fever and kept calling Žofie "Papa" even though she only knew Papa through photos and stories, Papa had died before Jojo was born.

Stephan said, "I'll take her home, Deet. I'll catch up with you later."

She and Stephan backed farther into the shadows as Dieter rushed down the theater steps, toward a gang of Nazis surging toward an old man who came out of a building to protect his shop window. A brownshirt began taunting the man, and others joined. One swung a punch at the poor old man's stomach, and he doubled over.

"God," Stephan said. "We should help him."

Already the man had disappeared under a swarm of brownshirts.

Žofie looked away, to men raising a Nazi flag over the Austrian Parliament, with no one there to stop them: no police, no military, not even the good people of Vienna. Were *these* the good people of Vienna? All these people shouting their support for Hitler, these boys who might have been peering in the store window to see the model train at Christmastime?

"We can't get home through the streets," she said.

Chaos. It was the one thing that even mathematics couldn't predict.

WITH SCISSORS SHE found in Grandpapa's barbershop without turning on the light, Žofie pried open the grate below the mirror. She led

Stephan through the ducts they'd traveled that first day they met, to an opening to the underground she'd later found but never taken, too afraid of getting lost by herself.

"Ooof," she said as she dropped into the cave-darkness, much farther down than she'd imagined.

Stephan dropped down too, and Žofie groped blindly for him, feeling a shock of comfort when her fingers found his sleeve. He took her hand in his. Again, comfort, and something more.

She said, "Now which way?"

"You don't know?"

"I've never been in the underground except with you."

"I've never been in this part," Stephan said. "Well, we're not going back up through the theater, not without a ladder."

They crept forward together, the trickle of water and the scamper of scurrying things all around them in the startling darkness. Žofie tried not to think about the thugs and murderers Stephan had told her about. What choice was there? Aboveground, the thugs and murderers had taken over the streets.

THE SOUNDS OF the crowds were distant, but Stephan could still hear horns honking and "Heil Hitler" repeated again and again as they emerged from the underground through the octagonal manhole near Žofie's apartment, Stephan lifting a single triangle ever so slightly and peeking out first to see that this back street was safe.

At her building door, Žofie keyed the lock. "Be careful going home, okay?" she said to Stephan, and she kissed him on the cheek and disappeared inside, leaving him lingering in the cold brush of the arm of her glasses against his skin, the warmth of her cheek, the soft dampness of her lips.

She'd kissed Dieter snot-nose full on the lips, though.

No, Dieter had kissed her.

In an upstairs window, a shadow man behind thin curtains threw his arms out, wrapping up the slight shadow girl who was Žofie-Helene arriving home to her father. Except that Žofie's father was dead. Stephan watched closely, making out the squat round body that was Otto Perger, the two shadows connecting in a hug of love and relief. He ought not to watch; Stephan knew that. He ought to turn and slip back into the underground, make his own way home. But he stood there as the shadow grandfather and granddaughter separated and spoke together, as Žofie raised up a little to kiss her grandfather on the cheek. Her glasses would be brushing her grandfather's cheek, her skin would be brushing her grandfather's skin.

She disappeared from the window, but her shadow reappeared a moment later, holding something. Faintly, the opening notes of Bach's Cello Suite no. 1 trickled out to join the distant horns and the cheering voices, the unknown future of whatever was to be Vienna after tonight. And still Stephan watched, imagining what it would be like to wrap Žofie's slight body up in his own arms, to feel the press of her breasts, to kiss her on the lips, on her neck, at the base of her throat where the infinity necklace her father hadn't actually given her touched bare skin.

EMPTY DANCE CARDS

The Hamburg inn's glossy oak taproom was overrun with beer-laden SS. Truus put a hand on Klara's across the table. The poor woman's fingers were trembling. Her schnitzel sat untouched on her plate.

"It's frightening, I know," Truus said soothingly, her voice low-pitched so that only Klara would hear. "But the Germans will allow only a five a.m. train, so no one will see the children leave, and it couldn't go today."

"Because I said 'package' rather than 'delivery.'"

"In this business things don't always go by the clock," Truus said gently.

Klara said, "It's just that . . . Mr. Van Lange is so nervous for me. And we can't stay here waiting forever, especially if— Do you suppose it's true? These men seem to think Hitler will invade Austria tonight, or perhaps already has."

Truus lifted her fork and collected a bite of schnitzel, thinking an Austrian invasion would explain why there wasn't a train for them. The trains might all be moving troops.

"That's not our worry tonight," she said. "Our worry is thirty German orphans."

They ate in silence for a few moments before they were approached by one of the SS, who kicked his heels together sharply and bowed so low that his head nearly touched Truus's plate.

"I am Curd Jiirgens," he said, his voice slurring.

The song that played was a bad omen: "Ah, Miss Klara, I Saw You Dancing."

Truus took his measure. She did not offer their names.

"Mutti," he said, addressing Truus, "may I ask your daughter to dance?"

Truus looked him up and down. She answered firmly but politely, "No, you may not."

The room fell silent except for the music, everyone turning to watch.

The owner of the inn hustled to their table, taking Mrs. Van Lange's plate although it was barely touched, saying, "Perhaps you ladies are ready to be escorted back to your room?"

THE ANSCHLUSS

When Stephan came up from the underground through one of the kiosks on the street, Nazi storm troopers had replaced the guards at the chancellery, and the crowds were even more raucous. Staying in the shadows of the buildings, he wound his way to the royal palace and ducked through the arches to Michaelerplatz, where a banner on Loos Haus read "The same blood belongs in a combined Reich!" He went the back way home from there, to find the curtains still drawn and the house dark, and still no Rolf.

He slipped back into the palais, quietly closing the door behind him, and crept up the stairs, hoping to sneak back in unnoticed, as if he'd been in his father's study next to the library all this time. He listened outside the open library door to Papa and Mutti arguing to the drone of the radio, Walter asleep in Mutti's arms and his rabbit on the floor.

"You have to take Walter and go on to the train station," his mother was insisting. "Lisl will have gotten the tickets. I'll send Stephan along."

"You're overreacting, you and Lisl both," his father said. "Who can my sister imagine will bother her? She's married into one of Vienna's most prominent families. And if I left, who would run Neuman's Chocolates? President Miklas will have order restored by daybreak, and you can't stay alone here, Ruche—"

Lisl burst through the front door and ran upstairs, rushing past Stephan into the library just as Mutti was saying Helga would take care of her and she could join them when she was well enough.

"Don't be a fool, Ruchele," Aunt Lisl said as Stephan, ignoring the ruckus spilling in from the door she'd left ajar, tried to slip in behind her.

"Stephan! Thank heavens," Mutti exclaimed as Papa demanded to know where he had been.

Aunt Lisl said, "The eleven fifteen to Prague was packed by nine o'clock—completely sold out before I got to the station. And there's nothing else tonight. Anyway, as soon as the train boarded, those awful thugs began pulling off any Jew who had a seat."

The grandfather clock struck a single chime, a half hour or one in the morning. The radio continued its low murmur, replaying part of an address Chancellor Schuschnigg had made earlier in the evening, saying that the German Reich had presented an ultimatum demanding that unless a chancellor chosen by them was appointed, German troops would begin to cross the border. "We have, because even in this solemn hour we are not willing to spill German blood, ordered our army, in case an invasion is carried out, to pull back without any substantial resistance, to await the decisions of the next few hours," the chancellor said. "So in this hour I take my leave of the Austrian people with a word of farewell uttered from the depth of my heart: God protect Austria!"

The chancellor had resigned, turning the government over to the Nazis? Austria was not even going to defend herself?

Voices from downstairs startled them. Stephan helped Papa quickly lift Mutti into her wheelchair, still holding the sleeping Walter, and Papa pushed her to the library door. It would be safer on the upper floors.

Already young men and boys swarmed the palais, voices echoing excitedly in the entry hall.

Papa backed Mutti into the library again and threw the lock.

From below came the thuds and crashes of furniture being upended, the tinkle of crystal breaking, not just a glass or a vase but perhaps all of the crystal and silver and china Helga had laid out on the table in case they might want a proper dinner. Raucous laughter followed. Someone played the piano, surprisingly beautifully. Beethoven's

Moonlight Sonata. Nazis called to each other about a cigarette box, a candlestick, the statues lining the ballroom. Some began chanting, "Heave-ho. Heave-ho," followed by a heavy thud that could be nothing less than one of the large marble statues toppling over onto the ballroom floor. The invaders cheered and cheered, several now stomping up the main stairs to the upper floors, to the bedrooms where Stephan supposed they hoped to find the family.

Something crashed overhead, followed by more laughter. Papa's money clip would be on the dresser. Mutti's jewels might be out too. It wasn't clear if the invaders were taking things or just reveling in being in the opulent house with its doorman who had always blocked entry. Where *was* Rolf?

Poor Helga on the servants' floor must be terrified. Would these hooligans harm the servants?

The library doorknob rattled. No one moved. It rattled again. Still, the radio continued its revealing murmur.

The piano played in the music room, the C-sharp—the note Stephan did think seemed like the moonlight on Lake Lucerne might sound if it were audible—now ominous.

A voice said, "Who's in there? Have you locked yourselves in?" It might be Dieter's voice, but Stephan couldn't believe that, not really.

A body bumped violently against the door, then again, followed by laughter, and shoving, and another thud at the door as different voices urged one and then another to step aside, they would be the one to break open the door.

"That statue," someone said. "We could use that to force the door."

A chaos of chatter and sliding feet was followed by laughter. The statue was marble. Like the one they'd toppled in the ballroom, it weighed over five hundred pounds. Žofie had calculated that.

Another body thumped against the library door.

"How about this table?" someone said.

Stephan listened as if by listening intently enough he could stop them. His mother's collection of silver trinkets clanged to the floor outside the door. And still the radio murmured, still the piano played.

Stephan moved to the doorway, his body one more barrier against them. His mother shook her head, trying to dissuade him, but no one moved or said a word.

The radio announcer called attention for an important announcement: President Miklas had given in. Major Klausner announced "with deep emotion in this festive hour that Austria is free, that Austria is National Socialist."

A roaring cheer sounded out in the street.

From down by the front door, someone whistled loudly.

The boy who sounded so like Dieter shouted, just outside the door, "Over the rail!"

A splintering crash in the marble entryway met with cheers and a stampede down the stairs. The front door slammed, leaving them to the muffled sounds from outside and the low murmur of the radio, and *Moonlight Sonata* still being played on the piano. The final two long, deep notes of the first movement sounded, followed by a moment of quiet. A last set of footsteps hurried across the entryway. The door opened, but did not close again. Had he left?

Before the stillness inside had time to settle, the voice on the radio giving way to a German military march, Stephan opened the library door and peered out. There was chaos everywhere, but no piano player.

He crept down the stairs, stumbling the last few steps. He threw the lock on the front doors. He leaned back against them, his heart thudding like some frantic visitor banging the knocker outside.

The entryway and the imperial stairway were awash in broken and dented things: furniture and crystal, paintings and sculptures, delicate silver flower bowls and sugar boxes, baby rattles, water vessels, thimbles and bottle stoppers and things that had no purpose whatsoever now irreparably dented. Scattered among it all were the trampled photographs and papers and letters that would be, in all the mess left in the invaders' wake, the sight that would make the tears pool in Mutti's eyes. Only the piano seemed unharmed, the player even having taken the trouble to pull the cover back over the keys, a task Stephan himself so often forgot. As he approached it, he came upon another mess of scattered pages. Faceup among them, trampled almost to illegibility, was a page on which was typed only a title: THE LIAR'S PARADOX.

Part II

THE TIME

BETWEEN

AFTER THE REFUSAL TO DANCE

Truus peered into the darkness outside the guest room at the little Hamburg inn just as Klara van Lange, awoken by the voices or perhaps up all night, asked what all the noise was.

"The boys from the bar are standing on the flat roof below our window, singing."

"At four in the morning?"

"I believe they mean to serenade you, dear."

Truus let the drape fall closed and climbed back into bed.

Minutes later, the alarm clock rang out. The two women got up and, without turning on the lights given the boys outside, shed their nightclothes and began to dress. Truus felt Klara watching her finish the hook-and-eye fastenings of her corset and choose a stocking. It was unnerving, to be watched in half nakedness, even in the darkness. From inside. From outside.

"What is it, Klara?" she asked, stocking in hand.

Klara van Lange looked away, to the window. "Do you suppose we would be doing this if we had children of our own?"

Truus slid her stocking over her toes and around her heel, over her calf and knee to her thigh, a bit of it catching in between the two intertwined bands of her center ring, but not laddering. She carefully clipped the stocking into place as, outside, the boys were giving up and leaving. In a moment Truus might turn on the light, or Klara might.

"You're still young, dear," Truus said softly. "There's still time for you."

CHOICES

The trolleys outside the Hamburg station were as silent as they had been the prior morning, the tracks below as empty. Truus and Klara van Lange entered again through the doors beneath that awful swastika, descended the same dirty stairs to the same dirty platform, brushed the same bench with a fresh handkerchief—the only bit of Truus that was fresh this morning; she hadn't packed for the delay. Again they set their overnight bags beside them and waited. It was not yet dawn.

Mr. Snowman approached and, without turning or pausing, whispered, "The train is delayed thirty minutes, but your package will arrive before it leaves."

Just as, finally, the train could be heard approaching, two supervisors—an older woman with gray hair and a younger one with a baby in her arms—led a gaggle of children down the same stairs Truus and Klara had descended.

Truus asked the younger supervisor to introduce the children as the gray-haired one checked names off a clipboard list and handed the paperwork to Klara. With a warm hand for each child—touch was so important to establishing trust—Truus told them they could call her "Tante Truus."

After all thirty had been checked off, the younger supervisor shot a nervous glance to the older one and said, "Adele Weiss." She handed the baby in her arms to Truus and hurried away, the child now in Truus's arms crying, "Mama! Mama!" and beginning to wail.

"Her paperwork?" Klara asked the older supervisor.

Truus cooed at the girl to calm her as the train hissed to a stop.

"We can't take a child without paperwork," Klara whispered.

Truus nodded toward the Nazi attendant just stepping down from the train to the platform. "Mrs. Van Lange, I believe you're on," she said. "I'll have help enough here getting the children onto the train."

Klara, with a dubious glance at the child in Truus's arms, extracted her ticket and approached the Nazi, whose gaze fixed on Klara's pretty calves and ankles under her shorter skirt.

"Entschuldigen Sie, bitte," she said to him. "Sprechen Sie Niederländisch?"

The train attendant looked for all the world as if Helen of Troy had just abandoned a train station bench to chat with him.

With little Adele Weiss on her hip, Truus took another child's hand and walked to the train carriage, the Nazi glancing up only briefly before returning his attention to Klara van Lange. Truus climbed aboard, and the supervisor began to help the children climb up to her.

"Thank you," the older supervisor said. "These choices we must make—"

"You've put the lives of thirty children—children who have no parents—at risk for the sake of one whose mother clearly loves her," Truus said. "Hurry now, let's get them all on the train."

As the supervisor handed the last child up to Truus, the woman whispered, "You do my sister a disservice, Frau Wijsmuller. You would have her risk her daughter's life along with her own."

WITH THE CHILDREN aboard and the train leaving the station, Klara van Lange began to weep.

"Not yet, dear," Truus said. "There is still the inspection at the border."

Truus thought to tell her she was too young and beautiful, too memorable, to be asked to do this again, but although there were volunteers enough to help refugees in the Netherlands, those who would cross the border were a rarer breed.

"I'd advise you to get used to this, but I never have," she said. "I wonder if anyone does."

She handed little Adele Weiss to poor Klara. "Hold the child. She'll make you feel better; she's that kind of child."

The other children all sat miraculously quietly. She supposed that was on account of the shock.

She said to Klara, "My father used to say courage isn't the absence of fear, but rather going forward in the face of it."

CLEANING DAY

Stephan peered out into the gray Vienna morning through a gap in the closed library curtains. A bundled woman was selling swastika flags on sticks, another offered large round swastika balloons, and the "Ja" banners for the plebiscite were already painted over with huge swastikas. Men on ladders hung the symbol from streetlights. Others plastered trolley-stop signs with "Ein Volk, Ein Reich, Ein Führer." Signs with the same slogan topped the trolleys, which also sported giant posters of Hitler. Just outside the palais door, an open-bed truck painted with a swastika came to a stop.

"Papa!" Stephan said, alarmed. Were they coming for them again?

His father, giving Mutti a dose of medicine, didn't register Stephan's alarm. He didn't even look up from Mutti, wrapped in blankets on the chaise by the fire with Walter and his stuffed Peter Rabbit curled up beside her as he forever was, as if he knew somehow that although no one would say it, their mother might not be here tomorrow. The five of them—Aunt Lisl was still with them—listened to the news on the radio while, throughout the house, the servants restored order.

Stephan gathered his courage and looked out again. A driver had hopped out of the truck and was offloading bundles of swastika armbands. Crowds gathered to get them and put them on.

It was shocking how well organized this all was, how many flags and cans of paint and armbands and balloons—balloons!—were here in Vienna without seeming ever to have arrived, to celebrate this moment the Germans wanted the world to believe was a spontaneous uprising from within Austria.

On the sidewalk beyond their gate and on the street Stephan crossed every day of his life, people on their hands and knees scrubbed away plebiscite slogans. Not just men but also women and children, the elderly, parents and teachers, rabbis. They were surrounded by SS, Gestapo, Nazis, and local police—many holding up their pant legs so as not to get wet as they supervised the work—while onlooking neighbors jeered.

"Herr Kline is a hundred years old, and he's never done anything but say a cheery good morning and let people who can't afford to buy a paper read at his stall," Stephan said softly.

Papa set the pill bottle and water glass beside Mutti's largely untouched breakfast. "They're making Vienna 'fit' for Hitler, son. If you'd been home—"

"Don't, Herman," Mutti scolded. "Just don't! You'll make it my fault, for being unwell. If I were well, we'd have left weeks ago."

"I can't leave in any event, Ruche," Papa said soothingly. "You know it's not your fault. I can't leave the business. I only meant—"

"I'm not a fool, Herman," Mutti interrupted. "If you want to use the excuse of the business to save me from blame, fine, but don't you dare make it Stephan's fault. We'd have sold the business and left if I were well."

Walter buried his face in his Peter Rabbit. Papa sat beside them at the edge of the chaise and kissed Walter's forehead, but still Walter cried.

Stephan returned to the window, to the awful view. Their parents didn't argue like this.

"All of Vienna loves Neuman's Chocolates," Papa said. "Those thugs last night, they didn't know who we are. Look, no one is bothering us this morning."

On the radio, Joseph Goebbels was reading a proclamation from Hitler. "I myself, as führer, will be pleased to enter Austria, my homeland, once again as a German and a free citizen. The world must see that the German people in Austria have been seized by a soulful joy, that their rescuing brothers have come to their aid in their hour of great need."

"We need to send the boys away to school," Mutti said in a voice so steady that it alarmed Stephan even as he recognized she meant to spare him alarm. "To England, I suppose."

THE CARD INDEX

A huge circular card index filled with hole-punched cards dominated the office of SD Department II/112 at Berlin's Hohenzollern Palace. The place was littered with Austrian newspapers, books, annual reports, handbooks, and membership files men consulted as they filled out colored information cards. A senior aide went through Eichmann's personal notes gathered from the contacts he'd been cultivating, while a second aide sat at a piano bench, inserting completed cards into the index, arranged alphabetically. At Eichmann's entrance, Tier at heel beside him, everyone stood, offering salutes and "Heil Hitler, Untersturmführer Eichmann." He'd been promoted yet again, to second lieutenant, and if he was still not the head of his department, he was at least in charge of this: gathering whatever information might be needed to provoke the Reich's Jews to emigrate. His view that the best solution to the Jewish problem was to rid Germany of its rats was finally getting its due.

He picked up copies of various publications and read random by-lines and other names to the aide loading the index. At each name, the aide spun the file until he located the corresponding card, then read aloud—Jews and Jew-lovers to a man.

"Käthe Perger," Eichmann read from a byline in the prior day's *Vienna Independent*, his attention caught by a blatantly anti-Nazi bit of trash on the front page.

The aide spun the index, extracted a card, and read, "Käthe Perger. Editor of the *Vienna Independent*. Anti-Nazi. Non-Communist. Supports Austrian chancellor Schuschnigg."

"Ex-chancellor," Eichmann said. "This Käthe Perger is perhaps a male journalist hiding behind the stink of women's ink?"

They could send the men to Dachau, but they'd have few places to hold women.

"The information is quite specific," the aide said. "Husband deceased. Two daughters, fifteen and three. The fifteen-year-old something of a mathematics prodigy, apparently. And she's not a Jew."

"The prodigy?"

"Käthe Perger. She's from Czechoslovakia, and her parents were Christians. Farmers. The father dead, but the mother still living."

The Volk. The blood of the Reich.

"The dead husband was a Jew?" he suggested.

"Also Christian, the son of a barber—and a journalist like his wife. He died in the summer of 1934."

"In Vienna?"

"He happened to be in Berlin at the time."

"I see," Eichmann said. The husband was one of the bothersome journalists who'd not survived the Röhm Purge. "One of the suicides."

The aide chuckled.

"Then good riddance," Eichmann said. "This Käthe Perger will be someone else's problem; we won't be faced with the prospect of arresting someone's mother. Our charge is the Jews."

"You'll take the catalog with you to Vienna?" the aide asked.

Eichmann said, "The list of persons we make from it. To Linz, I hope."

THE PROBLEMS YOU
FAIL TO ANTICIPATE

Truus gently bounced a sleeping Adele Weiss in her arms as she negotiated with an SS guard at the border station, thinking she could use that doctor's lucky "rock" right about now. Behind her, Klara van Lange did the best she could to keep the thirty children in line, waiting to board the train out of Germany and into the Netherlands.

"But again, Frau Wijsmuller," the guard insisted, "you do not have a child indicated on your passport. A Dutch child can travel with its mother without separate papers, yes, but the child must be indicated on its parent's passport."

"I tell you again, sir, that I haven't had time to change my passport." Wishing she'd found a sympathetic traveler whose passport did list children and arranged a short border adoption. Thinking she needed to finish with this man before the child woke and cried for her mother while still in Truus's arms. "Can't you see she has my . . ." Eyes, Truus had almost said, but the child was sleeping, this dark, petite-faced child who looked nothing like Truus.

"Ah, it is Mutti and her fine daughter!" someone said, the voice drawing Truus's and the guard's attention. It was the soldier from the inn—Curd Jiirgens, who had asked if he might dance with Klara. As the guard saluted, Truus pulled the baby closer. This Jiirgens would know she'd had no child at the inn. Lordy, what harm would one dance have done?

"I was sure I recognized you, and yes, I am right," Jiirgens said proudly. Then, in that officious way of senior officers, "Is there some problem, Officer? This lovely woman and her beautiful daughter don't dance, apparently, but nor do they complain when they well might."

He smiled at Truus as the soldier muttered, "Her daughter," looking from Truus to the sleeping Adele. Truus remained silent, afraid anything she said might alert the border guard to his misunderstanding, as Jiirgens offered his apologies to Klara van Lange.

"But surely your midnight serenade was apology enough!" Klara answered charmingly, distracting both men. And then the men were helping them board the children, Truus trying not to think what it might mean that Curd Jiirgens and his men had not moved from Hamburg toward Austria to support the invasion, but were instead here, at the border with the Netherlands.

A SHORT FEW minutes after the train left the German station, it stopped in the Netherlands. A Dutch agent boarded the carriage and, with a distasteful look at the seats all filled with children, examined the paperwork Truus offered, thirty perfectly valid entrance visas signed by Mr. Tenkink at The Hague. The station clock outside the window read 9:45 a.m.

"These children are all dirty Jews," the border guard said.

Truus might have slapped him if she weren't bringing a child across the border with no papers. Instead, she said in her most accommodating voice that if he had any doubt about the visas, she would refer him to Mr. Tenkink—keeping focus on the thirty children who had entry visas and not the one who did not.

The guard asked them to step from the train, which was to leave again in just a few minutes. There was nothing to do but what the man asked. Truus kissed the forehead of the child in her arms as he took their papers and disappeared. She was such a sweet baby, this little Adele Weiss. Edelweiss. A spiky white star of a flower that clings to Alpine cliffsides. It had been the sign of the Austro-Hungarian Alpine troops of Emperor Franz Joseph I during the Great War; Truus had met boys with the symbol sewn to their collars. Now it was said to be a favorite of Hitler's.

The child looked up at Truus with a thumb in her mouth, without complaint although she must be hungry. Even Truus was hungry, having left the inn long before breakfast was served.

Their train left without them, and the clock ticked onward, another hour of trying to keep tired and restless children amused before the guard returned. Truus handed the baby to Klara as the man approached again, supposing that if it came to it, she ought to say the baby was Klara's. Klara was of an age more likely to have a young child. Truus ought to have done it at the German border. Why had she not?

She answered the border guard's further questions: "The children will be taken directly to the quarantine barracks at Zeeburg, and from there to private homes." "Again, I am sure Mr. Tenkink at The Hague would be happy to explain that he personally authorized these children to enter the Netherlands."

All but Adele. Adele Wijsmuller, Truus told herself, suddenly worried she might already have told him the child's name was Adele Weiss.

As again he left with their travel papers, Truus repeated it to herself. *Adele Wijsmuller.* She said to Klara, "It takes all one's patience to keep one's thoughts to oneself."

Klara set her hands gently on the heads of two boys; as if by magic, they stopped tussling, smiled up at her, and began to play some friendly little game with their hands.

She said to Truus, "One's thought that these children are cleaner than that guard?"

Truss smiled. "I knew you were the right one for this challenge, Klara. Now if only that border guard would get about his job before the last train leaves. Finding a place here to put up thirty children for the night would be an impossible task even if they were Christian."

"Who would have imagined it would be easier to get out of Germany than into the Netherlands?" Klara said.

Truus said, "And it's the problems you fail to anticipate that defeat you."

THE SHAME SALUTE

Stephan stood with Dieter and their gang in the crowd, the horizon moving through the red of the German flag and on toward darkness before the first train arrived at the Westbahnhof station and soldiers emerged. The troops, led by a marching band, were barely visible down the block, but the crowd raised arms in salute and cheered wildly. Armored cars arrived from farther up the road with more Germans, some carrying torches, their stiff-legged steps up the Mariahilfer Strasse sounding a beat to the band's music as they approached. The crowd around Stephan grew even louder, Dieter and the other boys chanting over and over with them, "Ein Volk, Ein Reich, Ein Führer!"

Across the road, an old lady in a proper fur coat—someone Stephan might have passed any afternoon on the Ringstrasse—began to yell at a man who stood watching as silently as Stephan was, his arms, too, at his sides. The woman waved her raised hand at the man, insistent. The man tried to ignore her, but onlookers surrounded him, and he disappeared into the squall. Stephan couldn't see what happened. The man was just gone, leaving the lady in the fur coat again shouting, "Ein Volk, Ein Reich, Ein Führer!"

"Ein Volk, Ein Reich, Ein Führer, Stephan!" Dieter shouted right in Stephan's ear, and Stephan turned to see all of his friends saluting and shouting, and watching him.

He hesitated, alone in the massive crowd.

"Ein Volk, Ein Reich, Ein Führer!" Dieter repeated.

Stephan could find no breath for words, but he slowly raised his arm.

INTERTWINED

Truus stepped from the train onto the Amsterdam platform, baby Adele in her arms and thirty children still to be helped from the train. Joop took the baby from her and wrapped Truus herself in a fierce hug. Well, of course he'd been worried, and Mr. Van Lange right behind him, too, already at the carriage window, calling, "Klara?" and looking like he might cry with relief at the sight of his wife. The poor man hurried to the carriage door and began lifting the children down, welcoming them each to Amsterdam as he set them on the platform to be taken by the volunteers.

Joop cooed at baby Adele, saying he was Joop Wijsmuller, the husband of this crazy Tante Truus, and who was she? The child put a hand on Joop's nose and laughed delightedly.

"Her name is Adele Weiss. She's——"

She was not one of the thirty, but to admit that to Joop—that the child's mother was so concerned for her baby's safety that she'd turned her over to a stranger without so much as papers, real or forged? That Truus herself had risked bringing a child with neither exit nor entry visa over the border? That would only alarm him more, and to what end?

"She's quite the sweetest child," she said. Edelweiss. A rare flower.

Together they shepherded the children out to the electric tram, the wires overhanging all the city streets not, in Truus's opinion, an improvement over the horse-drawn trams, but at least none of these sixty little feet would step in horse filth. Only when everyone else was on the trolley did Joop hand little Adele up to her.

Truus, waving back at Joop as the trolley swayed and clanged into motion, thought of the beautiful wooden rocking cradle he bought the first time she was pregnant, the linens she sewed for it, the pillow sham she embroidered with a snowman on a bridge overlooking a canal and an overhang of tree branches, white on white so that you might not see the scene at all. Where were the cradle and linens now? Had Joop stored them out of sight? Or had he finally given them away?

THE ZEEBURG QUARANTINE barracks consisted of a villa, an office building, and ten barracks, each as dismal and uninviting as the next. They were meant to house unwell Europeans bound for the United States, but what choice was there, with so many children? Truus, holding baby Adele, helped the last children climb from the trolley, a girl whose long dark braids were tied with a red ribbon, and her brother with the same sad saucer eyes. All these children had sad eyes, even baby Adele, who quietly sucked her thumb in Truus's arms.

The two siblings balked when Truus directed them to separate barracks.

"We can share a bunk," the boy offered. "I don't care if I sleep with girls."

"I know you don't, dear," Truus said, "but they've set aside one place for the girls and another for the boys."

"But why?"

"That is an excellent question." Some of these girls were old enough to get into trouble, though, and some of the boys old enough to lead them to it. "I might have done it differently, but sometimes we have to live with other people's choices, even when we might make better ones ourselves."

Truus handed the baby to Klara and took the girl up in her arms, then stooped to her brother's level. "Sheryl, Jonah," she said, meeting each child's gaze directly so they could see that she was being honest. "I know it's frightening to be separated." *I know how frightened you must be*, she'd thought to say, but that wouldn't have been the truth; she could only imagine how terrifying this must be for a child who'd already lost her parents. She might just take them home with little Adele Weiss, her rare little flower, but Joop was right: if they started taking in orphans, it would be difficult to continue her trips to Germany.

Perhaps this would be her last trip anyway, though, with her own country's border now closed, no more entry visas to be had.

She removed her intertwined ring and separated its two bands. "This ring was given to me by someone I love as much as you two love each other," she said to the siblings. "Someone I can't bear to be separated from either. And yet I have to leave him sometimes, to help those who need my help."

"Like us, Tante Truus?" the boy said.

"Yes, wonderful children like you and Sheryl, Jonah," she said.

She took the girl's hand and put one of the bands from the ring on her thumb, a reasonably good fit, then placed the other on her brother's middle finger—a bit loose. She said a quick prayer that the ring bands wouldn't fall off and get lost, this gift from Joop that she never could wear comfortably after losing her first baby and yet couldn't bear to take off and put away. Hope was such a fragile thing.

"When I come to collect you to take you to your new home—and I promise I will find a family to take you both—you must give this ring back to me, all right? Now then, go on and find your bunks."

As they set off, she reached in her coat pocket for her gloves, feeling oddly exposed without her ring. She was just pulling one on when Klara van Lange rejoined her. She had not realized, as focused on the siblings as she was, that Klara had gone off.

"Well, they're all being settled," Klara said. "I had half a mind to take that little Adele home with me."

Truus pulled on the second glove. She carefully fastened the pearl buttons, buying time to gather herself. "They've taken Adele too?" she managed.

"Who wouldn't love such a beautiful child?" Klara said, her voice perhaps as unsettled as Truus's own heart. "But then the time would come when I would have to hand her back over to her mother, and I couldn't bear that, to let go of a child I'd fallen in love with. Could you, Truus?"

HITLER

Stephan climbed a streetlamp to better see. People everywhere—on the streets and in the windows and on the rooftops, on the Burgtheater steps and filling Adolf-Hitler-Platz, the newly renamed Rathausplatz—waved Nazi flags and offered Nazi salutes, all of Vienna throbbing with cheering as church bells pealed. Hitler stood in an open car, holding the windshield and waving. Two long lines of cars followed him up the Ringstrasse as soldiers, some in sidecar motorcycles, held back the crowd. The car turned in at the Hotel Imperial and Hitler stepped out onto a red carpet, greeted a few people, and disappeared through the fancy doors. Stephan watched—the empty car, the closed door, the shadow-men moving into a well-lit second-floor suite—all the while clinging to the lamppost, above the throng.

HITLER SAT ON a couch in the Royal Suite's high-ceilinged main room, its red drapes and white and gold furniture in a bit of disrepair. There were finer places to stay in Vienna, but he wouldn't have them.

"In the days I lived here, the Viennese had a sentimental way of saying, 'And when I die, I want to go to heaven and have a little hole among the stars to see my fair Vienna,'" he said as his inner circle settled around him and Julius Schaub knelt before him to remove his shiny black boots. "But to me, it was a city going to decay in its own grandeur. Only the Jews made money, and only those with Jewish friends or willing to work for Jews made a decent living. I, and a lot like me, nearly starved. I used to walk past this hotel at night when there was nothing else to do and I hadn't even money to buy a book.

I'd watch the automobiles and the coaches drive up to the entrance and be received with a deep bow by the white-mustached porter. I could see the glittering lights of chandeliers in the lobby, but even the porter wouldn't deign to speak to me."

Schaub brought him a glass of warm milk, and Hitler took a sip. Others ate. They were welcome to all the food and drink they wanted, so long as no one smoked.

"One night after a blizzard, I shoveled snow just for money for food," he said. "The Habsburgs—not Kaiser Franz Josef, but Karl and Zita—stepped out of their coach and grandly walked over a red carpet from which I had cleared the snow. We poor devils removed our hats every time aristocrats arrived, but they didn't even look at us." He settled back into the sofa, remembering the sweetness of the women's perfumes even in the frozen air as he'd shoveled snow. He'd been nothing more to those women than the slush he cleared.

"This hotel hadn't even the decency to send out hot coffee for us," he said. "All night long, each time the wind covered the red carpet with snow, I'd take a broom and brush it off. And each time I'd glance into this brilliantly lit hotel, and listen to the music. It made me wish to cry, and it made me angry, and I resolved that someday I would come back to this hotel and walk over the red carpet myself, into the glittering interior where the Habsburgs danced."

THE VIENNA INDEPENDENT

BRITAIN MOVING TO CLOSE ITS DOORS TO JEWISH IMMIGRANTS

Most other countries have already limited immigration

BY KÄTHE PERGER

March 15, 1938 — Amid the collapse of the London Stock Market on the news of Germany's seizure of Austria, the British prime minister has asked his cabinet to impose an entrance visa requirement for all citizens of the Reich.

The British Council for German Jewry, with the support of the Rothschild and Montagu banks, has long provided a financial pledge to allow Jewish refugees to emigrate to England without the threat of becoming a financial burden on the British public. But with the German occupation of Austria comes the fear of millions of arrivals, for which financial support would not be feasible.

Britain has also suspended immigration of all Jewish labor to Palestine until economic conditions improve. By order of William Ormsby-Gore, the British secretary of state for its colonies, no more than 2,000 Jews of independent means will be admitted to the colony in the next six months.

TRUUS AT THE
BLOOMSBURY HOTEL

As Truus and Joop entered an office marked "Central British Fund for German Jewry" in London's Bloomsbury Hotel, an impeccably dressed woman rose to greet them. "Helen Bentwich," she said, her voice smooth with wealth softened by social responsibility. "And this is my husband, Norman. We don't stand by formalities in this work, unless you insist."

Truus, in no position to insist on anything, responded, "This is *my* husband, Joop. What would we do without them?"

"Quite a bit more than we do with them, I suspect!" Helen said, and they all laughed.

Yes, Truus thought, instantly comfortable in this elegantly just-this-side-of-decay office with its improbably well-used Rococo writing desk and table, its worn tapestry chairs: this Helen Bentwich was, like dear Mr. Tenkink at The Hague, someone who would never say no to those who needed help if there was any possibility of yes. Helen's family, the Franklins, were bankers like Joop, only more so, part of the Anglo-Jewish "Cousinhood" of Rothschilds and Montagus that included not just powerful men—heads of banks and businesses, barons and viscounts, members of Parliament—but also women of influence. Her mother and sister had been prominent suffragettes, and Helen herself, who'd worked as the *Manchester Guardian*'s Palestine correspondent when her husband was the colony's attorney general, was now an elected member of the London County Council.

"You don't have to persuade us of the need to find homes for these children," Helen began as she cleared a chair of papers and invited them to sit. "But we'll need to move quickly."

Norman had just been part of a delegation received by the prime minister and home secretary to consider the plight of the Reich's Jews—a delegation that included Lionel de Rothschild and Simon Marks, the Marks & Spencer heir.

"No one doubts the benefits of admitting immigrants like their fathers," Norman said. "Without Marks & Spencer, where could we buy British-made-only gifts our wives can always exchange for their own better choices?"

He and Joop chuckled.

"But with this new flood of refugees . . . ," he continued. "It's a devil's choice: how to remain as humane as possible without . . . Well, we must be realistic. We can't risk an anti-Semitic response here in England."

"But these are children," Truus said.

Norman said, "The government fear that if children come, their parents will follow."

Truus said, "But these children are orphans," feeling the queasiness again, the fear that she would fail them.

Helen, with a discreet hand to her husband's arm, said, "There are thirty?"

"You've changed your mind, Truus?" Joop asked with the same hopefulness he'd shown the night he'd given her the intertwined ring, the hope for the baby she might have borne if only she'd eaten one thing or not another, or stayed in bed, or been more careful.

Truus said reluctantly, "There are thirty-one."

Helen tapped a single finger lightly on her husband's arm, a gesture so small that Truus might have missed it if Norman hadn't immediately stood and asked Joop to join him outside for a cigarette, saying, "As my Helen says, the ladies accomplish quite a bit more without us."

The two left, appearing a minute later on a terrace, where they settled at a charming little wrought-iron table amid bare branches, tired grass, and brown flower beds, the blooms of Bloomsbury not evident this early in the year.

"The thirty-first child is a baby without papers," Truus told Helen. "Her mother was one of the women who delivered the children to us in Germany."

"I see," Helen said. "And you are . . . considering adopting the child?"

Truus watched through the window as Norman offered Joop a cigarette, surprised to see her husband accept.

"I meant to go back to Germany for the child's mother," she said, "but Joop says—Joop says rightly—that if Adele's mother could leave, she would have. That if we keep the child . . . It's a 'devil's choice,' as your husband says: I can help rescue more children, or I can mother this one, but it would be unfair to risk leaving her motherless again even if I could bear the possibility. And she does have a mother."

"One who loves her enough to give her away," Helen said.

She set a hand on Truus's, the gesture so filled with understanding that it made Truus wonder why she hadn't thought to touch Adele's mother this warmly, to understand.

Truus stood and went to the window, beyond which Joop and Norman chatted easily as they smoked. When she turned back, she noticed atop some papers on Helen's desk a lovely snow dome inside of which was an empty Ferris wheel and, beside its ticket booth, a snowman. She lifted the glass globe and turned it upside down, setting off a little snowstorm.

"I'm sorry," she said, realizing her presumptuousness.

"I have forty-three of them at our house in Kent, many of them Wiener Schneekugels from Vienna, as is that one," Helen said. "A bit of an obsession, I'm afraid."

"And yet you keep only this one here in your office," Truus said.

Helen smiled sadly, a concession that this snow dome held special meaning, leaving Truus to wonder what it might be.

"My mother had one of the first ever made, with the Eiffel Tower inside. From Paris—1889," Helen said. "My father didn't like us to touch it, but my mother used to let me, and it would make me giggle every time to promise not to tell." Again, the sad smile. "Truus, I know it isn't my business, but . . . You look as queasy as I felt when . . . Well, I don't have children, but . . ."

Truus tasted the ruby at her lips as she touched her belly with her other hand, the one that still held the snow dome—realizing only as she did so that Helen was right, she was again expecting. Or had she known already, really, or suspected? Could she not face it alone, with no one to tell? Amsterdam was a smaller city than one might imagine, and even the most discreet of friends might inadvertently spill the secret to Joop.

"Then keeping this German child, Truus . . . ," Helen said gently. "Isn't your devil's choice already made for you?"

The tears sprang at her name spoken so gently. It was something, always, to be addressed by name so comfortingly. Her name and the trying not to think of that: a child growing up without her mother to feed her, to bathe her, to read to her from her favorite book and sing her to sleep.

She dabbed with her handkerchief, saying, "I've never . . . Oh, Helen. But I can't possibly tell Joop, can I? He couldn't bear to lose another baby."

Helen Bentwich stood and joined her, setting a steadying hand on her arm again as, outside, Joop knocked the growing ash from his cigarette.

"Believe me when I say I know how heartbreaking it is to lose any child," Helen said.

Joop's voice drifted up through the closed window, his laughter.

"Joop would have us keep Adele," Truus said.

They watched together as their husbands stubbed out their cigarettes and turned back to the door.

"I'll find a safe place for this little Adele," Helen said. "I can promise you that."

Truus said, "I don't think it's the child's safety Joop would mean to preserve in keeping her."

THE GATES OF HELL

Stephan slipped through the crowded Heldenplatz, Žofie-Helene's hand solidly in his lest the two of them get separated in the mob. The palace grounds were more crowded even than when Vienna mourned the death of Chancellor Dollfuss, men in hats like any decent fellow from Vienna might wear, and women too, circling from the horseman statue out as far as you could see. "One People! One Reich! One Führer!" The words might well echo through Stephan's head for the rest of his life. Only the road under the arch and into the palace grounds was cleared, the crowd held back there by soldiers as Stephan pulled Žofie along to the statue of Hercules and Cerberus, then cupped his hands to give her a boost. She scrambled up the stone and over Cerberus's three heads to straddle Hercules's neck, her thighs pressing into the hero's beard and stone shoulders, her shoes dangling in front of the massive stone chest. Stephan climbed up behind her and sat in the crook between the highest of the beast's raised snouts and Hercules's shoulder. If he leaned toward Žofie, he could see around the bus in the midst of the crowd to the balcony where Hitler was to speak.

Žofie reached down, her hand inadvertently brushing Stephan's thigh as she stroked one of the stone beast's three snouts, her mouth close to Stephan's ear now, so that when she said, "Poor Cerberus," it was painfully loud.

"When you're this close, you don't have to shout," Stephan said more measuredly into her ear, inhaling the scent of her—something grassy and fresh. "And poor *Cerberus*? He's a flesh-eating beast who keeps the dead trapped in the underworld, Žofe. Eurystheus ordered

Hercules to capture the creature because he couldn't possibly succeed at it; no one had ever returned from the Underworld."

Žofie said, "I don't think you can blame a mythical creature for being what the plot of the myth calls on him to be."

Stephan considered this. "Or them? Is Cerberus a him or a them?"

He drew out his journal from his coat pocket and made a note about mythical creatures serving plots that needed them. He'd like to have written about the smell of Žofie-Helene, and the way his palm in hers fit like a jigsaw puzzle, but he only fixed them in his mind to note later, when she wasn't there.

She said, "This is one of the best bits of our friendship: the things I say going into your journal to show up later in a play."

"You know no one else says things like that, Žofe?"

"Whyever not?"

Her face was close enough that he might stretch his neck up like the beast underneath him, and kiss her.

"I don't know," he said.

He used to think he knew so much, before he met Žofie-Helene.

She sat up straight again, to observe, and Stephan did too, but always with one eye to her. He was making notes in his journal—about the day and the crowd, the Nazi flags flapping in the stiff breeze, the old Austrian heroes honored in stone statues now surrounded by what seemed to be all of Vienna crowded into the square—when a motorcade entered the plaza through the arches from the Ringstrasse. Hitler stood in straight-armed salute in an open car, the sharp echo of his shadow following along beside him. The crowd surged, exploding into straight-armed salutes and a great roar of joy, which settled into a chant of "Sieg Heil! Sieg Heil! Sieg Heil!" Stephan watched silently, a fear bubbling in his chest as the car circled the stone Prince Eugene and came to a stop. As the führer entered the royal palace, Žofie watched as silently as he did, through smudged lenses.

"We don't say those kinds of things because we aren't as sure as you are that we're right, Žofe," he said quietly, his voice too low for Žofie to hear over the chanting crowd. "We say what everyone else says, or we say nothing at all, so we won't look like fools."

"What?" Žofie-Helene responded, the single inaudible word discernible from the movement of her lips as Hitler stepped up to the microphones on the palace balcony and began, "As führer and chancellor of the German Nation, I report before history the entry of my homeland into the Reich."

REMOVAL

Eichmann wondered if the dead men in the portraits hanging around them in Vienna's Israelitische Kultusgemeinde office might have more idea of what was in store for Vienna's Jews than the Jewish leaders gathered at the table did. He watched patiently as Josef Löwenherz, the community center's director, extracted reading glasses from a vest, catching his shirt collar so that it poked out untidily. The glasses did nothing to improve the look of the man's bug eyes and furry upper lip, his hairline retreating as surely as was his stature. Such a lawyerly thing to do, to read the document carefully, as if he might have some choice in the matter.

Löwenherz signed the document and passed it to Herbert Hagen, who signed for the Reich before passing it on to Eichmann. Eichmann's appointment here in Vienna was temporary; Hagen had made that clear. It was up to Eichmann to make himself indispensable, and this raid of these IKG offices on Seitenstettengasse was his first step toward that end.

Eichmann scrawled his name beside Hagen's, set his pen next to the silver bell on the dark wood table, and stood and saluted Hagen, who, having completed his part, left for some fancy meal or some fancy woman.

"All right then," Eichmann said to the Jews at the table, "there are boxes to be loaded."

Löwenherz stammered, "You mean for us to do the loading?"

It was Eichmann's own little joke, to complete this deed under the domed ceiling in the Stadttempel's ostentatious oval room. When the Jews had finished carting their membership lists and other evidence of subversive activities from the five-story stone building to removal trucks waiting in the narrow cobblestone lane, he ordered them back inside.

Löwenherz, sweaty now and clearly unhappy to have Tier in the sacred room, but not objecting, glanced up to the second-level balcony as if it might provide escape.

"I suppose the lesser Jews sit up there," Eichmann said.

Löwenherz answered, "The women, of course."

Eichmann laughed. "The women, yes, of course."

His men fastened the synagogue doors, and an aide began reading the short list of Vienna's Jewish leaders: Desider Friedmann, the IKG president; Robert Stricker, the publisher of Vienna's Zionist daily newspaper; Jacob Ehrlich; Oskar Gruenbaum.

"Adolf Böhm . . ."

Eichmann waited until the shocked Adolf Böhm had taken his place in the line before saying, "No, Herr Böhm, I have changed my mind about you." He was pleased to see the relief register on the writer's face. Yes, this would prove to be as effective as he'd planned, to have the man feel in his weak old heart the risk he would take if he did not cooperate. To let all those who remained free today feel that risk.

His aide read the last name, "Josef Löwenherz."

At the betrayal in Löwenherz's bug eyes, Eichmann nodded. This was no mistake. He had not forgotten the lesson learned at such cost to his dignity and advancement: that he needn't pay Jews for what he wanted from them.

Only after the arrested men had been enclosed in the darkness of the truck and it had rumbled off did Eichmann reenter Löwenherz's office, Tier at heel. He scanned the dark table and the fancy wallpaper, the paintings. "Yes, your time has come," he said to the men in the portraits. He took the silver bell from the table where his pen still sat and slipped it into his pocket, a souvenir of little value, but one he would put to good use.

He returned then to the elegant six-floor Hotel Metropole where, as a young man, he'd arrived by streetcar (a dirty, clanging monstrosity like the one passing beside him now) and been prevented from entering. Now the doorman held the door for him and bowed as he passed, while in the basement, currently fashioned as a Nazi prison, the Jews he'd just arrested cowered in cells, waiting for him to decide their fates.

THE JEWISH QUESTION
IN AUSTRIA

Eichmann waited two days, long enough for the wound to fester, before summoning six of the Jewish leaders he'd let go free, all led by an old and frail and terrified Adolf Böhm. Eichmann wasn't quite sure why he'd summoned the others—Goldhammer, Plaschkes, Koerner, Rothenberg, and Fleischmann. Perhaps just to let them all see that he could.

"You will step back," he demanded. "You are too close. Now, I'm charged with solving the Jewish question in Austria. I expect your unwavering cooperation. Herr Böhm, you are the Adolf Böhm who wrote the history of Zionism? I've learned much from your writings." He recited by heart a short passage of the man's writing he'd memorized the night before. "Kol hakavod," he said to the gaping Jews. "You're surprised at my Hebrew? I was born in Sarona."

Tier's ears perked. Eichmann couldn't have said why he'd claimed Jerusalem as his birthplace the first time he'd done so, but it had proven surprisingly effective at winning the trust of naive Jews.

"I understand, Böhm, that a second volume of your work has appeared recently?" he continued. "Perhaps you will do me the favor of having a copy brought to me? Now, there is no future for Jews in Austria. What would you recommend be done to streamline your emigration?"

Böhm's horrid old mouth gaped at him. "You want me to . . ."

"You have no opinion on how to help your people, Herr Böhm?"

"I . . . Well, I . . . It's not my—"

Eichmann rang the little silver bell on his desk, saying, "You're too old for my purposes in any event."

"AND YOU ARE WHO?" Eichmann demanded of yet another of the Jews in custody. This was the fourth prisoner he'd interviewed since dismissing Böhm and the leaders he hadn't arrested. Really, it was hard to imagine how these Jews had been any success.

The Jew, perplexed, stammered, "Josef Löwenherz."

Löwenherz. The IKG director. A man did look different after a few days in a cold cell. Eichmann fingered the silver bell—Löwenherz's own. The man stared at it but said nothing.

"There is no future for Jews in Austria," Eichmann said, a line now grown tiresome. "What would you recommend be done to streamline your emigration?"

"To . . . To streamline emigration?" Löwenherz stammered. "If . . . If I may say . . . Not that I would know better than . . . Well, it seems to me that wealthy Jews are reluctant to leave their comfortable lives, and poor ones lack the means to do so."

Eichmann set a hand on Tier's head. Quite amazing, how easily terror could be stoked by such simple gestures. In the first ten days after the Germans had arrived in Austria, one hundred Jews jumped to their deaths or took poison or shot themselves.

"So you are proposing we make the lives of wealthy Jews less comfortable?" Eichmann asked the man.

"No, I . . . I understand, Herr Eichmann, sir, that there are . . . What I mean to say is that many receive one of the various papers needed to obtain a visa to leave the Reich, only to have it expire before they can obtain the other necessary paperwork. Receipts for the payment of bills and taxes and fees. You see, we . . . The whole process must then be begun again."

"That is a problem, not a solution."

"Yes. Yes, but perhaps . . . Again, not that I would know better, but mightn't you organize all the offices for the necessary permits and payments into a single building? That might allow us . . . those you would grant permission to emigrate . . . to move with visa in hand just down the hall to pay for . . . to remedy . . ."

"Which would rid us of wealthy Jews, leaving us only with the lowest scum?"

"I . . . We are a community. It has always been our intention that wealthier Jews would help fund—"

"Yes, a tax," Eichmann interrupted. "A tax on wealthy Jews to fund emigration of the poor."

"A tax? Well, I meant—"

"A tax to be paid for an exit visa, and everything in a single building. Herr Löwenherz, I will see if I might arrange for your release after you've drafted me this plan."

"You want me to draft a plan for the emigration of Jews from Vienna?"

"A plan for emigration of Jews from all of Austria."

"How many, sir?"

"How many? How many? Did you not hear me? There is no place in the Reich for you Jews!"

Eichmann rang his bell, and an aide took Löwenherz away.

"We might call for all Austrian Jews to relocate to the Leopoldstadt ghetto, Tier, to make this easier," Eichmann said. "But no point in causing alarm by announcing that yet."

He called out to the hallway, "A list of Jew leaders we've imprisoned." And to Tier's perked ears, "We might release a few. Carrot and stick, Tier. Carrot and stick."

THE VIENNA INDEPENDENT

AUSTRIA OVERWHELMINGLY VOTES TO JOIN GERMAN REICH

Austria's final humiliation

BY KÄTHE PERGER

VIENNA, April 11, 1938 — Members to the first Great German Reichstag were elected by 49,326,791 voters in Austria and Germany yesterday. In the ultimate insult to our once proud and independent nation, 99.73% of Austrians voted for our own subjugation to the Führer in a choice between "yes" and "no." In Vienna, 1,219,331 voted "yes," while a mere 4,939 voted "no." The conquest gives Hitler mastery of central Europe in a world that will never know whether the Nazis were a majority or not.

Other nations, including England and America, rushed to recognize the conquest. With barely a murmur of protest at home or abroad, the U.S. State Department closed its Austrian legation before Germany could abolish it . . .

AT THE FERRIS WHEEL

Stephan checked his watch again as he stood with Papa and Walter outside the British consulate, Walter tossing his Peter Rabbit as two women just in front of them looked on disapprovingly.

". . . My sister got out before the British put in place this new visa requirement," the prettier woman was saying. "She's doing maid's work, but she's in England."

"Papa, I'm supposed to meet Dieter and Žofie," Stephan said.

His father examined the line, stretching forever ahead of them although they'd arrived even before the consulate opened. "Not at the park?"

Stephan stood silently, watching Walter toss his rabbit.

"Well, take Walter with you, then. Be back in two hours. And keep yourselves tidy."

Stephan said, "Peter stays here, Wall-man."

Walter handed his rabbit to their father without a thought to the indignity of a grown man standing with a stuffed doll in hand, but there was no dignity in Vienna these days.

"You can apply for your sons, sir; they don't need to be with you," the prettier woman said.

"Their mother wants someone to see what good, intelligent boys they are," Papa answered her in what Stephan thought of as his "I, Herman Neuman of Neuman's Chocolates" voice. But at the hurt in the woman's eyes, he said, "I'm sorry. I didn't mean to . . . I'm just . . . At the American embassy, I waited until nearly ten at night only to be told they see six thousand people each day for visas that won't be granted for years. But they told me the British still grant unlimited educational visas."

"For students admitted to university. Is your son bound for Oxford?"

His father hesitated, then said, "My Stephan is a playwright. He hopes to study with Stefan Zweig"—his words true, and yet the implication they left was as much a lie as Stephan's silence about the park.

STEPHAN, WITH WALTER in tow, spotted the long single braid hanging almost to Žofie-Helene's waist in the line at the Ferris wheel, the gondolas circling slowly as the ride was loaded. Everywhere in Prater Park, kids wore Hitler Youth uniforms: dark shorts, khaki cotton shirts, knee-high white stockings, and red armbands with black swastikas. Even Dieter, in line with Žofie, wore a swastika pin on his coat.

"Walter, I didn't know you were coming!" Žofie-Helene said.

"I didn't either!" Walter said. "Stephan promised Papa we *wouldn't* come to the park!"

Žofie tousled Walter's hair as she said to the next person in line, "You don't mind, do you? I didn't know his little brother was coming too." Then to Stephan, "We told them we were saving you a place in line."

Stephan said, "We'll wait. Walter hates Ferris wheels."

"I do not!" Walter objected.

"Fine. I hate Ferris wheels," Stephan said.

Dieter said, "Stephan, you've ridden this thing a hundred times."

Stephan said, "It makes me feel I've left my stomach on the ground."

"That's just the centripetal acceleration altering the normal force of the gondola on your body," Žofie-Helene said. "At the top you feel almost weightless, and at the bottom you feel twice as heavy. I can take Walter."

"The Wall stays with me," Stephan said. They'd reached the head of the line, and the attendant was opening the gondola door. "You go ahead. We'll wait," he insisted, holding Walter's hand tightly lest he object.

Dieter climbed in, and Žofie followed, the others behind them filling the car. Stephan watched them circle upward, Dieter putting his arm around Žofie, that ugly swastika pin nearly touching her sleeve as they waved down to him.

"I wanted to ride," Walter said.

"I know," Stephan said. "I did too."

STEPHAN STOOD WATCHING as Žofie-Helene sat on one of the promenade's long wooden benches. She patted the seat beside her, saying, "Come on, Walter. Sit with me," but Stephan grabbed his brother's hand.

Žofie stood and turned all in one motion, as if there might be a big spider there, and fixed on the shiny metal "Nur Für Arier" plaque. *Reserved for Aryans.* "Oh! Yes, Mama says it's disgraceful the way the Nazis treat Jews. She says we should all stand with them."

"Of course Stephan is standing with the Jews," Dieter said. "He's one of them."

Žofie-Helene said, "Don't be a cretin, Dieter."

"But he is. He sits behind a yellow line at school now, in the last row with the other Jews."

"He does not."

"With two empty rows of desks between them and us."

She looked to Stephan, who couldn't deny it.

"You . . . You're Jewish, Stephan? But you don't look Jewish."

Stephan pulled Walter to him. "What do you think a Jew looks like?"

"But . . . Then why don't you leave Vienna? Mama says any Jew who can is leaving, anyone with money, and you— Well, you're rich."

"My father can't leave his business. Without his business, we have no money."

"You could go to school in America. Or . . . isn't Stefan Zweig in England? You could study writing with Stefan Zweig."

Dieter said, "He could not."

"Why not?" Žofie shot back.

Stephan said, "We can't leave my mother anyway."

Žofie said, "When your mother recovers, then."

Stephan leaned close to Žofie-Helene, and whispered so that Walter couldn't hear, "One doesn't recover from cancer of the bones."

The words were barely out before he regretted them; he never spoke of Mutti's illness, much less to hurt anyone. Why had he wanted to hurt Žofie? He felt filthy, unworthy of her. He felt like the filthy Jew his teachers now called him—not Mr. Kruge, who taught literature, but the others.

He stepped back, wanting to apologize and yet not wanting to, wanting to ask Žofie what she meant in coming to the park with Dieter. Wanting to blame her for his lie to his father, although that wasn't right either; it was his own fault, his own foolishness in letting Dieter goad him into coming. So he just stood there, staring at her, and she stared back, his anger reflecting in her face as something else.

From up the wide promenade came the sound of cheering and, underneath it, a heavy *thud thud thud*. Marching feet.

"Let's go, Walter," he said with alarm.

"You promised—"

"We have to get back to Papa."

"I'll tell him you brought me to the park."

"Walter," Stephan said.

He reached down to take his brother's hand, but Walter scrambled out of his grasp and leapt at Žofie with such force that she fell back onto the bench, Walter more or less in her lap.

"Papa said two hours," Walter whined. "It hasn't been two hours."

Stephan tried to take his brother from Žofie, but she wrapped her arms around him, saying, "Stephan."

Already, the line of storm troopers was in sight.

"Now, Walter. Right this minute."

Walter began to cry, but Žofie, hearing the panic in Stephan's voice, or seeing the storm troopers herself, or both, released him. Stephan tried to swing him up onto his shoulders, but Walter squirmed and Stephan lost his grasp, and poor Walter fell to the ground.

"Walter!" Žofie exclaimed, scrambling to help him. "Walter, are you okay?"

And the storm troopers were marching in tidy formation straight toward them.

"Give Stephan your pin, Deet!" Žofie demanded, sitting back on the bench with Walter, trying to appear calm. "Quickly!"

Dieter only stared at her.

The storm troopers were stopping right in front of them, the leader demanding, "There is some problem here?"

"No. No, everything is fine, sir," Žofie answered.

The lead storm trooper looked from Žofie and Walter and Dieter on the bench to Stephan, still standing. Stephan felt the bareness of his jacket, the absence of a swastika pin like Dieter wore, the new "Vienna safety pin."

"We're not with him," Dieter declared.

"He is a Jew?" the man demanded.

Dieter said, "Yes," just as Žofie said, "No."

The man put his face right in Žofie's, so close that it was all Stephan could do not to grab him and pull him back. Walter, still in her arms, began to cry in earnest, not the showy tears meant to get his way, but absolute terror.

"And this little one, he is a scared little Jew brother sitting on a bench on which Jews are forbidden?" the storm trooper taunted.

"He's not my brother," Stephan said.

Žofie, with a steady voice, said, "He's mine. He's my brother, sir."

Stephan licked his lips, his mouth unbearably dry.

The storm trooper turned to the rest of his men. "I think this young Jew has come to this park in search of exercise, yes?"

Stephan didn't know if he was speaking of himself or Walter. He felt a small trickle of urine, but somehow managed to stem it before he visibly wet himself.

"You will show us how well you goose-step, then," the man demanded, clearly speaking to him now.

A crowd was gathering around them.

"I am being unclear?" the man demanded.

Stephan, with a dry swallow, goose-stepped forward, afraid to put distance between himself and his brother, but with no choice. He made a circle of the straight-knee kicks, returning to a spot ever so slightly closer to Walter.

"Again," the man demanded. "Surely you can do better than that. You will sing. It is easier when you sing. 'I am a Jew, do you know my nose?' You know this song?"

Stephan chanced a quick, pleading glance at Žofie. The man drew out his billy club.

Stephan goose-stepped forward again, away from them, the man shouting after him, "You must sing!"

Still, he goose-stepped silently, unable to bear more humiliation than that with Žofie and Walter watching.

When he turned back toward them, he saw Žofie-Helene's long braid hanging down her back, her hand firmly gripping Walter's smaller one.

His little brother, crying silently now, glanced back at him as Žofie mercifully led him away.

The storm trooper stepped right in Stephan's path, grabbed his foot as he marched, and pushed it upward. Stephan's planted foot came out from under him and he landed hard on his back, the air knocked out of him. The growing crowd jeered at him. Dieter too jeered.

"I said you will sing," the storm trooper demanded.

Stephan climbed up, straightened his glasses, and began goose-stepping again, this time singing the humiliating song now that Žofie and Walter were no longer there to hear.

The storm trooper drove him down the promenade, followed by the jeering crowd.

When Stephan grew so tired that he no longer could raise his legs high enough to please the storm trooper, the man again pulled his foot up, spilling him backward.

And again.

And again.

Stephan was sure one more fall would break his back. But each time, he would find Dieter's face in the jeering crowd and rise again.

He goose-stepped to the end of the promenade and turned around.

Halfway back again, or maybe more, or maybe less, Stephan peered up from the ground through skewed lenses, no longer able to find Dieter's face in the mob. He tried to conjure in the storm trooper's spitting mouth Dieter's lips fumbling the script lines he so meticulously wrote, Dieter's mouth calling him a Jew, Dieter's hand on Žofie's beautiful hair as he kissed her up on the Burgtheater stage. But there was no anger left, nothing to marshal against the storm trooper beating him and kicking him as, in the distance, the Ferris wheel circled its long climb around and around against the sky.

LETTING GO

Truus arrived at the bare grounds of the Zeeburg quarantine unit, where the children were already gathering in the cafeteria—all but the seven, including little Adele Weiss, who had tested positive for diphtheria and been quarantined. Adele's case was mild, the doctor had suggested the prior morning. She had the gray throat and the cough that were indisputably the disease, but her neck was less swollen than those of the other children, her breathing not badly labored, and she had as yet developed no lesions on her body.

And today was a good-news sort of morning: that very afternoon the healthy children would board the ferry to England, where Helen Bentwich had foster homes waiting for every one of them.

As Truus hurried along, she was startled by something flying from a window and splattering just at her feet. Was that . . . She examined it more closely, the bile rising in her throat, but that was the good news, the morning sickness. Was the gray blob a dumpling? She wasn't sure what troubled her more: that the food the children were meant to survive on here was of such poor quality that they threw it out the window, or that the amusements were so few that throwing food out a window passed for fun. This dumpling—or whatever it was—came from the diphtheria unit, where the children were not even allowed walks along the canal and the occasional treat of seeing a barge pulled from land by a team of men.

Inside the cafeteria, Truus addressed the gathered children, who cheered at her news and rushed off to the barracks to pack. It *was* a good-news day, she thought as she shooed one last lingering child off, saying, "I've a home for you and Jonah, Sheryl. Now run along and pack."

The girl said, "I can't leave him."

"Leave who, sweetheart?"

"Jonah."

"Of course you won't leave him." She reached out and took the hand with the thumb that sported one half of her ring. "I've a home for you both in England. Now hurry along. I won't let him leave without you, but you must allow time to return my rings!"

"Jonah is sick," the girl said, and silent tears slid down her cheeks.

"Sick? But he's had the vaccine."

The girl just stood there crying.

"Oh, sweetheart, I expect it's just a little . . ." She wrapped the child up in her arms, praying. Surely it couldn't be another case of diphtheria.

TRUUS HELD LITTLE Sheryl's hand as they entered the office of the head nurse. Yes, the girl's brother had awoken in the night with chills and a sore throat. He'd not begun to cough and as yet showed no symptoms beyond the gray tonsils. They'd considered quarantining the sister too, since the two were inseparable. But to expose an asymptomatic child to the illness?

"No, of course not," Truus said, already working through the implications of this child being diagnosed just as the others were to leave. She would have to tell Helen Bentwich. She would have to hope Helen would accept children who might in a few days show signs of illness they didn't currently. Helen was sensible. The doctor had pronounced it extremely unlikely at this point that others would become ill— assurance Truus took for the child she carried as well. All the children had received vaccines when they arrived. The ones that had become ill had only done so because it wasn't always possible to prevent exposure before the vaccine took effect. Surely Helen would see that the relatively low risk of a sick child arriving in England was a small price for getting all these others out of this godforsaken place and settled in homes. It was diphtheria, not smallpox or polio. And Helen was a woman who never said no when a yes was possible.

Truus touched her ring that the child wore on her thumb, pushing aside thoughts of those American children who'd died due to bad vaccine batches in 1901 and in 1919, focusing instead on the story about the Alaskan mushers, the Great Race of Mercy: twenty mushers and one hundred fifty sled dogs who'd raced 674 miles in five days to deliver antitoxin that saved the small town of Nome. This ring was not an omen; she'd become pregnant again only after she'd given it to these children—or had come to realize the pregnancy, which seemed the same thing. If the ring went to England with them, she would not likely ever see it again, but perhaps that was a blessing. Perhaps the ring was a curse for her, but wouldn't be on the hands of this boy and girl.

"You must trust me on this, Sheryl: I will make sure Jonah joins you in England as soon as he is well," she told the girl. "You can go ahead and make friends with the family so that when he comes you can introduce them, all right?"

The girl nodded solemnly, such a small child to be made to endure so much.

An assistant was found to help the girl back to her barracks. Truus would like to have taken her back herself, but she needed to visit the sick children, to explain to them that they weren't being left behind, there were homes for them in England too as soon as they were well.

"The others are recovering?" she asked the head nurse.

The woman opened the door to the unit: plain white cribs and beds lining the room's walls, all made with plain white sheets. A window was open on one side, where that dumpling had made its quick exit. One of the older girls sat on a bed, creating creatures out of what appeared to be the remains of her lunch. Two boys in the center of the room played a made-up game, the sole point of which seemed to be to catch some half dozen things tossed into the air all at once. Others, the poor dears all with their necks swollen, slept or read books or darned socks. Darning socks—that was what passed for amusement for the quarantined children, for heaven's sake. Truus supposed it was a good sign that some child in the unit had the gumption to toss a dumpling out the window.

"I'm afraid it was a rough night," the nurse said.

Truus braced herself, sensing what was coming and quickly counting: the girl and the two boys, Adele in— Had they moved her crib?

The nurse said, "I suppose it's a blessing that these children are orphans, that there are no parents to be told."

"An orphan," Truus said, feeling crushed, yes, but also awash with a relief she knew she shouldn't feel. If the child had no parents to be told, then it must be the toddler. "Poor sweet little Madeline?" she asked.

THAT NIGHT, TRUUS held back her tears, unwilling to break Joop's heart with the news. He would have taken little Adele Weiss into their own home. They would have been a family—that word they no longer spoke aloud. She wanted to tell him about Adele and she wanted to tell him about this other child too, the child growing inside her. And yet she couldn't, not yet, not until she was more certain, and certainly not tonight. Tonight, she could only hold her husband and try not to think of the little flower he'd loved the moment he held her in his arms.

FRIENDSHIPS COME AND GO

Stephan was typing in the library when Walter burst in, announcing, "Žofie is here again! She says to tell you she *really* wants to see you."

Stephan, looking up to see his brother in the mirror above the desk, caught a reflection of himself, his eye no longer the mess it had been but still yellow-orange streaked with purple, his lip where it had been split no longer swollen but with a scar the doctor said would never go away. He'd been lucky, actually. An old couple had come upon him lying unconscious in the park, and they'd woken him and helped him into a waiting motorcar, where the woman urged him to lie across the back seat to avoid being seen as they brought him home.

"Tell Žofe I'm not here, Wall?" he said.

"Again?" Walter asked.

Stephan stared at a line of dialogue on the page in his typewriter: *Sometimes I say things wrong just to see who will notice. Mostly nobody does.*

Walter backed out, leaving the door open so that Stephan could hear his every slow step down the marble stairway to the entry hall, his little-boy voice rising up from the entryway, saying, "Stephan says for me to tell you he isn't home."

Žofie-Helene didn't ask Walter to try again this time, or say that she just wanted to see him, to know he was okay. She said, simply, "Give him these for me, Walter?"

Stephan waited for the sound of the door closing before he returned his fingers to the typewriter keys. He stared at the page, but the words no longer came.

READING

Walter, with Peter Rabbit in hand, climbed into Mutti's fancy wheelchair in the elevator, opened one of the dozen identical booklets Žofie-Helene had brought for Stephan, and began earnestly to try to read to Peter. Only he couldn't read. He wanted to ask Stephan to read it to him, but Stephan was in a grumpy mood.

A KINDNESS

Truus sat in a window in a café on the Roggenmarkt square in Münster, Germany, beginning to feel conspicuous. The late afternoon when Jews were allowed to do their shopping, after Aryan Germans had what they wanted, was an odd time for a Christian Dutchwoman to be lingering over cold tea. Recha Freier appeared up the street, finally, seeming both bigger and yet more gaunt than Truus remembered, the black scarf over her head and the plain coat not particularly flattering for her masculine brow and face. She passed by without a glance into the café, but she reached up with a gloveless hand to adjust the unflattering scarf.

Truus waited until Recha was well down the street, then stood, nodded thanks to the waitress, and followed at the span of a block. Recha turned toward St.-Paulus-Dom, where Truus, following the instructions delivered to her back in Amsterdam, had left her car. Six weeks, she'd had to wait for this meeting. Six weeks since Adele Weiss had died.

Recha passed the cathedral and disappeared into a building farther down the block. Truus passed the full ten minutes in a nearby shop, inquiring about scarves. Only after her purchase was carefully wrapped did she circle the building Recha had entered, again following the instructions.

As the back door closed behind Truus, Recha said without greeting, "There are only three."

An unfamiliar chill ran through Truus, which might have been the unseasonably cold day, but she supposed was on account of her pregnancy. She followed the sound of Recha's voice to find her hidden in a small alcove from which both the front and the back entrances were visible.

"We've made arrangements for them to go to England next month," Recha said. "The woman helping the boy has undertaken to arrange a home but needs time to do so."

The woman would be Helen Bentwich, the boy Recha's own son Shalhevet. How had Recha found the strength to send her son to England with the intention that he would go on from there to Palestine, so far away? Truus was to take these three children to the safety of the Netherlands, and provide for them until they could be sent on.

"All right. I'll manage it somehow, but I— Listen, one of the last group, she died of diphtheria she contracted at the quarantine unit," Truus said, not wasting a moment lest they be interrupted. "Not one of the orphans, but little A—" *But little Adele Weiss*, she had almost said, even though she'd rehearsed this so carefully, a way to communicate the situation without using names. Edelweiss. A rare flower, beautiful but short-lived. "It was the child of the rescue worker; she put her baby in my hands for safety and . . ."

And Truus, in her arrogance, had taken the child, imagining she was saving her when, had she handed the child back to her mother, Adele Weiss would still be alive.

"Surely you understand that I must tell her myself," she managed.

Recha remained uncharacteristically quiet, leaving Truus to remember the little face lying in the crib in the quarantine barracks, still with her thumb in her mouth, and the tiny coffin.

"I need to tell her mother myself," she repeated softly.

"You mean this as a kindness. I understand this," Recha answered. "But it will be no kindness to put the mother at risk to salve your own guilt. We all must carry our guilts. I am sorry this one is yours to carry, but there it is.

"Now, the bishop is waiting to hear your confession, the sin of . . ." Recha paused, gathering herself. "The sin of loving one of your children more than the others."

Recha knocked twice on the wall beside them. In the pause before she knocked once again and disappeared through a hidden doorway, Truus tried to imagine that: having so many children that one might tug at your heart more than any other, that you might send one to safety while keeping the others close.

She walked out the front door, then, and down the block, and into the cathedral, into the dim, stained-glass filtered light and the stone chill, the lingering odor of incense and burnt candle wick, wood pews and leather kneelers, the improbable survival of faith.

CONFESSION

The little wooden confessional door slid open, revealing in shadow behind a screen a big man with more eyebrow than hair and a heavy cross on a heavy chain around his neck. Truus found herself wanting to weep in the dim, cramped space, as if the man's very presence suggested a possibility of setting her burdens down.

After a long silence, the bishop prompted, "Forgive me, Father, for I have sinned."

Truus managed, "The sin of . . . of loving one of my children less than the others."

Had she loved any one of the children she'd carried less than any other? Less than this child she carried now?

Had she loved Adele Weiss any less?

She looked through the grate, registering the bishop's silence.

"More than the others," she said. "I'm sorry. Loving one more than the others."

He peered at her, clearly torn between the code error and her obvious grief.

"I am sure, good lady," he said, "that your God finds your soul worthy of any forgiveness you might need."

He gave her a moment to collect herself before opening the door behind him, letting in enough light to reveal his long nose and thin lips, his comforting eyes. A child joined him in the little room, and peered through the screen from the inside, to Truus. She was a girl of perhaps seven, with straight lashes like Joop's over big brown eyes that held more fear than a child her age ought ever to feel.

"This is Genna Cantor," the bishop said.

The girl continued staring.

"Genna is the oldest," the bishop said. "She is going to introduce the others, aren't you, Genna?"

The girl nodded solemnly.

A second girl entered, so like Genna that they might be twins.

Genna said, "This is Gisse. She's six."

"Genna and Gisse," Truus said. "And you're sisters?"

Genna nodded. "Our biggest sister, Gerta, is in England, and Grina is our sister too even though she went to God before we were born."

The words spoken with a sureness of the existence of a God that Truus worked harder and harder not to doubt.

A baby was handed in to them then, her perfect little fingers reaching to her sister's face.

"This is Nanelle," Genna said. "She's the youngest."

Nanelle—a name impossibly close to that Truus and Joop had chosen when Truus was pregnant the first time; if that first child had been a boy, he was to be named for Joop's father, but a girl was to be Anneliese, whom they would call Nel. Perhaps that child had been the most loved, the only one for whom they had dared choose a name.

"Nanelle," Truus repeated to Genna. "I suppose your mother and father ran out of G names?"

Genna answered, "She's really Galianel. Only we call her Nanelle."

"Well, Genna and Gisse and Nanelle, I'm Tante Truus."

Tante Truus, the name she'd taken when she'd turned to social work five years into her marriage, when she'd come to think there would likely never be a Nel.

"Can you remember that?" she asked the girls. "Tante Truus."

"Tante Truus," Genna repeated.

Truus nodded to Gisse to repeat it too. It was an easier thing to ask a child to repeat an improbable name than to ask her to lie.

"Tante Truus," Gisse repeated.

"Nanelle doesn't talk yet," Genna said.

"No?" Truus said, thinking, Thank heaven. It was impossible to guide a baby's words.

"She says Gaga," Gisse said, "but we don't know which one of us she means!"

The two sisters giggled together. All right then. This was going to be okay somehow.

"So I'm Tante Truus, and I'm going to take you to Amsterdam. I'm going to have to ask you to do some funny things on the way, but I want you to remember through all of it that if you are asked, I am Tante Truus and you are coming to spend a few days with me in Amsterdam. Can you remember that?"

The girls both nodded.

"All right then," Truus said. "Which of you is best at pretending?"

PRETENDING

It was as cold as the devil by the time Truus approached the wooden guard hut, but cold and dark and dinnertime was the best time to avoid a thorough border search. She slowed the car, willing the two guards smoking cigarettes inside the hut to conclude what lazy soldiers so often did, that a single woman driving a car with Dutch plates might be waved across the border with no bother at all. But as her headlights illuminated a closed chain-link gate draped with a large fabric swastika fringed on the bottom in white, one of the soldiers emerged.

Truus, with her single passport already in one gloved hand, tidied the folds of her long skirt. She rolled the window down to the frigid night air, said good evening, and handed the guard her passport. She returned her hands to the steering wheel, already taking his measure as he shone his flashlight on her documents. His collar under his coat was tidy and square, and his boots were polished, and even this late in the day his chin bore no stubble. Likely a new recruit, as he wore only the trenchcoat that might be issued this time of year, never mind that the chill night called for something heavier. He was too young to be married, he and his colleague too, she supposed, and probably too idealistic to be bribed. Well, she had only her mother's real ring this time, anyway—she'd used all the paste copies, and there hadn't been time to arrange more—and in any event it was too big a risk to try to bribe one Nazi in the presence of another. Each would have to trust the other, and real trust was such a rare thing these days.

"You are going home, Frau Wijsmuller?" the guard asked.

Respectful. Well, that might help.

She felt the stiffness of the gas pedal and clutch under her feet, the warmth against her legs. A respectful border guard was less likely to ask her to step out of the car.

She said, "Home to Amsterdam, yes, Sergeant."

He flashed the light carefully around the car's interior, onto the coat sitting on the seat beside her, and into the empty back seat too. Truus tried not to show any expression but respect. He shone the light through the back window, examining the floorboard. He went around the car and repeated the check of the back floorboard on that side, then underneath the car. So thorough. What kind of God would arrange for her to have to pass through this meticulous boy's needle?

He returned to Truus's window. "Your coat?"

She lifted the coat beside her, letting it spread to show that it was just that, just a coat.

"You won't mind if I check under the seats?"

She draped her coat again on the seat beside her. "Of course you must check everywhere," she said, "although I hope you won't have to disturb the things in the boot. It's awfully packed."

The guard nodded to his comrade in the guard booth. The comrade reluctantly set his food aside, drew his weapon, and joined them, keeping his Luger trained on the trunk while the first opened it. Truus watched in the mirror until the flashlight beam caught the mirror glass and it became impossible to make out what the soldiers were doing. She let go her tight grip on the steering wheel and set her hands on her skirts.

"Steady, girls," she whispered. "Stay hidden." Thankful for just that moment that the girls were small. So small and so terribly thin.

The guard returned to the car window, leaving Truus to see in the mirror his companion standing with his gun in one hand and a carefully folded blanket in the other. Truus returned her yellow-gloved hands to the steering wheel.

"I wonder, Frau Wijsmuller, if you might tell us why you travel with so many blankets?" the guard asked, sounding more like a boy than a man, a poor young boy made to stand all night in the cold to prohibit people from leaving a country that didn't want them, a country that he'd been raised to believe in, the way Truus imagined her own child would believe in the Netherlands. Just a young, idealistic boy, doing his duty.

She said, "Would you and your colleague each like to take one? I don't believe there has ever been such a cold May night as this."

He called back to his companion, who took two blankets and set them at their post.

"Thank you, Frau Wijsmuller. It *is* such a cold night. You ought to put on your coat."

Truus nodded, but she left her coat on the seat beside her and her foot on the gas pedal as she watched the comrade return to the trunk.

The boy said, "You won't mind that we must empty the whole trunk?"

He returned to the back of the car and began removing the blankets one by one while the other kept his gun carefully trained on the trunk. Truus stared ahead at the cold silver of the chain link, the red and black of the swastika flag, the improbable white fringe.

THE SIMPLEST THING
IN THE WORLD

S tephan," his father said, "your mother asked you a question."
Stephan looked to Mutti, smiling across the table set with silver and china and the new crystal his father had purchased to replace
what had been broken the night of the Anschluss. His mother's chop
was untouched, her dumplings cut but uneaten, her cabbage salad
rearranged to appear more eaten than it was. But she had come to
the table tonight, when so often she was only there in the portrait on
the wall: Mutti younger even than Stephan was now, and Klimt still
painting in a more traditional style, his mother not draped in gold but
rather in white balloon sleeves and a hat that sat high atop her hair, not
a way she ever wore a hat, but it emphasized her perfect dark brows
and huge green eyes. Mutti would think Stephan's attention was on his
writing, and he would let her. She would work to make this new life
seem normal, and so would he.

"How did your play rehearsal go?" his mother repeated.

"We aren't going to do the play, after all," he answered, and to the
concerned expression in his mother's tired eyes, "Žofie is busy with
her maths."

Walter said, "She brought Stephan a whole bunch of copies of a
book, but he won't even read it to Peter."

His lousy play. She'd had it typeset on that Linotype machine in her
mother's office, or maybe she'd even set it herself, but that only made it
a dozen copies of a lousy play instead of just one.

His father started, "I don't think—"

"Friendships come and go even in the best of times," Mutti interrupted.

"It's just as well, Stephan, as we've found a tutor to work with you on your English for the summer. He can only give us an hour a day, so he'll have to work with you both at the same time."

"I get to study English with Stephan?" Walter said. "And Peter too?"

Stephan set his fork on his plate, as he'd been schooled to do, and with a forced lightheartedness said, "When we have tests, Wall-man, you have to leave your answers uncovered so I can copy them!"

Walter whispered to his rabbit, "Peter, you have to leave your answers uncovered so we can copy them!"

Mutti reached and took the stuffed rabbit's hand, though only weeks before Walter had not been allowed to bring Peter Rabbit to the table. "You must race to see who will be the best before you go away for school!" she said. "My money is on you, Peter."

"Ruchele, even if we had visas for the boys," Papa said, "I don't think they want to leave their mother to—"

"You can't ignore Hitler rolling down the Mariahilfer Strasse in his six-wheeled Mercedes limousine, Herman. You can't ignore more than a million of our neighbors voting for annexation."

"The plebiscite wasn't legitimate," Papa objected.

"Do you see anyone standing up to say so?"

STEPHAN HAD FINISHED his *Germknödel* and was surreptitiously scooping up the last little bit of plum filling and poppy seeds with his finger when Aunt Lisl burst in, suitcase in hand. Why hadn't Rolf taken it at the door?

"Michael is demanding a divorce!" she said.

Mutti said, "Lisl?"

"He can't be married to a Jew. It's bad for his business. He's thrown me out. He can't be married to a Jew, but still he means to keep my fortune."

Papa said, "He wouldn't *have* his business if he hadn't had your fortune to save it."

"He's transferred it into his name! He means to have my share of the chocolate business too."

"He can't just up and take half my stock," Papa objected. "It's in your name, Lisl."

"Calm down, Lisl," Mutti urged. "Have a seat. Have you eaten? Herman, do buzz Helga and get her to bring Lisl something to eat, and perhaps a brandy."

"Michael can't effect a transfer unless it's entered into the stock book," Papa said to Aunt Lisl, ignoring Mutti, "and I simply won't enter it."

"He's already had the paperwork drawn up, Herman," Aunt Lisl insisted. "He says if I refuse, he'll just have you arrested and sent off to a work camp. He says it's the simplest thing in the world, to turn in a Jew."

CHRYSALIS

Truus pulled the car to a stop at a small market just across the border. "We're in the Netherlands," she said.

Gisse, huddled in a ball on the floorboard underneath Truus's long skirts, climbed up onto the passenger seat.

"I was quiet," she said earnestly.

"You were perfect, Gisse," Truus said as she reached down to take the baby from Genna, who was wedged under her skirts and against the door on the other side. "You were all perfect."

She opened the door carefully lest Genna fall out, and the girl crawled out of the car, came around to the passenger door, and sat next to her sisters. Truus climbed out and pulled her coat back on, worrying now about the complications, the lack of Dutch entrance visas. The little store was closed, but she went to the public telephone booth at the road's edge and placed a call to Klara van Lange, to let her know she had three children. Four children, she thought, but the one child would go with Truus wherever she went.

THE VIENNA INDEPENDENT

GLOBAL MEETING OF REFUGEES PLANNED

Paris accepts U.S. proposal for meeting in Évian-les-Bains

BY KÄTHE PERGER

May 11, 1938 — The United States government has proposed a meeting of an intergovernmental committee to facilitate the emigration of refugees from Germany and Austria. It is to be held in Évian-les-Bains, France, beginning July 6.

All of Europe has been marking time, waiting for America to lead the coordination of efforts with respect to Jewish refugees, and suggest new ones. Expectations are high that, as host, the U.S. will open the conference with an offer of a grand solution. More than thirty nations are expected to attend.

It is believed that most of Germany's Jews would leave the Reich now if given a chance, but the barriers to immigration are rapidly becoming insurmountable. Fixed immigration quotas leave Jews with nothing but years-long waiting lists. Refugees to most nations, including the United States—where the State Department has refused to allow even the limited quotas imposed by the Johnson-Reed Act to be filled due to the challenging economic situation—are made to guarantee they won't ever require public assistance.

While immigrants must arrive with assets to support themselves for a lifetime, the Germans on April 26 passed their Order for Disclosure of Jewish Assets, requiring all Jews with assets in excess of 5,000 reichsmarks to submit a declaration of wealth by the end of June. Real estate. Personal possessions. Bank or savings accounts. Securities. Insurance policies. Pension payments. Every silver spoon and wedding gown must be itemized. Already, Germany claims, too many Jews have fled with wealth that properly belongs to the Reich. They now require all property of any Jew wishing to emigrate to be forfeited. . . .

RAISED HOPES

It was the heat, Truus supposed—as stifling for early June as it had been frigid the night she smuggled the three sisters out of Germany, just a month before. She sat across the breakfast table from Joop, trying to hide the worst morning sickness she had yet experienced. She'd meant to make him *broodje kroket* before she left this time, a nice sturdy breakfast, but when she'd woken, she knew she couldn't stomach the smell of frying. She instead made *wentelteefjes*, using the wonderfully sweet and cinnamony *suikerbrood* that was to have been tomorrow's breakfast. "French toast," a friend of hers had told her this was called in America, where it was served at fancy hotels but was not, her friend assured her, as good as Truus's. It was so easy on the stomach that Truus might eat it every morning until the baby came.

She would be showing soon; she would have to tell Joop. If she spent more effort on fashion, the pencil-thin silhouettes that were the rage might already have given her away. But women were always more aware of changes in their bodies than men were, and Joop was distracted with his work at the bank, the difficult financial climate on top of all the difficulties of the world. She might still have a week or so to be more certain before she raised his hopes.

"Italy and Switzerland have declined to attend the Évian Conference," Joop said, still reading his newspaper. "Romania has asked to be treated as a refugee producer."

Truus said, "I heard yesterday that President Roosevelt is sending a nobody as his representative."

"Myron C. Taylor," Joop said, looking up. "A former U.S. Steel

Corporation executive. Roosevelt is granting him the powers of ambassador, as if that will give him— Truus, you don't look well. I wish you would reconsider letting me go to Germany for you this time. I—"

"I know, Joop. I know you would go in my place, that you would rather go yourself. You are such a good man. But a woman traveling with children raises so much less suspicion than a man doing so."

"Perhaps Mrs. Van Lange could go?"

Klara was with child too, but Truus had no intention of conceding that a woman with child should not rescue children. She said only, "Mrs. Van Lange is quite clever, but she's not yet ready for solo flight"—although Klara often did surprise, with her unexpected competency.

"Not ready because it's gotten too dangerous," Joop said, "which is precisely why I should go in your place."

Truus forked together a bit of the eggy bread and the fruit, avoiding the cream. Even the *wentelteefjes* now seemed too much for her stomach.

"Joop," she said, "I mean this in the kindest way: you are a terrible liar."

"This lot don't have exit visas?"

He knew she brought children into the Netherlands without Dutch entry visas, but that was far less risky than smuggling them out of Germany without exit visas.

"Recha is arranging everything on the German end," she said.

"Then what need would I have to lie?"

Truus stood to clear their dishes and avoid Joop's question. In the motion, a cramp caught her off guard so surely that she had to set down the plate she had in hand. She felt the gush of warmth, and smelled it again.

"Truus!"

Joop stood and reached across the table, the plates clanging frighteningly to the floor.

For a moment, Truus imagined the small pool of red was just the strawberry compote. She thought to assure him it was her monthly, to spare him, but the pain made her double over, a new gush of blood drenching her stockings and staining her dress.

THE COST OF CHOCOLATE

Stephan was holed up in the cocoa cellar, staying cool in the summer heat and mapping out a new play, when he heard the commotion upstairs. He tried to ignore it—he was just getting this new idea down, and ideas had a habit of disappearing if not immediately committed to words. It was hard enough to hold on to the appeal of them once they were in ink in his journal, but if they didn't get that far, they didn't get anywhere.

He focused on the words he'd just written: *A boy who used to sit at the front of the class now sits at the back, behind a yellow line. He knows the answer the teacher is looking for, but raising his hand only provokes ridicule. No matter how right his answers are, they will be found to be wrong.*

He didn't know why he needed to revisit this, with school out for the summer. For Walter, he supposed. Poor Walter had cried every morning the last weeks of school. Peter needed to go with him, he'd insisted; if he left Peter at home, the rabbit wouldn't learn anything.

Above Stephan, the door to the cocoa cellar burst open, and shiny black boots tromped down the wooden stairs—a sight he'd almost gotten used to out on Vienna's streets but never imagined seeing inside Neuman's Chocolates. He closed his journal and tucked it under his shirt.

As the Nazis set to work inventorying the crates of cocoa beans—there were only four men, but it felt like an invasion—Stephan slipped up the stairs to find others swarming the bean roaster and the conch and the stone tables as the chocolatiers nervously watched. Were the men who worked for his father Jewish? Stephan didn't even know; they worked for Papa because they made great chocolate.

He ducked past the elevator and into the stairwell, relieved to find it empty.

Even before he reached the top floor, he heard his father's voice.

"My father built this business from nothing!" Papa was saying.

Stephan crept toward his father's office, to find Papa and Uncle Michael in a heated discussion.

"You have to understand that no one cares about that now, Herman," Uncle Michael was saying in a surprisingly gentle voice, so low that Stephan had to listen hard. "You're a Jew. If you haven't sold to me before these men finish their inventory and report the value, they'll seize Neuman's Chocolates for the Reich. And they'll still make you pay the taxes, with money you can no longer earn. I swear to you, that is what will happen, that is what they're doing. But I can take care of you and your sister—"

"By divorcing her and stealing from us?"

"I'm not divorcing her in a real sense, Herman. I'm just doing it in the eyes of the law, to save us both." Uncle Michael held out a pen to Papa. "You have to trust me. Sign the deed of sale before it's too late. I'll listen to whatever you tell me to do with the business. I'll take care of you and Ruchele and the boys just as I will take care of Lisl. She's my wife and you're my family, whether our relationships are state-sanctioned or not. But you have to allow me to help. You have to trust me on this."

THE WHITE SHEETS OF DEATH

Truus lay in the hospital bed, a ceiling fan stirring the muggy July day and a radio Joop had brought her the only relief from the white sheets on the iron bed frame, the white walls, the white-capped nurse coming in regularly to take her temperature.

"Your husband isn't visiting tonight?" the nurse asked.

Where *was* Joop?

The hemorrhage had been stopped before Truus bled to death, but an infection had left her too weak even to sit up. Without the radio, she would have been left with nothing at all to do but listen to the sounds of new babies being brought to new mothers, and to worry about the German children whose lives depended on her not languishing in a hospital bed, the white sheets of death tucked neatly into hospital corners as if clean, starched cotton could save anyone.

AT THE BORDER

Joop watched the swastika flag on the chain-link gate plummet into darkness as he killed his headlights. He levered the cool metal door handle, moving slowly, the gun trained on his temple through the open window. A bead of sweat trickled down his forehead, but he didn't dare brush it away. He slowly pushed the door open. The thin guard stepped sideways to keep the gun trained on him. Joop turned his legs. He set his feet on the ground. He stood carefully. He waited. He didn't have any children with him, any reason to be afraid.

He'd gone in Truus's place to try to persuade Recha Freier to allow him to take the children Truus would have brought across the border if she weren't hospitalized. He'd come without even telling Truus; she made it seem so simple that he hadn't imagined he couldn't rescue the children himself. It had seemed the only thing that might ease her grief at losing their baby, to know that other children would survive.

He trembled as, with the thin guard's gun still trained on him, a stockier one patted him down: chest, waist, privates.

"If you have been in Germany on your banking business, as you say," the stockier border guard said, "you will not mind coming with us while we confirm this."

Joop ventured a quiet, nonconfrontational, "I'm afraid the banker with whom I met will be long ago gone home, it being so late."

"We will of course move your auto in that event," the one holding the gun said, "so it won't block the road all night."

A DISTRACTION

The radio was a blessing and a curse: the news bleaker and bleaker. Truus was listening to a report from the world refugee conference, a bit of a recorded speech in a familiar voice—"My hope is to persuade this esteemed gathering of the need for all of the world to join in providing relief for the Reich's persecuted Jews"—when Joop's voice interrupted.

"You need to rest, Truus."

"Joop!"

He turned off the radio, sat carefully at the edge of her bed, and planted a gentle kiss on her forehead. She wrapped her arms around him and held him tightly.

"Oh Joop, thank the good Lord you're home!"

"Klara told you, didn't she?" Joop asked. "I telephoned from the first public booth I found after I got out of Germany. I told her I would come straight here."

"She came the minute she knew, to tell me in person. But hearing you're safe isn't the same as seeing that you are. What *happened*, Joop? Klara said you had your papers and you weren't bringing any children, and still the Gestapo kept you for questioning?"

"I'm so sorry, Truus. I'm an utter failure. I couldn't persuade Recha Freier even to see me, much less put children in my hands."

Recha already took so many risks; it was too much to ask her to deal with anyone she didn't know. Perhaps Klara van Lange would have had more success, but Joop hadn't asked her to go. Joop had wanted to do this himself, for her.

"It's the children Recha fears for, Joop," she said. "With so much going wrong . . ." Adele Weiss dying, and Recha the one who had to tell the poor mother. Truus ought not to be allowed to touch children. God clearly did not want her to. But she couldn't think about that now.

"At least you tried, Joop," she said. "Thank you for that."

"What if Recha had met me, Truus? What if she'd entrusted those children to me?"

He pulled a chair up beside her bed and took her hand. If he heard the sounds of the babies elsewhere on the ward, he didn't show it. She tried not to show it as well, tried to wall off the sound of a fussing child quieting as, she imagined, it latched on to its mother's breast.

"That was that nice Norman Bentwich we met in London on the radio," she said, not wanting to dwell on babies or on the danger Joop had been in. "You remember Norman?"

"And Helen," Joop said. "I liked them both."

"He's speaking for the British at Évian-les-Bains, where delegate after delegate has expressed sympathy but not a one has volunteered to take in refugees."

Joop sighed. "All right, Truus. I'll turn the radio back on, but you must promise you won't let it upset you."

She blinked back tears, trying so hard not to hear the baby coos. Were they real, or were they imagined? How could Joop not hear them too if they were real? It was this awful white bed, this awful white room, this day after endless day of whiteness driving her to imagine things.

"It's a distraction, to think of other things," she said. "Even horrible ones."

Joop squeezed her hand, on which she now wore only the plain band and the ruby, the two bands of the third ring still with the German siblings now both in England.

"We can try again," he said, "but I don't need a child. Really, I don't."

They sat silently, doing their best to spare each other the added pain of knowing of their own pain. He kissed her again, then, and turned the radio back on.

THE SERVANTS' FLOOR

I read your play, Stephan," the English tutor said. "It's quite good. The play, I mean. The English could use some work."

The three of them were in the library: Stephan with Walter and their tutor. Four, if you counted Peter Rabbit.

"Peter has to play the girl," Walter informed the tutor importantly.

"It's okay, Wall, I can play the girl if it bothers your rabbit," Stephan offered.

"Žofie-Helene used to be the girl," Walter told the tutor, "but now she spends all her time doing maths."

As the tutor paged through the playscript, Stephan listened closely to the murmurs of Mutti and Aunt Lisl in the entry hall, Aunt Lisl saying Uncle Michael had arranged for the family to stay in the palais, to have rooms on the top floor.

"Just our rooms, or the guest wing too?" Mutti asked.

"The servants' floor," Aunt Lisl said. "I know it doesn't seem like much, Ruche, but most people are being made to move across the canal to Leopoldstadt, where whole families are sharing single rooms."

Stephan looked to the ceiling high above him, the map of the world painted there, with a full-sailed ship of explorers charging across it. Beyond it were his parents' bedrooms, and his and Walter's. The servants' rooms were on the top floor, the attic floor that the elevator didn't reach.

"Here, Stephan, where you use 'amaze,' you might consider 'astonish,'" the tutor was saying. "The meanings aren't all that different, but 'amaze' suggests a more positive response than I think you mean. And here, with 'damage,' perhaps you'd be better served with 'ruin.' Again, they're similar, but 'damage' leaves the possibility that a thing can be fixed, while 'ruin' is more permanent."

"Ruin," Stephan repeated.

"Like the ruins of Pompeii. Your father told me you've been there, right? It was rediscovered after, what, fifteen hundred years? But it will never be put back together again."

"Ruin," Stephan repeated again, thinking that even in ruin, some things were perfectly preserved.

LISL WAS SITTING with Ruchele in the library when the Nazis arrived, one waving a swastika-stamped document granting him the palais. They watched through the doorway as, in the entry hall below, Herman handed over a set of keys: to the china cabinet, the silver closet, the wine cellar, his office here at home, his desk. The man's cadre of accompanying soldiers—some only boys, really—began the process of inventorying the artwork, starting in the entry hall with the Van Gogh self-portrait, the painter laden with a box of paints and brushes and a canvas on the road to Tarascon; the Morisot girl reading, which made Lisl think of Stephan's little friend, Žofie-Helene Perger; the Klimts—the Birkenwald birches from the artist's summer retreat in Litzlberg on Lake Attersee, and the scene of Malcesine on Lake Garda—and the Kokoschka of Lisl herself.

As the men laughed at the red scratches that were Lisl's own cheeks, Ruchele said soothingly, "They have no idea what they're looking at, no appreciation."

"No," Lisl agreed. "No."

Michael had promised her he would claim possession of her portrait, and the Klimt of Ruchele as well. How he would do that, she didn't know, but she chose to believe he would.

Hope. *Until the day when God will deign to reveal the future of man, all human wisdom is contained in these two words—Wait and*

Hope, Alexandre Dumas had written in *The Count of Monte Cristo*, a book she and Michael had talked about the first time they'd met.

Other men were set to inventorying every piece of furniture, jewelry, silver, and china; every linen (table and bed and bath); every clock; the contents of every desk and dresser; and the clothes Lisl had brought with her when she moved from the home she'd shared with Michael—a palais they'd bought with her money, which now belonged solely to him. They inventoried Ruchele's letters and Herman's too, and Stephan's stories. They even inventoried Walter's toys: one electric train set; one red rubber racer, Ferrari-Maserati model; forty-eight metal toy soldiers from a box of fifty Herman had bought him in London just last year.

One stuffed Peter Rabbit, much loved, Lisl thought. But Peter was safely in her nephew's arms.

On the radio, which had not yet been inventoried, in Herman's library, which had yet to be breached, the result of the Évian Conference was being announced by the Nazis: delegates from thirty-two countries, after nine days of meetings, had nothing to offer but abundant excuses for closing their doors to refugees from the Reich— "an astounding result from countries who have criticized Germany for our treatment of the Jews."

Ruchele whispered, "Two thousand Jews have already committed suicide since the Germans seized Austria, Lisl. What difference would one more make?"

"Don't, Ruche," Lisl said. "You promised me. You promised Herman. Don't—"

"But I'm dying," her sister-in-law said softly. "I will die. There is nothing to be done about that. If I were gone, Herman would take the boys. He'd flee Vienna. He'd find a way to live somewhere outside Hitler's reach."

"No," Lisl insisted, but an unfaithful little chip in her heart thought *yes*. If Ruchele died, her brother and her nephews would leave Vienna, and her with them. Michael had said she should flee Austria, that he could help her get out of the country with money enough to live on. But how could she leave every single person in this world she had ever loved?

Herman and Stephan were already carrying the Victrola out to the elevator, where a Nazi forbade them entrance. They carried it instead up the main staircase and around to the narrow servants' stairs, "helped" by Walter and his rabbit. It was the old wind-up they kept in the library, not the Electrola used to play music during salons and simpler gatherings that didn't require the hiring of a quartet. They were being allowed to keep only this one old player, and a very few records.

Lisl followed her brother up the stairs, whispering, "I think it would be better to move Ruchele now, Herman. It will destroy her to see them pawing through your books."

They placed the Victrola in the small, low-ceilinged sitting room that adjoined two servants' bedrooms next door to the room Lisl would use, at the opposite end of the floor from the staff staying on to serve the Nazis. She turned on the lamps to make it a little more cheery. At least they would have electricity, as the servants' floor wasn't separately metered, and the Nazis who would occupy the main floors weren't about to go without.

They returned to find the Nazis beginning to inventory every bit of Herman's library, but if the intrusion pained him, he bore it stoically— her book-proud brother for whom chocolate was a business and literature a joy. Lisl wondered if he'd had the sense to destroy the books by authors who were banned: Erich Remarque and Ernest Hemingway, Thomas Mann, H. G. Wells, Stefan Zweig, whom Stephan so loved.

Herman removed his suit coat and easily lifted Ruchele from her wheelchair, as if she weighed nothing. He set her on the library chaise, one of the few pieces of furniture they would be permitted to take upstairs.

As he and Stephan carried the heavy wheelchair upstairs, Lisl carefully folded Ruchele's blanket, cream-colored cashmere that was the only thing Ruchele could bear against her dry, translucent skin. A soldier watched every smooth crease Lisl made. Yes, it was a valuable blanket, and no, she would not allow it to be taken from her dying sister-in-law only to be shoved into some storage facility in Bavaria, to be put to no use at all.

Herman returned for Ruchele. He lifted her from the chaise and began up the stairs.

Ruchele looked back over his shoulder to the Nazis swarming the main floors. Lisl, with a nod to the soldier, followed them, blanket in hand. Her sister-in-law would not easily come down these stairs again.

At the top of the servants' stairs, Herman set Ruchele in the wheel-chair's cane seat. Walter climbed up into his mother's lap—clearly causing her pain, but she tousled his hair as if she were perfectly comfortable. Lisl unfolded the blanket she had so carefully folded and spread it over Ruchele, and Stephan took the handles and wheeled his mother toward their rooms.

The wheelchair wouldn't fit through the doorway.

Before Lisl could suggest they might try removing the brass wheel handles, Herman grabbed a fireplace poker from inside the room and swung it at the door trim.

Soot flew from the poker as it slammed into the wood.

The trim splintered, but remained affixed to the wall, now sprinkled with soot.

Herman swung the poker again, his shirt ripping at the arm just as the cast-iron poker hit the wood. He swung again. And again. And again. His rage poured into the effort, the wood collapsing and splintering, bits of it flying everywhere with the soot, splattering back onto his shirt and into his hair, littering the floor around him, landing even on Ruchele's blanket and Walter's little rabbit. The whole area around them was sprinkled with soot and wood bits, and the trim was completely battered, and still the door frame remained intact.

Lisl watched silently—they all watched silently—as Herman sank to the floor beside Ruchele's wheelchair, weeping. That was what terrified Lisl more than anything: the sight of her big brother, whom she had never seen anything less than composed even when they were children, now sitting on the floor in his torn shirtsleeves, covered in soot and wood chips, and weeping.

Ruchele touched Herman's hair as comfortingly as she had touched Walter's. "It's all right, darling," she said. "It will all be all right somehow."

Stephan—dear sweet Stephan—took the poker and gently applied it as a wedge to the smashed trim. The wood popped loose at the point of contact with the wall. Stephan repeated the move all up and down that side of the doorframe, until the battered trim could be pried off. He stepped into the room and removed the door trim from inside the little room, too.

Lisl took Ruchele's blanket carefully off her and shook it out over the railing, so that the splinters and soot floated down onto the Nazis working below.

Stephan returned to his mother's wheelchair, took it in hand, and pushed his mother from the hall into the room.

"Wall, can you and Peter go fetch Mutti a glass of water?" he asked.

After his brother left, Stephan said, "Papa, shall we get Mutti's chaise for her?"

And by the time Walter and his little stuffed rabbit had returned with a half-filled water glass and a long trail of drips on the wood floor, Ruchele was arranged on the chaise, with her blanket covering her legs.

Stephan disappeared, to return a minute later with the radio. Lisl had no idea how he had managed it; Jews were now forbidden radios.

He closed the door and set one of his father's saved books at its base to keep it closed, muffling the sounds of the whole of their lives being recorded in a Nazi ledger, to be scattered to Reich art museums or sold to fund Hitler's rampage or, because what they had was so often the finest, sent to Germany for Hitler himself.

RELEASE

Your wife will still need a lot of rest, Mr. Wijsmuller," the doctor said. "No travel. No stress. Recovery from—"

"Doctor," Truus interrupted, "I am here in the room with you and perfectly capable of taking my own instructions."

Joop put a hand on Truus's—a gesture meant to comfort, Truus knew, but also, annoyingly, to hush.

"Days at the hospital are terribly long, Doctor," he said. "We're glad to be going home."

After the doctor left, Joop began laying out the clothes he'd brought for Truus to wear home: a shift that would require no girdle, nothing to uncomfortably bind.

"Truus," he began gently, "you can't—"

"I am perfectly capable of understanding what the doctor said, Joop."

"And you'll abide by his instructions?"

Truus turned her back to him as if modest, and removed her hospital gown. She felt his warmth as he approached her, as he gently fingered the braid down her back. He wrapped it into a bun at the nape of her neck, and pinned it up.

"And you will abide by his instructions?" he repeated.

She pulled the dress on, thankful for its loose fit, and turned to him.

"I am perfectly capable of understanding what he said," she repeated.

He put his arms around her and tilted her chin up. "I'm not sure you're the better liar," he said, "but you are quite good at avoiding questions, and at keeping truths to yourself."

"I would never lie to you, Joop. When have I ever—"

"Recha is arranging the exit visas?"

"That isn't precisely what I said, Joop. I said—"

"You said in response to my question about exit visas that Recha was arranging everything. Not a lie, but meant to leave me believing an untruth." He kissed her forehead gently, then again. "That isn't what matters, though, Truus. You know that isn't what matters."

Truus felt the tears welling, despite every effort. "It's been so many times, Joop. I just didn't want to have you hope again until it was more certain."

He wiped away a tear spilling down her cheek.

"You're all I need, Truus," he said. "You are all I will ever need."

"I'm a woman who can't bear a child in a world that values nothing else from me!"

He pulled her to him, so that her cheek was to his chest, to his slow, steady heartbeat. "You're not, though," he said, stroking her hair as if she were the child they'd lost. "You are a woman doing important work, in a world that badly needs you. Only you have to take care of yourself first. You can't help others if you aren't well."

OLD FRIENDS

Otto Perger, at a bread stall at the Naschmarkt, turned to the quiet hush of a familiar voice. Stephan Neuman, waiting patiently at a meat stall just two down, was admonishing his little brother. The younger boy's nose was pressed to a case of chocolates at the stall between them, where Otto had just purchased chocolates for Johanna and Žofie-Helene.

Otto watched the older brother, oddly missing him. So many customers he could take or leave, but it had always made him smile to see Stephan show up at the barbershop door even before the boy and his granddaughter became such friends. Now, of course, the boy didn't come anymore, and Otto couldn't serve him if he did. Now even Žofie-Helene didn't see the boy.

Otto watched as the meat seller, ignoring Stephan, chose a nice piece of meat for a woman who had arrived after the boy. It was what so many adults did, tending to older customers while children waited. But when the seller finally served Stephan, he charged him twice the proper price for a single nasty gray chop.

Stephan objected, "But you just charged—"

"You want the meat or you don't want it?" the seller demanded. "It's all the same to me."

The boy looked defeated. That's what Otto thought as he watched the meat seller eye Stephan's money as if it might not be currency of the Reich. It was, he saw in the boy's expression, why Stephan had turned Žofie-Helene away again and again in the days after the humiliation in Prater Park, which Žofie-Helene had told her mother about and Käthe had in turn described to Otto. The poor boy could not bear to face Žofie after she had witnessed his humiliation; he could not imagine that that humiliation was not somehow his own fault.

"But why can't we get chocolates?" the little brother demanded. "We used to get them all the time! At Papa's, we—"

Stephan took his brother's hand and again gently shushed him, and pulled him to stand beside him while the seller wrapped the chop. "We'll get chocolates another time, Wall."

"Stephan!" Otto exclaimed, joining them as if he'd only just noticed them. "I haven't seen you in so long. I believe you may be in need of a haircut."

He stooped to the younger boy's level and handed him a chocolate. "You are just the person I need, Walter. The vendor has given me a second for free, and I'm far too old and portly to be eating two sweets myself!"

He surreptitiously slipped the other chocolate into Stephan's satchel as they shook hands. The boy was impossibly thin, impossibly older. Otto would like to have made sure Stephan ate the sweet himself, but he knew the boy would give it to his little brother. Otto wished he could buy a whole box of chocolates for them, but there would be so many things they needed more than candy, and it would do nobody any good for him to be seen helping them.

He glanced around. The meat seller had moved his attention to another customer. No one was paying them any mind. He returned his attention to the boys, noticing the scar on Stephan's lip. Where had it come from? It hadn't been there the last time Otto cut his hair.

"I believe I owe you a haircut for that time when, as my Žofie noted, I didn't really cut your hair," he said.

"Nor did you charge me, Herr Perger."

"Didn't I? Ah, memory doesn't fit as readily into an old brain as into a young one."

The boy's hair looked neat. Perhaps he was going to a Jewish barber, or perhaps his parents were trimming his hair. Otto couldn't say why he extended the boy the invitation for a haircut. He knew Stephan couldn't come, and he knew Stephan knew it. He supposed he wanted the boy to know he wished it weren't so.

"Well," Otto said, "the truth is, I would love to hear about your latest play, and I expect Žofie-Helene would as well. She quite likes being the star of the show, you know."

Stephan said, "There's no place to rehearse anymore except the Jewish center."

"I . . . Yes," Otto said. The boy who'd once brought his friends to rehearse in his family's ballroom was now confined to a few servants' rooms, without servants anymore, as Aryans under the age of forty-five could no longer work for Jews even if the families could pay them.

Žofie-Helene rushed up to Otto, a fussy Johanna in tow, saying, "Do tell me you've gotten the chocolates, Grandpapa. Johanna— Oh!"

Oh how I've missed you, Holmes, Otto thought, although he couldn't have said which of his granddaughter and her friend was Sherlock and which Dr. Watson.

Stephan said simply, "Žofie-Helene."

An awkward silence followed before the two spoke at the same moment, Žofie-Helene saying, "The Americans made a movie of Zweig's *Marie Antoinette*," and Stephan, "How are your proofs coming along?"

Žofie-Helene answered glumly, "Professor Gödel has left for America."

"Ah. He's a Jew?" Stephan said with an edge of accusation. Otto could hardly blame the boy.

"He . . . Hitler abolished the Privatdozent," Žofie-Helene answered. "So Professor Gödel had to apply for another position under the new order, and the university turned him down. I believe they dislike his connection with the Vienna circle."

"Not a Jew, but too friendly with Jews," Stephan said. "Something so many in Vienna are careful to avoid these days."

Žofie-Helene studied him frankly, through smudged lenses, unbowed. "I didn't realize," she said. "Until that day in the park, I didn't realize. I didn't understand."

Stephan said, "We have to be going," and he took his brother's little hand and hurried off.

Otto watched his granddaughter watch them until they disappeared, and then the space where they'd been.

He turned back to the chocolate vendor. "It seems I need two more chocolates," he said.

—SARA—

Lisl stood outside the servants' entrance of Palais Albert Rothschild at No. 22 Prinz-Eugen-Strasse, her umbrella raised against a late October rain turning toward the first slushy snow of winter. She pulled her fur coat closed, thinking of the many times she'd been driven up the U-shaped front courtyard to this home that filled a full city block, to enter through its main doors into a world of tapestries and mirrors and paintings, five-hundred-candle crystal chandeliers, the unforgettable marble staircase kept impeccable by a servant whose sole task was to polish it. She'd dined in the Rothschilds' silver dining room. She'd danced to music from the two orchestrions built into a niche off the gold-leafed ballroom, which together sounded like an entire orchestra. She'd basked in the art collection both here and at the even more stunning Palais Nathaniel Rothschild on Theresianumgasse. Now a banner strung over the gates between the street and the front courtyard declared this "Zentralstelle für Jüdische Auswanderung," the Central Bureau for Jewish Emigration; Baron Albert von Rothschild had been forced to consent to the appropriation of all his Austrian assets, including the five Rothschild mansions and the art in them, to gain his brother's release from Dachau and their safe passage out of Austria. And now Lisl stood in the line of applicants here, hoping for permission to leave the only country she'd ever called home.

As she waited, a fancy car drove up to the gates. Two Nazi soldiers hurried to open the heavy wrought iron. The car pulled to a stop in the cobbled courtyard, where an attaché waited with raised umbrella, getting wet as he held it over the car's back door.

Adolf Eichmann emerged. He set off across the courtyard, protected by the umbrella held over him by the increasingly drenched attaché as a second attaché took the place of the first, holding an umbrella over the open car door. Eichmann's slope-backed German shepherd climbed from the car and shook himself. The attaché held the umbrella over the beast as it followed Eichmann across the courtyard and into the palais.

LISL LOWERED HER umbrella and ducked into the back servants' entrance, glad to be out of the weather, if not yet to the front of the line. She followed its slow progress into a salon where she'd so often taken tea. The furniture and the art had been removed, replaced now by a folding table manned by a clerk surrounded by piles of furs, jewelry, crystal and silver, and other valuables.

When Lisl reached the front of the line, the clerk said blandly, "Your things."

Lisl hesitated, then handed over the fur she wore and the few jewels Michael had given her to bring.

The clerk tossed them onto the appropriate piles.

"Your umbrella," he said.

"My umbrella? But how will I get home in this weather, without even a coat?"

At the clerk's impatient expression, she handed over her umbrella, smiling politely although she burned with fury that she should need the permission of this little Nazi fool to do anything at all. Michael had schooled her to be on her best behavior. The Nazis often withheld permits even after an applicant had satisfied their every demand. She did not want to be left with nothing but a one-way trip to a labor camp.

The clerk looked to the next person in line, done with her.

She queued in the next line, remembering that somewhere here—was it on the second floor?—a small wooden staircase led up to the Rothschilds' private observatory, where she'd once peered through one of their telescopes to see the rings of Saturn. They had been as clear as if the planet were a toy on a table in front of her. How had her world shrunk now to such a small thing? Living in the upstairs servants' rooms with Herman and Ruchele and the boys. Going out to the market herself each afternoon, when Jews were allowed to pick through whatever the rest of Vienna had passed up. She was thankful, of course; but for Michael's efforts, she and Herman's family might have been moved to a grubby little place in Leopoldstadt. They had no kitchen at the palais, but Cook, who'd stayed on to serve the Nazis, did manage to make meals out of the meager bits Lisl bought, and Helga brought them up the back stairs—no longer on a silver tray, but they had never been more grateful for their servants' loyalty.

As Lisl waited in line, she saw through a passageway an attaché gently drying the paws of Eichmann's German shepherd. The dog's patience was rewarded with a piece of meat that would have made an entire dinner for Lisl and Herman's family.

Another clerk at another folding table said to Lisl when her turn came, "Your passport."

The nasty little clerk inked a stamp on a red pad, then pressed it to one corner of the passport.

As the clerk set the stamp aside—Lisl's passport now marred with a three-centimeter-high red "J," for Jew, never mind that her marriage had been in a Christian church, attended by all of Vienna society—Eichmann and his dry-pawed dog entered the room. Another Nazi followed, the two men watching as the clerk laid a second ink stamp firmly across her middle name, Elizabeth. Elizabeth, which sounded more British than Jewish. Perhaps that was why her parents had chosen it. When the man lifted the stamp, the name was overwritten with "—Sara—" in purple ink. Sara, a woman so beautiful that her husband had feared more powerful men might steal her away. Selfless Sara, who, believing herself barren, sent her Egyptian handmaid to her husband's bed. Sara who, after being visited by God when she was a hundred years old, bore a son herself. Lisl had known nothing of Sara's story until August, when the Nazis started this practice of stamping passports of Jewish women with the name, and those of Jewish men with "Israel."

The man with Eichmann said to him, "You see, it is working like an automatic factory, Obersturmführer Eichmann. You put in at the one end a Jew who still has capital—a factory or a shop or a bank account. He passes through the entire building, from counter to counter. When he comes out the other end, he has no money, he has no rights. He has only a passport in which it is written 'You must leave this country within two weeks. If you fail to do so, you will go to a concentration camp.'"

The clerk handed Lisl's passport back to her.

Eichmann eyed her the way men did, but said to her, "Don't think you might slip over the border now. The Swiss don't want you Jews any more than we do."

Lisl would have no need to slip over the border, though. She had insisted for months that she wouldn't leave Herman, who wouldn't leave Ruchele, but on September 23 Hitler had occupied Czechoslovakia's Sudetenland with not one country of the world standing up against him, and the next morning she'd allowed Michael to begin arranging her passage to Shanghai. It had taken more than a month, and he'd had to pay a small fortune to secure a berth for her on a ship leaving in just two days now. She hadn't even told Herman yet. She couldn't imagine how she would tell her brother that she meant to flee. But she was going through the process now, moving from one room to another.

She was lucky. She reminded herself of that as she passed into the next room. Her assets went to Michael, who would protect them until the world had righted itself. She had only to forfeit these few token things: the least valuable of her fur coats, a few carefully selected jewels, her umbrella that might have kept her dry, her name, her dignity.

RAID

It was not yet dawn, and cold for this early in November. Eichmann wore his greatcoat. He preferred to conduct these raids in daylight, with an audience to spread the message that really, everyone in Vienna ought to fear Adolf Eichmann. But he wouldn't risk the possibility of an outcry upon the public arrest of an Aryan woman—a mother and a widow, at that, albeit of the Lügenpresse, the lying press. The *Vienna Independent*, indeed.

The soldiers burst the door open, finally, and flooded inside. They began pulling out desk and file drawers and spilling out the contents, rummaging for incriminating material. They toppled desks and chairs, broke windows, and scrawled "Jew Lovers" on the walls and on the outside of the building, letters dripping from their carelessness with the paint. He let them have their fun. He too had been undisciplined in his youth—all those brawls in Linz before he fled to Germany. And youthful fury could be used to advantage. What could be more frightening than young men full of unbridled fury unburdened by an ounce of sense?

One of the Hitler Youth, a big, stupid-looking boy, pointed a pistol at the Linotype. The boy fired, then fired again, the bullets ricocheting off the hard metal.

"Stop it, you fool," Eichmann commanded, but the boy had given over to his lust.

"Dieterrotzni!" an older boy yelled.

The younger boy turned, still with the pistol pointed. The older boy took it from him.

"You nearly killed me, snot nose," the older boy said.

The boy shrugged, then lifted a metal chair and began to beat the machine with it.

ONE IS ALWAYS
GREATER THAN ZERO

Žofie-Helene was at the breakfast table with Mama, Grandpapa, and Jojo when the stomping of boots filled the building's stairway. Mama quietly stood, went into the bedroom, and lifted the little rug at the end of her bed. With the rug came the floorboards beneath it, fashioned on an invisible hinge. She climbed into the narrow space between their floor and the ceiling of the apartment below.

"You don't know where your mother is, you understand?" Grandpapa said to Žofie and Jojo as Mama pulled the hiding place closed. "She's out covering a story, remember, just as we've practiced."

At a rap on the apartment door, Žofie looked in alarm at her mother's coffee cup and porridge bowl.

Her grandfather answered the door to a swarm of Nazis.

"What can I do for you gentlemen?" he asked.

Johanna sat, terrified, at a table that now had only two settings. Žofie stood filling the sink with water, suds just covering her own and her mother's bowls, still full of porridge, and her mother's coffee mug.

"Käthe Perger," a man in a greatcoat demanded.

The German shepherd that had come in with him sat at the doorway, perfectly still.

"I'm sorry, Käthe is out, Obersturmführer Eichmann. May I be of help?" Grandpapa answered calmly.

Johanna began to cry for their mother. Žofie hurried to soothe her, her hands dripping soapy water across the floor.

The Nazis swarmed the apartment, opening closets and searching under beds, while Eichmann interrogated Grandpapa, who continued to insist that Mama wasn't there.

In Mama's bedroom, a Nazi stepped onto the rug.

"Grandfather Perger," Žofie said.

Otto glanced toward her. She had never in her life called him Grandfather Perger, although of course that was who he was. She blinked back at him, willing him to see the Nazi so close to her mother, to do something to stop the man lifting the rug.

"I tell you, she is out, covering a story!" Grandpapa shouted at Eichmann—shouted so loudly and disrespectfully that even the dog turned. "She is a journalist, one of the keepers of the truth. Do you not care for your country enough to want to know the truth of what happens here?"

Eichmann put a pistol to Grandpapa's temple. Grandpapa stood as perfectly still as Žofie-Helene did. Even Jojo didn't move.

"We are not Jews," Grandpapa said quietly. "We are Austrians. Loyal members of the Reich. I am a veteran of the war."

Eichmann lowered his pistol. "Ah, the father of the dead husband," he said. He turned to see everyone watching him. He seemed to like that, the power of being able to do whatever he wanted while everyone looked on.

He met Žofie-Helene's gaze and held it. She knew she was meant to look away, but she couldn't have done so even if she wanted to.

He sheathed his pistol as he approached her. He reached out and touched Johanna's arm, brushing hers as well.

"And you must be the young daughter who studies at the university?" he said to Žofie.

Žofie answered, "I'm enormously talented at mathematics."

The man laughed an irregular nonagon of a laugh, all sharp angles and unmatched lines. He reached out for Johanna's cheek, but she turned away, burying her face against Žofie's chest. Žofie wished she were as young as her sister, that she could bury her face in some-one stronger. She had never missed Papa more.

Eichmann touched Johanna's hair more gently than Žofie would have imagined he was capable of.

"You will be as pretty as your big sister," he said to her turned head, "and what you may lack in intelligence, you will perhaps make up with a modesty your sister lacks."

He leaned closer to Žofie, uncomfortably close, and said, "You will give your mother a message for me. You will tell her that Herr Roth-schild is happy for us to use his little palace on Prinz-Eugen-Strasse. He assures us the Jews are as interested in leaving Vienna as we are in helping them to do so, and he is content to have his home used by the bureau for Jewish emigration. He has, he finds, more homes than he needs. While he appreciates your mother's concern, he wishes to as-sure her that further press on the matter will not benefit him—or her. Nor will it benefit you or your sister. Can you remember that?"

Žofie repeated, "Herr Rothschild is happy for you to use his little palace on Prinz-Eugen-Strasse. He assures you the Jews are as inter-ested in leaving Vienna as you are in helping them to do so, and he is content to have his home used by the bureau for Jewish emigration. He has, he finds, more homes than he needs. While he appreciates Mama's concern, he wishes to assure her that further press on the matter will not benefit him, or her, or Johanna or me."

The man laughed his ugly laugh again, then turned to the door and said, "Tier, I believe we may have met your match."

"Žozo, I don't like that man," Johanna said as Otto watched through the window, needing to be sure the Nazis were good and gone. He watched them pile into their cars, an aide holding the door for the dog, and drive off around the corner. And still he watched, sure they would return.

Finally he pulled the curtain, turned out the light, and lifted the rug in the bedroom. Käthe emerged from her hiding place and, without a word, wrapped her arms around Žofie and Jojo.

"Käthe," Otto said, "you *must* give up your writing. Really you—"

"These people are being stripped of everything, Otto," Käthe interrupted. "They're being left with nothing but exit visas and the hope that someone from overseas will pay their way to Shanghai, the only place left with doors open to them."

"I can support you and the girls. I can give up my apartment and move in here. It would be easier and I would feel—"

"Someone has to stand up against the wrongs, Otto," Käthe said.

"You can't win this alone, Käthe!" he insisted. "You're only one person!"

Žofie-Helene said quietly, "But one is always greater than zero, Grandpapa, even if zero is more interesting mathematically."

Otto and Käthe both looked at her, surprised.

Käthe kissed the top of her daughter's head. "One is always greater than zero. Yes, that's right," she said. "Your papa taught you well."

KRISTALLNACHT

Another of the chilly little room's lightbulbs flared and went dark as Stephan contemplated his last pawn, afraid to look across the chessboard to his father trying to ignore the chaos raging outside. They'd done their best to restore the room's door to functioning, securing the wood frame with the retrieved bent nails and wedging old newspapers into the gaps, but still the stomping of boots downstairs on the main floors reached them through the crushed doorframe, while the outside came in—the noise and the cold—through the single thin window of the servants' sitting room.

He glanced up to see Mutti in her wheelchair, huddled under a blanket as she had been since the noise outside began, not long after four that morning. "Mutti," he said, "why don't you let me move you to the chaise, or even to bed?"

"Not now, Stephan," she answered.

Stephan rose from the table, removed his gloves and set them beside the chessboard, and put another coal in the brazier, a lame attempt to make a dent in the chill. It was no warmer in his parents' bedroom, the next-door servant's room, from which they'd removed the door trim to make the passageway wide enough to accommodate Mutti's wheelchair. There was not enough coal to light all three braziers, or even enough, really, to do more than keep this one very slightly aglow.

"I'm just going to make sure we closed the window in Walter's room," he said.

"*Our* room," Walter said. If his little brother didn't love their new accommodations any more than Stephan did, still he was thrilled that they now shared a bedroom.

"You just checked it," Papa said.

But already Stephan was in the little room, from which the door trim had also been removed. He took another quick look out the window, to riotous young men smashing storefronts, with no one stopping them. A man across the street was hauled out of his building. Stephan thought it was Herr Kline who used to own the newsstand, although he couldn't be sure with the mob around him. They loaded him into an open truck already filled with men.

Stephan felt more than saw Walter appear beside him.

"Hey, Wall," he said, lifting his brother before Walter could see what was happening.

He returned to the sitting room and its shade-drawn window, to the table and the chessboard where, without giving it much consideration, he moved his last remaining pawn forward one square to threaten his father's rook. His father slid his queen on the diagonal, capturing the pawn and Stephan's last chance to replace his lost queen. He knew he ought to concede. He could see he was defeated, and his father had taught him that if you could see how a game would end, whether you would win or lose, you should end it; chess was not about winning or losing, but about learning, and if you knew how a game would end there was nothing left to learn. But to end the game would be to return to the chaos outside and the stomp of boots now on the palais stairs. It made Stephan nervous, the sound of all those Nazis in rooms that used to be theirs. He would have said he'd grown used to it, but there was so much activity tonight, so many voices rising up to the servants' floor.

"Herman, Stephan, out on the roof quickly!" his mother whispered in alarm just as he registered the boot steps not just on the main floors now, but rising toward them.

Stephan opened the window, scrambled out onto the ledge, and, using the caryatid beside the window for a foothold, hoisted himself up onto the roof. He leaned back over to give his father a hand. His father teetered, losing his balance.

"Papa!" he said in hushed alarm, pushing his father back toward the tired little servant's room so he wouldn't fall. "Papa, here, take my hand," he said more calmly, urging his father to regain his balance and try to climb out through the window again.

"Go!" his father said. "Go, son!"

"But, Papa—"

"Go, son!"

"But where?"

"If we don't know, we can't say. Now hurry! Don't come back unless you're sure it's clear, you must promise me. Don't put your mother at risk."

"I— Hide, Papa!"

"Go!"

"Play the 'Ave Maria' when it's safe for me to come back. It's on the Victrola."

"It may never be safe," his father said, pulling the window closed, inadvertently leaving it open a crack.

"Herman!" Mutti urged.

Stephan, hanging over the roof's edge with his head upside down, watched through the window as his father climbed into the wardrobe. Walter closed the door behind their father—Walter who was far too young to have any idea what was happening and yet, despite all their attempts to shelter him, already did.

After just a second, his father opened the wardrobe and pulled Walter in with him.

As Mutti wheeled her chair over—thankfully, she was still in the chair—and secured the wardrobe's door, Stephan reached down and nudged the window farther open. If the Nazis followed him out onto the roof, he might get away. If they opened the wardrobe, his father was doomed.

Doomed. Stephan touched his lower lip, the unevenness where the split had healed imperfectly. Yes, he knew what these men were capable of.

He lay listening to the banging on the door, the invading of the apartment, the demanding, "Your husband, where is he?" He didn't think the Nazis would take a boy as young as Walter; they wouldn't want the trouble. But again and again, the Nazis went beyond what he could imagine they would do. Still, he couldn't help Mutti if he too was taken, and Mutti would not survive without help.

He scampered quietly across the roof toward the tree outside his old bedroom window and looked down through the tree branches. On the sidewalk below, a soldier patrolled with an ugly beast of a dog. It wasn't the dog's fault, though. The dog was only trying to please its owner. That was what dogs did.

A NIGHT OUT

Truus sat with Klara van Lange at the check-in table at the Groenvelds' house on Jan Luijkenstraat, where they were holding a fund-raiser for the Netherlands Children's Refugee Committee, the small sort of gathering often being hosted these days—although less often now that the weather had turned and a garden party was out of the question. The bins for donations sat behind them in the entry hall, heaped with clothes. The last couple had now been checked in. The dinner preparations seemed to be going along without incident, leaving Mrs. Groenveld free to stand by the check-in table, greeting guests. Truus watched as the youngest Groenveld boy was carted back to bed by his father, in this house where she so often brought the children from Germany. Somewhere in a drawer or a cabinet here was the comb they had used to remove lice from the hair of that little Benjamin (what had his surname been?) before deciding finally just to shave his head. Really, there had been nothing else to be done.

Dr. Groenveld returned to join his wife and Truus herself and Klara, who was visibly with child now. The good doctor began telling them of some boy named Willy Alberti, whom the Groenvelds had heard sing somewhere. Joop joined them too as they were hearing of the accomplishments of the Groenvelds' oldest son at the sport of *fierljeppen*, as if an ability to vault over a ditch using a long pole were something a young man ought to spend time practicing. But everyone was laughing at the story Mrs. Groenveld was telling about a vaulter ending up in the water at some past contest—which was apparently the fun of watching the sport.

Joop, beside Truus, was laughing and laughing, and Truus was laughing too. It was good for the soul, to laugh with friends.

When the story was ended, Joop, who was known for his enthusiastic, if less than elegant, dancing, said to Truus, "Well, my bride, at the risk of making myself tonight's sport amusement, would you perhaps dance with me? I promise to try not to vault right into the water, and I apologize in advance to your toes."

A waltz was playing, and Truus always did love a waltz.

"Do go, Truus," Klara said. "You've been doing nothing all evening but working while everyone else is enjoying themselves."

PAPA

Stephan lay flat on the roof, watching and listening, too shocked to be cold. All around the city, flames rose up into the sky, buildings burning, and yet there were no sounds of sirens, no fire trucks. How was that possible? Some blocks away, in the direction of the old Jewish neighborhood, a new flame leapt up and, with it, a cheer so raucous that Stephan could hear it even from this far away.

On the street below, a truck waited, its open bed filled with silent men and teenage boys. Rolf, who now opened the palais doors for Nazi visitors and, in inclement weather, held his umbrella over their heads, bowed to the Nazi thug who climbed from the truck. It seemed a lifetime before three Nazis emerged through the doors Rolf held open for them. Papa was not with them.

The Nazis joined the driver, lighting cigarettes and laughing together. Rolf again opened the door.

Papa emerged first this time, followed by a Nazi holding a Luger to his head.

The soldier with the dog opened the back gate of the truck, and two of the men in the truck bed reached down to give Papa a hand.

Papa turned to the soldiers. "But you don't understand," he said. "My wife, she is sick. She is dying. She can't—"

A soldier raised a club overhead and brought it down on Papa's shoulder. Papa fell to the sidewalk, the dog barking angrily at him as the soldier swung the club at his leg, and again at his arm, his stomach.

"Get up," the soldier demanded, "unless you want to see what dying really is."

The whole world seemed overcome with silence, the soldiers and the men and boys in the truck and even the dog seemingly suspended in that moment, while Papa lay unmoving.

You must do what they say, Papa, Stephan thought as hard as he could, as if he might move his father to do so out of sheer unspoken will. You can't give up like I did in the park. Realizing only as he thought it that it was true. Ashamed of his own willingness to give up. Would he even be alive if that old couple hadn't helped him?

Papa rolled over onto his side, screaming in pain. The dog, barking fiercely now, lunged toward him, stopped only by the length of his leash.

Papa brought himself up to kneeling, then slowly crawled toward the back of the truck. When he was close enough, two of the men reached down again, each taking one of Papa's shoulders. They hoisted him to his feet and held him upright. A third man reached out and put his arms around Papa's waist and dragged him up into the truck, others crowding back to give him room. Papa lay faceup, unmoving in the truck bed.

Stephan fought the urge to climb to the roof's edge so that his father might see him, to call out to Papa that he must not fight them, he must just survive.

The soldiers slammed the truck closed again, penning in his father, who disappeared from Stephan's sight now among the boys and men. The driver climbed back in, and the engine sputtered to a start.

Stephan watched silently as the truck headed down the long arc of the Ringstrasse, toward the canal and the river. It slipped in and out of sight behind trolleys and trucks and kiosks, finally disappearing altogether. Stephan watched the emptiness of the chaos left in its wake, the flames around the city and the cheering crowds, the impossibly mute fire trucks.

WAITING

Stephan crept back across the roof toward the servants'-floor sitting room window, staying low, trying not to make a sound, not to knock a slate free. He listened intently over the chaos of the night to hear what was happening inside.

"Peter and I can get it," he heard Walter say.

He leaned down over the roof's edge to peer into the window. Mutti was wheeling her chair to the Victrola, where poor Walter held Peter's little stuffed rabbit paw in one hand as he tried to right the table on which the Victrola had sat. Stephan was just reaching down to push open the window when the door from the hallway again opened. Walter hugged his rabbit close, to protect him, as Stephan pulled himself back up out of sight.

"Wall-man," a voice said. "Frau Neuman."

Wall-man? Stephan listened more intently.

Someone began resetting the chessboard, banging the pieces.

"We don't know where he is," Mutti said.

"How about you, Walter?" the same voice—Dieter's voice—asked. "Do you know where Stephan is?"

"He doesn't know either," Mutti insisted.

"I can help him," Dieter said. "He's my friend. I want to help."

Stephan wanted to believe him, wanted someone to help him, wanted not to be out alone on this terrifying night. There were no other voices but Dieter's and Mutti's. Maybe Dieter had returned just to help. But mixed in with the memories of exploring with Dieter on their bicycles, rehearsing plays together, searching cafés for

Stefan Zweig, was Dieter's face jeering with the others in Prater Park as the Nazi kicked Stephan, demanding he goose-step yet again.

Dieter knew as well as anyone how Stephan could slip out a window and down the tree to sneak out at night. Stephan hesitated, torn between the certainty that Dieter would climb out to find him—and help him? or load him into a truck?—and the fear of leaving Mutti and Walter to whatever Dieter might do to them.

"Even Peter doesn't know where Stephan is," Walter said.

Stephan wiped his face and looked to the horizon, the blazes all over the city. He was no match for Dieter's strength, and if he was found, Mutti and Walter would be caught in the lie.

He mapped out in his mind the quickest way into the underground. There was nowhere else to go. If he could get down the tree unnoticed, he could enter through the kiosk perhaps twenty-five steps down the Ringstrasse, twenty-five perilous steps, given the rioting crowds. Or he could slip down the back street to the manhole cover between here and the Michaelerplatz, a longer way to go but perhaps easier to avoid being seen. Or he could just trust Dieter. Was there really any other choice?

THE NEWS

Truus?"

Truus looked up from the radio on the narrow table, startled. Joop stood in his nightclothes, lit by the moonlight through the window.

"I didn't want to wake you," she said. She had kept the lights off and the radio so low she could barely hear it herself, even with her ear right to it.

"Come back to bed, Truus. You need your rest."

Truus nodded, but didn't move from her chair. It was preposterous. They'd had such a lovely evening at the Groenvelds' that when they'd come home they'd turned on the radio, to dance barefoot together in the apartment, as they sometimes did before they made love. But there had been no music. There had been only the awful news coming out of Germany, all of the Reich burning on account of the death of a low-level diplomat shot in Paris by some poor Polish boy upset that his parents were caught at the border, between a Germany wanting to send them home and a Poland refusing to take them.

Joop said, "The entire police force are out in Berlin and have been since eight this evening, and hundreds of Black Guards too. Surely the chaos is over."

"They're saying even women are being beaten," she said. "They're saying the gangs are drunk with destruction, that they've been chasing down Jews in the streets all day and night. Can you imagine? While we were laughing at dinner. While we were waltzing, with no idea in the world."

Joop shook his head. "If the German people don't stand up now, they are finished."

"Goebbels spoke a second time tonight, calling for order, but his words are having no impact."

"His words are a dog whistle," Joop said. "I said that earlier. Didn't I say that when we first heard what he said at that gathering in Munich? In the same breath as he announces the death of vom Rath, he blames it on a Jewish conspiracy and says the party won't organize demonstrations but nor will they hamper them."

"But it makes no sense," she said. "Why would this one death in Paris spark riots throughout the Reich?"

"That's what I'm saying, Truus. It isn't the cause of the riots. It's the excuse. When Goebbels said they wouldn't hamper demonstrations, he was *inviting* this violence. It's what the Nazis do so well. They create a crisis—like they did with the Reichstag fire in '33—which they then use to increase their military control. They want every German to see the havoc they can wreak at the snap of a finger. They want every German to know the violence they can bring to bear on any single person for the slightest perceived offense. What better way to silence citizens opposing the regime than with the prospect that their resistance will jeopardize their families and their lives?"

"It isn't just the Nazis now, though. They're saying crowds of ordinary Germans have been flocking into the streets to gape at the wreckage and to *cheer*. 'Like holiday makers at a fairground,' Joop. Where are the decent German people? Why aren't they standing against this? Where are the leaders of the world?"

Joop said, "You put more faith in politicians than they warrant. They cower at the slightest threat to their power, although of course no one but Hitler has any real power in Germany now." He kissed her head. "Really, Truus, you ought to come back to bed."

She watched him disappear down the hallway, headed back toward their comfortable bed in their comfortable home in their country that was free from terror. He was right. There was nothing to do tonight. She should follow him back to bed and get some sleep. But how could she sleep?

Joop emerged again, shrugging on his robe and bringing hers, saying, "All right then, go ahead and turn the radio up. Do you want the lights on?"

As he helped her into her robe, she shivered at the thought that she might have lost him, that the Nazis didn't need any real excuse to hold anyone they wished.

He turned the volume up, and pulled his chair around beside her, and took her hand. They sat listening together in the moonlight.

"Joop," she said, "I thought I might borrow Mrs. Kramarsky's car at daylight, just to go to the border."

"It's too dangerous now, Truus."

"You've seen these children."

"You'd put your life at risk. Really, Geertruida, the doctor said—"

"You would ask me to sit now, Joop? Just when it is so important to stand?"

Joop sighed. He went into the kitchen and put on coffee: the click of the cabinet door being opened, water from the tap, coffee grounds falling onto the metal of the percolator basket as the voice on the radio continued. He returned with two steaming cups, saying, "You'll just collect the children who've already made it out of Germany, like you usually do?"

Truus accepted a cup from him, hesitating as he again sat with her. She took a sip of the strong, hot coffee.

"Parents send their children on trains to Emmerich am Rhein," she said. "There's a farm on the border there. . . . It's too dangerous for the farmer and his wife to take in children, but . . ."

"They call you?"

Truus nodded. "The committee does, yes."

"You're the one who goes over the border to get them? You go into Germany to get children with no papers whatsoever?"

Truus nodded.

"Oh, Truus."

Truus unconsciously touched her ruby ring to her lips, then looked at it, slightly surprised to realize that the ring Joop had given her when she was first pregnant wasn't there, it was still with the refugee siblings.

"I know," she said, "but . . . Joop, I . . . I never told you, but . . . Little Adele . . ."

"You brought Adele on a train with thirty other children, Truus. You and Mrs. Van Lange did. You had papers for them—"

"Yes, but . . ." She took his hand, willing herself not to cry. "She didn't make it."

"What are you saying? I don't understand."

She looked to their joined hands on this sturdy table, his wide palm and strong fingers dark against her paler skin. "Adele . . . I . . . Diphtheria."

"No. No, Adele is in Britain. The Bentwiches—"

"She had a mother, Joop," she whispered, the tears spilling but still she met his gaze, his pain too now set free for this child who had never been theirs. "I might have left her in her mother's arms," she said. "I might have put her in yours."

THE "AVE MARIA"

Ruchele held Walter close as the Nazi boy returned through the window and took up the chore of restoring order to the apartment. He lifted the toppled table, then the Victrola. He placed the record back on the machine.

"Would you like me to turn it on for you, Frau Neuman?" he asked.

"No!" Ruchele cried out.

At the boy's startled expression, she said more calmly, "No, please. I don't think I could bear it, music." Dieter, she'd almost said, but if she called him Dieter, would he be offended? If she called him Officer, would it break the spell of guilt that surely was what kept him here helping them despite the risky position it must put him in with his new friends? "Thank you," she said.

"I'll put another coal on then," he said.

He opened the coal box. Only a few lumps remained. As he looked sadly up at her, he spotted Stephan's gloves, which had been knocked from the table. He picked the gloves up, saying, "If you know where he went, I can find him. I can let him know it's safe to return. It's so cold out. Did he even take a coat?"

She swallowed back the urge to accept this help, knowing she could expect to be offered no other.

"You're sure you don't want music?" he said. "It might soothe you."

Ruchele, careful not to glance in the direction of the dirty little window, now fully closed, said, "Thank you. Thank you so much, but no. Walter can manage that for us if we want music. Perhaps you could just open the window ever so slightly, for the fresh air?"

The boy opened the window slightly, and bowed, and left Ruchele holding Walter to her, listening for whether the quiet outside the door was Stephan's friend slipping back to join his comrades, or the boy stealthily waiting in the hallway for Stephan's return.

The clock struck the quarter hour, then the half.

"Walter," Ruchele said, "can you peek out the door and see if that boy is there?"

"Dieter snot nose," Walter said, not in his own voice but in his Peter Rabbit one.

He cracked the door open and peeked out, then opened it slightly wider and looked about.

"All right, then," Ruchele told him.

"I can make it go, Mutti," Walter said. "I can make it go."

"The Victrola?"

"For Stephan," Walter said.

"For Stephan," Ruchele said.

He went to the little machine and turned the crank—a task he'd always loved, but there was no joy on his face now, only studied concentration as he set the needle in place. The music crackled to life, the record damaged, but still the first strains of the "Ave Maria" played in the cold room.

"Climb into my lap so you can keep me warm," she told him. "Peter too."

He did so, and they sat waiting, Walter climbing from her lap each time the record reached its end to lift the needle and replace it, to once again begin the "Ave Maria."

FIGHTING FIRES

Stephan huddled inside Papa's cocoa bean cellar (his Uncle Michael's cocoa bean cellar now), his hands tucked into his coat pockets for the illusion of warmth. How long had he been underground? Surely it must be morning, the chaos of the night over even if there wasn't yet the sound of workers arriving in the chocolate factory overhead. He took the flashlight from the bottom of the stairs and climbed down the ladder into the cave underneath, pushing away thoughts of Žofie here as he made his way out through the lower cavern and the little tunnel, and up the circular stairs. At the top, he pushed up one of the metal triangles just enough to peek out. It was still dark. There were still people everywhere.

He slipped back down into the tunnel and hurried along to one of the open-grid grates, where he might see more easily without being seen. Even before he climbed the metal rungs in the tunnel wall, he heard the crowd.

At the top, as he looked up at them through the grate as if through prison bars, the revelers seemed even more drunk on their anger. *What hath night to do with sleep?* Hoodlums, Stephan wanted to call them, but they were the same people to whom, not so long ago, he would have apologized as he dashed down the Ringstrasse.

This crowd was gathered by one of the synagogues as if at the tree lighting at the Rathausplatz on Christmas Eve. There were no chestnut stands or punch stalls here, though. There were only people crowded around, cheering each spike of flame, and firefighters who stood, unmoving, just in front of Stephan. He watched through the metal grid, unable to understand why they didn't fight the fire.

A mob of brownshirts dragged a crippled old man from his apartment, his wife trailing them, begging them to leave her husband, that he could harm no one. The firefighters turned to watch, but didn't move to help the poor couple. No one moved to help.

"He's a good man," the woman pleaded. "I tell you, he's a good man."

One of the brownshirts raised an ax. Stephan couldn't believe it even as he watched the man swing it at the woman. Her husband groaned at the sight of his wife felled to the ground, the blood pouring from her arm.

Another Nazi put a pistol to the man's temple. "Now you are ready to identify for us your Jew friends?"

The man could do nothing but plead, "Ignaz! Ignaz, no. Ignaz, no," as his wife bled to death.

The Nazi pulled the trigger, the shot barely registering over the noise of the crowd as the man crumpled to the ground just at the grate, his lips still moving.

"I ought to finish you, but there are too many Jews in Vienna to waste two bullets on only one of you," the Nazi said as he kicked the man's head with his heel.

Something oozed from the man's ear, leaving Stephan feeling the vomit rise in his throat, but too afraid to move away lest he be found.

Another brownshirt said, "You better be careful or you'll have Jew brain on your boots," and the whole group laughed.

The firefighters turned back to watch the fire again, one saying, "We ought to do something before the flames spread to the other buildings and get out of hand."

"This mob would kill us for interfering," his companion said.

The crowd cheered at the sound of something collapsing—a roof beam, Stephan thought, although it was outside the frame of what he could see. All he could see through the grate beyond the man's head was spark and flame roaring up into the dark, smoky sky. A spark alit on the roof of the building beside the synagogue. Only then did the firefighters move to action, and only to keep the fire from spreading as the synagogue continued to burn.

BACK IN THE tunnels under his own neighborhood, Stephan peeked from the kiosk on the Ringstrasse up to the servants'-floor windows, hoping to hear the "Ave Maria." But there was only Rolf standing guard at the door for the Nazis now.

He returned through the underground to the chocolate cellar. He was so tired, so cold. He moved in shadow and silence up to his father's office. He stretched out on his father's office sofa, where, in the earliest days of Mutti's illness, he had often come after school, as tired in those days as he now was. He used to fall asleep on this couch to the comforting sound of Papa working at his desk, and wake hours later to the soft feel of a blanket Papa had spread over him, and Papa, working at his desk, smiling at him and saying, "Even a soul submerged in sleep is hard at work and helps make something of the world."

He wondered where Papa was now, where the truck had taken him.

He would wait here for Uncle Michael. Uncle Michael would help him figure out what to do.

NO ESCAPE

Stephan woke in the darkness to the sound of a woman's voice approaching, a familiar voice. He rolled silently off the couch and under it just as the office door opened.

The woman giggled. "Really, Michael, I couldn't."

Had Aunt Lisl come back from Shanghai?

"Why can't you?" Uncle Michael said in a teasing tone not unlike that he'd so often used to ask whether Stephan had kissed Žofie-Helene.

Stephan listened, holding his breath, as his uncle lifted the woman and laid her out on the sofa, which sagged toward him. His uncle's feet skimmed off shoes only inches from Stephan's face.

"Michael," the woman said, and Stephan recognized the voice of Anita, his father's secretary, to whose image Stephan had sometimes pleasured himself.

"Didn't you do this with Herman?" his uncle asked. "After Ruchele got so sick?"

"Michael," the woman said again, with a note of objection in her voice.

Her breathing grew deeper as Uncle Michael's trousers dropped to the floor around his feet, the belt buckle clanking against the wood floor so close that Stephan nearly gasped. The gasp, though, came from Anita, as the shadow of Uncle Michael stepped out of the puddle of trousers and the couch above Stephan creaked even lower under his uncle's added weight.

The woman's gasp turned to a moan, then, as it had so often in Stephan's dark bedroom, in his imagination. The couch overhead began to move rhythmically, slowly at first, and then faster and faster, until his uncle gasped quietly, "Lisl." And still Stephan could do nothing but lie there, absolutely still, trying not to think of his own shameful imaginings, pushing away the awful thought of his father with Anita on this same couch, where Stephan had so often found escape.

ABANDONED

Walter startled awake to silence and dawn light. He climbed from Mutti's lap, cranked the Victrola to restart the music, and retrieved Peter Rabbit from the floor.

NOTHING MORE THAN A NAME

Stephan watched the palais from the shadows near the newsstand, which now offered copies of *Der Stürmer* sporting a big-nosed cartoon caricature of a black-bearded man lifting the tail of a cow on a World Bank pedestal, around which money bags were littered. The chaos had settled into a bleak morning, the thugs no doubt sleeping off their foaming rage. Still, he moved carefully, guardedly, wondering where Herr Kline was and whether the newsvendor might be with Papa, until finally Walter emerged from the palais.

Stephan followed a half block behind him, keeping close to the buildings and with his cap low, comforted just to see his little brother walking to school. At the wide stone steps, Walter was shunned by the other boys, but at least they weren't tripping him and laughing when he fell, at least they weren't swarming around him, chanting, "Jew. Jew. Jew." Stephan watched and listened, knowing there was nothing he could do to help Walter, knowing he ought to back away lest he be drawn into defending his brother. That would do neither of them any good.

A Nazi at the top of the school steps stopped Walter at the door.

"But it's my school," Walter objected.

"No Jews."

Walter, confused, studied the man frankly. "We celebrate Christmas just like you do," he told the man, words their mother might have used.

"Tell me your name, boy," the man demanded.

"Walter Neuman. And your name, sir?" Walter said politely.

"Neuman, the Jew chocolate maker."

Walter took a step back, and then another, as if from a rabid animal.

With surprising dignity, he turned and patiently descended the steps. Stephan, feeling ashamed at his own cowardice, slipped back into the shadow of a building until his brother reached the corner.

"Wall-man," he whispered.

Walter's face lit like the chandeliers in the main entryway of the palais that had been their home, that would be their home again, Stephan told himself. He wrapped his arms around Walter, pulling him out of the vile Nazi's sight, saying, "It's okay. It's okay." His brother had never smelled so sweet.

"We played the music, but you didn't come home," Walter said. "Dieter put the Victrola back up, and after he left, we played the music."

"Dieter did?"

"He said not to tell anyone," Walter said. "That man said I couldn't go to school. Mutti would want me to go to school."

He pulled his brother to him again, this boy who had been so young just two days before. "She would, Wall. You are such a good boy."

Walter said, "Do you think Mutti would wake up if we brought her something to eat?"

"How long has she been sleeping?" Stephan asked, working to keep the alarm from his voice. What if it wasn't sleep?

"She couldn't get into the bed and I'm not big enough to help her out of the wheelchair. I got Rolf to help move her this morning. It made him grumpy."

"Don't worry about Rolf, Wall. He's always grumpy."

"He's more grumpy now."

"We all are. Listen, Walter, I want you to do something for me. I want you to go back home to Mutti. Don't tell Rolf or anyone else that you've seen me. Whisper to Mutti that I'm okay, that I can't come back in daylight but I'll be back tonight, I'll come up the tree and through the window. Tell her I'm going to get Papa a visa. Tell her I'm going to get us all visas."

"You know where Papa is?"

"I'm finding out."

"What is a visa?" his brother asked.

"Just tell Mutti," he said.

"I want *you* to tell her."

"Shhhh!" Stephan said, looking around nervously.

"I want to go with you," his brother said more quietly.

"All right," Stephan said. "All right. I could use your help today anyway. But first I need you to go tell Mutti I'm okay. Don't admit to anyone else you've seen me, but tell Mutti. If anyone else asks you, tell them you forgot something you need for school."

"My new pencil?" Walter said. "I was saving it for you, Stephan, in case you needed it to write a new play."

"Your new pencil," Stephan agreed, hugging his generous little brother to him, thinking of all the pencils he'd forgotten at all the café tables where he used to order coffee and a pastry without a thought.

He watched surreptitiously as Walter walked past Rolf and into the palais. He kept watching, as if he might be able to do anything if his brother was questioned. He barely breathed the whole time, afraid that Walter wouldn't return, that the Nazis in the palais would come out and arrest him, that Walter would return to say he couldn't tell Mutti because Mutti wouldn't wake.

When Walter emerged, looking for all the world like a young boy on his way to school again with a new pencil in hand, Stephan pulled his brother to him.

"I whispered to Mutti," Walter said, "and she woke up and she smiled."

THE LINE, WHEN they reached the American consulate, was impossibly long, but Stephan couldn't risk taking Walter home and returning again. He could barely risk standing in this line, but there was no alternative.

"All right, Wall-man," Stephan said. "Hit me with a word quiz."

"Peter Rabbit is better than me at English," Walter said.

"But you're awfully good at it too, Wall," Stephan assured him. "Go ahead."

IT WAS DARK outside the consulate windows when Stephan, holding a sleeping Walter over his shoulder, took a seat across the desk from a gourd-headed American with wire spectacles. Mutti would be worried, but there was no choice; they couldn't put to waste all that time standing in line just because it had been the end of the school day, or late afternoon, or dinnertime.

"I'd like to apply for a visa for my father, please," he said.

The consulate employee frowned at him. "Not for yourself and your—"

"My father has already applied for us."

Patience, he told himself. Patience. He hadn't meant to sound so abrupt.

"Sorry," he said. "Sorry."

"And your mother?" the man asked.

"No, I . . . She's sick."

"It takes time. Perhaps she'll be well—"

"She won't be. She won't get well. That's why we haven't left before, because Papa wouldn't leave Mutti. But now he has no choice."

The man took off his spectacles and studied Stephan. "I'm sorry. I'm really sorry. I . . ."

"My father, he needs a visa immediately. We can wait, but he's been sent to a work camp. We think he's been sent to a camp. And if he has a visa, they might let him leave Austria."

"I see. Do you have family in the United States? Anyone who could give you an affidavit of support? It goes much faster if you have family to vouch for you. Otherwise it can take years."

"But my father can't leave if he has nowhere to go."

"I really am sorry. We're doing the best we can, working until ten every night, but . . . I'll take your information. If you can find someone to vouch for you, come back and I'll get it added to your file. It can be anyone."

"But I don't know anyone in America," Stephan said.

"It doesn't have to be family," the man said. "People . . . We have telephone books here from New York, from Boston, from Chicago—all over America. You can use them anytime. You can note the addresses of people who share your name and write to them."

"To strangers?"

"It's what people do."

THE VIENNA INDEPENDENT

NAZI VIOLENCE AGAINST JEWS

Synagogues burned, Jewish businesses vandalized, thousands arrested

BY KÄTHE PERGER

November 11, 1938 — Some thirty thousand men throughout Germany, Austria, and Czechoslovakia have been arrested in the last twenty-four hours simply because they are Jews. Many were severely beaten, and several have reportedly died. The men have, apparently, been transported to labor camps, although the details of this are not yet known.

Women have also been arrested, although in fewer numbers, and indications are that the women arrested here in Vienna are all being held somewhere in the city.

More than 250 synagogues throughout the Reich were destroyed by fire. All Jewish businesses have been shuttered, if they still have shutters, if they haven't been smashed to bits . . .

THE TWINS

Truus knocked a second time at the door in the Alster section of Hamburg, having come by overnight train in response to a frantic letter received by the committee. A Dutch Jewish family had written on behalf of relations that two babies were in danger from the Gestapo in this beautiful house in this lovely neighborhood. How Mr. Tenkink had managed to get Dutch entry papers for these twins despite the ban, she didn't know. She supposed the children's relations must be well connected, although not so well connected as to have obtained German exit papers too. How they got out of Germany was in Truus's hands.

She tapped the brass door knocker a third time. It was opened by a sleepy-eyed nurse still in her nightclothes. Truus introduced herself and explained why she had come.

"For the babies?" the nurse said.

Had she come to the wrong address?

"The missus doesn't receive anyone before ten in the morning, and certainly the babies are too young to receive visitors on their own," the nurse said.

Truus stuck her boot heel in the threshold before the woman could close the door. "I have come from Amsterdam at the request of your mistress's relations, to rescue the babies."

"To rescue them?"

"You'd best get your mistress for me."

Truus held the nurse's gaze until the nurse opened the door.

"I WAS QUITE frightened when I contacted my aunt," the twin's mother explained to Truus as they sat together, finally, in the library. "If I exaggerated, it was from real fright."

Truus allowed the silence to grow uncomfortable. She rose then and pulled from the shelves two volumes she'd seen while she waited for the woman—stories by Stefan Zweig and Ernest Hemingway—and placed them firmly in front of the woman. "If you are so very frightened," she said, "you might start by taking the precaution of at least hiding that which would bring the wrath of the Gestapo down on you."

"Oh, well, they're only books," the woman said.

Truus smoothed the skirt of her navy-blue pinstripe suit and, with it, her anger. "The children have not been mistreated by the Gestapo?"

"They have not," the mother said unapologetically.

"You might ask yourself if they're safe with a mother who will, in a moment of fear, invent for her children a horror other children are truly experiencing, wasting resources that would save other children's lives."

"You must not have children, or you would understand! None of us are safe here," the woman wailed, her composure gone and in its place the same pleading expression Truus had seen on the face of Adele's mother at the train station, the same expression she felt in her own guilty heart.

Truus turned away, to the empty space on the bookshelf. "You must see the position you have put me in," she said softly. "I've come on an overnight train with permission to bring two abused babies to safety on an emergency basis. If I show up at The Hague with two perfectly healthy children who have suffered no harm, I will lose my credibility. And if I lose my credibility, that will be the end of my ability to help any child."

"I'm sorry," the mother said. "I'm so sorry. I didn't imagine . . ."

"We don't always, do we?" Still thinking of Adele, and of her own lost children, still thinking of what she would have done to save all the babies she'd lost even before they were born. "I'm sorry I cannot help you, I truly am," she said. "Your nurse might be able to get your babies to safety in Switzerland. People seldom question a nurse crossing a border with children who aren't hers. They can't imagine a mother would want so desperately to get her children to safety that she would turn them over to someone else's care with the possibility that she will never see them again."

OUTSIDE AGAIN, TRUUS searched in her handbag for the address of the Dutch consul-general in Hamburg. She no longer needed this Baron Aartsen's help getting the twins out of Germany, but she was here, and dressed for Hamburg too in her suit and her blue pumps, her yellow gloves and a flamboyant hat she wore because even the Gestapo tended to be daunted by a woman in a flamboyant hat. She might as well salvage something of the journey by introducing herself to the man. He might prove helpful somewhere along the way.

"ARE YOU HERE AT LAST?" the baron asked without so much as a greeting or introduction when she was shown into his office.

His words so startled Truus that she turned to see if someone else might be behind her. But it was only the two of them, Truus and this friendly-faced, prematurely gray-haired aristocrat.

"I've been waiting for you," he said.

Truus touched a gloved hand to her hat, as if her balance might be found in its brim. There had been no safe way to alert him that she was coming to collect the babies, and no point in it. She'd been given his address and told to contact him if she had trouble getting the babies across the border, without any assurance that he could help if she did.

"But however did you know I would come?" she asked.

"It was high time for a good woman from the Netherlands to come help us out here, wasn't it? Do come with me."

Truus, tamping down her astonishment, fell in beside him, chatting amiably as he led her to the chancellery. There, the waiting room was overrun with Jewish mothers and their children, all waiting to appeal for papers to the Netherlands.

He called for the attention of the mothers, most of whom had already turned toward them.

"This is Geertruida Wijsmuller," he said. "She's come from the Netherlands to fetch your little ones."

He chose six youngsters as surely as if he had been expecting Truus to arrive to fetch them: five boys and a girl, all of the eleven-to-thirteen-year-old variety Truus most adored—old enough to see the world with some intelligence, and young enough still to have ideals and hope. The baron had already arranged paperwork from the Germans allowing them to travel, or what he said was proper paperwork. He also had, inexplicably, seven first-class tickets for a train to Amsterdam.

"You leave at two forty-five," he said, checking his watch.

"You have visas for them to enter the Netherlands?" Truus asked.

"If I had, I wouldn't need you, Mrs. Wijsmuller, now would I? I'm afraid you'll have to change trains at Osnabrück, to one coming from Berlin and bound for Deventer, but there will be a carriage reserved for you."

Truus thought it inexcusable to spend so much money for first-class tickets, but the baron declined to change them for cheaper fares when they arrived at the station.

"I assure you, you will be glad for the arrangements," he said. "It is so difficult to get out of Germany these days."

"And it's easier for those who travel in first class?" Truus asked, wondering how she would be expected to get these children across the border and into the Netherlands if the consul-general himself couldn't arrange it.

BEGGING FOR PAPA

Uncle Michael sat in Papa's chair, turned sideways from Papa's desk, his eyes closed and his hands rubbing Anita's bottom under her skirt, as Stephan stood frozen, trying to blot out the memory of the sound of them as he'd hidden under the couch. Was that only yesterday? He tried not to think of the glimpse of Žofie-Helene's thighs in the tunnel that first time, and still the memory stirred in him as he watched Anita's face, the pleasure in the tilt of her jaw and her hair falling down her back the way Žofie's did. Stephan had always written his female leads to be played by Žofie with her hair loose, free of her usual braids or bun.

Anita opened her eyes. "Oh!" she said, meeting Stephan's gaze with her own startled blue.

"See, you want a little more too," Uncle Michael said.

The woman moved his uncle's hands away, saying, "Michael, you have company."

His uncle turned toward him. For the briefest moment, Stephan imagined he was still somehow the Uncle Michael who would pull a butterscotch candy from his pocket and say, "A sweet for my sweet son" or, as Stephan grew older, ask about the play he was writing or the music he liked.

"What are you doing here?" his uncle demanded. "You can't be—"

"They've arrested Papa," Stephan said as the secretary scurried past him and out the office door.

"You have to go. You can't be seen here," Uncle Michael said. He glanced out the window. At the bank across the street, a long line of people waited, although the bank was closed. "I'll get you money, but don't—"

"Papa needs a visa," Stephan said.

"I— What do you think, that I can just ring up some official and say my ex-brother-in-law needs a visa?"

"You promised to take care of us. I can stay in Vienna with Mutti, and Walter can too. But Papa has been arrested. Papa needs to leave."

"I'll get you money but I can't get you a visa. I can't be seen asking for visas for Jews. Do you understand? You can't be seen here. Go on, and don't let anyone see you go."

Stephan stood staring at his uncle sitting in Papa's chair, the Kokoschka of Aunt Lisl with her scratched cheeks now hanging above Papa's desk at this business Stephan's grandfather had built from nothing at all when Uncle Michael's family had had every privilege. He wanted to go back home and crawl into bed, as he had late the prior night, but it was too dangerous for Mutti and Walter to have him seen coming and going; there was little to do but climb the tree and slip in through the window late at night, and sleep a few hours, and slip back out before sunrise.

His uncle said, "Go on. Leave. I'll get some money to your mother somehow, but you need to turn for help to your own kind."

"My own kind?"

"You're a Jew. If I'm caught helping you, I'll be sent off to a camp too. You are a Jew."

"You're my uncle. I don't have anyone else to turn to."

"They're helping Jews at that Jewish community center, the place just down from the apartment your grandfather lived in while he was building the palais."

"In Leopoldstadt?"

"While he was building the palais, I said. Listen to me, for God's sake. The one on this side of the canal. Now go on, before anyone sees me helping you."

SEARCHING FOR PAPA

Stephan kept close to the damp walls as he made his way through the underground darkness. He came to the crypts behind the locked gate under St. Stephen's Cathedral; he'd made a wrong turn somewhere. He retraced his steps and headed toward the Talmud school. He peeked up through a manhole cover, closer. He carried on to another manhole cover and peeked out onto the narrower streets and older, shabbier buildings of the old central city where the Stadttempel and the IKG offices were. He could see the door to the Jewish center, but two SS there watched as Hitler Youth taunted women and children, pelting them with stones.

Stephan ought to help the mothers and children. He knew that. But he only waited until the SS left. He gave them several minutes, to make sure they weren't returning, before pushing up the heavy grate and hurrying across the street and into the IKG offices himself.

Inside, in an entrance hall with worn stone floors, a line of people several deep rose up the open stairway to a warren of offices. Unmatched baskets labeled A–B, C–D, and on through the alphabet sat on tables along the back wall, all heaped with index cards. A hush fell over the crowd as the fact of Stephan's presence registered with them. Most Jewish boys his age had been arrested with their fathers, and he didn't wear a skullcap.

"I'm trying to find my papa," he said.

Slowly, cautiously, people came out of their frozen stillness. An organizer helping people fill out cards returned her attention to the woman she was helping, who couldn't fill out the card herself because she couldn't write. As the organizer wrote, others questioned her, but she kept her attention focused on the illiterate woman who was hoping to find a loved one who, like Papa, had disappeared in the raids.

"Please, everyone, we are doing our best," the organizer called over the din. "Herr Löwenherz was also arrested again. We don't yet know where anyone is. You can wait in line here if you need help, but it would be easier for all of us if you would take a card and fill out the information for whoever is missing. Name. Address. How we can reach you. Put the card in the pile with the first letter of the missing person's surname. We'll let you know as soon as we know anything."

Nobody left the line.

Stephan took a card and, with a pencil from his satchel—Walter's new pencil—wrote down his father's information.

A younger woman was saying to an older one behind her, "He said just go to Shanghai and he would find us. That was the last thing he said: just get the children out of Austria. You don't need a visa for Shanghai, you can just go. But there are no passages to be had."

"I heard you can get Cuban visas for a price," the older woman said, "but the Nazis have taken everything we own."

Stephan finished filling out the card for his father and placed it in the M–N basket, and turned to go as another organizer emptied the I–J basket into a larger bin. A card spilled to the floor, unnoticed, to be trampled as the line moved ever so slightly forward.

Stephan retrieved the card he'd filled out for his father and waited.

The organizer reappeared and emptied the K–L basket into the bin, and disappeared again. When she appeared once more, for the M–N basket, Stephan placed the card for his father directly into the bin in her hands.

She stared at him, surprised.

"Neuman. Herman Neuman of Neuman's Chocolates," he said, hearing in his own voice his father's. They were fine people, his family: their wealth came from their own chocolate business established with their own capital, and they kept their accounts always on the credit side at the Rothschild bank.

THE BOY WITH CHOCOLATES
IN HIS POCKET

None of the newspaper staff but Käthe Perger herself and her assistant editor, Rick Neidhardt, had shown up for work in the aftermath of the chaos. Fear had flooded every corner of Vienna. Anyone seen to help a Jewish neighbor was defying the new Nazi laws, with "help" so broadly defined that simply reporting the truth in a newspaper could land you in jail or worse. How could Käthe ask her staff to continue working? She might as well ask them to stand in line to be beaten and imprisoned.

"So how are we going to do this with just two of us?" Rick asked her.

She studied the task list they'd made, the only sound Rick's clearing throat.

"All right, Rick," she said, "why don't you—"

She looked up from the list and stopped short, startled by the cloud of fright in Rick's face as he stared away from her, toward the door.

She gave a small gasp herself before she recognized the boy who stood inside the office. She would have sworn she'd closed the office door—and it *was* closed—but the boy stood there, waiting. The boy, who was almost a man now.

"It's okay, Rick," she said, resisting the urge to bolt to Stephan and wrap him in a hug of her own relief. "It's Žofie's friend." Žofie's friend, not a friend of Žofie's, but one is always greater than zero.

"I'm sorry to bother you," Stephan Neuman stammered, "but I'm . . . My father . . . I thought you might know where they've taken the men they arrested?"

Käthe said, "But you're not . . . ? Most of the older boys were arrested with their fathers."

The boy waited. He was a smart boy, unwilling to give up his secret to avoiding arrest.

She said, "Our best information is that some have been taken to a German labor camp outside Munich, near Dachau, so not too far away. But others may be in transit to Buchenwald, or even as far as Sachsenhausen. We're doing what we can to find out."

"I heard the Nazis might allow my father to return if I can arrange papers for him to emigrate. I don't know what to do," the poor child said, his eyes welling.

Käthe approached him slowly, so as not to alarm him, and put an arm around his shoulders. "No, of course not," she said. "Of course not. No one does, Stephan. I think . . . I'll find out what I can, I promise. Can your mother—" Lord, the boy's mother was confined to a wheelchair, and dying; it had been Käthe's small obsession, to keep track of this only friend of her daughter, even if the friendship had not survived this awful time. "No, I'm sorry, of course not," she said. "And your aunt, she's gone to . . ."

"Shanghai."

Rick said, "Maybe the consulates?"

Käthe squeezed the boy's shoulder reassuringly. She returned to her desk and began writing addresses on a piece of paper. "Start with the Swiss, the British, the Americans."

"I spent all day yesterday at the American embassy. They will do nothing."

Rick said, "The American backlog is horrendous."

"Go to the others, then," Käthe said. "Apply for a visa for your father, but also for the rest of your family. Tell them your father has been arrested. It will . . . They may give his application special attention. Apply everywhere, quickly. I'll find out what I can about your father. Telephone me—"

"We no longer have a telephone," the boy said, his voice cracking, as if he believed the shame of this to be his and not that of all of Vienna who happily claimed as their own the Jewish homes seized all over the city while the proper owners were made to cram into tiny, dark apartments on the island of Leopoldstadt. How could their world have changed so drastically in so little time? At the start of the year, Austria had been a free country, its leader and its people resolved to remain such. And how could she have been so impossibly wrong about her neighbors? How could she have failed to see this hatred under the surface, waiting for the excuse to express itself that Hitler offered?

"It's okay, Stephan," she said as Rick opened the office door, trying, she could see, to hurry the boy's leaving without appearing to do so. "It's okay. Come see me, then. If I'm not in, I'll leave a note about whatever we've learned here on the desk, with your name on it."

Rick sputtered, "Not . . . We'll . . ."

He glanced out the door to the Linotype machine, functioning again but scarred from its recent Nazi battering. The thing sat silent, a reminder of the impossibility of their own task to which, Rick was right, they needed to return. You could help one, or you could help many, but there wasn't time to do both, even if you could stomach the risk.

Käthe opened a desk drawer. "I'll tape it to the underside here. If I'm not in the office when you come, pull the drawer out and reach under it, okay?"

Stephan, dejected, turned to leave.

"Stephan . . . Just for a little bit, stay low," Käthe said. "You aren't in a Jewish neighborhood, that's good; the most brutish among them seem to be concentrating on the Jewish neighborhoods." Perhaps that was what had saved him from arrest? "And don't tell anyone about this, for their safety. Do you understand? Don't tell your mother. Don't tell Žofie-Helene. Don't tell anyone."

Please don't tell my daughter, she thought as she watched the boy leave. Please don't put her in danger. Which was ridiculous, of course.

This boy who had befriended Žofie could not possibly put her in more danger than her own mother's self-righteous certainty already had.

As the boy slipped out of the office and back onto the street, Rick turned to her, his fear rotting to unspoken accusation.

"I know. I know, Rick," she said. They could not allow themselves to be distracted by a single victim; they had too much to do. "But that boy . . . He was just a boy with chocolates in his pocket only months ago. He was Žofie's first real friend, the first child who didn't see her as a freak. And because he didn't, his friends didn't either."

"He just appeared like a specter," Rick said. "Did you even see or hear him enter?"

Käthe smiled just a little, despite everything. "I expect you can blame Žofie for teaching him that. She likes to imagine herself Sherlock Holmes."

PRINCESS POWER

At the Hamburg station, as Truus waited in line with the children to exchange German currency for Dutch, she tried to imagine what Baron Aartsen had meant to do if she hadn't come to see him. He might have taken the children himself, but it was one thing for a simple Dutch-woman to be caught taking children across the border on forged German orders, and quite another for that person to be a Dutch diplomat. It was of course possible that the orders were real. Truus appreciated the baron allowing her a plausible claim to believe they were—or at least the ability to state truthfully that she did not know they were forged.

"I'd like to exchange sixty reichsmarks for guilders," she told the customs officer when her turn came.

"For whom?" the clerk asked.

"For the children," Truus said. Each German was allowed to take ten reichsmarks from the country, and Baron Aartsen had thought even of this, giving her the money for each child. But in her experience, German border control was far more likely to seize reichsmarks they could easily pocket and spend unnoticed than to seize Dutch guilders whose exchange would have to be recorded and explained.

"These children are your children?" the clerk demanded.

They weren't her children, of course. The travel orders for each of the six identified them as Jewish.

"Jewish children don't need money," the clerk said, and without fur-ther attention to her, he moved to help the next person.

Truus intertwined her gloved hands, tamping down her fury, before stepping away from the window. There was nothing to be gained by arguing with him.

She walked over to the ticket counter with the children. "I need a ticket for Amsterdam for tomorrow, please," she said.

She in fact had all the tickets she needed, but she could change the extra ticket in Amsterdam and receive her refund in guilders, effecting the currency change in a roundabout way. She felt rather proud of her resourcefulness as she shepherded the children onto the train.

AT OSNABRÜCK, THEY transferred to the train to Deventer, boarding the reserved carriage, which was, it turned out, one of two right next to each other, the second carrying the Dutch princesses Juliana and Beatrix home from a visit with their grandmother on her estate in Silesia. The train, because it was carrying the princesses, would not stop in Oldenzaal, just over the border, but rather would continue nonstop all the way to Deventer, where, it being far from the border, Dutch border patrol were not likely to be present, or to be attentive if they were. This was why the baron had been so intent on her being on this, the princesses' train.

The baron had not, apparently, counted on Dutch border guards entraining in Bad Bentheim, two men appearing at the front of Truus's carriage to check papers. Truus turned to the children and said calmly, and loudly enough for the guards to hear, "Go wash your hands, children, and then I'll comb your hair."

"But it's the Sabbath," objected the oldest boy, a pill of a child who had nearly made them miss the train for his wailing over a ring his father had given him for his bar mitzvah, which he'd somehow lost. *See that you do not despise one of these little ones, for I tell you that in heaven their angels always see the face of my Father who is in heaven,* Truus reminded herself. She tried never to judge the children harshly—they were always in difficult straits—but sometimes they did test her patience.

Out the window, there might or might not have been a sliver of sun still up behind the clouds.

"The Sabbath is over," she said. "Now, go on."

"You can't make the Sabbath be over just because you're bored of it," the boy said, words Truus imagined the boy's father meant for requests to go out and play and not for a journey to save his life.

"I can, actually," Truus said, with another glance out the window. "But fortunately for us, the sun really is down, young man." Saving me the role of playing God, she thought.

The boy looked dubious, but his gaze went up the carriage aisle to the men.

Truus continued for the guards' benefit, "You are riding in the carriage next to the princesses. We may need to go with these two nice gentlemen to ask the princesses if you ought to be allowed to continue on to the Netherlands. So go on, wash up."

Taking advantage of the border guards' uncertainty as the children headed off in the opposite direction, she said, brooking no resistance, "These children are going to Amsterdam. They're expected at the Jewish hospital there."

"Madam—"

"Your names," she said as if she were the guard and they the passengers.

As they gave her their names, she pulled from her bag a pen and a small notepad. "It's Saturday, sirs," she said, repeating their names for effect. "The Hague is closed, so you cannot inquire on our behalf today, nor can you tomorrow, as it will be Sunday. But rest assured that if we are made to disturb the princesses, Mr. Tenkink at Justice will know all about it first thing Monday morning." She removed her yellow gloves and took up the pen in earnest. "Now, you'll spell your names for me, please."

They stepped back to allow the children to return to their seats, then bowed and left, apologizing for disturbing them. As they closed the carriage door behind them, Truus set a comb to the oldest boy's head as gently as she imagined his mother would have done.

BLOOMSBURY, ENGLAND

Helen Bentwich slid a new page and the triple carbons into the typewriter carriage and continued typing. She was a lousy typist, but she'd sent Ellie home at three in the morning, after her poor assistant had crossed over to being an even worse typist. At least she'd had the foresight to have Ellie set up the carbon stacks before she left. That took a lot of time, building stacks of four pages and three carbons, but it could be done even while asleep on one's feet.

"It's time, Helen." The voice was Norman's, but still it startled her. There had been nothing but the sound of typewriter keys striking paper for hours, that and the occasional gong that might or might not have been Big Ben, a good mile away.

Out the window, morning was dawning the usual gray of London wintertime.

Norman hung a suit bag from the doorknob, then came up behind her and stroked her hair so gently that she longed to close her eyes and sleep. She made a mistake, perhaps because of the interruption or perhaps because she was a lousy typist. With no time left, she back-slashed over the error.

"Appearances matter," Norman said.

She finished the page and pulled the sheets from the typewriter, set one in each pile, and tossed the used carbons in the trash bin. The last copy was barely dark enough to read, but it was what it was at this point. She fed in another set of blank pages.

"I'm not a typist, Norman," she said, "It's the content that matters, anyway."

Norman said, "I meant *your* appearance, not the plan's."

Helen, striking the keys as hard as she was able, typed in capital letters on the clean new page: MOVEMENT FOR THE CARE OF CHILDREN FROM GERMANY.

She stood and turned over each of the four stacks of pages beside her typewriter so that they were facing up, then pulled the title pages from the typewriter carriage and set one neatly atop each stack.

"Dennis will meet us there," she said. "You have the summer camps arranged?"

She took the jacket off the hanger he now held out to her.

"You don't want the blouse?" he asked.

She flipped the Ferris wheel snow globe over and righted it, the gentle float of suspended snow ever soothing as she set it back on this desk that had been her grandmother's. That was something she would never be, a grandmother.

"There are so many things I want, Norman," she said, "if only there were time."

"I still think you ought to speak yourself, Helen," he said. "Viscount Samuel does as well."

She smiled and kissed him on the cheek. "Darling, I only wish the committee would put as much faith in a woman's words as you and my uncle do."

He took the copies of the plan and squared the edges of each into neat stacks, which he placed in folders. "These are your words, whoever delivers them," he said.

She shrugged on the fresh jacket. "Do keep that to yourself," she said, "if we're to have any hope of success."

A WOMAN OF VISION

When Helen Bentwich entered the Rothschild dining room, the men around the table all stood: the Executive Committee of the Central British Fund.

"Norman, we've saved you the head of the table," said Dennis Cohen, who had helped Helen formulate the plan but had slept the night while she and Ellie committed it to the page, which was just as well; Helen really could do things faster without the men involved, without the need to grant each of their suggestions more consideration than it deserved.

Rothschild asked Simon Marks if he might move down a seat to make room for her, and before she could object, the Marks & Spencer heir was holding the chair for her.

Even as, with Helen seated, the men resumed their seats, Norman began, "The proposal sets forth the plan we described to Prime Minister Chamberlain by which we will bring children of the Reich to safety here, asking nothing of the government beyond that they provide British entry visas."

How the meeting with the prime minister about this plan had come about still surprised Helen. When the Cabinet Committee on Foreign Policy met to consider what might be done in light of Germany's night of violence, it had seemed the answer they reached was "not a blessed thing"; Foreign Secretary Halifax said that any British response could provoke war, and Prime Minister Chamberlain that Britain was in no position to threaten Germany—or so Helen heard from Norman, who heard it from Rothschild, who heard it from someone in the government. Helen had watched from the gallery herself when the matter came before Parliament. The chamber had devolved into squabbling, Colonel Wedgwood demanding of his peers, "Have we not been discussing these refugees for five years? Cannot the government show the feeling of this country by attempting to do *something* for the victims of this oppression in Germany?" and MP Lansbury shouting, "Are we not *Great* Britain? Is it impossible to say to the world that Great Britain will take them and find them a place to start life afresh?" The Earl of Winton and the home secretary, though, had babbled on about the dangers of provoking an anti-Semitic response in Britain, and the prime minister pointed out that even the Dutch were accepting only refugees who were assured passage on to other countries. "This is not a matter for the British government, as the right honorable gentlemen realize, but I have no doubt we shall be taking into consideration any possible way by which we can assist these people," the prime minister concluded, leaving Helen to wonder exactly for whom it was "a matter," if not the British government. But where Helen had heard naysaying in the prime minister's words, Norman had seen an opening, and soon enough yet another delegation—Jews and Quakers together this time, led by Helen's uncle and Lionel de Rothschild—were meeting with Chamberlain at No. 10 Downing, proposing in concept the plan now presented in tidy stacks of paper before them.

"Prime Minister Chamberlain brought our proposal to the full twenty-two-member Cabinet yesterday," Lionel de Rothschild was now telling the committee. "The home secretary expressed concern that the greater need was for elderly Jews, and the foreign secretary banged that drum too, but our offer of financial support is for the children, of course, and the prime minister assures me he made that clear. Now, the plan calls for the rescue of five thousand? And how much of the need does five thousand address?"

"We think sixty to seventy thousand German and Austrian children under the age of seventeen need to be brought to safety," Dennis Cohen answered.

There was a long silence as this was digested.

Norman said, "We expect the greatest number will be under the age of ten. We've confirmed that two summer camps in Harwich can be opened to receive those we can't send directly to foster homes, with the idea that the children would then be placed in private homes as promptly as possible. The Inter-Aid Committee for Children from Germany would arrange placements. The expertise they've gained finding homes for almost five hundred prior to the recent violence—"

Simon Marks interrupted, "It's a long way from five hundred, half of whom were Christian and came over the course of years, to five thousand in just a few weeks."

"They're the best we have," Norman said. "They haven't, of course, our fund-raising capability, so that will be on us."

"We're certain we want to ask only for the children?" Neville Laski asked. "I continue to believe if we brought whole families—"

"There is too much fear that if we bring whole families, they'll never leave," Lionel de Rothschild insisted. "We will state publicly that we mean to bring the children on a temporary basis, until it's safe for them to return to Germany. But the prime minister understands that we must be prepared to accept the possibility of permanent unofficial adoption of younger children and permanent residence for girls who might enter into domestic service or marry British boys. He expects they would require older boys to re-emigrate."

Norman began, "Mrs.—," but caught Helen's look, or just caught himself, mercifully. "Several of us," he began again, "have been discussing how to fund such a large undertaking. We've already used the prod of publishing contributor names in the *Jewish Chronicle* ad infinitum. We feel it's necessary to consider an appeal in the non-Jewish press."

"To the public at large?" the chief rabbi asked with a hint of alarm.

Dennis Cohen said, "Even if we could raise the money, finding homes for five thousand children—"

"We're proposing to house Jewish children in gentile homes?" the chief rabbi demanded. "But what about their faith? Their religious training?"

Everyone stared at him, perhaps as stunned as Helen felt.

"Rabbi, do you not understand the emergency we face?" she said, surprising even herself. "Would you prefer five thousand dead Jewish children, or some portion of those five thousand tucked into extra beds in Quaker and Christian homes?"

Dennis Cohen said soothingly, "Our preference of course will be for Jewish homes, Rabbi, but I for one will be grateful for anyone of any faith who will help. The public at large will be invited to offer accommodations, with the minimum standards of the London County Council for foster homes for British children to apply."

"We might put them in guest houses or in schools rather than in gentile homes," the chief rabbi suggested.

"Where these young children—already torn from their families— will receive no affection whatsoever?" Helen demanded.

Dennis Cohen said, "We'll rely on the Reichsvertretung in Germany and the Kultusgemeinde in Vienna to select the children based on vulnerability."

"It will be the older boys who are most vulnerable," Helen cautioned, "and the youngest girls whom the British will want to take in."

Norman said, "We'll bring those we can, and trust God to provide."

"Trust God," Helen muttered; that was a big ask, given all that He had already denied.

Lionel de Rothschild said, "As time is of the essence, may we have a vote on whether to present the Bentwich-Cohen plan to the government?"

POLISHED BOOTS

Käthe Perger looked up, startled to see a Nazi in a long, dark coat and polished boots striding through the newspaper office with his German shepherd, headed directly toward her open office door. A gang of SS trailed him, several already surrounding the Linotype, considering how best to load it onto their truck, which, Käthe saw, waited on the street.

The dog stood perfectly still as Adolf Eichmann, in her doorway now, said, "You are Käthe Perger."

Käthe met his gaze. As his words had not been a question, she didn't feel he required a response.

"And your staff are not here this evening?" he asked.

"I have no staff left, Obersturmführer Eichmann," she said. It was close enough to the truth.

"You will come with me, then," he said.

EMPTY DRAWERS

Even in the dim light, Stephan registered the smashed desk and the scattered and broken remains of drawers. He righted a drawer that was still more or less intact. There was nothing inside. There was nothing on paper anywhere in Käthe Perger's newspaper office, which was covered with signs prohibiting entry. Everything had been carted off as evidence.

At the sound of voices approaching outside, he hid under the largest bits of the desk as best he could, just as a flashlight beam shone from the doorway, bobbing quickly around.

He listened to the two men entering, talking and laughing, the *chhhh* and *wooop* of a match striking and leaping to flame, the smell of cigarettes.

"That crazy bitch who used to be forever poking into other people's business, she got what she deserved," one of them said.

Stephan breathed shallowly, holding himself so still that his entire body ached, as the two chattered in the bored way of men trying to convince themselves they aren't as vile as they actually are. They left, finally, and still Stephan stayed under the smashed desk, waiting, his heart slowing to something closer to normal.

When it seemed they must be lounging in some other wreckage, smoking another cigarette and laughing at another misfortune, he climbed out and quickly flipped over the bits of drawers in the darkness, running his hands all over each. He tried his best to be methodical in the chaos, setting each piece of drawer aside after he'd examined it so as to mark it as searched.

His fingers caught on splinters but found nothing.

Just as he was despairing, his fingers brushed a small slip of paper taped to the underside of a mostly intact drawer, tucked away in the corner. It might be nothing more than some kind of furniture tag.

He felt more carefully, using his nail to edge up the tape. When he had it free, he pulled out his flashlight.

He froze—voices at the window again. He hadn't heard them coming.

He remained perfectly still. The voices carried on down the street, fading.

He tucked the freed bit of paper, whatever it was, securely into his pocket lest he drop it, and finished the search in the darkness, too afraid now to turn on the flashlight. He found three loose scraps of paper, which he tucked away as well before slipping out of the office and, as quickly as he could, into the underground.

He ought to wait until he was back in the palais that night, but he found his legs were weak, he found he needed to know the truth himself before he took it to Mutti and Walter. He crouched at the edge of the tunnel, hiding behind a pile of debris. He unfolded the first slip of paper he'd found, the one that had been attached to the drawer.

He flicked on his flashlight. A circle of light fell on the words.

He died in transit to Dachau. I'm so sorry.

THE WESTMINSTER DEBATE

It was half seven, and Helen Bentwich, in the gallery, was already exhausted from the long day of speechifying when Parliament finally took up the refugee question. Philip Noel-Baker in his passionate if long-winded way began to make the case with the awful specifics: a man and his family burned to death; a boarding school at Caputh utterly demolished at two in the morning; patients driven from the Bad Soden home for consumptives wearing nothing but their nightshirts; the inmates of the Jewish hospital at Nuremberg forced to line up on parade. "If these acts had been the spontaneous excesses of the mob, the German government might be expected to punish the offenders and make reparation to the victims," he said. "Instead, the German government completed the dreadful business by issuing a decree blaming the Jews themselves for the destruction and imposing upon them an eighty-four-million-pound fine. Most sinister of all, the German government have begun to arrest all Jewish males from the age of sixteen to sixty." He wouldn't "pile up horrors," but the House must understand that men and boys in labor camps were made to work seventeen-hour days on rations that wouldn't feed a child, and were subject to tortures he would not specify. Helen didn't want to know the details of the tortures either, but she'd heard them, and she couldn't imagine why the members of this chamber were so delicate that they ought to be spared as they made decisions that would save lives, or not.

It was ten at night before Home Secretary Hoare moved specifically to the Kindertransport proposal. "Viscount Samuel and a number of Jewish and other religious workers came to me with an interesting proposal," he said. "They pointed back to an experience during the war, in which we gave homes here to many thousands of Belgian children, playing an invaluable part in maintaining the life of that nation."

Helen whispered to Norman, "Those children were brought with their families, when they had families."

Norman put his lips so near her ear that she could feel his breath, and whispered, "It's easier to persuade a man to do what he believes has precedent."

"This delegation believes," Hoare continued, "that we can find homes in this country for a large number of German children without harm to our own population—children whose maintenance could be guaranteed by the delegation's funds or by generous individuals. All the Home Office need do is grant necessary visas and facilitate their entry. Here is a chance of taking the young generation of a great people, and of mitigating the terrible suffering of their parents. Yes, we must prevent an influx of undesirables behind the cloak of refugee immigration. The government therefore must check in detail the individual circumstances of adult refugees, a process bound to involve delay. But a large number of *children* could be admitted without individual checks."

The discussion was excruciating: Would the British taxpayers not be encumbered with financial responsibility for the children? Ought the number be limited? What about the Czechs? What about the Spanish refugees? Mr. David Grenfell insisted, "The large and powerful nation of Germany cannot be allowed to strip its Jews of everything and dump them over the frontier, to say, 'I do not want the Jews in my country; you must take them.'" But the question was eventually put: Would this House, in view of the growing gravity of the refugee problem, welcome a concerted effort among nations, including the United States, to secure a common policy for the temporary immigration of children from the Reich?

"A 'concerted effort'?" Helen said to Norman. "But there are no other nations with which to concert."

"All in favor . . ."

EXIT, NO VISA

Stephan, hearing footsteps on the stairs, sprang from bed, grabbed his coat and shoes from the chair beside the bedroom window, and scrambled out to the roof while Walter—who had also been sleeping fully clothed on account of the cold rooms and the need to be ready for anything—clutched his Peter Rabbit tightly and scurried silently into Mutti's room, Mutti's bed, just as they'd practiced. The thugs burst in, not even slowed by the shabby door, their flashlights so bright that the window now below Stephan shone as if the lamps inside were lit, even though the men were still in the center sitting room.

"Where is the boy?" a deep voice demanded.

They must be in Mutti's room then, as Mutti could not so quickly have gotten out of bed and into her wheelchair, even if she'd had Stephan's help.

Stephan crouched as motionless as possible, his coat and shoes in his hands and the roof cold against his stockinged feet as the thin layer of ice on the roof melted into his socks.

"We're happy to take the little one in his place," the man said.

Even the Nazis wouldn't harm a dying woman and her little boy, Stephan told himself as he reached down to close his bedroom window as silently as possible, shutting out the sound of his mother two rooms over saying she did not know where he was, that she assumed he'd been taken to the camps—his mother putting herself at risk so that he could get away while Walter said nothing, the poor little guy terrified, or brave, or both. It was all Stephan could do not to climb back in and demand that Mutti and Walter be left alone, but he had promised Mutti this. They could not survive without him, she had insisted. She needed him to find a way to get them out of Austria. She couldn't do that herself, and Walter couldn't do it, so Stephan must save himself first. Walter had said he and Peter could take care of Mutti. He was such a little boy, but he was determined. He could empty a bedpan. He could help Mutti change clothes. He could do so many things a five-year-old ought not to be asked to do.

Stephan scrabbled silently across the slippery roof toward the tree by his old bedroom window, the way down to the street.

A soldier patrolled with a dog on the walk near the tree. The dog's ears perked as they passed through the golden glow of the streetlamp, his shadow so long that he looked like a creature from another world.

Stephan backed slowly away from the roof's edge and ducked behind a chimney, where the sound of his breathing might not reach the dog's hearing. He tucked up against the brick, the slight warmth of it, the protection of its shadow.

There was not a star in the sky.

He scanned the roof's chimneys as he tugged on a shoe, trying to see in the darkness. Was that smoke rising from that chimney? From the next one? He was tying the shoe when he heard a window open.

He hurried to one chimney and felt it—warm. Then another, also warm. Already, someone was pulling himself up through Mutti's servants'-floor window onto the roof.

"Crap, it's cold," the Nazi called down toward the window.

And slippery, Stephan thought. He might be able to push the soldier off the roof and hope it looked like a fall.

"Any sign of him?" a higher voice asked—two of them now up on the roof. No hope of pushing two, much less having that coincidence go unnoticed.

He could make out the shadows of them in the darkness, but they wouldn't yet see him; he had their voices to help locate them, and his eyes had had time to adjust, while they'd just climbed from the light.

Keeping them in sight, he crept toward a third chimney. It was cold, as mercilessly cold as his one shoeless foot.

His coat! He must have left it by the first chimney.

A bright light flared across the rooftop, a flashlight coming on, then a second.

Stephan scrambled up over the top of the chimney and wedged himself just inside, the brick rough against his thin shirt and slippery from soot at the same time, and cold against his one stockinged foot.

He set the other shoe in his crotch so that he could better brace himself with his hands.

The deeper-voiced Nazi called down to the soldier patrolling with the dog on the ground below. No, no one had come down from the roof.

The two spread out, their voices coming from different directions on the massive roof and their flashlight beams occasionally crossing over Stephan's head. They began to talk about the other roofs around them, as if Stephan might actually have leapt the entire gap of the street.

The higher voice came from near the first chimney now, near Stephan's forgotten coat.

Stephan's thighs were burning from holding himself up in the chimney. A five-story chimney. Could he climb down it, or would he fall, his legs already exhausted? Could he get past the flue? If he could, the room it serviced might well be empty. The chimney was cold, after all. A room somewhere in the center of the palais, given the chimney's placement. The kitchen? The windowless kitchen, where he would be trapped, unable to get out of the palais unnoticed. He ought to have found a cold chimney at the building's edge, one that might lead to a room with a window, an exit. But there had been no time.

He adjusted a little, trying to strengthen his grip. The shoe at his crotch slipped. He reached out to grab it before it could clatter against the metal flue below, and slipped himself. He barely caught the shoelace with his left hand.

He quickly stuck the laces between his teeth and pressed his arm back against the cold brick to stem his slide. His right knee was shaking with the effort, or the cold, or the fear.

The Nazis were laughing. What were they laughing at? Had they found his coat?

The high voice said, "I told you we were no gymnasts!"

They considered together where he might have gone. And still, Stephan braced himself inside the chimney, the shoelace between his teeth oddly steadying.

There was a groan, and laughter, and the thud of the Nazis tumbling back inside the little apartment. It was just a game to them, an adventure.

He waited some time after the voices ceased before edging himself up a little higher in the chimney and peeking over its edge. He climbed from the chimney and lay flat on the roof, waiting and watching, willing his legs to stop quivering. He was still lying there when he heard the creak of the window. It was safe to go back inside! He wouldn't have to return to the awful underground.

The opening notes of Bach's Cello Suite no. 1 drifted up to him.

Stephan listened through the opening notes, the plaintive longing in the bobbing, broken chords that were not the "Ave Maria." Finally he pulled his second shoe on over his wet and soot-covered sock. He crept across the roof to find his coat, and he pulled it on and slipped down the tree. He hurried to the nearest Ringstrasse kiosk and down the narrow steps inside it, only breathing the smallest relief when he reached the cold and dreary, rat-infested underground.

VISCOUNT SAMUEL'S APPEAL

The Bloomsbury Hotel's run-down old ballroom was crowded with folding tables and filled with the din of sixty women processing immigration papers with all due speed. They had devised a system with color-coded two-part cards, one part of which would remain in England while its counterpart was sent to Germany, a card for each child. "Turn it up!" someone said. "Helen, your uncle is on the BBC, starting his plea!"

"Well, leave it on then, but do keep working," she said. "All of Britain opening their doors to take in children will do no good if we can't get them out of Germany."

The women kept to their tasks, listening as Helen's uncle spoke on the radio. ". . . Heartbreaking though separation is, almost all the Jewish parents, and many 'non-Aryan' Christians, wish to send their children away, even as they can find no refuge themselves."

By mentioning the Christians, Viscount Samuel meant to make the proposition more attractive, Helen knew.

"A world movement has been launched for the rescue of these children," her uncle said.

A world movement in which only Britain moves. But surely other countries would follow their lead.

"The case is urgent," Viscount Samuel continued. "We therefore appeal to the nation herself to take these children and care for them, to board them in private homes. Will the churches, the Jewish communities, and other groups now come forward and each offer to be responsible for some of these children, who are being thrown upon the mercy of the world?"

WISHES BIG AND SMALL

Stephan curled up on a crate of cocoa beans and wedged his bare hands between his thighs, trying to keep warm. He woke, shivering, after a minute or five, or fifteen, or several hours. Time didn't pass in the underground darkness, without any cues to mark its changing. In his groggy state, he reached for the chain to the overhead electric bulb, only realizing just in time that it would cast a light at the door at the top of the stairs. Was anyone upstairs in Neuman's Chocolates to open it and discover him?

He ought not to stay here, he knew that, but it was dry and it was familiar, and where else could he go? He wanted to return home and crawl into his own bed, not the bed in the servant's room he shared with Walter but his own bed with his own favorite pillow and newly pressed sheets, his books and his desk and his typewriter, all the paper in the world, all the dreams. How could this not be a nightmare? How could he not be sleeping, about to wake up, still in his pajamas, to go to his desk and his typewriter, to capture the nightmare before he lost the details that might make a story if only this weren't real?

He collected the flashlight from the hook at the bottom of the cocoa cellar stairs; he could keep the beam away from the door and he could turn it off more easily than the overhead. He kept an ear to the upstairs as he took the crowbar and pried open one of the crates.

He took a handful of cocoa beans from one of the jute sacks, then carefully closed both the sack and the crate so that if you didn't know it was short a handful, you wouldn't notice. He put a couple of the beans in his mouth and chewed—hard and bitter. He wished he had water to wash them down. So many wishes, big and small.

He poured the rest of the handful into his coat pocket and was just returning the crowbar to its proper place on the hook when he heard voices overhead—workers coming for the day's cocoa beans. Startled, he killed the flashlight and slipped quickly under the stairs and down the ladder. As he heard the door overhead creak open, he realized he still held the flashlight. He stuck it in his pocket, hoping they wouldn't miss it.

He crawled through the tunnel to the underground, trying to think where else he might hide. From the tunnel's far end came other voices—"This way!"—and running. Nazis searching the underground for men and boys in hiding, like him.

Trapped, he scooted backward to the tunnel's inside end, sure the pounding in his chest would give him away.

Nazi boots sounded outside the tunnel, running just feet away from him.

OTTO

Otto scooped Johanna up and kissed her.

"I want Mama," the little girl said.

"I know, sweetheart," Otto said. "I know."

Žofie, who'd become so subdued since her mother was arrested, so adult, asked him if he'd gotten in to see their mother.

"I've confirmed your mother is being held here in Vienna," he said. "Why don't you let me finish making the dinner?"

"It's only *kulajda*," she said.

Kulajda. It was Žofie's favorite. Whenever they visited her Grand-mère Betta, she came back talking about how Johanna and she got to gather the eggs from the henhouse for their grandmother to poach, one egg set carefully in each bowl of creamy potato soup.

"You just relax, *Engelchen*," he said. "Read for a little while."

Her copy of *Kaleidoscope* was on the table. He took it into Käthe's bedroom and put it back in the hiding place under the rug. He brought her, instead, *The Memoirs of Sherlock Holmes*.

Žofie sat at the table with a graph book full of equations, shunning even Sherlock Holmes. Johanna settled beside her, sucking her thumb. Otto turned on the radio to listen while he finished the soup: Foreign Minister von Ribbentrop was heading to Paris to sign the proposed Franco-German peace accord; an enormous number of secondhand books were available due to the closing of Jewish bookstores; and a curfew on Vienna's Jews had just been imposed.

Žofie-Helene looked up from her graph paper. "When will they let Mama go?"

Otto set the stirring spoon down, and took the chair beside her. "She just needs to promise she won't write anymore."

Žofie, frowning, returned to her equations. Otto returned to the stove, to the satisfaction of being able to care for them, at least.

Long after Otto assumed Žofie-Helene was well lost in her mathematics, she said, "But she's a writer."

Otto stirred the soup slowly, watching the line of swirl appear, and blend, and disappear. "Žofie," he said, "I know Stephan gave you that book. I know it means a lot to you. But it's banned. If you take it out again, I'll have to burn it in the incinerator."

The telephone started ringing then, of course it did, just when it was least convenient.

"I don't need to keep the book," Žofie said. "I'll take it down to the outside rubbish bins myself after dinner. I promise."

He nodded—yes, that would be for the best—and answered the telephone.

"Käthe Perger?" a woman asked, her voice crackling through the static. An overseas line?

"Who is this?" Otto demanded.

"I'm sorry," the woman answered. "It's Lisl Wirth, Stephan Neuman's aunt. I hoped I might find Žofie-Helene, actually. I'm calling from Shanghai. I've just received a call from my sister-in-law that Stephan is . . . They came to arrest him and he fled, but now Ruchele is being forced to move. She thought Žofie might know where Stephan—"

"Surely someone else can help find him," Otto said.

"No one knows where he is," the woman insisted. "And Ruchele— Even her maid has had to leave because Christians can no longer work for Jews. It's only her and Walter. She simply can't manage. She thought Žofie might know where Stephan . . . She doesn't want to know where he is, she—"

"Žofie-Helene has no idea where Stephan is," Otto said.

"My sister-in-law just wants to get a message to her son so he'll know where to find her."

"My daughter-in-law is imprisoned because of you people! You must leave us alone!"

He hung up, his hand trembling.

Žofie-Helene stared at him. "I can find Stephan," she said.

Johanna sat watching him too. She removed her thumb from her mouth and said, matter-of-factly, "Žozo can find Stephan."

Otto stirred the soup again. It didn't need stirring, but he needed to stir.

"You don't know where he is, Žofie," he said. "You will stay here and do your proofs, and when your mama is released we'll go to your Grandmère Betta's. Your mother can't stay here. When they free her, we'll go to Czechoslovakia."

SEARCHING FOR
STEPHAN NEUMAN

Žofie-Helene slipped out of bed, still in her clothes. She pulled her secret-things box from under her bed and set the book she'd been reading to stay awake until Grandpapa was sleeping back inside, the Stefan Zweig stories she'd promised Grandpapa she'd throw out. It was both true and not true that she'd kept her promise: she had taken the book down to the rubbish bins outside the building, but then she couldn't bear it, and she'd brought it back up. *Kaleidoscope*. She'd so often wondered why Stephan had given her the second volume of the collection rather than the first. She might have asked him, but the puzzle of it pleased her, the deducing, the untangling of the mental knot. He might have chosen it for her because of the title; he would have known the title would appeal to her, all the reflecting surfaces tilted toward each other so that one simple thing became many, the image repeated over and over to become something else, something beautiful.

She tiptoed into the kitchen and removed a knife from the block. She edged a drawer open and fumbled in the dark for a candle and a box of matches. She gathered her coat and pink plaid scarf, and she was about to leave when, as an afterthought, she took the remains of the bread left over from dinner, still in its paper wrapper from the bakery, and slipped it into her coat pocket.

Outside, she rounded the corner, lifted a triangle of the octagonal manhole cover, and slipped down the stairway into the underground—which was so dark and spooky that she had to light a match. It wasn't enough light to tell much, but it did at least send the rats scurrying away. She set off in one direction, but soon had to wrap the scarf over her mouth against the stench. She'd gone the wrong way, headed toward the sewer rather than away. She turned around and wound her way stealthily forward. If she was found by someone, she would say she was searching for her cat.

After a time, she stopped and listened: someone snoring. She crept toward the noise until she could see the source—a big heap of a man. She backed away and carried on, relieved to reach one of the passageways illuminated by a work light. Once past it, though, the darkness was even worse.

She hated to use the candle, which she'd brought for Stephan, but it was surprising how much light it made. She found her way past the convent and the gate by St. Stephen's, the stack of skulls she avoided looking at although perhaps she should have looked, perhaps it would be less haunting if she replaced the memory of borrowing Stephan's bravery with her own.

At the tunnel to the cocoa cellar, she paused, inhaling. *Keep your mouth open, just let the chocolate sit in your mouth. Leave it there, make it last, taste every moment.* She'd wanted to take Stephan's hand that first time in this underground, but how did you take the hand of your only friend without ruining everything?

She knelt on the cold stone and crawled into the tunnel she'd been so delighted to discover that first time.

"Stephan, are you there?" she whispered, both wanting him to be and not. The friendship paradox. How could he survive down here in the cold and damp? How could he sleep down here with the ever-present rats?

"It's me, Žofie-Helene," she whispered. "Don't be afraid."

The lower cavern was empty. She held the candle toward the ladder to the cocoa cellar. The rungs were not particularly dirty. They'd been recently used. Elementary.

She climbed the ladder slowly, carefully. She heard something. She blew out the candle flame and listened, then took the last rungs as stealthily as she could. At the top, she peered into the darkness. She heard nothing.

"Stephan?" she whispered.

There was no answer.

She lit another match, and turned to the sound of some creature scurrying off.

She groped in the air until she found the string to the overhead bulb, which lit the cavern so brightly that she had to close her eyes.

A new flashlight hung by the stairs, but the cavern was otherwise unchanged. There was a small gap between the cocoa crates at the far end of the cellar. They might have been left askew when they were first loaded into the cellar, the last work of a tired laborer at the end of a long day. She moved closer. Nothing there. If Stephan was living here, he was leaving no trace beyond the relatively clean ladder rungs. But where else could he be living?

She returned reluctantly to the ceiling bulb, bracing herself against the return of darkness. The cold. The animals you couldn't see. Their sharp little teeth, and the diseases they bore. She waited a minute, hoping the light would draw Stephan, before turning it off and descending the ladder again.

Where could Stephan possibly be sleeping, if not in the cocoa cellar? Someplace warmer, and without rats, she hoped. But she had no idea where that might be.

She took the wrapped bread from her pocket, unwound her scarf, and tied one end of the pink plaid like a purse around the little package. She tied the other end to the ladder, to affix the food up off the floor, out of the reach of vermin, she hoped. She crawled back through the low tunnel, and stood and scratched "S—>" in the stone in several places, hoping to help Stephan find the food. She began to scratch more letters, then instead returned to the cavern, untied the bread and put it back in her pocket.

She climbed the ladder back into the cocoa cellar, groped in the dark again for the overhead. After her eyes again adjusted, more quickly this time as she'd been fewer minutes in the dark, she took the pen from the clipboard and wrote on the paper bread wrapping: *Your mother is being made to move to Leopoldstadt. I'll find out where and leave a note and a blanket. Leave me a note about anything else you need.*

The book. Why hadn't she brought it for him? Next time, she would bring him *Kaleidoscope*.

She returned the pen to its place, exactly as she'd found it. She braced herself against the darkness, pulled the string, and climbed back down the ladder. She tied the bread package and, reluctantly, the candle and matches back up into her scarf, which she again tied to the ladder rung. She groped in the darkness until she found the low tunnel, crawled through to the underground, and groped her way the short distance to the rubble pile and the circular stairs. At the top of the stairs, she pushed one triangle of the octagonal manhole cover up and peeked out. Not seeing anyone, she slipped out onto the street as fast as she could and headed home.

THE CLOAK

Truus poured tea for Norman and Helen Bentwich and offered
them biscuits. She offered the silver box of cigarettes, too; it
tended to put a man at ease to allow him to smoke.

"This is awfully cloak-and-dagger," she said. "Joop will be devastated
to be left out."

Helen responded, "We thought you might like time to consider our
proposal on your own."

Truus understood that by "we," Helen meant "I."

Norman said, "Several agencies now operating together under the
umbrella of the Movement for the Care of Children from Germany
have persuaded our Parliament to allow an unlimited amount of temporary immigration from the Reich into England."

"Unlimited!" Truus said. "That is amazing news!"

"Unlimited in number," Norman Bentwich said, "although limited
in scope. The children will be accepted only as transmigrants—"

"A grudging welcome," Helen said, "and a ridiculous stipulation,
given that there is no other country to which the children will be able
to emigrate. The requirement seems to be window dressing without
any actual immigration drapery required. They urged us that it would
be in everyone's interest that the children be widely dispersed rather
than concentrated in cities like London or Leeds. 'It will behoove none
of us to create a conspicuous Jewish enclave,' was the way it was put."

"We're handling the British end of things," Norman said. "Arranging
sponsors for as many as possible, and temporary housing and support
in Britain for the rest. The Reichsvertretung have already begun the
selection of children in Germany. But the effort in Austria is more

complicated. The head of Germany's Jewish Office there, a man named Eichmann . . ." Norman tapped his cigarette in the ashtray. "He poses a particular challenge, apparently."

Helen said, "The Kultusgemeinde and the Friends Service Committee helping them feel that someone from the outside might be more effective in persuading Eichmann to allow Austrians to leave. A Christian."

"We hope to be able to fund and accommodate perhaps ten thousand children," Norman said. "And given how many children you've rescued—"

"Ten thousand children and their parents?" Truus said.

Norman, with an uncertain glance to his wife, extinguished his half-smoked cigarette. "The prime minister believes children might more easily learn our language and ways. They might, without their families, integrate more easily into our society. I understood that the children you've rescued have been unaccompanied?"

"'The prime minister believes' there is room in England for children but not their parents?" Truus replied, astonished. "'The prime minister believes' parents ought to turn over their precious children to strangers?"

"Do you have children, Mrs. Wijsmuller?" Norman demanded.

Helen, as startled at the question as Truus was, or more so, said, "Norman! You—"

"Joop and I have not had that blessing, Mr. Bentwich," Truus said as evenly as she could manage, blinking back the image of the beautiful wooden rocking cradle, the linens, the snowman embroidery she'd found in the attic one day when Joop was at work.

"I assure you," Norman Bentwich said firmly, "that no child will be taken whose parents do not freely send him. We are not barbarians."

"No, there are no barbarians in the world anymore," Truus said. "None that anyone will call out as such. Appeasers everywhere, but no barbarians."

Bentwich said indignantly, "I don't believe you are in a position to lecture Britain on the extent of its generosity. You Dutch allow across your own border only German Jews with visas in hand to settle elsewhere."

"But separating families? Surely . . ." She turned to Helen, remembering little Adele Weiss dying in that crib at Zeeburg, without even her mother to comfort her. "Helen, cannot the mothers be found positions as domestics? Or . . . We hear rumors of allowing more Jewish immigration into Palestine? Surely you have some influence in that, given the years you two spent there."

"Unfortunately, Palestine is seen to be too politically sensitive to offer a solution," Norman answered.

Seen to be. So he didn't agree, but there was nothing he could do about it.

Helen said gently, "The government have agreed to grant bulk visas so children can be brought quickly. It is something, Truus. These children are in dire circumstances. The council are concerned for their lives."

Truus said, "But not for the lives of their parents."

Norman Bentwich stood and went to the window, to the bright, unseasonably warm winter day. It was what Joop too did when he was angry or frustrated. What she herself did.

When he turned again to her, the backlight from the window made his face impossible to read.

"These parents will do anything to save their children," he said. "They are happy for the generosity of strangers to keep them safe until this horror finds an end."

Helen set a hand gently on Truus's own, saying, "I would do the same, Truus, and you would as well."

Truus took a careful sip of tea. She selected a biscuit from the plate, but found she couldn't stomach it. The face of Adele's mother kept coming to her: yes, she'd wanted Truus to take her child, and she hadn't at the same time. Why hadn't Truus simply pulled the mother onto the train too? Why hadn't she thought to bring the mother, to count on her own resourcefulness to somehow get Adele's mother out of Germany?

"Helen," she said, "I . . . You've never done this. You have never taken a child from her mother's arms. I cannot imagine there exists a more horrible task on this earth."

Norman Bentwich stepped toward her, emerging from the silhouetting effect of the bright window light, demanding, "Can you really not?"

THE DAGGER

On a bridge over the Herengracht, a father held a child over the rail so she could poke with a long stick at a gaily colored toy sailboat stuck in the middle of the canal. The child's coat wasn't even buttoned, and she was held so precariously that Truus had half a mind to scoop her up before she could fall into the cold water. She had half a mind to push the father over the bridge. Really, what was the man thinking? So many parents took their children for granted, assuming no harm would ever befall them. But a gaggle of parents watching him from nearby cheered as the bright little wooden boat was dislodged and set back on course to the far quay, where their own children poked with sticks at their own bright little boats, occasionally scurrying across the bridge to Truus's side to send a boat back across.

"I admire the work Helen and Norman Bentwich are doing," Joop was saying to her. "But really, Truus, to Vienna *tonight*? With no planning whatsoever? Without so much as an appointment to see this Eichmann character?"

Joop wasn't a man who allowed passion to show in public, which was the reason she'd chosen to discuss the Bentwich proposal out here, along the canal. There had been planning involved, of course, not by Truus but by Helen Bentwich, who had persuaded the men of the committee that Truus was the woman for the job they thought ought to be left to a man. Her friend Helen—a funny way to think of someone she'd met only once before, but there it was.

"It's one thing to bring a few children out through a border crossing you know is weak," Joop said, meeting her gaze directly, "but you're talking about multiple trips—not just five minutes over the border but all the way to Vienna."

"Yes, Joop, but—"

"Do not defy me on this."

The force of his words startled her. He meant them. He meant the words he had so often said he would never mean. He meant them not because he was determined to control her, but because he was afraid for her.

She smiled reassuringly to the group of parents now watching from across the canal, the father again with them while his child poked her sailboat along the shore.

"I would never defy you, Joop," she said gently. "It's one of the many reasons I love you, because you would never put me in the position of having to." The gentlest of reminders, with a sweetener of humor to help it go down.

His expression softened to something like apology. "But really, Truus."

They watched as the girl, whose boat was again out of reach, appealed to her father. He was too involved in conversation to take notice. The girl appealed to an older brother, who abandoned his own boat to shepherd hers back within reach.

"What would you have me do, Joop?" Truus answered, again in the subdued voice, the soothing voice. "It's fine to save three children or it's fine to save thirty, but I shouldn't try to save ten thousand?"

"The Gestapo will know everything you do, Geertruida! Where you go. How and with whom you spend every minute. There will be no room for misstep." He hesitated, then said, more gently, "Never mind that the doctor advises against traveling any long distance."

Truus brushed back the pain of that—the doctor who had saved her life but not their baby's. Their last chance, she supposed. Her last, unexpected chance.

She took Joop's gloved hand in her own. "The fact that I make light of risk doesn't mean I take it lightly, Joop," she said. "You know that."

They stood together as, on the far side of the canal, the little boy's and girl's father joined them. He used his daughter's stick to haul in her boat, held it until the bulk of the water had drained from it, then repeated the process for his son. The brother took his little sister's hand, and she said something that made them all laugh. The father picked up the boats and sticks, and the three walked off toward the bridge and over it.

Truus looked up through the bare trees to the barren sky, now tarnishing with evening.

"Joop," she said, "imagine if these Austrian children I'm being asked to collect were our children—"

"They aren't, though! They aren't ours, and no amount of saving other people's children will replace having our own. You must stop imagining it will!"

People again turned in their direction. Truus just kept staring across the murky canal, her hand in the anchor of his. He didn't mean the words, the hurt. It was just the sense of loss bubbling out. He too might be visiting with other parents if only she hadn't failed him. He too might teach a child how to swim before she was taught to launch a toy boat into the water, a child he never would have allowed to tie on an ice skate and wobble out onto a canal until it had been frozen for at least a week. He too might button a top button, kiss a bruised elbow, laugh at something that was funny to a toddler, and perhaps to an adult.

Joop pulled her to him, wrapped his arms around her, kissed her hat at the crown of her head. "I'm sorry. I'm sorry. Forgive me. I'm sorry."

They stood together like that as parents called for their youngsters and the little boats were brought in, water streaming from their gaily painted wooden hulls, and the boaters disappeared in threes and fours and fives back into their homes, to have dinners together around family tables, the little boats left to dry in bathtubs after their final voyage before winter set in. A train whistle sounded in the distance, sharpening the quiet of the now-gray sky and the gray water, the gray buildings, the gray bridge. The sun set so quickly these days.

"Perhaps this is why God chose to deny us children, Joop," she said gently. "Because there would be this greater need, this chance to save so many. Perhaps He's saved us the burden of having to choose to risk leaving our own children motherless."

ALL THE INK

Stephan, with Žofie's pink scarf around his neck and a blanket over his shoulders, watched from behind a pile of rubble as the shadow that was Žofie-Helene paused in the underground passageway. *Žofie,* Stephan wanted to say, *Žofie, I'm right here.* But he said nothing. He only watched the shadow turn and crouch, and disappear into the tunnel to the cocoa cellar.

He put the scarf to his nose and breathed in, watching and listening. Water dripped in one direction and another. A car clicked over the octagonal manhole cover at the top of the circular stairs Žofie had come down. He didn't know how long he waited. He no longer had any sense of time.

"Stephan?" she said, her voice startling him.

He stood watching the shadow of her, which he could make out now that he knew she was there. He didn't move or say anything. It was for her safety, yes, but for his dignity, too. He didn't want her to see him like this: cold and dirty from living underground, unable to bathe; relieving himself closer to the sewer so as not to soil the place where he slept or to give anyone an idea of his whereabouts; so hungry that he might eat bread his mother might need to stay alive.

The shadow of her moved, her footsteps pattering almost inaudibly toward the stairway, then climbing the metal steps. Light filtered down as she opened the manhole cover at the top and disappeared, leaving him alone again.

Finally he crawled through the low tunnel. Only when he was well inside did he flick on his flashlight. He squinted against the brightness, giving his eyes time to adjust.

She'd left a new supply of bread and butter. She'd brought him a notebook and a pen too, and Stefan Zweig's *Kaleidoscope*.

BACK IN THE underground stables, he settled in the safest spot, between the two tunnel openings. He pulled the horse skull toward him and set the flashlight there, pointed at himself. In the splash of light, he could read the writing on the bread wrapper. A Leopoldstadt address where Mutti and Walter now lived.

He opened the bread wrapper and put his nose to it, to inhale the yeasty smell. He sat there for a long time, imagining the taste of it, before wrapping it back in its paper and tucking it into his pocket.

He tilted the light to better shine on the book: the second volume of Stefan Zweig's collected stories, which he'd given to her even though he didn't really have a second copy, he just liked having her have it. He sat staring at the cover. Zweig's books were banned by Hitler. Žofie ought not to have kept it.

He opened the book and flipped the pages by memory to his favorite story in the collection, "Mendel the Bibliophile." He again adjusted the flashlight, then read the first few pages, to the line he loved about the small things that jog to memory every detail about a person—a postcard or a handwritten word, "a sheet of newsprint faded by smoke."

He opened the exercise notebook—a graph-paper journal of the kind in which Žofie did her equations—and let his fingers linger on the page. He wished the book weren't blank. He wished she'd left a note for him. He wished it were one of her own exercise books, with an old equation in her sprawling writing on the page.

He took off his gloves and took the pen in hand, smooth and cool. All the paper he'd taken for granted. All the ink. All the books he'd been able to pull from the shelf any time he wanted. He adjusted the flashlight yet again and repositioned himself so that the spot of light shone on the blank page. He tucked his face deeper into Žofie-Helene's scarf and wrote, *You don't show it to your friends, but you're showing me, so logically I'm not your friend.*

He wrote at the top of the page, centered for a title, *The Liar's Paradox*.

He wrote, *Her braid hanging down her back as she left Prater Park*.

He wiped his nose with the back of his wrist, remembering Walter's little face looking back at him over Žofie's shoulder, Walter seeing his big brother reduced to goose-stepping for the Nazis. He wiped his nose again, and his eyes. He nestled his face back into the soft cashmere of Žofie's scarf, and wrote, *The pure white skin at the nape of her neck. Her smudged glasses. The smell of fresh bread. The smell of her.*

I PROMISE

Truus carefully folded a blouse and placed it neatly in the overnight clutch, a lovely soft leather bag that had belonged to her father. He'd owned a drugstore in Alkmaar, where he sometimes gave his customers medicine they needed but could not afford. He had never hesitated simply because their skin was a different color or their God some version other than his. And yet she supposed he would be expressing the same worry Joop was now.

"Worry isn't the same thing as failure to value what you do," Joop said. "And if I ever thought I could do it in your place, or that anyone else could, I saw in Germany how wrong that is."

She turned to him, listening as closely as her parents had always listened to her. It was an honor, to be listened to closely, to be heard. One could honor someone without agreeing with them.

"But you can't ask me not to worry," Joop continued. "I won't ever stop you from doing what you must. I knew who you were when I married you. I believe I knew who you were even before you knew yourself." He put his arms around her, pulling her head to his chest so that she heard the impossibly slow beat of his heart. "You must trust me to be as strong as you are," he said. "Even if I am a much poorer liar."

He tipped her chin up. Her eyes crossed in her attempt to focus on him, as surely as they had the first time he'd kissed her, so many years ago now. He was such a good man. What a different woman she would be but for the good people in her life.

He removed the skirt she'd just placed in the suitcase and substituted another. "You must trust me on this skirt too."

Joop wasn't one to buy clothes for her; it was meant to be a Christmas present, he said, but he wanted her to have it now. The fabric did match the blouse, and there was no point in questioning him on a thing that didn't matter.

He put his arms around her again. "Promise me you will tell me everything," he said. "Promise me you'll allow me to know when I ought to worry, so that I won't have to worry all the time."

Truus leaned back slightly, to better see him. "I do promise," she said.

He kissed her, his lips so warm and soft that she wondered that she could bear to leave him for an empty bed in an empty hotel room, in a city under Nazi control.

"And I promise you the freedom to make your own way, as I always have." He smiled wryly. "Not that you would leave me any choice."

THE LEOPOLDSTADT GHETTO

Stephan slipped into a ground-floor apartment stacked like a junk shop with furniture, several families packed into a very few rooms, many observing the Sabbath. In a bleak little room at the back—a room crowded with a few pieces of his own family's furniture—Mutti slept in the single bed, her arms wrapped around Walter. Stephan knelt beside them.

"Shhh . . . ," he said. "Mutti, it's me."

Mutti gasped awake, then reached up as if to a specter and put her hand to his neck. Her touch, dry and papery but offering more warmth than he'd felt in days, left such an ache in his throat that he was unable to speak for a moment.

"It's okay," he managed. "I'm okay. I want you to know that I know where to find you. I'm going to find a way to take care of you."

Mutti said, "It doesn't matter for me, Stephan. It doesn't matter for me, but only for Walter."

He put a bit of bread and a small pat of butter wrapped in paper in her hands, along with a jar of tomatoes marked in Žofie-Helene's handwriting, brought from her grandmother's farm in Czechoslovakia last summer, he supposed. He was glad to have the food out of his own hands and into Mutti's before he could give in to his own hunger. How many times had he left a pat of butter even larger than this unnoticed on his plate at Café Landtmann, a strudel half eaten at the Central? How many chocolates had he eaten, with his initials atop the chocolate in fleur de sel or his name in little chips of toasted almond, or a musical note in gold ganache, or even a tiny little piano painted with a variety of frostings? How many times would he have scoffed at preserved tomatoes? His mouth watered now at the idea of them, the idea of any food other than the small bits of stale bread and cocoa beans he'd been surviving on for days.

"I'll take care of you both, Mutti," he said. "You and Walter. I'll find a way, I promise. If you need to find me, send Walter to tell Žofie-Helene."

"She knows where you are?"

"It isn't safe for anyone to know, Mutti, but she knows how to get me a message."

"You've seen her?"

"No," he said, a half-truth.

He wondered if Mutti would eat the bread, or if she would leave it all for Walter. She was impossibly thin.

Mutti said, "They're beginning to release some of the men they arrested. Perhaps it will be safer for you?"

"At least it will be easier to visit you here, without Nazis living downstairs," Stephan said. "And here, you have others to help you." The thinnest of silver linings on clouds banishing all light.

VIENNA

Truus exited the plane to the top of the passenger stairway and a view of the Vienna skyline: St. Stephen's Cathedral, the spire of City Hall, the Prater Park Ferris wheel. It had been too late last night to catch the KLM, so she had had to fly Lufthansa through Berlin. Now it was the Sabbath; she would have to wait until sundown to meet with Vienna's Jewish community leaders. But that gave her time to clean up and to get her bearings. She descended the stairs, crossed the tarmac, stood in line to show her passport, and found a taxi. No, she assured the driver, her overnight clutch would be fine on the seat beside her, there was no reason to bother with the boot.

NOT WITHIN OUR PURVIEW

Ruchele sat in her wheelchair in the lobby of the British consulate as the line moved slowly forward. It had wrapped around the block already on their arrival, even though it had not yet been dawn, and the Sabbath too. Now Walter was at the top of the stairs, almost to the head of the line of women in scarves and, today, men in skullcaps— men who'd been released from the camps. Ruchele felt an inexplicable urge to scream at them for surviving what Herman had not, but it was Herman's trying to save her that had killed him. Herman had objected to being taken away from her, and they'd beaten him for that, and he'd survived the beating but not the long ride in the cold, awful truck bed.

Walter called down to her through the rail, "Mutti! Peter and I are here," the smile on his thin little face the first he'd offered since she woke him. This was impossible, the hours of one step forward and, slowly, another. But the impossible must be possible now; the impossible was required just to survive.

The three men who'd spent the hours behind them in line descended the stairs, the crowd in line between them stepping back to make way.

"All right, Frau Neuman, are you ready?" the older one asked.

At Ruchele's ashamed nod, he lifted her from the chair and carried her up the stairs.

The others followed with her chair, the whole of the lobby falling silent so that, for the first time that morning, the only sounds were the voices of visa applicants and administrators upstairs.

When she was resettled in her chair, with the waiting crowd again murmuring in their low, despairing tones, she looked expectantly up the line. It continued into a large room and around its perimeter—still a long wait before they would reach someone who would have spent the long morning listening to story after story, someone who might be sympathetic or might be so fatigued that even a dying woman and her young son would be unable to chip his heart.

Walter climbed into her lap. He closed his eyes and, exhausted, fell into the slow, steady breathing of a sleeping child. She kissed the top of his head. "You are such a good boy," she whispered. "You are such a very good boy."

RUCHELE, AT LAST at the head of the line, woke Walter. She polished the sleep from his eyes and the wetness from his lips, thankful they would be seen before the consulate closed—early today on account of the Winterhilfe decree requiring Jews to be off the street before the opening of the Christkindlmarkt that afternoon. At a nod from the next open desk, she wheeled this last little distance herself, not wanting her conversation with the immigration clerk to begin with him addressing anyone who helped her rather than speaking to her.

"My husband applied for British visas already," she began, hoping he would meet her gaze. He didn't. "But we hear Britain is preparing now to allow Jewish children into the country even before visas are issued, that an effort to transport children from Germany has begun, and one is being planned for us."

The man shuffled things on his desk. Like so many people, he was uncomfortable speaking with someone in a wheelchair.

She made herself as large as she could, to suggest strength. But she was large and strong only in her own mind.

He said, "Frau . . ."

"Neuman," she said. "Ruchele Neuman. My sons are Stephan and Walter. This is Walter. You see what a good boy he is, waiting patiently with me all these hours. My husband has . . . he was killed by the Germans in transit to a camp."

The man glanced up, his gaze flicking over her face before fixing on a spot somewhere above and beyond her left ear. "I'm so sorry for your loss, madam."

She shifted Walter so that, for a moment at least, the man would face the good boy he seemed intent to deny.

"Please," she said, "I don't want your pity. I want help getting my sons to safety."

The man shuffled papers again—papers that had nothing to do with her. She had as yet been offered no forms to fill out.

"I believe that a scheme such as you mention is being organized," he said, "but it has nothing to do with the British government."

Ruchele, confused, simply waited until, finally, he met her gaze.

"But it can't be done without your government," she said. "Who would issue or waive the visas?"

"I'm very sorry, madam," he said, addressing his desktop again. "I can only suggest you contact the committee."

He wrote a London address on a slip of paper and handed it to her.

She said, "You can't—"

"I'm sorry," he said. "It is not within our purview."

He nodded to the next in line, leaving Ruchele with nothing to do but wheel her chair to the top of the stairs. There, Walter climbed down and politely tapped the arm of a man in line and said, "Excuse me, sir. My mutti needs help getting down the stairs."

Out on the street, Ruchele thanked the men who had helped carry her, and Walter took the handles of her wheelchair. He couldn't see over it, but they had made it all the way from Leopoldstadt to the consulate this way, Ruchele telling her son to turn one way or another, to slow for a street corner, to stop at the edge of the walk to let Nazis pass. They would have to hurry now, to be off the streets before the Winterhilfe decree took effect.

A VERY GOOD BOY

It seemed to Walter that he had been pushing Mutti in her wheelchair forever; it had grown so heavy. Mutti had grown silent too, when all the way to that place with the long line she had told him what to do and what a good boy he was. He lost his grip and the chair tilted forward, over a curb Mutti hadn't warned him of.

"Mutti?" he said. He looked around the chair to see his mother slumped forward, her eyes closed. "Mutti? Mutti!"

A car swung wide around the corner, to avoid them. The one behind it honked. Passersby too gave them wide berth. It was because he'd yelled, because he was crying now, which good boys never did in public. He didn't want to cry, but he couldn't stop. If only Mutti would wake up, he would stop crying, but she wouldn't wake up and no one would help him wake her, because he was being such a very bad boy.

He moved Mutti's feet and climbed onto the footholds to push her shoulders up. Her head tilted back, so that her neck was all stretched white and horrible.

"Mutti, please wake up," he said. "Mutti, please wake up. Mutti, I'm sorry I yelled. Mutti, please wake up."

He took Peter Rabbit from Mutti's lap and kissed his soft rabbit lips to her cheek, the way she always liked. "Mutti," Peter Rabbit said, "can you please wake up? I will make Walter behave. I promise. Mutti, will you wake up for me? I'm a good little rabbit."

Walter wiped the snot from his nose on his sleeve before remembering he wasn't supposed to do that, he was supposed to use the handkerchief in his pocket. "I'm sorry, Mutti. I forgot," he said. "I forgot."

He pulled his handkerchief from his pocket like he was supposed to, and he unfolded it like Papa taught him, and he blew his nose and wiped his eyes. He set Peter Rabbit upright in Mutti's lap and touched the linen to Peter's whiskery rabbit nose too, then carefully folded the square back along the pressed lines, and returned it to his pocket. He climbed down from the footholds and lifted Mutti's feet back up on them, and looked ahead to see where the street ended and the sidewalk started again.

He pushed the wheelchair across the street, trying to ignore the cars honking at him.

Finally, a tall, stern woman who looked like Walter's last teacher but wasn't, stopped.

"Is this your mother, son?" she asked. "I think we'd better get her to hospital."

Walter looked up into her kind face. "She isn't allowed at hospital," he said.

"Oh, I see." She glanced furtively about, then dipped her hat to shield her face. "All right, let's hurry. I'll help you home, but then you'll have to run for someone else."

She pushed the chair quickly, Walter scurrying to keep up with her, saying "Sorry, sorry" to the other strollers.

The woman hesitated at the bridge across the canal.

A man from their apartment building, seeing them, stepped in and took the wheelchair in hand, muttering thanks to the woman. He wheeled Mutti to their room, Frau Isternitz from the next room joining them.

"Can you find your uncle, sweetheart?" Frau Isternitz asked him. "The one who leaves the envelopes for your mother tucked under the bench on the promenade?"

"Peter doesn't like the park," Walter said.

"Your uncle would be at his office or at his home."

"Peter isn't allowed to visit Uncle Michael."

"He— I see. All right, can you find your brother then? I'll send someone to fetch Dr. Bergmann."

Walter sprinted off as fast as he could, crossing the bridge out of Leopoldstadt without even thinking whether he was allowed.

WALTER

Otto opened the door to find Stephan's little brother—what was the boy's name?—standing in a thin coat without a scarf or gloves or hat.

"It's Mutti," the boy said.

He stooped to the little boy's level. "Is she . . ."

"She's with Frau Isternitz from next door," the boy said. "She won't wake up."

Žofie came to the door and wrapped her arms around the boy, who began to cry.

"It's okay, Walter," she told him. "We'll make it okay. You run back and hold your mama's hand. You run back and hold her hand and I'll find Stephan—"

Otto, looking first to make sure no one saw them, pulled the boy inside the little apartment, Käthe's apartment where he had been caring for his grandchildren for days now since she'd been arrested. "Žofie-Helene, you cannot—"

"Grandpapa Otto is going to go with you, Walter," his granddaughter told the boy. "He's going to collect our soup first, to take it to your mother."

She pulled on her coat. Otto tried to hold her, but she slipped his grasp and took off.

Walter took off after her. She was already down the stairs, with the boy not far behind.

"Žofie-Helene!" Otto called out. "No! I forbid you!"

He scooped up Johanna and ran after them, hurrying down the stairs and out the door and around the corner, where he caught sight of Walter. The poor little boy stood there, alone in the empty street. Žofie-Helene was gone.

The boy turned to him, and looked up at him bravely.

"Žofie will find Stephan," the boy said hopefully.

"Žozo will find Stephan," Johanna said.

Walter slid his hand into Otto's.

Otto felt his insides crumble as surely as the clods of dirt he'd dropped onto his son's grave. He shifted Johanna more securely on his hip, still holding tightly to the little boy's fragile fingers, which might have been his own son's fingers only yesterday. It was something no parent ought to have to endure: the death of a child.

"Let me . . . Let me get the soup," he said. "Let me settle Johanna with the neighbors." Unsure who would take her; even the friendliest of their neighbors was afraid now to help the family of a subversive journalist who'd been taken into custody. But to take his grand-daughter with him to help Jews? "Come with me, Walter. Let's get inside. Let's get you warm for a minute, then back to your mother. If she's woken, she'll be . . . She'll be very worried."

THE HOTEL BRISTOL

Truus left her coat on, trying to shake off the chill of her arrival, as she unpacked her overnight bag, setting her toiletries out in the empty bathroom, laying her carefully folded nightclothes on the empty bed as she waited for the hotel operator to ring her back. International calls could take only a few minutes to connect, or they could take as long as three or four hours. She hung her fresh blouse in the hotel room's empty closet and was reaching for the new skirt when the telephone rang. She felt a wash of relief despite knowing how high the charge for the call would be. Just a quick call to let Joop know she'd arrived.

Even as the operator was announcing him, Joop's beautiful voice was ringing, "Truus!"

She told him the flight was a bit bumpy and the long layover in Berlin unpleasant, but she had arrived well enough and found her way easily to this perfectly comfortable hotel.

"You will be careful, Truus? Just stay in the hotel until your meeting with this Eichmann character?"

There wasn't actually a meeting set up with Eichmann, not yet. The hope was that the man might open his door at Truus's knock even though he'd declined to listen to the leaders of Vienna's Jewish community. But Truus would not remind Joop of that now.

"I'll need to chat with the folks here for just a few minutes after the Sabbath ends," she said lightly, trying to put him at ease.

"Not in the hotel then."

"No, although I'm told they do look the other way for American Jews."

"Geertruida—"

"In any event," she interrupted before he could lay his fear for her like a paste on her own skin, "I need to see the facilities for organizing this, or to get them organizing if they aren't already. I can't just scoop up thousands of children and hide them in the train loo while I bribe border patrol."

She'd meant to make him laugh, but he only sighed.

"Well, be there at sunset and get back to the hotel before it gets too dark?" he said.

"There are hardly thirty minutes between sunset and the curfew, Joop. I won't be late."

"Have something to eat. Get some rest. I love you, Truus. Do please be careful."

After they'd hung up, Truus opened the French doors for the fresh air. She stepped onto a balcony overlooking the Ringstrasse. The winter sun was slanting low, a wetness threatening. Still the boulevard was full of strollers, and the doors of the stunning opera house next door were open wide, the matinee just ending, she supposed. She watched and listened to people chatting, people laughing. She wondered what the production had been.

She would just find a light bite to eat in the hotel's restaurant, she decided, before making her way to the Jewish district to find the leaders with whom she needed to meet.

The elevator operator said politely in response to her asking for the ground floor, "It's a pleasant afternoon for a stroll, madam."

"Oh no, I'm only going into the hotel restaurant," she answered.

He glanced at her coat, still on, her yellow day gloves.

Downstairs, the heavy wood-paneled doors to the dining room were posted "Juden Verboten." A large portrait of Hitler frowned over tables that were largely empty.

She no longer had an appetite. Perhaps she hadn't ever.

She returned to the elevator and waited. Just as it arrived, though, she changed her mind and headed for the doors onto the Ringstrasse.

"It's a pleasant afternoon for a stroll, madam," the doorman said, as if they all rehearsed the line at the start of their shifts and, by force of insisting upon it, could make visitors believe that this dreary Vienna day was something else.

She asked the doorman if she might walk to the place where they sold the snow domes. She still had perhaps an hour before sunset and the end of the Sabbath.

"Snow domes?" he said. "I wouldn't know, madam, but you might try the Christkindlmarkt. It's returned to Am Hof this year, down Kärntner Strasse past St. Stephen's. But the nicest stroll is to the right, beyond the Opera to the palace, the Volksgarten and the Burgtheater, and across the Ringstrasse to Parliament and the university."

"And to the left?" she asked.

"To the left, there is the only the Stadtpark. Little else but private homes all the way to the canal."

"And beyond the canal?" she asked, the mention of it making her long for home and for Joop.

"Madam, to cross the canal into Leopoldstadt would be . . . inappropriate for a proper lady such as yourself."

"I see," she said. "Well, perhaps I'll just stroll along the Ringstrasse."

She headed to the left, leaving his disapproval behind.

She'd hardly taken five steps before one of the can rattlers shook his collection tin at her. "None shall starve nor freeze," he said, the same Nazi slogan heard all over the Reich this time of year, to provide food, clothing, and coal for less fortunate citizens during the holiday season, they claimed, but it was in fact the biggest scam ever presented in the guise of charity. Even famous actors and actresses like Paula Wessely and Heinz Rühmann were called into service to support it, with no real ability to decline.

"A reichsmark for the children?" the man asked.

Truus pulled her handbag to her as if he might raid it. A reichsmark for Hitler, Göring, and Goebbels, more like it, she thought.

"How nice," she said. "I am indeed here to help Vienna's children."

The man smiled broadly.

"Your Jewish children," she said.

The man's smile disappeared. He shook his collection tin angrily as she walked on.

NO WAY OUT

Žofie-Helene once again turned off the light in the empty cocoa storage room. The food she brought Stephan each day was being taken, the food and the blanket and the pen, the exercise book, the copy of *Kaleidoscope*. Sometimes Stephan left her a note on a wrapper, scraps of butcher paper she kept in the little box under her bed. She knew he was living down here somewhere, but she'd searched the Talmud school ruins, all three levels of the underground convent, and everywhere else she imagined might be dry enough to live in. *Where are you, Stephan?* she wanted to shout throughout the whole underground, but she only waited for her eyes to adjust, then groped her way back down the ladder. She crawled out through the low tunnel and stood in the underground passageway, wishing she could smell the chocolate still, wishing she could taste it in the darkness, have it reflected over and over again on her tongue. It was so dark here, so much darker, it seemed, than the first time she'd come, with Stephan. Even a kaleidoscope would reflect only endless darkness, with no edges, no pattern, no repeat.

She stood stock-still, sensing movement. Just vermin of the small animal kind, she told herself. She hesitated to move forward until her eyes had adjusted. She ought to use the flashlight in the cocoa cellar next time rather than the overhead light. It would be safer.

Were those voices? She was shocked into stillness. Which direction were they coming from?

A hand covered her mouth. She tried to scream, but it was too tight. She was pulled backward. She struggled to be free, trying to scream still, the hand tasting of dirt and filth.

"Shhhh . . ." Right in her ear as her feet dragged over the edge of a rubble pile.

Still with the hand over her mouth, still with the terror right up in her throat, the voices growing closer, echoing in the tunnel from the direction of her apartment. If she could scream, would they hear her? Would they help?

The breath on her neck reeked of dirt and bitter cocoa. The hands held her so tightly that there was no moving, no turning.

"Shhh . . ."

The voices grew nearer. A dog barked. Not a friendly bark.

The hands restraining her pulled her backward and up the circular stairway. She went voluntarily now, away from the terrifying bark— not one dog but several.

The voices closer and closer, the dogs barking so loudly, so sharply.

The hands urged her up the steps, and she moved as silently as she was able, more afraid now of those coming.

The sound of something bumping against the manhole cover, just the quietest metallic *thunk* against one of the triangles, but still it alarmed her. Would the dogs have heard that over their own ruckus?

She looked up. Nothing but darkness and silence overhead, a blessing. Sounds from the street might give them away.

They waited at the top of the steps, ready to flee but afraid to. On the street overhead, the muffled voices of men approaching, then passing by.

From the tunnels, the barking dogs grew even closer. Men running. Men shouting.

Footsteps running so fast, a single person. The steps passed and faded.

The dogs' barking echoed so frighteningly now that it might be fifty dogs. An army of footfalls followed, and the underground lightened with bobbing flashlight beams. Voices shouted now, just below: "You little Jew!" "We know you're here!"

Were they calling up the stairway?

Just as quickly the dogs and the boots and the voices faded in the other direction.

"Stephan?" she whispered.

The hand over her mouth again, not threat but warning. She remained frozen, listening, waiting for what seemed so very long.

Footsteps, slower ones, came again from the direction of home, a man lighting his way with a flashlight, saying, "You must leave it to a Jew to live in such filth."

You will give your mother a message for me. You will tell her that Herr Rothschild is happy for us to use his little palace on Prinz-Eugen-Strasse.

She braced herself for the irregular nonagon of a laugh, but there followed only the one set of footsteps. The companion to whom the man spoke was the dog all of Vienna had come to fear.

When it was absolutely quiet again, Stephan sucked at his finger, cleaning it as best he could before setting it to Žofie's lips, trying to impress on her the continued need for silence, the ever-present need for silence. He put his lips just to her ear and whispered as quietly as possible, "You can't come here, Žofie."

She whispered into his ear, "I . . . I never imagined . . . ," her voice so soft, so warm. How long had it been since he'd sat listening to the "Ave Maria" with her, since he'd watched her explain her complicated equations to those two professors, or fed her chocolate, or listened to her read lines he'd written just for her?

She whispered, "That's why you don't stay in the cave below the storage room? Because there isn't a way out."

Her fingers brushed his cheek, but he leaned away. He ran a hand through his hair. He was so filthy.

"Those men aren't Baker Street irregulars," he whispered, trying to make the point without alarming her too much. "You can't be found helping me."

Far away in the tunnels, shots sounded, startling even in their faintness.

Almost as startling: the warmth of Žofie's fingers intertwining with his. Had she taken his hand, or had he taken hers?

A single additional shot sounded, followed by silence.

He felt Žofie's breath on his ear again.

She whispered, "It's your mother, Stephan."

AT THE CANAL

The Danube Canal was still and murky, the bridge across it open but the road beyond the bridge cordoned off. People passed Truus on this side of the canal as they might any Saturday evening, offering friendly St. Nicholas Day greetings as the occasional car or trolley passed. But beyond the cordon, the cobbled streets of Leopoldstadt were emptier than the streets back home were even on evenings when the canals were frozen over, even when the rain had its way.

Truus walked first one way, then the other. Still, she saw absolutely no one in the neighborhood across the bridge. The sun was just set, the streetlights coming on and the Sabbath ended, and still the quarter remained abandoned.

Beginning to worry as the gray sky faded and the curfew approached, she asked a passerby, "Is no one out because of the Sabbath?"

The woman, startled, glanced across the canal. "Because of the Winterhilfe decree, of course," she said. "Ah, you are a foreigner. I see. This is the Saturday before St. Nicholas Day. No Jews are allowed on the streets, so we can all enjoy the Christkindlmarkt undisturbed."

Truus looked back over her shoulder as if the hotel doorman might be able to see the whole of the long fifteen blocks around the curve of the Ringstrasse, or as if Joop might be able to see all the way from Amsterdam. The Jews of Vienna were confined indoors, the children forbidden to gather with friends to play tag in the snow just beginning to fall? She ought to stop here, then. She ought to turn back. There would be no one to meet. However would she even find them? She would only wreak terror by knocking on doors to ask where the Jewish leaders might be found.

It was the problems you failed to anticipate . . .

Still, she crossed over the bridge, the sky now as dark as the water. She slipped past the cordon, her heart pounding so much more rapidly than her husband's ever did, even when they made love.

HIDING IN SHADOW

Stephan pressed his back to the cold stone of the building, hiding in its shadow, watching. He couldn't help Mutti, he couldn't take care of Walter, if he was arrested and sent to a labor camp. And Jews were forbidden to be out tonight.

The figure was a woman. He relaxed only slightly when he realized that. What was a woman doing on the streets of Leopoldstadt now? A prosperous woman, from the look of her. It was hard to tell in the darkness, but her bearing alone suggested she was a woman of substance.

He watched her continue down the street, the woman walking slowly now, as if she might be expecting what was likely to come.

A moment later, two SS officers came hustling after her, demanding to know what business she had in this neighborhood.

Stephan took advantage of the distraction to slip in the door of his mother's building. He hurried down the dark hall, trying not to think about what he and Walter would do if Mutti too was gone.

THE CELL

Truus was escorted through the delivery entrance of the Hotel Metropole and into the hotel basement prison, past cell after cell of silent shadows. *Even though I walk through the valley of the shadow of death, I will fear no evil.* A door closed behind her before she could get her bearings, and she was alone. *For you are with me. You are with me.*

She knocked on the door.

The guard did not so much as glance up from his newspaper. "Shut up," he said.

"Excuse me," she said, "I am sure you will want to mind your manners with me. Now, you must let me out and return me to my hotel."

THE INTERROGATION BEGINS

A s I have said twenty times now to as many people, sir, I am visiting from Amsterdam," Truus repeated to this newest young
Nazi who had "joined her" in the bare basement interrogation room
to which she'd been brought perhaps an hour after being put in
the cell. She intertwined the soft yellow leather of her gloves gently to
make her own point: Do you not see how well I am dressed? The metal
chair was hard against her tailbone, the smell of wet laundry pervasive.
Tools of torture waited in the form of the wide leather military
belts her interrogators hitched their thumbs to, with their metal buck-
les as big as tea saucers, their swastika and eagle adornments that could
knock out a person's teeth. *You prepare a table before me in the presence
of mine enemies.* She set her gloved hands on the table between herself
and her interrogator. "I arrived by aeroplane today," she said. She was
not just anyone. She was a Christian Dutchwoman who traveled by
plane. Had any of them ever traveled by air?

The man looked from her gloved hands to her handsome coat—a
bolster against the chill room. He met her gaze and kept it, waiting for
her to look away.

When he turned, finally, to another of the soldiers, she was careful
to keep the triumph from her eyes or even her posture, the set of her
hands. It was her advantage, being a woman. What proud man ever
imagined himself bested by a woman, even when he had been?

He met her gaze again. "This," he said, "will not explain why you
wander the Jewish ghetto at a time when Jews are forbidden in the
streets."

THE PROMISE

Stephan sat at his mother's bed, spooning soup for her in the dingy little room—a closet, really, smaller and darker and more airless than they would have asked the lowest chambermaid to endure back at the palais.

"Promise me you will take Walter," Mutti said weakly. "You will find a way out of Austria, and you will take him with you."

"I promise, Mutti. I promise."

He would promise anything to make her stop talking, to make her save her strength.

"And you'll stay with him always. You'll watch over him. Always."

"Always, Mutti. I promise. Now eat this soup Herr Perger brought, or Žofie will scold me."

He breathed in the dill and potato aroma of the soup, trying hard not to want to eat it himself, and failing.

"I love you, Stephan," Mutti said. "Never doubt that. Someday this will be over and you will write your plays, and I don't think I will ever see them performed, but—"

"Shh . . . Rest, Mutti. Frau Isternitz will take care of Walter tonight while you rest."

"Listen to me, Stephan." Mutti's voice had a sudden strength that made him glad to have declined a serving of the soup himself, leaving more for her. "You will sit beside Walter in the dark of a theater as the curtain rises, and you'll touch Walter's hand, and you will know I'm there with you, Papa and I are there."

THE INTERROGATION
CONTINUES

Why am I to doubt that you are a Jewess?" demanded this new interrogator—Huber, his name was, and everything about him said he was in charge.

Truus answered politely, "You might simply look at my passport. As I have told your colleagues, you will find it back at the Hotel Bristol, where I am staying."

Huber frowned at the mention of her posh hotel. He eyed Truus, who was still sitting upright in the same uncomfortable metal chair she'd been in all the night and the early morning.

"Why are you really here, Frau Wijsmuller?" he demanded. "What agenda have you brought from the Netherlands?"

"Again, as I told all your various colleagues," Truus answered patiently, "I am in Vienna on behalf of the Council for German Jewry. I am sent by Norman Bentwich of England for a meeting this morning with Obersturmführer Eichmann. I urge you—"

"A meeting with Obersturmführer Eichmann?" Huber addressed the men, "And no such meeting is scheduled?"

The interrogators looked from one to the other.

"Who arrested this woman?" Huber demanded.

No one admitted to the action, although the arresting officers only minutes before had stood proudly for their feat.

"Has no one thought to see if this meeting is indeed to occur?"

"We're to trouble Obersturmführer Eichmann in the middle of the night?" the man who'd first interrogated Truus asked.

"You might have called his attaché, you fool."

Huber turned and left the cold little room, the interrogator trailing like a dog who has messed a rug. The others too filed out, leaving Truus alone in the room.

She remained immobile but for a quick glance at her watch. Nearly morning. Joop would soon be rising and dressing, cutting himself a bit of the *hagelslag* she'd made for him before she left, and sitting alone at the narrow table. In a little apartment on a neighboring canal, Klara van Lange and her husband would soon be sitting at their own breakfast table, making plans for the baby they were expecting. Klara would not forget to take a dinner to Joop. She had promised, and Klara van Lange was as good as her word.

Huber and his men at last reappeared.

"Frau Wijsmuller," he said, "I'm afraid Herr Eichmann's attaché states that your appointment does not appear on the obersturmführer's calendar."

"Doesn't it?" Truus said. "I suppose this attaché must be quite confident that he has made no error about it, of course. I understand Herr Eichmann is disinclined to forgive those who deny his will. And then there is of course the matter of the foreign press."

"The foreign press?"

"It would be a shame for the foreign press to have this story of a proper Dutchwoman bringing St. Nicholas greetings to Obersturmführer Eichmann from Britain and the Netherlands only to find herself spending the night in a cold, uninviting jail."

Yes, quite a shame.

After leaving Huber ample time to stew in the possibility of a mistake where there was none, as well as the real threat of bad press, Truus continued, "Perhaps you might like to check with Herr Eichmann? Or I might call and wake him myself?"

Huber begged Truus's leave and stepped outside the room to consult in a whisper with his men. When they returned, the arresting soldiers all bowed to her, a courtesy not previously offered.

"Do forgive these boys for this mistake, Frau Wijsmuller," Huber said. "I will personally make sure that the calendar error is rectified to include your meeting with Herr Eichmann. Now let me send an officer with you to see you safely back to your hotel."

AND NOW, YOUR SKIRT

Truus stood waiting, watching silently, as Eichmann wrote at his desk in his office at the Palais Rothschild, a room that once must have been a salon for receiving guests, given its size and its floor-to-ceiling windows, its statuary and art. The man hadn't acknowledged her presence even when his clerk announced her arrival. The dog sitting beside his desk, though, had yet to move his gaze from her, as surely as she had yet to move her gaze from his owner.

Eichmann looked up, finally, annoyed.

"Obersturmführer Eichmann, I am Geertruida Wijsmuller. I come on urgent—"

"I am not accustomed to doing business with women."

"I'm very sorry that I've had to leave my husband behind," Truus answered without a hint of sorrow about the matter.

Eichmann returned his attention to his work, saying, "You may leave."

Truus took a seat, the dog's ears perking in alarm despite her careful movement, not so much on account of the dog as in an effort to keep her knees from view. Really, what had Joop been thinking, substituting for her perfectly respectable second skirt this shorter fashion? As if her calves might prove as useful as Klara van Lange's.

Eichmann, without looking up again, said, "I have given you permission to leave. It is not an advantage I afford everyone."

"Surely you won't mind hearing me out," she said. "I've made quite a journey to speak with you, to arrange for a number of Austrian children to emigrate to Britain—"

"These are your children?" he demanded, now meeting her gaze.

"These are children Britain would—"

"Not your own children?"

"I haven't been blessed with—"

"You'll explain to me, I am sure, why a respectable Dutchwoman troubles herself to come all the way to Vienna to arrange that children who aren't even hers might travel to a country she is not—"

"Sometimes it's what we cannot have, Obersturmführer Eichmann, that we most appreciate."

The dog sat slightly more forward at her interruption, words she hadn't thought until she spoke them, and yet they were the truth.

Eichmann said, "You are, I am sure, quite experienced at helping the chaff of humanity?"

Truus, working to tamp down the anger that mixed with her sorrow into something explosive, said, "It's been my family's practice to help others for as long as I've been alive. We took refugee children into our home during the Great War, children who would be your age now. Perhaps you were similarly kept safe?"

"You'll know then that you need certain documents to effect your purpose. You'll have brought them for us to consider?"

"I have an undertaking from the British government to issue—"

"Nothing in hand? And how many children do you mean to take?"

"However many you will allow."

"Frau Wijsmuller, be so kind as to let me see your hands," Eichmann said blandly.

"My hands?"

"Remove your gloves so that I can see them well."

Hands, Aristotle's tool of tools. *He is at my right hand, I shall not be shaken.*

She hesitated but unfastened the pearl button on her left glove and loosened the scalloped cuff with its delicate black accent, then the creamy yellow French leather. She pulled the soft protection from her blue-veined wrist, her square and sturdy palm, her fingers as freckled and crepey as the backs of her hands.

Eichmann nodded for her to remove the other glove, and she did so, thinking *Blessed be the Lord my strength, which teacheth my hands to war, and my fingers to fight* . . .

Eichmann said, "And your shoes."

"Obersturmführer, I don't see—"

"You can tell a Jewess by the shape of her feet."

Truus wasn't in the habit of baring her feet, not to anyone but Joop. But then, she wasn't in the habit of revealing her calves either. She removed first one shoe, then the other, leaving only her new sun-beige winter stockings for cover.

Eichmann said, "Now walk for me."

She wondered how she had let it get this far, one step after the next as she walked slowly the long length of the room and back again. It was the fault of the skirt, perhaps. If the skirt she'd traveled in had not been filthy from being worn not just all night on the flights to Vienna, but again all a second night, in the cell and through the awful interrogation, she might have donned it again this morning and just told Joop a little white lie. But it did bolster her confidence, truth be told, that Joop still imagined her a woman who could distract a man with a short skirt and a show of calf.

Eichmann said, "And now you will lift your skirt over your knees."

Truus glanced at the dog, remembering Joop's words, that she must trust him on this skirt. She gathered Joop's confidence and her own sense of dignity together, and she raised her skirt.

"Unbelievable," Eichmann said. "A woman so pure and yet so crazy."

She glanced at the dog, whose expression suggested he might agree with her: Unbelievable. A man so crazy and impure.

Eichmann called toward the open door, "Let the Jew Desider Friedmann come in."

A man with large eyes and a healthy mustache in a small face entered, turning the kettle curl of a black felt homburg around and around in his hands as he watched the dog. He was, Truus knew from Norman Bentwich, one of the leaders of the Kultusgemeinde, the Jewish community organization that was to help select the children if Eichmann could be persuaded to let them go.

"Friedmann," Eichmann said to him, "do you know Frau Wijsmuller?"

Friedmann, with a quick, nervous glance from the dog to Truus, shook his head.

"And yet you happen to be here at my office this morning, just as she has shown up."

Friedmann only looked again from the dog to Eichmann.

Eichmann said, "Frau Wijsmuller appears to be a perfectly normal Dutchwoman. She comes to collect some of your little Jews for Britain. Yet she brings no documents to suggest this request is well considered."

Eichmann reached over and petted the dog's head, the pointy ears and pointy snout. Pointy teeth too, Truus was sure, although she had yet to see them.

"Let's make a little joke of this, shall we, Friedmann?" Eichmann continued. "By Saturday, you'll arrange that six hundred children will be ready to travel to England."

"Six hundred." Friedmann practically gasped the number. "Six hundred. Thank you, Obersturmführer."

"If you have six hundred by Saturday," Eichmann said, "Frau Wijsmuller may take them away. Not one child short of that."

Friedmann stammered, "Sir, I—"

"And Frau Wijsmuller must take them herself," Eichmann continued. "She will stay here with us in Vienna, to take them herself."

Friedmann, unfathomably terrified, managed, "But it isn't possible in so few days—"

"Thank you, Obersturmführer," Truus interrupted, still standing in her stockinged feet, with her yellow gloves in her hands. "And after this first six hundred?"

Eichmann laughed—the large, mean laugh of a man used to being denied what he wanted, yet wanting the world to think otherwise.

"After this first six hundred—but no less, not five hundred and ninety-nine, my pure and crazy Frau Wijsmuller?" His gaze raked her, from her face to her bare hands, her calves, her unshod feet. "If you have arranged for Vienna to be rid of six hundred, perhaps I shall be happy to leave the removal of all our Jews to you. Or perhaps not. Now you may go."

As Desider Friedmann bolted for the door, Truus resumed her seat in the chair across Eichmann's desk from him. With slow deliberation, she replaced her shoes on her feet, and tied them. Just as deliberately, she pulled on one yellow glove, carefully buttoning the pearl button at the scalloped cuff, then donned the other glove, all the while ignoring the dog's perplexed gaze.

She stood easily and walked to the door through which Herr Friedmann had already disappeared.

"One suitcase each," Eichmann called after her.

She turned back to him. He was writing again, paying her little attention, or purporting to. "Nothing of value," he said without looking up. "No more than ten reichsmarks for each child."

She stood waiting until he did finally look up at her.

"Should you ever find yourself in Amsterdam, Herr Eichmann," she said, "do come have coffee with me."

ARRANGING THE LAST LAUGH

As Truus left the extravagant palais with Friedmann, who had been waiting outside Eichmann's office for her, she was already beginning the mental list-making. She had come to Vienna to arrange the transport of the children, but with no notion that she would be immediately bringing them herself. She waited for Friedmann to speak first, though. He'd experienced so much of the vile man's capabilities, and she so little. And she felt bad for having interrupted him in front of Eichmann, although she didn't regret it. Sometimes a weakness can be a strength.

Friedmann spoke only after they'd walked down the U-shaped drive to the street and rounded the corner onto the Ringstrasse, the palais well out of sight. "It's not possible to arrange so quickly for six hundred children to leave Vienna," he said, "much less to house them in England."

Truus waited for a trolley to pass—a trolley this Jewish man was perhaps now forbidden to ride.

"Herr Friedmann," she said as the rumble faded, "you and I will have the last laugh at Herr Eichmann's 'little joke,' although we'll have to be quite circumspect about it, of course." She crossed the road at a brisk pace now, Friedmann beside her. "Britain will require no visas or German travel documents," she explained. "The Home Office will need only two-part identity cards, color-coded and prestamped, which will serve as travel permits. One half of each will be retained by the Home Office, with the other to accompany the child, personal data and photograph attached. We need submit only a nominal roll for a group visa."

"The task of gathering so many children, though, Frau Wijsmuller."

"Of course you must begin this moment to get the word out however you can," Truus agreed. "Let people know they can get their children to safety but cannot change their minds or they'll put others at risk." Thinking it through as she spoke. "As many older children as you can manage, children who won't need tending and can help tend. No child younger than four, not for this train, not with so little time. Nor older than seventeen. Six hundred, and as many more as you can manage, just in case—but again don't allow the possibility that any parent may back out once committed. We'll need doctors for medical exams, to ensure the children are healthy. Photographers. Good people of whatever kind you can gather to explain and record. A space in which to process, with tables and chairs. Paper and pens."

Friedmann pulled up short, causing Truus to have to stop and turn back to him.

"I tell you, it would be impossible in any event," Friedmann said. "But to travel on the Sabbath? Observant Jews—"

"Your rabbis must persuade them otherwise," Truus interrupted. "Your rabbis must persuade parents how precious their children are."

THE SHAPE OF A FOOT

Truus peeled off her coat and hung it in the hotel room closet as she waited for the operator to place the call, wondering despite herself about the shape of the elegant Helen Bentwich's hands and knees and feet. When the telephone rang, she lifted the receiver with her gloved hand, reluctant to bare her fingers even with Eichmann now half a city away. She thanked the operator and explained his proposal to Helen, who listened in steady silence. Only when Truus had finished did Helen ask, "Are you all right, Truus?"

"Six hundred children to leave Vienna by Saturday. Can you be ready when they arrive?"

"I assure you," Helen said, "that if the children were this minute to knock on Britain's door, I would tear it off its hinges, if that was needed."

Truus placed a second call. As she waited for the operator to ring back, she watched out the French doors. On the Ringstrasse below, a mix of Sunday strollers and troops marched by.

"I need you to help me arrange transportation for six hundred children by Saturday," she explained at Joop's "Hello."

"On less than a week's notice, Truus? But—"

"That's all the time I've been given."

"A full train and two ferries? You can't get six hundred people on one ferry."

"Children, Joop."

"You cannot get six hundred children on a single ferry."

"Two ferries, then."

"Six hundred children and their minders? You can't bring this many children across the border on your own, much less get them to England."

"Adults from Vienna will be allowed to accompany the children."

"What if they don't—"

"The adults have families here," Truus said. "They know that if anyone fails to return, not only will no further children be allowed to leave, but their own families will be at risk."

"But this Eichmann fellow can't mean to hold you to this impossible deadline. You have bargaining power too, Truus: a place to send some of his Jews."

"Joop, I can organize the children to be ready to leave as soon as the transportation is available. I can do that. This man, he . . . He maintains his power through intimidation. He cares more for his power than for anything. I have no doubt that if we're one minute late or one child short, he will cancel the transport. The threat was no doubt some sick pleasure in the making, but now that he has made it, his power depends on seeing it through."

After they hung up, Truus walked into the bathroom and, with her gloved hand, turned the tub faucet. She watched the stream from the tap, the steam filling the bathroom. Only when the tub was full and the tap shut off again did she return to the main room and begin to undress.

Still with her gloves on, she untied her shoes and removed them, and set them aside. She unclipped one sun-beige stocking, rolled it down her thigh, over her knee, down her calf and over her heel, off her foot. She folded it carefully, and set it on the hotel room's little writing desk. She did the same with the other stocking, her blouse, the shorter skirt Joop had bought her, that Eichmann had made her lift, and even her handkerchief, smoothing the fabric precisely before adding them one by one to the tidy pile on the desk. She took off her brassiere and her corset too, but set them aside with her shoes. She had only the one brassiere, the one corset. She removed her underwear last, carefully smoothed the cotton and folded it, and set it atop the rest. Just as care-fully, she placed the stack of clothing into the trash bin beside the desk.

She removed her yellow gloves from her hands only then, and set them beside the corset. Now naked but for her two rings, she returned to the bathroom, and climbed into the tub.

AN ENTERTAINMENT

Otto brushed the hair clippings from the SS officer's shoulders as the man said, "It is a joke, of course. Obersturmführer Eichmann is giving us all an entertainment: scurrying Jews! If only this crazy woman would take the Jew parents as well."

Otto chuckled falsely as he removed the cape. There was nothing to be gained in challenging these men. "You must tell me where this is, so I too can have a laugh," he said.

"On Seitenstettengasse. The synagogue where they had to extinguish the fire, the one hidden within other buildings that might have burned with it."

As the customer left, Otto turned the sign on the door to "Closed" and picked up the telephone.

A WOMAN FROM AMSTERDAM

Otto entered the bleak little room reluctantly. Frau Neuman sat in her wheelchair, as thin and white and frail as the sugar sculptures in the tea shop windows that seemed about to crumble with the next breath on them, but never did. Walter sat reading a book to his stuffed rabbit, whose little blue coat was askew—such a young boy, and already he could read. The room was overfull with furnishings, but the bed was neatly made, an attempt at dignity. It would have been little Walter who made it, Otto supposed. Little Walter who cared for his mother, although here at least they had the help of neighbors.

"Frau Neuman," Otto said, "I have word that someone here in Vienna—a woman from Amsterdam, I believe—is organizing an effort to . . . to place Jewish children with families in England, where they can go to school and be . . . and be safe until this dreadful time can pass. I thought of Stephan and Walter. I thought that, if you would allow me, I might take them to sign up. They—"

"You are a godsend, Herr Perger," Frau Neuman interrupted, leaving Otto startled at the ease of her concession to letting him take her sons away for what she must know would be the rest of her life. He'd spent the tram ride from the Burgtheater marshaling arguments, searching for words that would be both gentle and persuasive.

"But you must find Stephan," she continued. "He isn't—"

"Yes," Otto agreed. "I thought I could take Walter—"

"Without Stephan?" Tears pooled in the poor woman's sunken eyes, the words clearly a struggle, and not just on account of her health. "But of course one child safe, that would be better—"

"Žofie-Helene will find Stephan, I promise you that, Frau Neuman. I called her the moment I learned of this effort. She and Johanna are already holding a place in the line for your boys. We'll find Stephan, and I'll arrange to send the boys together so that he can watch out for Walter. But we must go now."

"Walter," the boy's mother said without hesitation, now with a strength that surprised Otto, "let's get your suitcase."

Walter handed Frau Neuman his little stuffed rabbit and wrapped his arms around her neck.

Otto said, "I believe this is just to register. I'll send Žofie-Helene for a suitcase for Walter if it's more than that, but I am quite sure this is just to register."

The poor woman removed Walter's arms from her neck and kissed him desperately.

"You must go with Herr Perger," she said to the boy. "Be a good boy and go. Do exactly as he says."

Walter said, "Peter will stay here to watch over you, Mutti."

ANY CHILD WHO IS IN DANGER

Otto eyed the long line. There couldn't be six hundred already, could there? Not if you excluded the adults, he didn't think. "There they are, Walter!" he said, spotting Žofie-Helene standing with Johanna in her arms.

Walter looked mutely up at him. The boy hadn't said a word since they'd left the little apartment. He was so young. How could he possibly imagine what they had in mind for him?

Otto led the boy to join his granddaughters, Johanna saying as they reached them, "Žozo, I'm cold."

Žofie-Helene snuggled her to be warmer. "It's okay, my little *mausebär*," she said. "I'll keep you warm. I'll take care of you."

A woman in front of them in line—a striking young mother with lilac eyes and perfect eyebrows, fine collarbones, and a baby in her arms—said, "Aren't you a good big sister?" Did the mother really mean to send her infant away to England? She stood with an older woman whose granddaughter, a little redhead whose left eye turned in, hung on her skirts.

"Do the children need to be here to be registered for the transport?" Otto asked them as he took Johanna from Žofie.

"Why is that woman watching us?" Žofie-Helene asked, and they all looked in the same direction at the same time—the grandmother with the cross-eyed redhead and the beautiful mother with the baby and Otto himself, as if Žofie's words had put point to their sense that they were being watched.

A pale, foreign-looking woman stood apart from the line some distance away, seeming to belong here, and yet not—a woman with a strong chin and nose and brow, a mouth so wide it might be cruel were it not softened by gentle gray eyes. She shifted, registering the discomfort in the faces returning her gaze, then lifted one yellow-gloved hand in acknowledgment and carried on into the building, striding as easily as if she owned the synagogue.

"They do," the grandmother said. And at Otto's puzzled expression, "The children do need to be here to be registered for the transport. They're taking photos and giving medical exams."

"Žofie, I need you to go find Stephan," Otto said. "Get him to come here and get in line. Walter and Johanna and I will hold the place, but run and get him if you can. I've told their mother I would register them both. That's what they're doing here. They're organizing for Jewish children to get to safety in England."

"And others," the pretty mother said.

"Other places than England?" Otto asked.

"Other children. Not just Jews."

Otto put a hand on Žofie's shoulder before she could run off, saying to the women, "They're taking non-Jews?"

"The children of Communists and political opponents."

"Do you think they might take my granddaughters? Their mother has been arrested for publishing a newspaper critical of the Reich."

The women eyed him skeptically.

"Our Žofie-Helene, she's a mathematics prodigy," he said. "She's been tutored at the university since she was nine. By Professor Kurt Gödel, who is very famous. She could study in England."

The grandmother said, "We're not the ones you have to convince."

"Any child who is in danger," the lilac-eyed mother said. "That's what Herr Friedmann said. They have to be healthy, is all. Healthy and not yet eighteen."

Otto struggled with his own conscience, and quickly lost.

"Žofie-Helene, you need to stay here," he said.

"I'll be back, Grandpapa. I won't miss our turn, I promise. If I can't find Stephan quickly, I'll come back." And she was running off already, leaving Otto calling after her, caught between wanting to stop her lest something happen to her and knowing that if something happened to young Stephan, he would never forgive himself.

"I'm cold, Grandpapa," Johanna said.

Otto pulled the child to him, cold himself now. Cold with the fright of the choice he faced, the choice Frau Neuman had confronted so boldly. Could he send his grandchildren off to a country where they didn't even speak the language? And if he did, would he ever see them again? Would Käthe ever forgive him, or would she want him to send them away?

Walter handed his scarf up to Johanna. "You can have my scarf," he said. "I'm not too cold."

OUR DIFFERENT GODS

Truus entered the main synagogue on Seitenstettengasse, where the long line from outside continued around the burned-out shell of the main hall and snaked upstairs to circle the women's gallery, which had survived the night of synagogue fires. It was up there that she found Herr Friedmann orchestrating volunteers at folding tables and others with clipboards in hand, sending children one way or another. A teenage girl disappeared behind a curtain for a medical exam. A boy was having his photo taken. Herr Friedmann ushered Truus to a quieter corner, still in view of the line.

"How did you get the word out so fast?" she asked.

"So many of us are confined to a single neighborhood," Herr Friedmann said. "The miracle is that these parents have told each other. The problem will not be finding enough children, but having too many."

"And the medical exams?" Truus asked. "We need to assure the British that the children are healthy—truly healthy. Any problems in this first transport will jeopardize any future—"

"As healthy as malnourished children can be," Herr Friedmann interrupted. "Our doctors will make sure of that. It is the blessing of our doctors being deprived of earning their living in Nazi Vienna that they are free to show up here on a moment's notice, as they have."

"There will clearly be no issue with gathering six hundred," Truus said. "The question will be sorting which should go. Can we assess who are at highest risk and take them on the first train?"

"The most at risk are the oldest boys," Herr Friedmann said. "Those in work camps whose mothers stand in line for them."

Older boys would be the hardest to place in Britain. Families would want to take in babies, but they simply couldn't manage to transport babies in this short amount of time and with so few adult chaperones.

"Can we assess the health of boys in camps and get their photos taken?" she asked.

Desider Friedmann conceded that they could not.

"All right, then we are back to where we started: children here, between four and seventeen," Truus said. The cutest little ones, she thought, but did not say. Cute little children the parents of England could imagine were their own. "Let's make sure we take enough older girls to help with the little ones on the train. The older girls will be relatively easy to place. They can serve as informal domestics when they get to England."

Desider Friedmann said, "These children are not meant to be domestics, Frau Wijsmuller."

The faces of the mothers across the room were filled with dread and hope. Any one of them would be happy to serve as a domestic in England, to be near her children. Informal domestics. The idea had not been Truus's own.

"Herr Friedmann, we must be practical," she said. "These first children must be placed quickly."

Friedmann said, "I'm told there are holiday camps—"

"If the holiday camps fill, the British will be reluctant to accept more children unless there are homes already arranged for them." Another idea not her own. But Norman and Helen Bentwich had been right: Who was she to question Britain's generosity in welcoming these children in whatever manner they would? Her own country would grant them no more than passage by train from the border with Germany to ferries at Hook of Holland. "And arranging homes takes more time than we have," she said. "Well, perhaps we could note the quality of the children's table manners and the extent of their English? Children who can speak English will be easier to place, and good manners will stand them in good stead. We might even teach them a few English phrases and give preference to quick learners."

"We have only until Saturday," Herr Friedmann said.

"Yes, of course," Truus said. So much to do. So many children.

"There must be more than six hundred children in line already," Herr Friedmann said, "and we are to decide who escapes? We are to play God?"

The long line wrapped around the women's gallery, down to the burned-out main hall and out the door onto the street—so many parents waiting patiently for the chance to send their children off to a land where they knew no one, with customs they couldn't fathom, a language they did not speak. Adorable youngsters who would be easy to place, some of them, but also unruly boys, and girls like the cross-eyed redhead Truus had seen in the line outside. She ought not to have stared at the girl, but it had broken her heart to imagine that beautiful child lined up for prospective parents to choose, or not.

She said to Herr Friedmann, "'Who has known the mind of the Lord so as to instruct him?'" She started to say "Corinthians," but it was the New Testament, the word of her God but not his. She said instead simply, "Who are we, Herr Friedmann, to question the order in which God brings his children to us?"

PAPER TRAIL

In the cocoa storeroom, Žofie-Helene took a middle sheet from the clipboard and tore it into pieces, working quickly in the dim light of the storeroom flashlight, aware that at any moment someone from Neuman's Chocolates upstairs might come down and find her. She wrote on one scrap *Come to the synagogue behind St. Rupert's now! We're in line for a train to England with W—*

She scratched out the W and wrote *your brother.*

She repeated the message on the other scraps, then pocketed them and hung the clipboard back in its place. She took the flashlight with her as she ducked under the stairway and descended the ladder into the lower cavern, where she folded one of the notes in half and balanced it over one of the ladder rungs.

Back in the tunnel, she tucked a note into the octagonal manhole atop the circular stairs. She hurried up the tunnel to the crypt under St. Stephen's to tuck a note there. One at the convent. The Talmud school. Where else had Stephan been keen to show her?

With the last note still in hand, she hurried back to see where Grandpapa was in line. She still had some time.

She pulled the flashlight from her coat pocket again and hurried through the tunnels in the other direction, all the way to the exit across the canal from Leopoldstadt, nearest the apartment where Stephan's mother now lived.

BINARY

Žofie-Helene hurried to the head of the line at the synagogue, where Grandpapa waited with Johanna and Walter behind the lilac-eyed mother with the baby and the grandmother with the redheaded girl.

"Ach, Žofie-Helene!" Grandpapa exclaimed.

The people in line all turned. Žofie expected the grandmother might hush Grandpapa as she'd hushed the redheaded girl so many times. Even the staff at the registration tables and the people with the clipboards frowned at Grandpapa's outburst.

As the grandmother was called to one of the registration tables, Grandpapa set Johanna down, pulled out a handkerchief, and scrubbed at Žofie's face. The lilac-eyed mother was called too now, to the other table.

"I searched everywhere," Žofie said to Grandpapa. "I left notes. I know he'll be here in a minute. We can just wait like you said I—"

"We cannot wait, Žofie," Grandpapa said. "We cannot wait."

The grandmother with the redheaded girl was now demanding to know why the children must be made to travel on the Sabbath. The lilac-eyed mother began weeping at the other table as the woman who had watched them in the line—the one with the beautiful yellow gloves—spoke to her patiently, saying she was sorry, honestly she was, but for this first transport they simply could not take babies. The gloved woman took the mother's arm, easing her away from the table. "There isn't the capacity to arrange care for them in this short time," she said. "The children must be at least four. At least four and not past seventeen."

Four, the smallest prime squared. Žofie fixed on the comfort of the number. And seventeen, the sum of the first four primes and the only prime that is the sum of four consecutive primes.

The attendant at the table motioned for Žofie and Grandpapa to step forward, introducing herself as Frau Grossman and handing Grandpapa some forms to fill out. Grandpapa took two for Johanna and Walter, and handed a third to Žofie to fill out for herself.

Grandpapa asked if he might have a fourth form to fill out for Walter's brother, whom he hoped would join them shortly. Frau Grossman responded that she could only register children who were present.

Žofie dawdled over the form, stalling for Stephan.

Frau Grossman said to Grandpapa, "The little girl isn't Jewish?"

Grandpapa said, "No, but—"

"And she is only three," Frau Grossman said.

"She will be four in March, and her sister—"

"I'm sorry, sir," Frau Grossman interrupted. "The boy is Jewish?"

Frau Grossman looked impatiently to Žofie, who with another glance over her shoulder—the lilac-eyed mother was watching her so intently that it was disconcerting—reluctantly turned over her form. There was still no sign of Stephan.

A man was saying to the grandmother with the redheaded girl, "Yes, I understand it's a cruel choice, but the transport is to leave on the Sabbath. Rest assured it is not our choice. You must commit your granddaughter, though, or step aside and leave the space for someone who will. If anyone backs out, the whole six hundred will be prohibited from leaving."

Frau Grossman said to Grandpapa, "I'm sorry, we're processing only Jewish children here. Non-Jews are to be—"

"But we've stood in line for hours already," Grandpapa objected. "And we're here with a Jewish boy who has already lost his father and whose mother is ill. We can't be in two places at once!"

"Nonetheless—"

"My grandchildren's mother has been arrested for the simple act of writing the truth!"

The woman with the yellow gloves stepped over and took the paperwork from Grandpapa, saying, "It's okay, Frau Grossman. Perhaps I can help Herr . . . ?"

"Perger. Otto Perger," Grandpapa said, trying to calm himself.

"I'm Truus Wijsmuller, Herr Perger," the woman said. Then to the other workers, "How many is this?"

Frau Grossman consulted with the woman at the other table, each counting the number of pages they'd filled out and the number of names on their most recent, partial pages.

"Let's see," Frau Grossman said. "Twenty-eight multiplied by nine is—"

"Five hundred and twenty-one," Žofie said. She was sorry the minute she'd blurted it out. The longer they took, the more time Stephan had to find the notes and show up here.

The woman smiled condescendingly at her. "Twenty-eight multiplied by ten is two hundred and eighty." Then to the others, "Subtract twenty-eight and that's two hundred and fifty-two."

The woman at the other table said, "Two hundred and fifty-two doubled is five hundred and four. Plus your ten and my seven is . . ."

The woman in the pretty yellow gloves, with a kind smile at Žofie-Helene, said, "Five hundred and twenty-one."

The beautiful mother with the baby, still watching, also smiled.

"It's a prime number," Žofie said, trying to keep them talking. "Like seventeen, the highest age of children you are registering. Seventeen is the only prime that is a sum of four primes. If you add any other four consecutive primes, you always get an even number, and even numbers are never primes because they're divisible by two. Well, except two, of course. Two is a prime."

The two other women took in the long line still waiting to register. "More than six hundred," Frau Grossman said. "Hundreds more."

The gloved woman came to Žofie and took her hand, the leather gloves softer than skin against Žofie's fingers.

"And you are . . . ?" the woman asked.

"I'm Žofie-Helene Perger," Žofie said.

The gloved woman said, "Žofie-Helene Perger, I'm Geertruida Wijsmuller, but why don't you call me 'Tante Truus'?"

"You aren't my aunt," Žofie said.

The woman laughed, a lovely, elliptical laugh like Stephan's aunt Lisl's.

"No, I'm not, am I?" the woman said. "But Frau Wijsmuller is a lot for most children to say. Not for you, of course."

Žofie-Helene considered this. "It's more efficient."

The woman laughed again. "'More efficient.' It is, isn't it?"

"People call me 'Žofie,' because it's more efficient," Žofie said. "My friend Stephan sometimes calls me just plain 'Žofe.' I don't have an aunt, but he does. His aunt Lisl. I like her a lot. But she's in Shanghai now."

"I see," Tante Truus said.

"She's Walter's aunt too. Walter and Stephan are brothers."

She waited for Tante Truus to ask about Stephan, but the woman only turned to take in Walter.

"Well, why don't you two step over here and we'll get your photographs taken?" Tante Truus said.

Grandpapa handed the woman Johanna's paperwork.

Tante Truus said, "I'm really sorry, Herr Perger, but for this train, please believe me when I say it isn't possible to include toddlers. We hope to include them on the next one."

Johanna said, "I'm a big girl. I'm three!"

Grandpapa said, "Her sister would be with her, and she's a good girl, she's no trouble."

"I'm sure, Herr Perger," Tante Truus said, "but I simply cannot . . . There isn't time for discussion with everyone. Please understand. We must draw lines and hold to them."

"I . . ." Grandpapa glanced at the long line behind them. "Yes, I'm . . . I'm sorry. Of course."

Tante Truus extracted a linen handkerchief and wiped at Žofie's face a bit more, then unwound her braids and fluffed her hair.

"Smile for the photographer, Žofie-Helene," she said.

The flash popped, leaving stars of light dancing in Žofie's eyes.

Tante Truus took Žofie's hand and led her behind a screen, where she was to undress so that a doctor could examine her. Žofie wanted to tell her that she was not a baby, that Walter needed more help than she did. But she only skinned off her shoes, which seemed to fascinate Tante Truus even though she'd told her to undress.

"Are you in charge here, Tante Truus?" Žofie asked as she pulled off her stockings and carefully folded them, wanting to stay in Tante Truus's good graces. "Mama is in charge of a newspaper. People never expect it, a girl in charge. She says it can work in her favor."

"Well, in that case I suppose I should be in charge here," Tante Truus said. "I do like things to work in my favor."

"Me too," Žofie said. "I'm quite talented at mathematics."

"Yes, I saw that," Tante Truus said.

"Professor Gödel has left the university, but I still help him with his generalized continuum hypothesis."

Tante Truus peered oddly at her, the way people so often did.

"You know, about the possible sizes of infinite sets?" Žofie said. "The first of Hilbert's twenty-three problems. My friend Stephan is as smart with words as I am with mathematical concepts. He could study writing with Stefan Zweig if he went to England. He ought to have been in line with us, so perhaps when he gets here you could just put him with Walter and me?"

Tante Truus said, "Ah, so this is where you were going. And why isn't your friend here himself?"

"He's not in a camp," Žofie assured her. She'd heard people in the line say there wouldn't be time to get boys from the camps.

Truus asked, "Where is he, then?"

Žofie met her gaze, unwilling to betray Stephan.

"You must understand, I can't just move someone in line ahead of the others," Tante Truus said. "That wouldn't be fair. Now take your clothes off, Žofie-Helene, so the doctor can see that you're healthy."

"Stephan is in hiding!" Žofie blurted. "It's not his fault he isn't here!"

"I see," Tante Truus said. "And you know where he is?"

"He can have my space," Žofie said. "I can stay here with Jojo."

"Oh, sweetheart, I'm afraid I can't do that. See, each card is specific to a child. The other half of your card is in England, and only you will have permission to—"

"But Stephan will be eighteen and he'll be too old!" Žofie gulped back the sob climbing up her throat. "You can send his card for mine and say you made a mistake. Even I make mistakes."

The woman pulled her close and hugged her the way Mama sometimes did. Žofie couldn't help herself; tears spilled from her eyes to be absorbed by the woman's clothing, which was nearly as soft as the gloves. It had been so long since Žofie had seen Mama.

"I think this Stephan is lucky to have such a good friend, Žofie-Helene," Tante Truus said, and Žofie felt the woman's lips press to the crown of her head. "I wish I had a . . . a friend like you."

The doctor peered around the privacy screen. Tante Truus helped Žofie quickly out of the rest of her clothes.

"Okay, breathe deeply for the nice doctor," Tante Truus said. "Then quick as you can, dress again and run and get your friend. Bring him directly to me. I can't register him without a photo or a health certificate, but you just pretend the line isn't there and bring him to me."

The doctor listened to Žofie-Helene's breathing, which she did as quickly as she could.

"More slowly," he said. "Deep breaths."

Žofie closed her eyes and let her mind fill with numbers, the way she did at night when she couldn't sleep. What came to mind as he set the stethoscope aside and finished the examination, tapping her knees with the little mallet and looking in her ears and nose and mouth, was a simple problem: if each child took, say, four minutes to process and there were two processed at a time, that meant there were two hours and thirty-four minutes for her to find Stephan. Two hours and eighteen, actually, since she and Walter were already past the table, and two others were registering now.

"Žofie-Helene," Tante Truus said, "I'm going to help your friend as best I can, but I can't put him ahead of anyone given a number before he arrives. You must promise me that you'll get on the train, with Stephan or without him. If you don't, six hundred other children will not be allowed to go on account of you. Do you understand?"

Five hundred and ninety-nine others, Žofie thought, but she didn't say anything as now she didn't want to waste the time.

She pulled her clothes back on, saying at the same time, "It's binary. Six hundred or zero." Zero, her favorite number usually, but not now. "I understand," she said, "and I promise I'll go to England even if Stephan is number six hundred and one. I'll take Walter."

"Binary, heavens!" Tante Truus said. "Hurry, then. Fast as you can!"

THOUGH BANISH'D,
OUTCAST, REVILED

Žofie-Helene sprinted off to the nearest entrance to the underground, trying not to think of what her life would be like without Stephan, but awash with memories: that day Grandpapa had pretended to cut Stephan's hair; Stephan's birthday, when she hadn't known it was his birthday, when she hadn't known that he lived in a big palais on the Ringstrasse with a doorman and famous paintings and an elegant aunt; the first time she'd read one of his plays, the feeling that, even though it wasn't about her, she was understood; that night on the Burgtheater stage, when she'd closed her eyes and pretended it was Stephan rather than Dieter kissing her; the moment Stephan had looked at her as he goose-stepped up the Prater Park promenade, when she'd known from the shame in his eyes that he needed her to lie to the Nazis and take Walter away. She hadn't even been afraid that day. The fear had only bubbled up in her later, when Stephan had refused to see her, when she came to realize that in saving his brother she had lost her one friend.

The moment she reached the darkness of the underground, she began to sing. She sang quietly, the words from that day in the royal chapel, the voice of the single boy left alone in the choir loft, the voice of an entire choir echoing the music back under the unfrescoed rib vault, like the beautiful weight of the intersecting barrels carried on the piers so that the thrust was transmitted to the outer walls.

"Ave Maria, maiden mild," she sang softly. She wasn't much of a singer, not like the boys in the choir. Still, she sang more loudly, "Listen to a maiden's prayer."

She stopped and listened. She heard nothing.

"Thou canst hear though from the wild," she sang, even more loudly, her voice the one now echoing as she flicked on the dim flashlight and hurried through the cold darkness. "Thou canst save amid despair. Safe may we sleep beneath thy care; Though banish'd, outcast, reviled."

EVEN APART

Truus, just arrived back at her room at the Hotel Bristol, had not even sat down to remove her shoes when the telephone rang. The operator apologized for disturbing her at this hour, but she had an urgent call from Amsterdam. Would she take it? As Truus waited for the call to be put through, she pulled off her gloves, then sat and removed first one shoe, then the other. She unclipped one stocking from her garter and rolled it down, the rayon on the outside and the wool and cotton underneath for warmth giving way to her pale, exhausted thigh, her knee, her calf, the dry skin of her heel snagging on the fabric. She flexed her naked toes, the arched bones, the clear nails. A plain, Christian foot. How could a Jewish foot possibly be more or less remarkable?

She folded the stocking and set it on the dresser. The clothes she'd thrown away the night before sat as neatly folded as she'd left them, but on the dresser rather than in the trash bin now. Well, of course the hotel maid would have been confused.

Joop's voice crackled in the receiver, demanding, "Where have you been, Truus? I've been trying to reach you all day!"

Truus exhaled the dank air. "Six hundred children, Joop," she said.

She sat back in the chair, one leg bare, the other still the sun-beige of her stockings. She might just tip her head back and close her eyes and sleep, upright and half dressed.

"All right," Joop said. "The steamer *Prague* will lie ready at Hook of Holland. But only the one ferry. I'm sorry. I can't get a second on such short notice."

"Six hundred, or not a one, Joop. Eichmann could not be clearer."

"But that makes no sense. He wants to get rid of Vienna's Jews and

England will take them. Why demand they all be gone by Saturday? Why not Sunday or—"

"Saturday is the Sabbath," she said wearily. "We are to find six hundred families willing to hand their children over to strangers to travel on the day their religion forbids it, to go alone to a world in which they will certainly be lonely and frightened. And if a single parent has a change of mind at the last minute, the whole scheme collapses."

"He can't be that cruel."

"Joop, you cannot believe the humiliation he—"

The truth, the details, would only make her husband worry for her, and worry would do them no good.

"We haven't begun to see the extent of this man's capacity for cruelty, Joop."

"What humiliation, Truus?"

She stood and, with the receiver tucked under her chin, gathered the clothes folded on the dresser and placed them, still in their tidy pile, back into the empty trash bin.

"Truus?"

She reached into the bin and pulled the shorter skirt he'd given her from the other clothing, and held it to her chest. She wanted to tell him. She wanted to take the burden off her own soul, but she couldn't bear to place the weight of it on him. He had borne so much already. There was so much he deserved that she might never be able to give.

"Truus," he said gently, "remember, we're stronger together, even when we're apart."

PACKING

Žofie chose three of her mathematics notebooks and set them in her empty suitcase on her bed. She stood before the little bookshelf her father had built her, trying to decide how many of her Sherlock Holmes books she had room for. She liked "A Scandal in Bohemia" best, and the novels—*A Study in Scarlet*, *The Sign of the Four*, *The Hound of the Baskervilles*, *The Valley of Fear*—but Grandpapa said she must choose only two. So she selected *The Adventures of Sherlock Holmes* for the stories, and *The Sign of the Four* because it had the number four in its title, such a comforting number, and also because she liked Mary Morstan and the mysterious six pearls and the ending, where Mary doesn't get to become one of the richest women in England, but she does get Dr. Watson.

Johanna appeared at Žofie's side, saying, "Žozo," and handing her a framed photograph of the two of them with Mama, Jojo still a baby, in Mama's favorite frame. She tried to think of the hidden photograph in "A Scandal in Bohemia" for the distraction, so she wouldn't start to cry.

"It will be cold in England," Grandpapa said. "You will need more clothes. And remember, nothing valuable."

He took the photo from her, removed it from its expensive frame, and set the bare photo in the suitcase, inside the top notebook so it wouldn't get bent.

Žofie lifted Johanna and held her close, nuzzling into the warm, yeasty smell of her little-girl neck.

"Johanna can't come," she said to Grandpapa. "Stephan can't come. And Mama isn't here to say goodbye."

"I want to go with Žozo," Johanna said.

Grandpapa folded Žofie's favorite sweater and set it in the suitcase, beside the notebooks. He added skirts and blouses, panties, and socks, all the while speaking soothingly, saying, "Your mother will be released soon, Žofie. I've been assured she will be released soon. But Austria is no longer safe for us. She'll want you to go to England. When she's released, we'll all go to Czechoslovakia to stay with your grandmère until we can get visas to join you."

He closed the suitcase, to make sure it wasn't overfilled, then opened it again.

"Just think of everything you have to look forward to, *Engelchen*," he said. "You can see the Rosetta Stone at the British Museum."

"And the Rhind Mathematical Papyrus," she said.

"Sherlock Holmes's house on Baker Street."

"I could give my space to Stephan and come to Grandmère's with you and Mama and Johanna," she said. "Then there would still be six hundred."

Grandpapa put his arms around the two of them, and held them safe and together. "Frau Wijsmuller has already explained, Žofie, that the cards have been processed with the Germans. They have to match here as well as at the border leaving Germany, and in England. But Stephan will be on the next train."

"There might not be a next train before he's eighteen!" She pulled back from Grandpapa, still with Johanna in her arms. "Tante Truus wouldn't promise there would ever be a next train!"

"If we don't finish packing and get to the station, there certainly will be no next train, or even a first," Grandpapa scolded.

Johanna began to wail. Žofie-Helene pulled her sister's face to her chest, as Mama used to do to protect them, to comfort them.

Grandpapa, with tears in his eyes too now, said, "I'm sorry. I'm sorry." He reached out and stroked Jojo's hair. "It's as hard for me to say goodbye, Žofie-Helene, as it is for you to leave."

Žofie felt herself begin to cry despite all her promises to herself that she wouldn't, that her crying would only make Grandpapa and Jojo sadder. "But you'll have Mama and Johanna," she said, "and I'll only have Sherlock Holmes, who isn't even real."

"But you'll have Cambridge, *Engelchen*," Grandpapa said in a more comforting voice. "I think you will have Cambridge. It's where your mother would want you to go even if we didn't have to leave Austria."

Žofie set Jojo down, got a handkerchief, and blew her nose. "Because I'm very good at maths," she said.

"You are extraordinary at maths," Grandpapa said. "Surely someone in England will see that and help you find a mentor there."

He took one of her blouses from the suitcase and returned it to the dresser.

"You are extraordinary, period," he said. "Now look, I've made room for one more Sherlock Holmes book and another of your maths notebooks. You'll want some pencils too. But hurry now, it's time to go."

LEAVE-TAKING

Stephan, in his coat and Žofie-Helene's pink plaid scarf, kissed his mother's forehead.

"You'd better go or you'll miss the train," Mutti said. "Take good care of him, Stephan. Keep him with you, always."

Stephan said, "The Wall will take care of me, won't you?"

Mutti buttoned Walter's coat and tied his scarf.

"But really, Stephan," she said, "promise me."

Stephan looked away, to the two suitcases waiting side by side at the door. His held only a single change of clothes and his notebook and pencil, and the copy of *Kaleidoscope* that Žofie had kept even though it was dangerous to have. It was too dangerous to be taken on the train too, but it didn't matter.

"I know you're young," Mutti said to him. "But you must be the man now."

She pulled Walter to her, inhaling deeply. "You do what your big brother says, everything he says," she said to him. "You promise me?"

"I promise, Mutti," Walter said.

She took Stephan's hand again. "Promise me you'll hold his hand all the way to England," she said. "Find a family to take you both."

Stephan met her gaze, knowing he needed to seem to her to be marking her face, remembering her forever. If he hadn't hesitated when he first heard Žofie singing . . . If he'd run faster . . . But then Mutti would have been left with no one.

"I'll keep him safe," he said.

That much was true.

"You and Stephan will go to a family together, Walter," Mutti said.

"And Peter too?" Walter asked.

"Yes, and Peter too. You and Stephan and Peter," Mutti said. "You will all live together with a family. You'll take care of each other."

"Until you come to England to be the mommy again," Walter said.

"Yes, sweetheart," Mutti said, her voice catching. "Yes. Until then you will write me lots of letters, and I will write you back."

Watching her work so hard not to cry, Stephan wanted to cry himself. He wanted to tell her not to worry, that he would still be here. He would take care of her. She wouldn't be alone.

"Teach him to be a man like you are, Stephan," she said. "You are such a good man. Your father would be so proud. Make your brother know how much we love him, how much we love you both, no matter what happens."

Walter took out his handkerchief and unfolded it carefully, and put it to Peter Rabbit's eyes. "Peter wants to stay with you, Mutti."

"I know he does," Mutti said, and she hugged Walter and Peter one last time.

Stephan lifted the two suitcases.

"His hand," Mutti insisted.

Stephan gave Walter the lighter suitcase, his own suitcase, and took Walter's heavier one in his own hand. He intertwined his fingers with Walter's, around one of Peter Rabbit's ears.

"Walter won't remember us," Mutti said quietly. "He's too young. He won't remember any of us, Stephan, except through you."

NUMBERS

Westbahnhof station was already crowded when Stephan arrived with Walter. Everywhere, women held tightly to children clutching stuffed animals and dolls. Men in black hats and black beards and sidelocks said Hebrew blessings over young heads, but most of the families looked more like Stephan's, most might have been any Vienna family but for the small suitcase on the platform beside each child.

A mother who looked something like Mutti stood quietly in the crowd, a basket in one hand and a baby in the other. A father took a wailing child from his mother's arms and scolded him to behave like a big boy. Everywhere, Nazis patrolled, many with dogs straining at their leashes.

A man called names from a clipboard. A woman draped a numbered card fastened to a string over a boy's neck, like a necklace, and affixed a tag with a matching number to his suitcase. The child, suitcase in hand, walked away from his parents, to the waiting train.

The woman they'd been told to address as Tante Truus was arguing with one of the Nazis. The official was saying the cars would be sealed, to be opened only for the document check at the border leaving Germany.

"The train must be sealed for the safety of everyone," the official said.

"But we're allowed only six adults and there are ten cars," Tante Truus objected. "Ten cars with sixty children each! Now you're telling me the adults won't be able to move from one car to another to check on the children?"

"It's an overnight train," the official said. "Surely they will sleep."

Stephan was caught off guard by the sight of Žofie even though he'd known she would be here. He'd have been horrified if she hadn't come. The train couldn't go without every one of the six hundred, and she was one. She looked more grown up than he had ever seen her, with her hair long and loose down her back, still damp from having been washed, and her breasts below the necklace she always wore straining at the buttons of her coat. Even as she kissed her sister again and again, her big green eyes behind her glasses remained intent on her grandfather, who was telling her first one thing and then another, trying to pack a lifetime of advice into a goodbye, the same way Mutti had.

A quiet settled over the station as Eichmann walked through with the awful dog at his side. Stephan shrank back as Tante Truus stepped forward.

"Good morning, Herr Eichmann," Tante Truus said.

"Six hundred, Frau Wijsmuller," Eichmann said without stopping. He disappeared up a staircase to the upper-level offices.

Slowly, the station returned to life, more subdued now.

Stephan wrapped Walter in a wordless hug. "Wall-man," he said. He wanted to be like Žofie-Helene's grandfather, he wanted to make sure Walter knew everything he would need to know for the rest of his life. But he could not form a word beyond this nickname for his brother. It seemed not enough. It seemed he ought at least to say his brother's name. But to say "Walter" would alarm him. Wall-man. Steady and solid.

Still holding tightly to Walter's hand, as he had since they'd left Leopoldstadt—as Mutti had asked him to do all the way to England—Stephan walked over to join Žofie and her grandfather and sister. Only then did he kneel down to Walter's level, to tell him the truth.

"There was no room for me on this train, Walter." Using his name now, so he would know how serious this was, and working so hard to keep his eyes steady. He so wanted to cry, but he needed to be the man his mother imagined. "But Žofie-Helene will be with you," he continued.

"She'll take care of you just as if she were me, and I'll be on the next train. I'll be on the next train, and I'll find you as soon as I arrive in England. I'll find you wherever you are."

The tears began to stream down Walter's face. "But you promised Mutti you would hold my hand all the way to England!"

"Yes," Stephan admitted, "but Žofie-Helene is me, see?"

"No she's not."

"Walter, Mutti wants us to go to England. You know that, right? You promised her you would be a good boy all the way to England."

"But with you, Stephan!"

"Yes, with me. But the thing is, they can only take six hundred on this train, and I'm number six hundred and ten."

Žofie-Helene said, "It's a very lucky number, Walter, six hundred and ten. It's the sixteenth number in the Fibonacci sequence."

Walter looked up at her with the same doubt Stephan himself felt. She meant to reassure him, Stephan knew that. But the last lucky number today was an even six hundred. Why hadn't he run faster?

"Žofie-Helene is going to be me just for this little bit," he said. "Just until I can get to England."

"Peter and I can go on the next train, with you."

"But you can't, that's the problem. If you don't go on this train, none of the others can go. None of us will ever go."

"It's binary," Žofie-Helene said quietly. "Six hundred or none."

"But I'll be on the next train," Stephan assured him, without promising. He had resolved at some point—maybe when he'd learned earlier in the week that he'd been too late for the first train—that he would do whatever he needed to do to get Walter on the train with Žofie, that he would lie if he had to, but he would try his best to stay with some kind of truth. "Until I get there," he told Walter, "Žofie-Helene will take care of you. Žofie-Helene will be me." He pulled out a handkerchief and wiped Walter's nose. "You just remember that, Wall. Žofie-Helene is me."

That much was true, just as what he'd told Mutti had been true: that he would make sure Walter got safely to England. Žofie-Helene had promised to keep Walter with her, to take Stephan's place.

"Žofie-Helene is me," he repeated one more time.

"Except she's smarter," Walter said.

Stephan smiled up at Žofie. "Yes, Žofie-Helene is me, but much smarter." And so much more beautiful, he thought. "She's me until I can join you, and I'll be on the very next train, since I'm the sixteenth number of the Fibonacci sequence. I don't know how many more they will take, but I'm sure it will be at least ten."

"And we'll go to a family together?"

"Yes. Exactly. I'll find you in England, and we'll go to a family together. But until then, you do whatever Žofie says, just like she's me."

Walter took his own handkerchief out and touched it to Peter Rabbit's nose.

The man with the chart called a girl with bright red hair, and the aides draped her with a numbered placard and tagged her suitcases.

Žofie-Helene said, "I think we're next, Walter. Are you ready? You'd better give your brother a final hug."

Stephan held Walter close, breathing him in one last time as Žofie kissed her sister a dozen times more.

The man called, "Walter Neuman. Žofie-Helene Perger."

Žofie handed her sister over to their grandfather, but the poor little girl began to wail, "I want to go with Žozo! I want to go with Žozo!"

Stephan wanted to wail too. He wanted to grab Walter's hand and Žofie's too, and run. But there was nowhere to run to.

Herr Perger said, "Be a good girl and make the way ready for your sister. We'll get her on a train to you as soon as she turns four. Your mother and I will write. We'll be coming too, as soon as we can arrange visas. But, Žofie, we will always be with you, no matter what. Like your father always watching over you as you do your maths, we will always be there."

Žofie-Helene took Walter's hand with the rabbit ear, the same way Stephan always did. The two walked the few steps to the man with the clipboard. They ducked their heads as the women draped numbered placards around their necks.

Number 522—that was Walter. And number 523—that was Žofie-Helene. Stephan fixed the numbers in his mind, as if they meant anything at all.

NECKLACE

Žofie straightened Walter's number on the string around his neck. "Number five hundred and twenty-two! That's a very special number," she said. "It's divisible evenly by one, two, three, six, and . . . let's see . . . also eighteen, twenty-nine, eighty-seven, one hundred and seventy-four, and two hundred and sixty-one. And of course it's divisible by itself, five hundred and twenty-two. So that means it has ten factors!"

Walter looked up at Žofie-Helene's number.

"Mine is a prime number," she said. "It's not divisible by anything but one and itself. But that's special in its own way."

Still Walter frowned. "Peter doesn't need his own necklace?" he asked her.

Žofie hugged Walter to her, then kissed his Peter Rabbit. "Peter gets to ride for free on your ticket, Walter. How about that?"

She took his hand and they queued up at the train carriage Herr Friedmann had directed them to, behind the redhead from in front of them in line when they registered. As they waited, Tante Truus came over.

"Žofie-Helene, you are a good, smart girl," she said. "For this car, I'm putting you in charge. Do you understand? There will be no adult, so you will have to make very smart decisions for everyone. Can you do that for Herr Friedmann and me?"

Žofie nodded. Tante Truus, looking at her, seemed suddenly alarmed. Had she said something wrong? But she hadn't said anything at all.

"Sweetheart, you can't take that necklace," Tante Truus said.

Žofie fingered her infinity symbol necklace, her father's tie tack that Grandpapa had made into a necklace. It was the only bit of her father she had left.

"Take it to your grandfather," Tante Truus said. "Go quickly now."

Žofie ran back and handed the necklace not to Grandpapa but to Stephan. She kissed him on his scarred lips, which were wet with his tears and slightly swollen, and so soft and warm they made her insides go soft and warm too. It was all she could do not to cry.

"Someday you'll write a play that makes people feel like that music does, I know you will," she said, and she hurried back to the line, took Walter's hand, and climbed onto the train.

A SEVENTEEN-YEAR-OLD
JEWISH BOY

All around the station, parents waited expectantly, devastated to be saying goodbye to their children while so many others—parents who'd helped pack suitcases for *their* children in the awful hope that they would get the chance they had not yet been given—were devastated not to be saying goodbye. So many little Adeles. So many mothers' faces filled with the same sad hope that Adele's mother had shown that morning in the Hamburg station. Truus wondered how Recha Freier had told Adele's mother about the child's death, and how Frau Weiss had borne it, how much she must blame Truus for taking the child from her, or blame herself for giving Adele up to be taken. How could this be the right thing to do, to take children from their parents?

She scanned the station for Eichmann, wondering where the cruel man was now.

"We can't pull the child from his bed and put him on the train," Frau Grossman was saying to Truus and Desider Friedmann, her voice low lest the Nazi patrol overhear. "The lot of them would have the measles before they arrived in Harwich, and the whole effort would halt. Surely there is another seven-year-old boy we could send in his place."

"Obersturmführer Eichmann has the cards," Truus said. "The Germans will check them before the train is allowed to leave Germany."

So many grieving parents waited for a final wave goodbye to children who now might not even leave on account of one sick little boy. It was the problems you failed to anticipate . . .

"We'll have to find a child who can pass for the child in the photo," she said, "and who is very good at pretending."

"But the risk if the lie is found out," Herr Friedmann objected with a nervous glance up to a second-floor window overlooking the platform.

Truus followed his gaze to the man and his dog standing perfectly still up there, observing. She thought, oddly, of her mother standing at their window in Duivendrecht on that snowy morning two decades ago now. She supposed this man was laughing even though she had no snowman this time. His laugh would be of a far different sort than her mother's had been.

"What choice do we have?" she said softly. "Without him no child will leave, not now and likely not ever."

The three of them scanned the faces of parents searching the train windows for their children, others wishing for that chance, praying for that chance.

Truus caught sight of the older boy whom that dear little Žofie-Helene—Žofie, to be more "efficient"—had brought to her, only too late for him to be allowed on this first train. What was his name? She prided herself on being good at names, but six hundred was so many to remember, and he wasn't even in the six hundred. He stood, with a suitcase on the ground beside him, watching the carriage into which Žofie-Helene had taken his little brother. Truus did remember him—the little boy, Walter Neuman. Walter Neuman and his brother, Stephan.

Truus followed Stephan's gaze to see Žofie, inside the train carriage, wiping the condensation from a window, then little Walter holding a stuffed animal up to look through the glass while Žofie helped another child settle.

"That boy, Stephan Neuman," she whispered to Herr Friedmann and Frau Grossman, and before they could object, she took the placard and luggage tag and hurried over to Stephan.

"Get on the last car, Stephan," she whispered, handing him the numbers. "I'll be there in a minute. If you're asked before I get there, say your name is Carl Füchsl and they've made a mistake on your age. Go on, quickly."

The boy took the placard and grabbed his suitcase, repeating, "Carl Füchsl."

"The boy is ten years too old!" Herr Friedmann objected as the boy hurried to the train.

"We've no time," Truus said, careful not to look to Eichmann at the window, to avoid the appearance of doing anything out of the ordinary on this queer morning. "We must get this train on its way before there is any hint of a problem."

"But he's—"

"He's a clever boy. He's successfully evaded arrest for weeks. And I've put him in the last carriage, with me."

"Yes, but—"

"He is a seventeen-year-old Jewish boy, Herr Friedmann. He'll likely age out before we can arrange a second train."

She turned the list over to a Nazi official, to be taken to Eichmann for his approval before they could leave.

THE OTHER MOTHER

Žofie was trying to get a mute little thumb-sucking boy to take a seat when Walter called out, "Stephan!" and climbed over the child on the seat next to him. He raced down the aisle toward the carriage door.

"Walter, no! Stay on the train!" she called, hurrying after him, seeing Stephan now out on the platform, veering from the carriage behind them toward Walter.

Stephan bounded into their car, lifted Walter high in the air, and laughed, the scar on his lip almost disappearing with the wide stretch of his smile. "I'm here, Wall! I'm here!"

Žofie, at the carriage door, searched the crowded station until she found Grandpapa, his back to the train. Johanna watched Žofie over Grandpapa's shoulder.

"Žozo, I want to go with you!" Johanna called out.

"I love you, Johanna!" Žofie called back, trying so hard not to weep now, not to think that she might never see Jojo or Grandpapa or Mama ever again. "I love you!" she shouted. "I love you! I love you! I love you!"

A woman on the platform whose children had not been called became hysterical.

Stephan took Žofie's hand as Nazis emerged from every corner and surrounded the woman and her children, the barking of dogs fierce around her, fierce all over the station.

One of the dogs broke his leash, or was let go. He was on the woman, ripping at her clothes as Nazis beat her with batons.

In the panic, parents rushed the platform.

"Žofie-Helene," someone said, a woman's voice.

The woman from the registration line, the baby's mother with the lilac eyes, stood weeping just outside the train. She set a picnic basket into the carriage, at Žofie's feet.

"Thank you," Žofie said reflexively.

From inside the basket came a cooing noise.

The mother looked up at Žofie, as panicked as Žofie herself felt.

"Shhhhhhh," the mother said. "Shhhhhhhh."

She said something else, but Žofie was no longer listening, Žofie, sobbing now, was calling out, "Jojo! Grandpapa! Wait!"

Grandpapa disappeared around a corner, Johanna with him.

"Please take care of her, Žofie-Helene Perger," the lilac-eyed mother said.

The mother stepped back as a Nazi closed the carriage door, locking them in. The clank of the train brakes releasing sounded, and they began to move slowly forward. Outside the carriage door's window, the lilac-eyed mother watched as the space between them grew. A father climbed onto the side of the moving car, calling to a child. Other parents ran beside the train, weeping, waving, calling out love, as the train picked up speed.

Inside the car, the children watched silently as the father let go and tumbled to the ground beside the tracks. They watched as first the parents and then the station receded. As the snow-dusted Ferris wheel grew smaller and smaller. As the Vienna roofline disappeared.

FIVE HUNDRED

Snowflakes hit and melted on Stephan's window, beyond which it was nearly as dark as the underground back home. The train clacked over the tracks, slowing and rocking at a curve. Children in the rows ahead ate food their parents had packed, or chatted or sat quietly, or practiced English, or slept, or pretended not to cry. Walter lay in Stephan's lap in the back row, with his head on Peter Rabbit up against a window. In the row across the aisle, Žofie changed the baby's diaper, at the same time retelling a Sherlock Holmes story to three children crowding the seat ahead of her.

Stephan set Walter on the seat and took the dirty diaper into the toilet, which smelled worse than the soiled diaper. One of the little boys must have missed his mark as the train rocked, or more than one. The smell reminded Stephan of the underground, of his own shame. He rinsed the diaper in the toilet, then wrung it out and flushed, and rinsed again.

Back in the carriage, he draped the wet diaper over the arm of the seat beside Walter, then took the baby from Žofie, to give her a break. He sat next to a little boy who hadn't spoken, who hadn't even, as far as Stephan had seen, taken his thumb from his mouth.

"Number five hundred, even," Stephan said to Žofie.

"We can't think of him that way, as just a number," Žofie said. "Even such a beautiful number."

Stephan didn't know how thinking of him as "thumb-sucking boy" was any better.

He tried to get the boy to tell him his name, but the boy only looked up at him, still sucking his thumb.

"Would you like to hold the baby?" Stephan asked him.

The boy watched him, unblinking.

Žofie squeezed in beside them, one of the bottles of milk from the baby's basket in hand. "That was the last diaper," she said, taking the baby back from Stephan, as if she needed the child's warmth, or someone to care for.

"Walter and I have handkerchiefs we can use," Stephan said. "And the other boys too, I bet." He stroked the thumb-sucking boy's brown curls. "Do you have a handkerchief, pal?"

The child only stared as, outside the window, the lights of a town reflected off a river. A large castle on a hill appeared. They passed through a station—Salzburg—but didn't stop.

Stephan said to Žofie-Helene, "Stefan Zweig used to live here."

She said, "We're almost to Germany."

The train grew silent, the children who were awake watching out the window.

"Do you really think I will, Žofe?" Stephan asked.

Žofie, jostling the baby to sleep, looked at him but didn't answer.

"Write plays," he said. "Like you said in the station." When she'd kissed him, her lips smoother than the smoothest chocolate.

Žofie studied him, her straight lashes unblinking, her frank green eyes steady behind her eyeglasses, which were uncharacteristically unsmudged. "My father used to tell me that no one really imagines they're Ada Lovelace," she said, "but someone is."

Out the window, troops marched on the road in the dark.

"Ada Lovelace?" Stephan said.

"Augusta Ada King-Noel, Countess of Lovelace. She described an algorithm for generating Bernoulli numbers that suggested that the British mathematician Charles Babbage's Analytical Engine might have applications beyond pure calculation, which was all Babbage himself imagined it might do."

The sound of marching outside the window faded, leaving only the clack of the train and the quiet of the children's fear. Germany.

"Maybe you really could meet Zweig in London," Žofie said. "He could mentor you like Professor Gödel mentored me."

She turned to the boy then, number 500. "Did you know Sherlock Holmes lives on Baker Street?" she asked him. "But I suppose you're too young to appreciate his stories, aren't you? Well, perhaps you would like to sing? Do you know 'The Moon Has Risen'?"

The boy's eyes over the hand to his mouth studied her.

"Of course you do," she said. "Even Johanna knows it."

She touched the baby's cheek. "Don't you, Johanna?" she said. And she began to sing softly, "The moon has risen; the golden stars shine in the sky bright and clear."

Slowly, other children joined her. The little boy didn't sing, but he leaned into Žofie. His thumb settled slowly from his mouth as he fell asleep, his placard with the beautiful number 500 still around his neck.

DAMP DIAPERS

As the train arced around a bend, approaching the border between Germany and the Netherlands—approaching freedom!—Stephan pulled still-wet diapers and handkerchiefs off the seat backs, already searching for a place to hide them from the German border control check. It felt like he had been riding this train forever: all the long hours yesterday after they left, absorbing the unreality of leaving; the whole night trying to sleep on the seats, with forever one child or another needing comfort, even Peter Rabbit needing comfort, although Walter was otherwise heartbreakingly stoic; the long day today without even much food, most of what the children's parents had sent already eaten. He opened a window to throw the diapers out, thinking surely someone would provide new diapers, real diapers, when they crossed into the Netherlands. Along the road beside the train tracks, helmeted troops marched all the way up the curved arc of track to the engine belching black smoke and a white jet of steam, and back as far as he could see in the bright light of this second day, all the way across the winter-pale rolling hills to woods that seemed impossibly far away.

He closed the window and turned to Žofie, who was trying to rock the baby to sleep. He was feeling the kind of panic now that the doctor must have felt in Zweig's *Amok* before he threw himself on the woman's coffin, dragging himself and the coffin to the bottom of the sea. Both of them dead on account of a baby. He remembered Papa's voice as they sat together by the fire in the library back in Vienna, in his old life,

Papa saying *You're a man of character, Stephan. You won't ever be in the position of having a baby you ought not to have.*

Papa had been a man of character, and now he was dead.

Stephan went to the other side of the train to throw out the diapers, but there were people along the tracks there too: a man in a leather cap, so close to the train that he startled Stephan; a sausage vendor with a customer standing beside his flat tin cart; a nurse walking a baby in a pram, a child no doubt wearing dry, soft diapers rather than thin handkerchiefs. He tried to imagine what his father would have him do, what a man of character would do.

He opened his own suitcase and stuffed the diapers and handkerchiefs in with his clothes, his notebook, and his book of Zweig's stories. Perhaps the wet diapers would dampen the banned book beyond recognition, but then there would still be the diapers, the evidence of a baby they ought not to have.

Žofie was tucking the sleeping baby into the picnic basket.

Stephan closed his suitcase.

Žofie slid the picnic basket between the seats, making it as unobtrusive as possible.

"Now everyone remember," Žofie said to the other children, "be very nice to the soldiers and don't say a word about the baby. The baby is our secret."

The thumb-sucking boy, number 500, said, "If we talk, they might take her away."

"That's right," Žofie said, clearly as surprised as Stephan at the boy's subdued but surprisingly certain voice. "Good boy. Good boy."

The train jerked to a stop, the steam swirling outside the window cloaking them in what seemed suddenly like nothingness, like being alone in the world. But they weren't alone. They could hear the voices of the soldiers they couldn't see, German voices calling out to board the cars, to search every child and every suitcase, to make sure each child was properly documented.

"The numbers must match the identification," a man was commanding over a megaphone. "They must carry no contraband, nothing of value that properly belongs to the Reich. You will bring any Jew who has defied us directly to me."

TJOEK-TJOEK-TJOEK

Truus stood at the head of the carriage and called, "Children." Then louder, "Children." And finally, in a volume her parents had admonished her never to use with the children they'd taken in after the war, *"Children!"*

The carriage fell silent, all eyes on her. Well, there had never been more than a handful of children at home, and there were sixty here, and nine carriages more to address after they unsealed this one. Her first order of business, of course, must be to find Stephan Neuman who was not really Carl Füchsl before the Nazis did. He would be on the next carriage forward, with his brother and Žofie-Helene Perger; even in her first alarm after the carriage door was sealed off from all the chaos on the platform and Stephan Neuman was not there, she'd known that was where he was. Now she needed to get him on the carriage Carl Füchsl was meant to be on before unnecessary attention focused on him.

"I know it has been a long journey already," she said more gently to the children. All day and all night and half the day again, with the hardest bit at the beginning, the saying goodbye. "We'll be in the Netherlands soon, but we're not there yet. You must stay in this carriage now, no matter what happens. Stay in your seats, and do what the SS ask of you, with your finest manners. When they have finished, the train will start again, and you'll hear a change in the sound of the train. Its wheels . . ." She circled her forearm like a piston. "Here in Germany the wheels sound *tjoek-tjoek-tjoek-tjoek*. But when we get to the Netherlands you will hear *tjoeketoek-tjoeketoek-tjoeketoek*. *Then* you'll be there. Until then, no one is to get off the train."

DISAPPEARING TWINS

As the steam cleared, Stephan saw Nazis already boarding the other carriages, battering the children with their voices, and perhaps more. Stephan couldn't see what was happening on the other cars. He could only hear children crying, but that might be simply from fear.

Two toddler boys—identical twins—appeared on the platform, escorted away from the train by the SS.

Walter said, "Where are they taking those boys?"

Stephan put his arm around his brother. "I don't know, Wall," he said.

Walter said, "Peter and I don't want to go with them."

"No," Stephan said. "No."

CHILDREN, UNNUMBERED

Truus stepped from the train to the platform, to an SS officer demanding, "No one is to get off the train." Already, others in the station were watching: an attendant in a bright blue uniform with silver epaulets, a woman who must be the owner of the dozen matching suitcases on the luggage cart between them, a man on a bench behind them who lowered his *Der Stürmer* to better see.

"No one will get off, dear. I'll see to it," she assured the SS, even though she herself had just done so. "Now don't you dare scare these children."

She glanced forward to the next carriage, which hadn't, mercifully, been boarded by the guards yet. If only she could make this fool of a man move more quickly, so she could get Stephan Neuman in the proper carriage before anyone realized.

"You have the paperwork?" the man demanded.

She handed him the folder, saying, "There is a packet inside for each car. They should be fairly well organized, but with six hundred children, it isn't easy. One or two may be on the wrong car."

She heard the woman with all the luggage say "Judenkinder" with distaste.

She glanced to the train again. SS, seen through the windows of one of the carriages, were tearing through luggage, dumping suitcases out, and making the poor children undress, for heaven's sake.

"Your men are terrifying the children!" she said.

The SS leader watched his men on the train indifferently. The man on the bench folded his *Der Stürmer*, he and the others observing what could be seen through the train windows too.

"We are doing our duty," the SS said.

"They are not doing their duty," Truus insisted, refraining from saying "you" despite his identification of himself with his soldiers. Better not to reprimand him personally. "They are behaving very badly," she said.

Frau Grossman hurried toward her, frantic. Truus signaled her with a bend of her wrist not to interrupt.

"Go on, then," she said to the SS leader. "Right now, stop them before any more children wet themselves from terror, or your men will have to help us with the changing of six hundred children's clothes."

That did get his attention, and that of the onlookers, who turned startled faces back in her direction. She didn't suppose the soldiers would actually help children change soiled clothes, but nor would he want to have to continue guarding the train while she and the other escorts changed the children themselves, with everyone in the station watching.

As the SS hurried off, calling to his men—"You will check the luggage but you will not frighten the children!"—Truus thought of all the things she ought to have done differently. She ought to have arranged for paid border guards to travel on the train with them rather than having to stop for this kind of fiasco; she might enlist Baron Aartsen's help in arranging that for future transports, different guards each time, whom she would reward with gifts for their wives after the children were safe. She ought to have brought something to more easily call the children's attention to her, perhaps her yellow umbrella she could raise high, more obtrusive than her yellow gloves, but with hundreds of children she could not be subtle.

"Truus," Frau Grossman was saying frantically, and Truus turned to her now that the SS was taken care of.

"I'm sorry," Truus responded, "but I have to get Stephan Neuman—"

"They've taken two of the boys, the identical twins!" Frau Grossman said.

"The Gordon boys? How did they get on this train? They weren't in the first six hundred."

"I don't know. I was getting everyone settled and they sealed the door and the train left and they were just there, standing by the door identically crying!"

"The good Lord help us," Truus said, balancing the need, hoping she was right about the Neuman boy's instinct for survival. "All right, come with me. You'll explain that they threw their numbers out the window. Boys will be boys. I'll handle the rest."

"But I . . . I was so terrified. They asked me why these children didn't have numbers, and I told them they weren't meant to be on the train."

Truus could feel the color drain from her face. "All right," she said. "All right."

"The boys' parents—"

"We'll not be judging the parents," Truus said. "We might do the same. Let me see if . . . No, come with me. Perhaps we can persuade the Germans to allow you to return with these boys to Vienna and let the rest of the train go along to the Netherlands. We can't ask for more. We can't risk the whole train. Thank God they're a cute little pair."

THE EICHMANN PARADOX

The man pushed his way into Michael's office, his dog beside him. Anita trailed behind them, trying to announce this guest arriving on a Sunday, when the office was closed. As Michael stood to greet him, the man eyed the portrait hanging behind the desk, the Kokoschka of Lisl. Michael had claimed the portrait as his own, although of course it had been painted before he ever met Lisl. It belonged to Herman and, as such, was valuable property of the Reich.

"I need six hundred chocolates for a gathering at the Metropole tonight," the man said without personal address, introduction, or apology.

"Tonight?" Michael said, startled not so much by the short time he was being given on a day when his chocolatiers were not even there as at the fact that Eichmann had come on this modest errand. Michael was only there himself to see Anita. "Of course, Herr Eichmann," he said, trying to recover. "It would be the pleasure of Neuman's Chocolates to provide—"

"Neuman's Chocolates? I was assured this was no longer a Jew business."

"Wirth Chocolates," Michael corrected himself, uncertain whether to admit the mistake or pretend it hadn't been made.

The man was in a rage, and by all accounts had been since the train full of children left the station the prior day. Michael had seen Eichmann leaving Westbahnhof station with his awful dog after the train disappeared down the tracks. It was the last of a dozen times Michael had trod the same path that day, hoping for a glimpse of Stephan and Walter, wishing he'd arranged for them to go with Lisl to Shanghai.

He might have done it even as late as when she'd left those few weeks ago. How much greater risk would it have been to have arranged for three passages? But he hadn't. Then, after the night of violence, there had been no passages to be had, and any non-Jew asking about tickets to Shanghai would have been eyed with suspicion if there were.

The boys were gone now, on the train somewhere between Vienna and the Netherlands. He hoped this man would hold to his word to allow them out of Germany, but he thought it as likely or more that some excuse would be found to stop the transit, and then what would happen to them?

He said, "Six hundred—yes, we can do that." He glanced at his watch. He would call in the chocolatiers. They would have to skim a selection from the stocks meant to be delivered to customers. "Of course we would be honored to provide a selection of all of our chocolates for you this evening."

"Six hundred decorated with a train," Eichmann said.

"All six hundred?" Michael blurted. "Yes, of course," he amended quickly, with no idea if his chocolatiers could produce that many chocolates in just a few hours, each tiny train hand-painted with a variety of frostings, but what choice was there? "Perhaps you'd like a sample box to take home to your wife and children?" Michael offered, made nervous now not just by his own blunder—questioning anything this man demanded—but also by the way the man again eyed the portrait.

"You have children, Herr Eichmann?" Michael asked, filling the awkward silence, thinking he ought to have left the painting in the closet with the other, to preserve a credible claim that they had been hidden there by Herman, to whom no further harm could be brought. "My—" My godsons, he'd nearly said. Stephan and Walter. "I don't have children myself, but I believe we have little chocolates painted with the Prater Park Ferris wheel that are quite popular with—"

"You Viennese and your ridiculous Ferris wheel," Eichmann said angrily. "Six hundred trains delivered by seven this evening."

He turned and left the office, the dog at perfect heel beside him.

Mercifully, Anita stood with the elevator gate open—not a smart girl by any means, but she did have an uncanny sense for what was needed. As the elevator door closed off the man and beast, she mouthed to Michael, "He was made to leave his wife and children back in Germany."

HIDING INFINITY

The children sat, silent and wide-eyed, as a border guard entered the carriage. Stephan, on the back seat, held Walter's hand firmly in his. Žofie-Helene sat across the aisle with the thumb-sucking boy beside her and the basket with the baby at her feet. The mercifully silent baby. But if the soldier began tearing through the car, if the children started screaming like children on the other carriages had, the baby would wail. She was just a baby.

Stephan wished Tante Truus were here with them. He wished she knew about the baby, knew how to explain the baby. But she'd disappeared with one of the other adults, following the twins Walter did not want to join any more than Stephan did.

"Everyone will stand," the border guard demanded.

They all obeyed, and the guard looked them over, his eyes lighting when he noticed Žofie-Helene. Stephan didn't like that at all: the way the man eyed Žofie's long hair and her big green eyes, her breasts straining at her blouse.

The guard, as if sensing his thoughts had been read, turned his gaze to Stephan. Stephan, with Walter's hand in his, looked to the carriage floor.

Her necklace, he remembered. Žofie-Helene's necklace that was too valuable to be taken on the train—her necklace that Tante Truus had sent her back to leave with Herr Perger—was in Stephan's pocket.

The guard, still watching Stephan, said, "I will call your name, and you will repeat it, and only when I nod will you sit."

The guard began reading from a list, checking after each name to see which of the children repeated it, and nodding. Stephan, after each name, tried to judge whether he might surreptitiously take a seat. Carl

Füchsl wasn't meant to be on this car; what had he been thinking? He was ten years older than the boy whose name he was to listen for, a boy who was supposed to be on another carriage. And he hadn't even thought to tell Walter or Žofie about it.

The guard, as if suspecting that Stephan meant somehow to deceive him, glanced back at him again and again as he read the list, and, one by one, the children sat.

I'm an impostor, Stephan thought. I'm an impostor who will be given away by my unsuspecting brother. I'll be beaten this time the way Papa was beaten, or shot the way that man was shot outside the burning synagogue as he watched his wife bleed to death.

The guard called out the name of the cross-eyed redhead Walter said had been in front of them in the line when they signed up. The man stared at her, disgusted, before checking off her name. He repeated her name and told her she could sit.

"Walter Neuman," the guard called out.

Walter repeated his name, and the guard looked at him still holding tightly to Stephan's hand, his Peter Rabbit held to his chest.

The guard made a check mark on the list and said, "You may sit, but the rabbit stands."

Walter, terrified, clung to Peter and stared.

The guard said, "You Jews have no sense of humor."

Stephan leaned down to whisper to Walter, "Peter rides on your ticket, he does whatever you do," thinking it didn't matter about himself but he had to keep Walter safe.

"Žofie-Helene Perger," the guard called.

Žofie repeated, "Žofie-Helene Perger."

The guard looked her up and down but didn't nod, as if he wanted her to sit before he'd allowed it, to have that excuse to do something to her. Stephan didn't want to think what it was the guard might do. He felt Walter's little hand in his. He couldn't afford to think about what the guard might do to Žofie-Helene.

Žofie stood calmly, waiting—so sure and beautiful, like he imagined the woman from Zweig's *Amok* must look. Everything here running amok, like it did in the story. The necklace. The baby. The *Kaleidoscope* that was too dangerous to have been brought, but he hadn't been coming on the train when he'd packed his suitcase, he'd been number 610. He watched the guard, seeing the obsession of the doctor from Zweig's story in the man's hungry look at Žofie, or perhaps in his own reaction to the guard's hunger.

Looking through her smudged glasses.

The notebook. Everything he'd written in it. They would need nothing more to condemn him than his own writing, even if they believed him to be this Carl Füchsl he was not, even if they accepted the mistake of ten years on the paperwork, even if Walter did not, in failing to understand what had not been explained to him—why hadn't he thought to explain it?—give him away.

The border guard took a step toward them.

Still, the baby was quiet.

The guard approached Žofie, closer, then closer and closer until he was in the aisle between Stephan and Žofie, facing Žofie but so close that Stephan could reach out, Stephan could put his hands around the man's skinny neck. No more a man than Stephan himself, he realized, and Mutti's voice echoed, *I know you're young, but you must be the man now.* All over Germany, boys were masquerading as men.

The guard reached out and touched Žofie's hair, the way Stephan had longed to touch it since he'd seen her at the station, her hair flowing loose and wavy down her back.

The guard nodded.

Žofie stood regarding him.

Don't do it, Žofie, Stephan thought. Don't do anything. Just take your seat.

Stephan raised Walter's hand in his, so that Žofie might see it, and he coughed, a quick, stifled sound.

Neither Žofie nor the guard turned. From outside, the sounds of the search. A dog barking.

Stephan put a finger to his lips, willing Walter to remain silent. "It's okay, Wall," he said, whispering loudly, as if he meant not to be heard.

Žofie and the guard both turned at the sound of his voice in the silent carriage.

When the guard turned back to Žofie, he nodded again and, mercifully, Žofie sat.

The guard returned to the front of the carriage and read the last few names one at a time. Stephan watched with growing dread as each child took his seat.

Only Stephan was left standing.

The guard said, "You are not on the list."

Stephan said, "Carl Füchsl."

Walter looked up at him. Stephan swallowed nervously, willing his brother not to give him away. The seconds ticked as slowly as centuries. Sweat trickled down his back, and gathered on his hairless lip. Why hadn't he listened to Tante Truus? Why hadn't he done what she'd told him to do?

The guard looked him up and down.

Stephan stood absolutely still, Walter's hand in his, which was damp, too, wet skin against wet skin.

The guard examined his list as if the mistake might be his—nearly as afraid as Stephan was, in his own way. When had the world begun to run on nothing but fear?

"Carl Füchsl," the guard repeated.

Stephan nodded.

"You will spell it," the guard demanded.

Stephan tried not to show the alarm he felt: a boy would never misspell his own name.

"C–A—"

"Your surname, you fool," the man said.

Žofie said, "He's number one hundred and twenty."

The guard turned to her.

"It's five factorial," she said.

The guard stared at her, uncomprehending.

"We're all identified by number," she said. "It will be easier to find him by his number."

The guard eyed her for an uncomfortable moment, then turned and left the carriage. Stephan watched him step down to the platform, then go to consult with an officer.

He said to Walter, "It's our secret, Wall, but if anyone asks, I'm Carl Füchsl, okay?"

He took Žofie's necklace from his pocket and stuck it in the seam of the seat behind him, where no one was sitting, no one else could be blamed. There was no hiding the book or the notebook, but he could hide the necklace, at least.

He repeated, "I'm Carl Füchsl. Number one hundred and twenty."

"It's five factorial, a very lucky number," Žofie-Helene said.

"I'm Carl Füchsl," Stephan said a third time.

"Forever?" Walter asked.

"Just until we get to England," Stephan said.

"After the boat," Walter said.

"Yes, after we get off the ferry," Stephan agreed.

"Is Žofie-Helene still you, then?"

The guard reappeared at the front of the car. "You are on the wrong carriage, Carl Füchsl," he said. "Now you will all open your luggage and empty your pockets."

Stephan, with no choice, opened his suitcase along with the others. The edges of his book's pages were wavy with the dampness from the diapers. His journal too was damp, but not likely so damp as to be unreadable.

As the guard went through other children's suitcases, Stephan surreptitiously wrapped the diapers around the book and the journal, then wrapped the whole mess up in his single change of clothes.

The guard picked through the children's belongings, tossing them so that they landed on the dirty carriage floor. No one questioned him. When he found a photo of one of the children's family in a small silver frame, he made the child strip his clothes off, and he shook them out. When he found nothing else, he pocketed the frame, photograph and all, and continued on to the next child. He found a gold coin hidden in another girl's coat lining, and he smacked the child hard across the face so that her lip split open. Tears rolled down her cheeks, but she remained silent as he pocketed the coin.

Just as the border guard reached Žofie and Walter and him in the last row, the smell of excrement filled the air.

The guard looked to the little thumb-sucking boy.

Please, make the mistake, Stephan thought.

The guard looked from the boy to the basket at Žofie's feet. He looked to Žofie, then to the basket again. He licked his lips and swallowed, a hard Adam's apple bobbing in his skinny, hairless neck.

Stephan held Walter's hand tightly and said, "The basket is mine."

"It's not," Žofie insisted. "It's mine."

They all waited for the border guard to demand they open the basket. In the silence, the baby cooed. Just one small sound. One unmistakable baby sound.

The guard looked as terrified as Stephan felt.

"What is taking so long here?" a voice demanded.

A second border guard entered at the front of the car, and the first snapped to a salute, saying, "Heil Hitler!" He glanced at the basket; he didn't want to be the one to turn in a baby, Stephan could see that in his face now, but he couldn't be caught letting an unlisted child go, and there were no babies listed for this train.

"Ugh," the second border guard said. "These dirty Jews, they don't even know how to use a toilet."

The whole car watched him.

"If they're all in order here, we're rid of them," he said to the first guard. "They'll be the problem of the Dutch."

IN ANOTHER DIRECTION

Žofie leaned over, trying to quiet the baby still in the basket as the train crept out of the station, toward a red hut and a dirty white fence hung with a Nazi flag. Was that the border with the Netherlands? The train stopped suddenly, knocking Žofie's head against the seat back in front of her. The train lurched forward, and stopped again.

The children sat silently, waiting, the only noise the baby, who fussed as the train jerked.

The train began to move slowly backward, away from the red house.

Walter said to Stephan, "Are we going back home to Mutti?" with the same hopefulness a small bit of Žofie felt too, the part that imagined that if she had a second try at this she could at least bring her sister with her, that if a baby with no one at all to take care of her could come, then Jojo could too.

The train stopped again. From outside, the clanking of metal being struck by a hammer rang out.

The children sat perfectly still and quiet, terrified.

The train lurched slightly again; it was hard to tell in which direction, but it was only the one little bit. Žofie looked to Stephan. He had no more idea than she did what was happening.

The train began moving so slowly that she couldn't tell which way they were going. There ought to be some paradox for this, she thought as she watched the red house, trying to tell if it was getting closer or farther away. But if there was one, she couldn't call it to mind.

The train whistle sounded, the train moving forward now, Žofie was pretty sure of it. The little red house was getting closer, wasn't it?

She watched expectantly, focused on the swastika flag, the red house, the coal piles behind it.

Stephan came to her seat, settled next to her, and pulled Walter up into his lap. He put his arm around her shoulder, his touch somehow heavy and light at the same time. The Stephan-is-touching-me paradox. He didn't say anything. He just sat with his arm around her, and Walter held Peter Rabbit to her face and made a kissing noise, quietly, and she tried not to think of the Peter Rabbit she never did buy for Jojo.

Slowly at first, then more quickly, the flag and the red house and the coal piles grew larger in her vision, although of course not in reality. They were passing the house, the sound of the train on the tracks changing from *tjoek-tjoek-tjoek-tjoek* to *tjoeketoek-tjoeketoek-tjoeketoek*, when a jubilant "Hurrah!" sounded from the carriage behind them, where Tante Truus was. The children around her, hearing the others, took up the cheer, "Hurrah! Hurrah! Hurrah! Hurrah!"

CARL FÜCHSL

The train stopped again just minutes later, this time at a station in the Netherlands, where there were no soldiers and no dogs. A woman in a white-fur-collared coat approached the carriage with a huge tray of packages of some sort in hand. She tapped on the dirty window three seats ahead of where Žofie sat, and one of the older children opened it. The carriage doors were still locked.

"Who would like cookies?" the woman asked, and she began handing the packages to the little hands reaching out the window. She told them there were baked goods and butter and milk coming, but they could eat the cookies now, they could eat as many cookies as they wanted, even before they had proper food.

"Not so many that it will make you sick, though!" the woman said brightly, and she held the tray up to the window, and the three children there passed the packages back to everyone before they took ones for themselves.

All the length of the carriage, other windows were lowered.

Žofie saw, outside her own dirty window, Tante Truus enfolded into the arms of a man who kissed the top of her head. Žofie felt the weight of Stephan's arm still across the back of her hair, his hand on her shoulder. She thought of Mary Morstan, of Dr. Watson talking of his sad bereavement in "The Adventure of the Empty House," and later moving back in to No. 221B Baker Street with Sherlock Holmes. She couldn't say why she felt so sad when everyone was so happy.

The doors were unsealed, and more women boarded with more food and with hugs and kisses, strangers mothering these strange children in this strange new country. Walter hopped down from Stephan's lap, and Stephan hurried after him. The little thumb-sucking boy did too, leaving Žofie alone with baby Johanna, who slept in the basket despite all the commotion.

Johanna was such a good baby. Žofie wanted to take the infant in her arms, but she was afraid these women might take her away.

She watched through the dirty window as, out on the platform, Tante Truus spoke to the man who had kissed her head, then left him and boarded the front carriage, taking one of the chaperones with her. A minute or two later, she debarked the front carriage and climbed onto the second one.

Women escorted children from the front carriage. Not all of them. Just a few.

In the carriage around Žofie, children returned to their seats, carrying milk cartons and chattering, released from the prison of their fears. Žofie wanted to feel that way too. Stephan and Walter and the boy who never had told her his name returned with a carton of milk for her. She set it on the seat beside her before anyone else could sit there.

Stephan looked from the milk carton to her. She looked away from the little bit of hurt there in his eyes. He sat in the seat across the aisle, and the boys climbed up next to him.

Tante Truus boarded their carriage and called for everyone's attention. The carriage quieted, all eyes turned to her. She explained that most of the children would be going on through the Netherlands all the way to Hook of Holland, where they would board a ferry for England. There wasn't room for all of them on the first ferry, though. There was only room for five hundred. So her friends had arranged for one hundred of the children to stay in the Netherlands for just two days, until the ferry returned for them.

"I want to go wherever you go, Stephan," Walter said.

Stephan leaned close to him and whispered, "Can you remember to call me 'Carl' until we get to England? It won't be long now."

Walter nodded earnestly.

Tante Truus said a friend of hers named Mrs. Van Lange would come to read from a list of names, and those children were to go with the ladies. There would be hot chocolate for them in the station, she said, and beds for them to sleep in. Suddenly all the children wanted to stay in the Netherlands.

Žofie was surprised to see that Tante Truus's friend was pregnant. She stood at the head of the carriage and read a dozen names of children who were then taken in hand by the ladies, their suitcases found. She seemed so nice that Žofie considered telling her about the baby. Surely if she was about to have her own baby, she would let Žofie keep Johanna.

Mrs. Van Lange called the name of a child in the seat in front of her—one of the girls who'd been so intent on the Sherlock Holmes story she'd told them. When a woman came and took her hand, her seatmate began to cry.

"It's okay," Žofie whispered to her. "You can sit with Johanna and me." And she lifted the child up and sat her in her lap. The baby was still quiet. No one here had seen the baby.

They watched out the window as the children walked across the platform. Žofie tried not to think of those little twin boys who were taken away in Germany.

After the children who were to stay had exited the carriage, the rest of them settled in, waiting for the train to set off again. After a long wait, though, Mrs. Van Lange returned, calling out, "Carl Füchsl? Is Carl Füchsl on this carriage?"

Žofie felt a shock of alarm. Walter couldn't lose Stephan. She couldn't lose Stephan herself.

"Carl Füchsl?" Mrs. Van Lange repeated.

Žofie glanced across at Stephan still sitting there, holding tightly to his brother's hand.

"Carl Füchsl," Mrs. Van Lange said yet again.

One of the other women consulted with her.

"I know, but he wasn't on the car he was supposed to be on," Mrs. Van Lange explained to the woman, who suggested perhaps the child had gone mute, as several of the children had.

"Listen, children," Mrs. Van Lange called out. "If you are near Carl Füchsl—number one hundred and twenty—please tell us."

Stephan surreptitiously turned his number so it wasn't visible. No one answered.

"We'd better get Mrs. Wijsmuller," Mrs. Van Lange said.

TOGETHER

Truus boarded the carriage Klara van Lange was on, the second to the last, saying, "One of the children is missing?" Klara was now further along in her pregnancy than Truus had ever been, but would not be dissuaded from their work—albeit only on this side of the border now.

"Carl Füchsl," Klara said.

"I see," Truus said.

She scanned the children in the carriage, finding Stephan Neuman in the back row. The boy held his brother in his lap. Of course he wouldn't leave without his brother. Well, Stephan Neuman was a complication, and the complication didn't end here, anyway. The boy was out of German hands, but he still needed to be gotten into England. She couldn't risk that there might be some delay, as he would turn eighteen in just a few weeks.

"Let me see the list," she said, and she took it from Klara and scanned it. "All right," she said to the children, "who would like to stop here for hot chocolate and a nice warm bed?"

Nearly every hand went up. Well, of course they did. What child wouldn't want off this train, now that it was more or less safe?

Žofie-Helene said, "Tante Truus, Elsie here was quite devastated when Dora was called and she wasn't. They're friends from Vienna. I think their mothers registered them together so that they could stay together."

Stephan Neuman looked alarmed as Truus headed toward them down the aisle of the carriage, saying, "Elsie, would you like to go have a cup of hot chocolate and some cookies with Dora?"

The child clung to Žofie—torn between the girl and her friend—but already Žofie was setting the child in the aisle and urging her forward, seeming as alarmed that Truus might take Stephan as Stephan himself was. How could they fail to see that she meant to take another child?

"It's all right, Stephan," she said to the boy. "You can go ahead to England with your brother."

The little brother, little Walter Neuman, raised his rabbit and said in a pretend rabbit voice, "He's not Walter's brother. He's Carl Füchsl."

Truus scooped up the little girl and turned, not wanting the dear little boy to see the laugher in her eyes. Heavens, that was just what she herself needed: a stuffed rabbit to take responsibility for the little lies she sometimes needed to tell.

Had this little Elsie soiled herself? But no. Truus supposed this was the smell of sixty children in a single train carriage for a day and a night and a day again.

As she reached the front of the carriage, she turned back. Was that the sound of a baby? Lord, now she really was imagining things.

She glanced out the window to the anchor of Joop, trying to push back the memory of those new babies being delivered to new mothers while she lay alone under the white sheets in the white-walled hospital room. It must be seeing Klara van Lange so pregnant that brought it on.

"Oh dear, we're forgetting Elsie's suitcase," she said.

Already, Stephan Neuman was hurrying up the aisle with the suitcase, making an unreasonable clatter in the process.

There it was again. A baby cooing, she could swear it.

Stephan delivered the suitcase to her, and with it a long soliloquy about how much Elsie had liked the Sherlock Holmes story Žofie-Helene had told her, for heaven's sake, while seeming to be trying to hurry her along out of the carriage.

"Thank you, Stephan," she said in a tone meant to hush him, so she could better hear.

The poor boy looked chastened. She oughtn't have been so short. Was she hearing things?

The children sat silently. Too silently.

She turned little Elsie over to Klara, to take the child into the station and find Dora. She would tell Joop about the substitution herself.

She turned back to the carriage and stood silently watching, waiting. The children stared back at her. No one spoke.

Their silence might be hope or fear. She oughtn't suspect these children of trying to hide something from her. Why would they hide anything, now that they were safely out of the German Reich?

Again, the sound of a baby, coming from the back of the carriage.

Truus wandered slowly up the aisle, listening.

Again, the cooing of a child, moving toward a fuss.

She examined each seat, still wondering if the sound of the child wasn't in her imagination alone.

At the back, there between Žofie-Helene's feet, was a picnic basket. From inside it came again the gurgle of a baby.

Truus exhaled relief: she hadn't gone off her rocker, she wasn't imagining babies who didn't exist.

She reached for the basket.

Žofie-Helene, trying to block her, accidentally knocked it, setting the child inside to fussing in earnest. The girl, with defiance in her clear green eyes, opened the basket, lifted the infant, and snuggled her into silence. Truus stood watching, unable to believe there was a baby here, even now that she could see the dear little thing reaching for Žofie's eyeglasses.

"Žofie-Helene," she said, her voice not much more than a whisper, "where in heaven's name did this baby come from?"

The girl didn't answer.

Truus called up the aisle, "Klara!" Thinking the child would have to go to the orphanage with the one hundred until she could sort this out.

But Klara was outside, of course, taking little Elsie to join her friend Dora.

"She's my sister," Žofie said.

"Your sister?" Truus repeated, confused.

"Johanna," Žofie said.

"But, Žofie-Helene, you didn't . . . A picnic basket? You didn't have a picnic basket—"

"When I ran back with the necklace like you told me," Žofie said. "I got her then."

Truus watched the girl, so comfortable with the baby. She did have a sister, Truus remembered that. It had been devastating, to have to tell the grandfather that the sister was too young. So much devastation stuck in her memory from that day.

"Your sister is a toddler, Žofie," she said, remembering. *I'm a big girl. I'm three.*

The baby took the girl's finger in her grasp and made a sound that might have been laughter. How old would a baby have to be to laugh?

"If Britain can take a whole train of children," Žofie said, "they can take one more baby. She'll stay on my lap on the ferry. She won't need a seat."

Truus looked from Žofie-Helene to Stephan. Where had this child really come from? Žofie guarded the poor little thing as surely as if the child were her own.

The girl had been so intent on saving this boy. But they were impossibly young. Surely they couldn't . . .

Truus reached over and edged the blanket back from the baby's face, to better see. A baby with no papers. Just a few months old. You couldn't tell anything about such a young baby.

DISMANTLING

Yes, six hundred train chocolates," Michael said to the assembled chocolatiers. "I do understand that Arnold alone usually decorates the trains, but unless he can do them all himself in a very few hours—"

Better to deliver six hundred imperfect trains than to miss the delivery.

Six hundred. The party the chocolates were to be made for, he now understood, was a celebration of Eichmann's "success in ridding Austria of six hundred little Jews."

Six hundred, Michael thought, including Stephan and Walter.

"Use whatever chocolates we have," he directed the chocolatiers. "It's the train Obersturmführer Eichmann cares about, not the filling."

"Yes, you can explain to the others why their orders will be short," he said. To most of Vienna now, the fact of Eichmann placing such a sizable order of Wirth chocolates would raise their stature, and the others would understand it was a request not to be denied.

AFTER HE'D FINISHED with the chocolatiers and made arrangements for the delivery, Michael told Anita he was not to be further disturbed, and he returned to his office. He closed and locked the door, then sat on the couch for a long time, taking in the portrait of the Lisl he'd fallen in love with. The dark hair and dark, sultry eyes. The lips that, with a simple brush against his neck, drove him mad with desire. She had slept with Kokoschka, he supposed, although he'd never asked her about it and she had never offered, and he didn't actually want to know.

It was in her cheeks, the scratched rage there that was not Lisl's, but rather the painter's. So perhaps she hadn't slept with him; perhaps the rage was at her refusal.

He quietly lifted the portrait from the wall, set it on the floor, and began to pry the backing from the frame. He dismantled the painting careful step by careful step, removing the canvas even from its backing.

When the painting was freed of its moorings, he slid the empty frame into the closet, to be disposed of after dark late some night.

He pulled out the other painting, the one he'd stored in the closet, and he dismantled it in the same careful manner.

He rolled the two canvases carefully together and tied a string around each end, then put on his overcoat and slid them underneath. He carefully buttoned them inside, feeling the hard thump of his heart at this crazy risk, and he walked out of the office, down the stairs, and out of the building, onto the Vienna street.

AT THE HOTEL METROPOLE

Eichmann sat alone, only Tier beside him, at the sole table on the upper level of the grand Hotel Metropole dining room, the wall of glass windows behind him, the chandeliers at his level, and, below, every German of any importance in occupied Vienna. His guests were finishing a fine meal as the band played. He would speak in a moment, just a few words to proclaim the triumph of ridding Vienna of six hundred of its little Jews at the expense of the British. It *was* his triumph; he had commanded that it would be done only on his terms, and so it had been.

"On my terms, Tier," he said.

He would have the Jew Friedmann brought in tonight and kept in a cell in the basement for a night or two, he decided as he frowned out over the people sitting together below, laughing and visiting. Why had he allowed these people to bring their spouses, with Vera still in Berlin?

A waiter came to deliver him the first dessert, as he'd instructed. The man bowed and set the crystal dish before him: a special torte made by the chef in Eichmann's honor, dressed with Vienna's finest chocolates, each decorated with a train.

Below him now, waiters cleared the dinner dishes as others stood at the ready, with trays of identical tortes to serve to the guests only after Eichmann had eaten his own and given his speech.

He raised his fork and carved off a bite even as the waiter poured coffee from a silver server into his china cup. He wished to get on with this, to get it over with. At the bitter smell of the coffee, though, he set the fork back on the plate, the torte uneaten. The nerve of that horrible Dutchwoman, suggesting she might be worthy of drinking coffee with him.

He pushed the coffee away.

"I find I'm no longer hungry," he said to the waiter. "You may remove my coffee and feed my torte to Tier."

THE LIGHTS OF HARWICH

Young Walter Neuman was the first. The ties of the *Prague* were hardly thrown off and the shore was still well in sight when the North Sea seized the boy's stomach. Truus was helping another child settle in a ferry bunk not ten feet away. The boy's brother had just opened his suitcase and extracted a horrid bundle that, as he unpeeled the layers, turned out to be the baby's diapers, all carefully rinsed but still quite soggy, and similarly wet handkerchiefs, and, at the bundle's core, a journal and a book. She thought the boy might cry at the state of the book, its cover expanding from the dampness of the wrappings, the pages wavy and stuck together.

His little brother set his stuffed Peter Rabbit on Stephan's knee and used the rabbit's paw to open the book and turn a clump of pages.

Stephan said, "I'm not sure even Peter can read this anymore."

He laughed so bravely. Then little Walter said he was going to be sick, and promptly made good on the threat by retching right onto the opened pages. That had been hours ago. The first, but far from the last.

Truus emerged now onto the ferry's deck, a child's hand in each of hers. "The fresh night air will help, if we can stay warm enough," she assured the children, "but do stay back here on the bench, away from the railing and the sea."

The little boy—number 500, his tag read underneath the streak of vomit she wiped away with an already filthy handkerchief—took his thumb from his mouth long enough to say, "I'm going to be sick again."

"I don't believe there is anything left inside you, Toma," she said comfortingly. "But even if there is, you stay here. Stay back from the railing."

This sea was no easy crossing in the best of weather. Truus might be sick herself if she could afford to be, if there weren't so many children to tend to. How had she imagined she could manage this? The children sick, or crying, or mercifully asleep from exhaustion. What a dreadful first impression they would make on the good people of England.

"Can I say hello to the baby?" petite little thirteen-year-old Erika Leiter asked. She was a furniture-maker's daughter, one of the few children who would go directly to a sponsor in Camborne rather than wait at one of the summer camps until a home could be found.

Truus followed Erika's gaze to see Žofie-Helene standing at the ferry's rail, as green at the gills as any of the children.

"Don't move!" she commanded the children, and she rushed over and took the infant from Žofie-Helene.

"I promised her mother I would keep her all the way to England," Žofie said.

"The two of you will be *swimming* to England," Truus said. "You come find me when the sea is done with you, and I'll put her back in your care. Now, be careful. Why don't you step back from the rail? Take a seat on one of the benches."

"I don't want to be sick all over the deck," Žofie said.

"I assure you one more will make no difference," Truus said.

She took Žofie's arm with her free hand and guided her back away from the rail and the sea below it, to a vacant seat on the bench beside Erika. "Keep your eyes on the horizon," she said. "It will help you feel better."

Žofie-Helene sat with the other two, facing the sea. After a moment, she said, "Those are the lights of Harwich, I suppose."

Just visible in the distance: a faint, blinking light that might be the coast of England, in which case they had perhaps another hour. "Maybe the lighthouse at Orford Ness," Truus said. "Or Dovercourt—that's quite near Harwich. You won't see Harwich until we round Dovercourt, though, as it's in a protected bay."

"It's a line from a Sherlock Holmes story, 'His Last Bow,'" Žofie said. "'Those are the lights of Harwich, I suppose.'"

"Is it?" Truus said. "Well, you just keep your eyes on the light and it will help you feel better. Now, I'm going to take the babe to one of the other girls."

She took the infant not to another girl, though, but instead to a quiet spot out of the view of Žofie-Helene. She sat on a bench herself and slowly rocked the child—Johanna, Žofie-Helene had taken to calling her, Žofie's own sister's name. Truus really ought to separate the two. This would come to no good end.

There was no place for the baby in England yet, and the thought of explaining another child, of asking the English to take care of a baby they weren't expecting and had no home for . . . Really, she ought to take the child back to Amsterdam until arrangements could be made for a home for her.

"You might like to live in Amsterdam, mightn't you, child-with-no-name?" she cooed, trying to push back the memory of little Adele Weiss in the tiny coffin. Truus hadn't told even Joop about the tiny coffin.

She began to sing to the child then, a popular old song, "The moon has risen; the golden stars shine in the sky bright and clear."

She looked up, startled, half expecting to see Joop frowning down at her, although of course Joop was home alone, asleep in his pajamas, a single plate waiting on the table for the solitary breakfast he'd make with a bit of bread from the bread keeper and chocolate sprinkles from the jar. It was a child standing before her, vomit down the front of his coat. Several more children gathered around her then, and a teenage girl came running, exclaiming that two of the boys were fighting.

"One of them bit me, Tante Truus!" the girl said.

She showed Truus her hand—superficial bite marks. Truus reluctantly turned her seat and the baby over to the girl.

"Hold her until I come back," she said. "I'll see about the boys."

Then to the sick child, "Come with me, dear heart. Let's get you cleaned up."

And when she was done with settling the squabbling boys and cleaning up the child, she slipped back down to check on the children belowdecks. There were Stephan and his brother, Walter, fast asleep together with the stuffed rabbit. On the floor was the book—beyond saving. She tipped it to see its spine: a volume by Stefan Zweig titled *Kaleidoscope*.

The end of a gold chain Stephan never should have brought with him dangled from his pocket. Truus ought to reprimand him for it. He'd put the whole transport at risk, bringing both a gold chain and a banned book on the train? But then he hadn't expected to be on the train; the poor boy had come to send his brother off alone. And it was done now, and he'd gotten away with it somehow, and these boys had come from such wealth—not just material wealth, but wealth of family—and they were left with so little, not even this book that the boy had sacrificed for the baby's sake.

She tucked the chain more securely into his pocket and stroked his hair, thinking Joop would have liked to have a son like this boy. Joop would have loved to have a son.

HARWICH

The air was cold against gloves and hats and coats buttoned to chins as the ferry floated in toward the dock at Harwich. A film cameraman and photographers recorded the children watching somberly from the *Prague*'s rail as waves splashed and seabirds circled and called. Truus's heart broke for these poor dears now that they were in sight of the safety of England—safety without their parents, without their families or friends, in a country where so few of them knew the language, and none of them the customs. They would go to good homes, though, surely. Who but good people would take refugee children from another land and another religion into their lives for what might be years?

Truus, seeing Helen Bentwich waiting on shore with a clipboard, left the lining up of the children by number to the other adults. She'd considered starting with the problem children first—the baby and Stephan Neuman—but decided in the end to bring the children down single file by number. It was what Helen had requested, and although some little piece of this niggled at Truus—these children with names and personalities and desires, with futures now, being reduced to numbers on cards hung at their necks—there was some benefit in having the process well under way before any explaining was required. She was relieved that it was Helen to whom the explanation would be made. Helen, the woman who never said no. There were so few of those in the world these days.

Truus felt she ought to say something profound to the children, but what was there to say? She settled for telling them what good children they were.

"Your parents are all so proud of you," she said. "Your parents all love you so much."

The dock lines were thrown down and tied, the plank lowered to connect these children to the country that would be their new home. Truus took the hand of the first child—little Alan Cohen, with his number 1 card at his neck—and began slowly down the gangway. The children followed in frightened silence, the youngest ones clutching the single baby dolls or stuffed animals they were allowed to bring, as was Alan. Of course they were frightened. Truus was a bit frightened herself, now that it was done, now that she had been a part of separating these children from their parents. *My God, my God, why have you forsaken them?* But of course these children weren't the forsaken ones; like Jesus, these were the children who would live again.

She reached the bottom of the plank, she reached England, with little Alan Cohen's hand holding tightly to hers.

"I didn't know you would be here, Helen!" she said. "What a treat, and a relief."

The two women embraced, with Truus still holding Alan Cohen's hand.

"I couldn't resist coming, knowing you would be here," Helen Bentwich said.

"Heavens, I wasn't sure I would be until this minute!" Truus said, and they laughed.

"Mrs. Bentwich, may I introduce you to Alan Cohen?" she said, handing over the boy's hand to Helen, who took it in hers and held it fondly, reassuringly. Truus said to the boy, "Alan, das ist Frau Bentwich."

Alan regarded Helen cautiously. Well, of course he did.

"Alan is from Salzburg," Truus said. The boy's family had been moved to Vienna after the German invasion, to the Leopoldstadt ghetto in which the Germans were gathering Austria's Jews until they could decide what to do with them, but his home was Salzburg, and

Truus wanted to honor that, Truus wanted Helen to know that each child was an individual, not a number, even number one. "He's five years old, and he has two younger brothers. His father is a banker." His father had been a banker in Salzburg until his livelihood was forbidden him, but Helen Bentwich would know that. Helen's family were bankers too, and Jewish, and well aware of the way Germany was depriving its Jews of everything.

"Willkommen in England, Alan," Helen Bentwich said.

Truus could have wept at the sound of the boy's name repeated, the child welcomed in his own language.

As Truus took up the hand of the next child in line, seven-year-old Harry Heber, Helen gently stroked the head of Alan Cohen's stuffed . . . well, it was hard to say what it was; it had been loved beyond recognition.

"Und wer ist das?" Helen asked the boy. *Who is this?*

Alan said brightly, "Herr Bär. Er ist ein Bär!"

"Why he *is* a bear, isn't he?" Helen said brightly. "Well, Mr. Cohen and Mr. Bear, Mrs. Bates here is going to help you onto the bus." She pointed to two double-decker buses waiting a short distance away. "The other children will join you, but I'm afraid that as you are the first, it might be, for just a minute . . ."

Truus eyed what seemed, despite the long distance the boy had already traveled, an impossibly long stretch of emptiness between them and the waiting buses. She said to the boy in his own language, "Alan, why don't you and Mr. Bear wait here for just a minute while I introduce Harry and Ruth to Mrs. Bentwich, then Mrs. Bates will help the three of you. That way, you and Mr. Bear won't have to wait alone on the bus. Would that be all right?"

The boy nodded solemnly.

Helen and Truus exchanged an understanding glance.

"Mrs. Bentwich," Truus said, gently squeezing Harry's hand, "may I introduce you to Harry Heber?" Again handing over the boy's hand to Helen. "And this is Harry's big sister, Ruth. They're from Innsbruck, where their family are drapers." The poor father at the Vienna station had said a blessing over his precious children. "Ruth likes to draw," she said. The girl had told Truus about the charcoal pencils in her suitcase; it was all the girl had now: a few clothes and her drawing pencils. But Ruth and Harry did have each other. A sibling was more than many of the children had.

TWO BUSES HAD been loaded and Truus had said goodbye in her heart to more than one hundred of the children, the older ones bound for Lowestoft and the younger for Dovercourt, when Stephan Neuman reached the front of the line. He held in his hand only the single suitcase, freed of the soggy diapers and handkerchiefs, leaving only the one change of clothes, the soggy journal, and the ruined book.

"Mrs. Bentwich," she said to Helen, "may I introduce to you Stephan Neuman. Carl Füchsl had measles. We felt it better to substitute a healthy child rather than bring you a boatload of disease."

Helen said, "Thank you for that, Truus!"

"Stephan's father—" Stephan's father had been a chocolate maker before he died in the awful night of violence against Germany's Jews. "Stephan's family have given the world some of its best chocolates, and Stephan himself is a fine writer, I'm told," she said, remembering Žofie-Helene pleading the boy's case at registration. "He's seventeen, and his English is excellent. Now, I know you are sending the older children who haven't yet been placed with families to Lowestoft, but Stephan's younger brother, Walter, is back in line with a friend of theirs who is also quite responsible. Perhaps you'll send Stephan and their friend, Žofie-Helene Perger, with Walter to Dovercourt? I imagine you need some older children to help mind the younger ones, and one who speaks English would be such a help."

Helen crossed off Carl Füchsl beside number 120, inserted Stephan's name and age in his place, and noted Dovercourt.

Truus said, "You go ahead on the bus, Stephan."

"I promised my mother I would not let Walter out of my sight," Stephan said in perfectly competent if accented English.

Truus said, "But you weren't even meant to be on the transport."

"I told her I was. I did not think she would let him go otherwise. And she is . . ." He swallowed back emotion. "And my mother is dead."

Truus put a hand on his shoulder, saying, "Tot, Stephan? Das habe ich nicht gewusst—"

Stephan, flustered, said, "No, not dead. Is . . ."

Truus, seeing that the word, whether he knew it or he didn't, would not come to his mortified, exhausted tongue, explained to Helen that the boys' mother was sick, not wanting to say precisely how sick but trying to convey in her expression that these boys would soon have no one but each other. How many of these children would face that prospect? But Truus couldn't change that; she could only do what she could do.

Helen Bentwich said, "Stephan, why don't you wait by the bus for your brother, then. I'll make sure you and he can stay together."

THE LINE WAS nearing its end when Truus, introducing each child to Helen by name, came to Žofie-Helene and the baby, with little Walter as well. The baby was quiet, perhaps sleeping. She was such a good baby. Who wouldn't want to take in such a good baby?

"Mrs. Bentwich, may I introduce you to Žofie-Helene Perger," she said.

"Helene, like my name, although mine isn't so beautifully pronounced," Helen said.

"Žofie has been good enough to take care of this baby all the way from Vienna," Truus said. "The infant was . . ." Good Lord, she was going to cry right here, right now, just when these children most needed her to be strong.

Helen touched a hand to her arm, steadying her as surely as she had that first day they met, as Truus stood in Helen's office with the snow dome in hand and allowed herself for just that moment to imagine a child who might look like Joop, who might someday build a snowman, or throw a snowball at her, and make her laugh.

"The infant was put on the train by its mother," Truus managed, still unable to fathom that, to imagine the depths of despair that would lead a mother to set such a helpless child in the hands of a girl not much more than a child herself, without so much as a name or any hope of being able to find her again. A mother who imagined she was giving her child over to be brought to safety when in fact the child might slip from a girl's arms, she might fall over the rail of the ferry and into the sea. She might be put to bed at night by a woman who could love her as her own, only to die in a cold quarantine unit in a foreign country. She might die in a quarantine unit when she so easily might have lived with a childless couple who would have loved her, who might somehow have managed to free her mother, to reunite mother and child.

Žofie-Helene said, "She is put on the train in a . . ." She turned to Truus. "How do I say *Picknickkorb*, Tante Truus?"

"In a picnic basket," Truus managed.

Žofie said, "I do not know it was a baby."

Helen eyed the girl, doubt in her gaze. Well, of course it seemed an improbable story, and it was a different story than the girl had at first told Truus. Truus considered again the friendship between Žofie and Stephan, the boy nearly eighteen, and quite clearly in love with her, the girl not much younger, and sweet on him too.

"Well, we have no idea who the child is," she said to Helen. That much was true, for herself at least. "She'll be the first to be placed, I wager: a baby with no claim to her."

Helen studied Truus for such a long moment that Truus had to fight every instinct to turn away.

"What name shall I put for her, then?" Helen asked.

"Johanna," Žofie-Helene said.

"Unnamed baby," Truus said firmly. "Her new parents will be unburdened in their choice of names. I believe if you send them both to Dovercourt, Žofie-Helene will care for the child until she is placed."

Žofie stood silently as Helen checked off her name.

"All right then, you may head for the bus," Helen said.

"Should I wait for Walter?" the girl asked in her own language, addressing Truus. "He was ahead of me. He's five hundred and twenty-two, and I'm five hundred and twenty-three."

Truus smiled. The girl was a fine girl, and who was she to judge, given the life Žofie had been condemned to for the past year, her father dead and her mother God knows where and the family not even Jewish, the mother putting her own family at risk for the sake of others. And she believed the girl, actually. The simplicity of the picnic basket story had the ring of truth: a baby thrust at the last moment into the care of someone who could rescue her, given over only when the mother was left with no alternative and no time to change her mind.

"Mrs. Bentwich, Žofie is going to wait while I introduce you to her friend Walter Neuman," she said, taking Walter's hand now. "He's the younger brother of Stephan Neuman, who has been waiting so patiently all this time."

Helen Bentwich glanced to the bus, where the older Neuman boy was watching. She stroked the head of Walter's stuffed Peter Rabbit. "And who is this fellow?" she asked. "Und wer is er?"

"Das ist Peter," Walter said, and went on to explain in his own language, "Žofie told me he didn't need his own necklace, that he could ride for free on mine."

Žofie nodded encouragement. "It is a special number," she said. "It has ten . . . we say *faktoren*? One, two, three, six, eighteen, twenty-nine, eighty-seven, *Einhundertvierundsiebzig, Zweihunderteinundsechzig, Fünf-hundertzweiundzwanzig.*"

Helen Bentwich laughed delightedly. "Willkommen in England, Walter und Peter," she said. "You are both quite lucky, I see!"

Truus watched as the three children joined the older boy, Stephan lifting Walter into his arms with such joy, and spinning him around, and kissing first the boy and then the stuffed rabbit while Žofie-Helene laughed and the baby woke; the baby made a lovely baby noise that wouldn't bother a soul even if the child kept you awake all night.

"An unclaimed baby, Truus," Helen said.

Truus looked away, to the steely water lapping against the side of the ferry that would take her home, alone.

Helen said, "Have you considered taking her back to Amsterdam?"

"The baby?"

Helen gave her a look. "It isn't too late," she said, raising a hand to catch the bus driver's attention, motioning him to wait. "Until the bus leaves, I can change the list."

Truus watched the children disappear into the bus, trying to imagine their lives here. The baby would be fine. Some kind woman just like Truus herself would long to have a baby. Some woman just like her would see the child as a blessing from God. Some woman would fall in love with the baby, and carry the guilt of secretly hoping no parent would ever come to claim her. What were the chances of that? What would Hitler do to his Jews if there was a war? "If"—as if there were any doubt war was coming, despite the whole world pretending otherwise.

She looked to the short line of children still waiting on the plank, then to the ferry, to the long stretch of sea she would cross again, with no sick children to tend to on the return, nothing to keep her mind from its own painful path through what she had and what she didn't, the family she and Joop would likely never have.

"There are still a hundred children waiting in the Netherlands, another ferry to arrange," she said. "And so many children still in Austria."

Helen took her hand fully in hers just as Truus had taken each child's hand before bidding them goodbye, sending them off to their changed lives.

"Are you sure, Truus?"

Truus was sure of nothing. Had she ever been? As she watched, unable to answer Helen, to say it wasn't the baby that was so hard to set free, a light snow began to fall.

Helen squeezed her hand, understanding somehow what even Truus herself didn't quite understand, and she waved to the bus driver, and the engine coughed to life. A child was calling out from the bus, then—Žofie-Helene was calling from one of the upper deck windows, "We love you, Tante Truus!" And the bus windows, top and bottom, were suddenly filled with waving children calling out, "We love you, Tante Truus! We love you!" There was Walter, waving Peter Rabbit's hand in goodbye. And there was Žofie-Helene, holding the baby up now, waving her motherless little fingers as the bus rumbled off, Žofie-Helene waving too.

DOVERCOURT

Stephan watched out the window, Walter on his lap, as the bus passed under a sign that read "Warner's Holiday Camp." They carried on down an entry road wet with the melt of the light flurry already ended, leaving the world looking colder and yet no more beautiful. The bus pulled to a stop at a compound with a long, low central building and worn, gabled cottages lining a windswept beach.

"Peter is cold," Walter said.

Stephan wrapped his arms around his brother and the stuffed rabbit. "Don't you worry, Peter," he said. "Look, you can see the smoke coming from the fireplace in the big building. I think that's where we're going."

But the children from the bus ahead of them were carrying their suitcases to the little cottages, which had no chimneys at all. Only adults emerging from cars headed toward the larger place.

A woman with a clipboard stepped onto the bus.

"Welcome to England, children!" she said. "I'm Miss Anderson. Please tell me your names as you debark. When I give you your cabin assignment, take your belongings with you."

The children exchanged confused looks.

Žofie whispered to Stephan, "What is 'debark'?"

Stephan didn't know "debark," but he gathered that the woman meant for them to go from the bus to the little cabins. "Die hütten," he said. Surely there would be electric heat in the cabins.

Žofie said, "You go first, but wait for me?"

Stephan and Walter went down the stairs, Žofie and the baby right behind them, and merged into the line of children from the lower level of the bus.

"Stephan and Walter Neuman," Stephan said when it was their turn.

Miss Anderson said, "Walter Neuman, you're in cabin twenty-two, child."

She double-checked her list again. "I don't have a Stephan Neuman," she said. "You've gotten on the wrong bus. This is Dovercourt. The older children are being sent to Lowestoft."

"I'm Carl Füchsl," Stephan said, not sure how to say it more clearly in this second language. "He has . . . *masern*? He is sick. Mrs. Bentwich told me to help with the younger boys."

Miss Anderson eyed him, perhaps assessing whether he was up to the task. "All right, cabin fourteen."

"Tante Truus said my brother and I would be together."

"Who? Oh, all right. Stand here while I arrange the rest of the busload, then we'll sort out a cabin for you both."

Stephan thanked her in his best English, and he nudged Walter, who said "Thank you" in English too.

As they stepped to the side and Miss Anderson addressed Žofie, a man and woman approached Walter.

"Look, George, what a cute little boy!" the woman said.

Stephan said, "We are brothers."

The man said, "Darling, we've already chosen a boy from the German lot. I think one five-year-old is as much as Nanny can manage at her age. We're meant to go inside and collect him."

Miss Anderson, who'd been speaking with Žofie-Helene, said, "Goodness, is the entire bus full of children we aren't to have expected? All right, stand over there by those boys and let me process the rest of the children."

The woman who thought Walter was cute exclaimed, "A baby? George! Oh, I would love a baby who could be our own. They told us there would be none. Please, let's get him before anyone else does."

"These children are just arrived from Austria," her husband said. "They haven't even bathed."

The wife touched the baby's face, saying, "What's your name, little one?"

Žofie-Helene said, "My sister's name is Johanna."

The wife tried to take the baby from Žofie, but Žofie held tight.

"You're awfully old to have a baby sister, aren't you?" the woman said, stepping back as if Žofie might be diseased.

Žofie regarded her with an expression Stephan had never seen in her eyes before: uncertainty. She was so smart. She always knew everything, in their own language.

The woman took her husband's arm and set off for the main building, saying, "Heavens, they're sending us ruined girls."

Stephan stood watching, wanting to rise to Žofie's defense even though he couldn't exactly parse what the woman might mean. Ruin. Like the ruins of Pompeii, which would never be put back together again. You couldn't restore something that was ruined, but a thing could be ruined and yet still perfect.

AN EXIT VISA OF
ANOTHER KIND

Ruchele began weeping long before Žofie-Helene's grandfather finished what he'd come to say, that all three of the children had arrived safely in England.

Otto Perger set aside his hat, which had been in his hands. Ruchele pulled herself into as small a person as she could manage lest he touch her. She did not think she could bear any tenderness.

Herr Perger said, "They're at a holiday camp in Harwich until they can be placed with families."

Still, she wept and wept—an indulgence, she knew. She ought to pull herself together, but there was no doing it. There was so little left to pull, in any event.

Herr Perger said, "It is so hard to have them gone, I know."

Ruchele gathered herself enough to say, "It is such a relief to have them safe. Thank you, Herr Perger."

He smiled a little. "Otto," he said. "Please."

She ought to respond with her own given name, but she couldn't make herself do so. It wasn't, as she knew he would imagine, that even here, even stripped of everything that had given her dignity, she felt herself above him. She did not. She saw that she once had, and she regretted that. She would have liked to apologize, but she had so little energy left, and still this one task to hand off.

She pulled from the top bureau drawer some forty thin little envelopes containing letters she'd written on borrowed paper, with stamps Frau Isternitz had bought for her with the last of the money Michael had provided. Stephan's and Walter's names were on the envelopes, which were otherwise unaddressed. The simple movement caused her pain, but she brushed away Otto's help. He must not think her weak. If he were to see anything of her—better that he didn't, but if he did—it must be her strength, her resolve.

She held out to him all but a last, unstamped envelope.

He sat staring at them, refusing to take them, as if he knew what they meant, what she would ask of him.

"Herr Perger," she started, "it's so hard for me to get out, and I have so little time left—"

"No, I won't take them," he insisted.

"It's unfair for me to ask, I know," she conceded. "I'm a Jew."

He could be jailed for the simple task of mailing a letter for her.

"It isn't that," he said. "Of course it isn't that, Frau Neuman. You mustn't—"

"I would give them to someone here," she said, "but we are . . . No one imagines we will stay. My husband is dead already, Herr Perger, and I will die in any event. You must see that I am dying: I'm left a whole room here to myself."

She gathered every bit of strength she had to produce a weak smile. She hoped it was a smile. It had been so long since she'd smiled.

"Please do me this kindness?" she begged. "If not for me, then for my sons?" So thankful for his fondness for Stephan. "One letter to be mailed each week, so they will continue to know I'm safe."

"You might—"

"So they can attend to starting their own lives in England and caring for each other, without worry for me." Words that came in a whisper, in pain both physical and not. "The last letter is written in a different hand, to tell them I am gone," she managed. "They will expect it, Stephan will, and I don't want them to hurt for not having heard from me."

He touched fingers uncertainly to his goatee. "But . . . But how will I know when to send it?"

Ruchele watched him, saying nothing. He was an old man, his eyes behind the round, heavy glasses beginning to go rheumy. If she were made to put it into words, he would balk. Anyone would balk. Even an old man who might understand.

"Frau Neuman, you . . ." He set his hands on her hands, on the letters. "You mustn't do—"

"Herr Perger, what I must do in life is ensure that my sons will grow up to be fine young men." The firmness of her voice startled her as surely as, she could see, it startled him. She said more gently, "I cannot thank you enough for your role in allowing me that. Now you must leave me to rest with the good news that my sons are safe."

She tucked the letters into his hands.

"They aren't addressed," he said.

"I don't know where they will be, but perhaps you will write Žofie that you are addressing and mailing them for me because it's so hard for me to write? Žofie, I think, will always know where Stephan is."

The tears pooling again. How could this strange little girl fill the hope she had for Stephan and, with him, Walter?

"I'll come back tomorrow," Otto Perger said. "I'll bring you food. You must eat, Frau Neuman."

"Please, don't trouble yourself further for my sake," she said, "except to mail the letters over time."

"But you must keep your strength. Your sons need you to be strong."

"I will receive all the care I will need from my neighbors, and you would only jeopardize yourself."

He searched her face. He knew without knowing—she could see it in his eyes behind the lenses, she could feel it in the slight additional pressure of his grip on the letters. He wanted to know, and he didn't.

She kept her gaze steady. If she kept her gaze, kept her strength for this last moment, he would be reluctant to return, to intrude.

"In a few days, then," he said.

"Please," she said, "the letters are all I need from you."

"When I receive news from Žofie-Helene. Surely you will want to know when I hear from her. And I'll want to know what you hear from Stephan and dear little Walter."

She nodded, fearing he might not leave if she objected, and now that the letters were in his hands, she needed him to leave. What would she do if he changed his mind? What would she do if she changed her own mind?—a thought that came with this talk of letters from her sons.

He stood reluctantly, turning back at the meek little door. She closed her eyes, as if unable to stave off sleep.

When the door shut quietly behind him, she drew from the remaining envelope a photograph of Stephan and Walter together. She kissed each face, once, and then again.

"You are such good boys," she whispered. "You are such good boys, and you have brought me so much love."

She tucked the photo into her clothes, next to her bosom, then removed the tissue inside the envelope, and unwrapped the last of Herman's razor blades.

Part III

THE

TIME AFTER

RABBIT NUMBER 522

Stephan sat at the edge of Walter's bunk. "Come on, Wall, time to move," he said gently. "The other boys are long gone." He pulled the covers back. "It's a new day, a new year!"

Walter yanked the blanket back over his head.

"We've already missed breakfast," Stephan said. The first breakfast of 1939. In just weeks, Stephan would turn eighteen. And then what? If he and Walter weren't placed with a family before he turned eighteen, would they place him?

"Peter isn't hungry," Walter said. "Peter says it's too cold to eat."

Smart rabbit, Stephan thought.

He said, "I have a new letter from Mutti."

The camp post office at one end of the main room in the big building was closed on Sundays, but Stephan had saved the letter that arrived the day before, wanting to have it for after the prospective parents left today. It was exhausting, a whole day of sitting and politely chatting with strangers who held your future in their hands, or tossed it away. So far, his and Walter's futures had been tossed. But this was only their third Sunday, and last week almost no prospective parents had visited, as it had been Christmas Day. Back home there would have been the big Christkindlmarkt with gingerbread and glühwein and decorations, people coming from all over the country to see the tree in the Rathaus-platz. At home, they would have decorated the tree with gold and silver ornaments and stars made of straw, and lit the tree and exchanged presents on Christmas Eve, and sang "Stille Nacht! Heilige Nacht!"— the tune the same but the words so different from the ones the English sang. Some boys from a college near the camp had taught them the

English version, a way for them to begin to learn the language. Stephan wondered who Mutti had sung with, or if Mutti had sung at all.

He sat Walter up and pulled a second sweater over the shirt and sweater he'd slept in, then his coat and scarf. His hat and gloves were already on; they'd both slept in their hats and gloves, Stephan's arms wrapped around Walter's in the same bed because they were warmer together. He had all the boys in the cabin sleep with their hats and gloves on, sharing beds for warmth.

When Walter was dressed, Stephan handed him his Peter Rabbit, then took Walter's number placard to loop over his brother's head. Walter ducked to avoid it. He'd become obstinate about the damned number. Not that Stephan blamed him. Stephan hated wearing his tag too, hated being reduced to something numerical and cold, no matter how special Žofie tried to make their numbers seem. But it was the rule: the children at Dovercourt had to wear their numbers, always.

"I know," he said gently. "I know, but . . ."

He took the placard and tripled the string, saying, "How about if Peter takes a turn wearing it today?"

Walter considered this idea, then nodded.

Stephan looped the string over Peter's head: rabbit number 522.

It was somewhat warmer in the main building thanks to the fireplaces, but still the children ate breakfast with their coats on, finishing kippers and porridge at long tables. A radio played music as two of the older boys took down the Christmas tree. One of the ladies in charge called in English to three children arguing over table tennis, "You'd best behave or we'll send you back to Germany."

The children turned to her, but if they understood what she was saying, they didn't show it. Walter asked what the woman had said, and Stephan explained.

Walter, confused, whispered, "If I'm a *bad* boy, I can go home to Mutti?"

Stephan's throat suddenly ached. "How would I survive here without you to keep me from freezing at night, Wall?"

"You could be a bad boy too," Walter said. He addressed his rabbit. "Peter, could you be a bad rabbit?"

"But that would make Mutti sad," Stephan said. "How could she come to England if we went home?"

"Can we read Mutti's letter now?" Walter begged.

Stephan pulled the envelope from his coat pocket with mittened fingers, their names written in Mutti's hand but the address, like the first two, in Herr Perger's. Mutti's first letter had come with a note from Žofie's grandfather telling them not to worry about their mother, that he was helping her—helping her at great risk to himself and Johanna, Stephan knew; if Herr Perger was jailed for helping a Jew, who would take care of Žofie's sister? Their mother was still in Nazi custody.

Stephan searched the room for Žofie, but she wasn't here yet, although the chalkboard that the staff used to post the list of the children chosen to go to homes each week was covered with equations that hadn't been there when Stephan left the night before.

"We can read Mutti's letter now if we read quickly," he said to his brother. "But no crying, okay? Maybe the family to take us will come today, in just a few minutes."

Walter said, "If they pick us, we get to move to a house with heat for Peter and me and a library for you."

Stephan handed him the letter. "We hope about the library, but heat certainly," he said. "Now, you read this time."

"Peter wants to read," Walter said.

"All right, Peter, then."

Walter, in his Peter Rabbit voice, read, "'Dear dear sons, We miss you in Vienna, but it comforts me to know you are together in England, and will always take care of each other.'" It was the way Mutti's first two letters had begun, letters they read and reread together so that Walter now had them memorized. Walter was becoming quite a good reader; they had read so much together in the last few weeks, with so little else to do. As most of the books at the camp were in English, though, Walter was becoming a better reader in English than in his own language, a fact Stephan only realized as Walter looked to him for help. Of course, the books they read were in print while Mutti wrote in script, handwriting difficult even for Stephan to decipher. He too sometimes had to fall back on memory.

Stephan wiped Walter's tears with a handkerchief—a former train diaper—saying gently, "Come on, Wall. Tears only at night."

Žofie and the baby joined them, the baby wrapped in blankets some of the ladies had brought for her. Stephan removed Žofie's glasses, fogged from the change from the cold outside to the slightly warmer inside air. He cleaned them with his mittened fingers and returned them to her face.

"Who knew it could get colder?" he said.

"It continues to get colder after the solstice even though the days are getting longer now because the summer heat stored in the land and sea continues to dissipate," Žofie said.

Walter said, "Stephan and I slept together in all our clothes and still I was cold! Peter was freezing. He only has one little jacket. But maybe a family will pick us today."

Žofie said, "I bet they will, Walter. This feels like your week to me."

At the chalkboard, one of the ladies took up the eraser and cleaned off the equations. Stephan took Walter's hand, and the four of them joined the children gathering around her, a girl exclaiming, "Me! Me! Me! I'm going to a family!" as the chalk screeched on the board. When the list was done, the line of children at the door—who would be taken back to their cabins to pack their things—consisted only of girls and toddler boys. The rest began to settle at the tables. The prospective parents were about to arrive.

"Okay, Wall-man," Stephan said, "let's hear it."

"Good afternoon. It's very nice for you to visit us," Walter said, his English clearer than it had been the prior Sunday. Practice did make better, if not perfect.

"Perfect," Stephan said to build his brother's confidence. "Now, where do you want to sit this week?"

"I want to sit with Žofie and Johanna," Walter said. "All the parents come to see Johanna."

So as always they sat beside Žofie and the baby, in the chairs that had been turned away from the tables, the last of the breakfast dishes now cleared in preparation for another long, sad Sunday of what Stephan had begun to think of as "the Inquisition." Still, he watched hopefully as the doors opened and the prospective parents came in.

NINETEEN CANDLES

Stephan woke with a start, disoriented by the dreary little cabin and his brother tucked up against him in the bunk. Today was his eighteenth birthday. If he were still in Vienna, he would no longer be allowed in the Kindertransport program. He was already in England, but he hadn't yet been placed with a family. Would they send him back?

He closed his eyes and imagined waking up in his own warm bed, in the palais on the Ringstrasse that he'd never considered might belong to anyone but his family, even after the Nazis had taken it. He imagined descending the marble stairway under the crystal chandeliers, touching each sculpture at each turn all the way down to the stone woman at the bottom, the one with breasts like Žofie's. He imagined passing the paintings in the entry hall—the birch trunks with their funny perspective; the Klimt of Malcesine on Lake Garda, where they sometimes spent summer holidays; the Kokoschka of Aunt Lisl. He imagined entering the music room, Bach's Cello Suite no. 1 playing—his favorite. He imagined a cake made with his father's finest chocolate and cooked by Mutti even last year, when she'd had to take to her bed the entire day from the exhaustion of making a simple cake. His father would light his birthday candles as he had every birthday of Stephan's life, until this one. Nineteen candles, it would have been, one for each year and one for luck. And Stephan would have watched out the window for Žofie, with a new play in hand for her to read. He ought to write another play. He ought to write one in English, his new language. But he wasn't sure he could bear to write about this place.

He wouldn't say anything to anyone about it being his birthday. Not to Walter. Not even to Žofie-Helene.

He dressed in the freezing room, and woke all the boys and helped them dress, and hurried everyone across the cold yard to the main building. He set the boys loose to play, Walter going off with them, he was glad to see. He watched his brother for a moment before looking around for Žofie, who stood at the end of a long post office line.

He joined her and they waited patiently, amusing the baby. When their turn came, Stephan was handed a letter and a package, which he barely had time to be surprised about before Žofie said, "Look, Stephan!" and thrust an envelope at him—one addressed not in her grandfather's back-slanting hand like his own envelope was, but in a gracefully looped script.

She handed the baby to Stephan and tore open the envelope.

Stephan set his letter and package on one of the long tables lest he drop the baby. His letter was as always addressed in Mutti's handwriting to both Walter and him, with the address in Herr Perger's. He would save it until Walter was done playing; he was glad for his brother to be making friends. But the package was addressed to him alone, not also to Walter, and in a tidier hand than Mutti's or Herr Perger's. With no postmark?

"It's from Mama!" Žofie-Helene exclaimed. "They're in Czechoslovakia! Mama was released last week and they went immediately. They're out of Hitler's reach."

She began to cry, then, and Stephan, with the baby in one arm, awkwardly put his other arm around her, hugging her and the baby together. "Hey, don't cry," he said. "They're safe."

Žofie only sobbed more violently. "They're all together," she said, "and now they won't ever come to England, not even Johanna."

Stephan took the letter with his free hand and scanned it. "Your mother says they'll apply for English visas from Czechoslovakia, Žofe. It won't take long; it's much faster for non-Jews. I bet they'll be here by spring."

STEPHAN DIDN'T THINK again about his own mail until Žofie had stopped crying and was sitting down for porridge and milk poured from the big white jugs. As he eased the package open, Žofie grinned.

"It's your birthday!"

"Shhh," he said, and she looked suddenly alarmed. Eighteen.

He extracted from the brown paper outer wrapping a book, carefully gift-wrapped and ribboned. He peeled back the paper to reveal a brand-new volume: Stefan Zweig's *Kaleidoscope*—the book that had been his father's, that his father had given to him and he had given to Žofie, that Žofie had brought back to him during those awful days when he was living in the Vienna underground.

"What a beautiful book," Žofie said.

Stephan opened the cover and turned the pages. "It's in English."

Žofie said, "It's signed, Stephan. Look. It's inscribed by Stefan Zweig. 'From one writer to another, with birthday wishes from a woman who admires you very much.'"

"'From one writer to another, with birthday wishes from a woman who admires you very much,'" Stephan repeated.

"It's from your mother?"

Stephan eyed her skeptically. Was she being coy? His mother would have identified herself in the inscription. His mother would have written "love" rather than "admire."

He combed through the cast-off wrapping, thinking if it really wasn't from Žofie, whoever sent it must have included a note. But there was nothing more to indicate where it had come from. No card. Not even a name or a return address on the package.

"It didn't come in the post," he said. "No postmark." Which meant it had to be from Žofie.

"It was hand delivered?" Žofie said.

"Žofie," he said, "I hate to tell you, but no one here knows it's my birthday today except you. Even Walter doesn't remember, or realize."

The expression on her face: the sudden shame. She didn't have anything for him. Of course she didn't have anything for him. None of them had anything.

"I bet it's from your mother," she said.

But who besides Žofie even knew that this was the very book he'd brought with him, that his copy had been wrapped in wet diapers, then vomited on by his brother? Who besides Žofie might imagine he'd kept the ruined volume? Ruined. Unable ever to be read again.

"You must be right," he said, unconvinced. "And the letter is definitely from Mutti!" *It* was postmarked Czechoslovakia. Herr Perger must have had it to mail for Mutti when Žofie's mother was released and they fled Austria. He supposed he should count himself lucky that Herr Perger had remembered to mail it at all. He hoped his mother would be able to find someone else to mail her letters. They were what kept Walter going, washing his face every Sunday morning and putting on his best clothes, taking off his coat to sit in the big, cold room to be picked over again. He supposed he ought to wait to open the letter with Walter, but Walter was playing happily, and it was his own birthday, after all.

He opened the envelope, extracted the thin paper inside, and read: *Birthday greeting from Vienna.*

Mutti was sorry she couldn't send him a gift to mark the occasion, but he was a man now, he was eighteen, and she wanted him to know how very proud of him she was.

THE UNCHOSEN

Žofie-Helene sat yet again at a long table with baby Johanna, watching Stephan. Grandpapa would have said he needed a haircut, but then all the boys still at the Warner's Holiday Camp now needed haircuts. Žofie liked this more casual Stephan, though. He looked spiffy, if cold too, without his coat and gloves.

He took Walter's coat off and straightened his shirt collar and blazer. "One more time, Wall-man," he said.

Walter said, "Peter doesn't like the way the grown-ups look at him."

"I know," Stephan said. "I'm beginning to feel like a rotten apple in the market too. But it hasn't been that long. One more time, c'mon."

"Good afternoon. It's very nice for you to visit us," Walter said without enthusiasm.

Žofie snuggled into the baby's neck, thinking of the real Jojo at Grandmère Betta's now, with Mama and Grandpapa. Maybe someday Stephan would make a play about this, one with a character like this pleasant-looking woman already approaching Walter. He was such a cute little boy. He would already be with a nice family if Stephan would only let him go, but each time she tried to raise it with Stephan, he only said he had promised his mother, and anyway, she was one to talk. But surely now that he was eighteen—too old for a family even if he was pretending not to be—he would let his brother go.

The woman said to Walter, "What's your name, little boy?"

Stephan answered, as he always did, "He's Walter Neuman. I'm his brother, Stephan."

Žofie sighed.

Walter said, "Good afternoon. It's very nice for you to visit us. This is Peter Rabbit. He comes with us too."

The woman said, "I see. You boys want to stay together?"

This was what the parents always said when they realized they would have to take Stephan with Walter.

Žofie said, "Stephan is a very talented playwright."

"A baby!" the woman exclaimed. "I thought there weren't any babies!" She dangled her keys in front of Johanna, and the baby reached for them, cooing.

Žofie let her take Johanna. She always let people she liked hold the baby. It was hard for them to give the baby back.

"Oh yes, I do believe I have just the home for you," the woman said to Johanna.

Žofie asked in her best English, "Where do you live?"

The woman, taken aback, repeated, "Where do I live?" She laughed warmly, the kind of elliptical laugh Žofie associated with the best kind of person. "Well, we have a place on The Bishops Avenue in Hampstead, don't we, dear?" she said. "And Melford Hall in the country."

Žofie said, "That sounds very nice."

"It is, yes. It is indeed."

Žofie said, "Is it near Cambridge?"

"Melford Hall? It is actually. Yes."

"I could be the baby's nanny," Žofie said. "I took care of Johanna while I was working with Professor Gödel. At the University of Vienna. I helped him with a generalized continuum hypothesis."

"Oh! I . . . But . . . Well, I don't know how Nanny Bitt would like that. She's been with us since my Andrew was born, and he's about your age now, I'd venture. Are you . . . the baby's . . . sister?"

Žofie-Helene watched her, trying to decide how best to respond. Something different was needed, she knew that, but she didn't know what.

Johanna reached for her then, saying, "Mama!"

The woman, startled, handed Johanna back to Žofie-Helene and hurried off.

Žofie called after her, "Johanna and Žofie-Helene Perger."

She turned to Stephan, who was staring at Johanna.

"I didn't know the baby could talk," he said.

Žofie said, "I didn't either!"

She nuzzled in the baby's warm little neck, saying, "You're a smart Johanna, you are."

THE PRAGUE GAZETTE

LIMITED REFUGEE BILL FOR CHILDREN PROPOSED IN U.S. CONGRESS

Bill urgently opposed by organizations concerned for needy Americans

BY KÄTHE PERGER

PRAGUE, CZECHOSLOVAKIA, February 15, 1939 — A bipartisan bill has been introduced into America's Senate by Robert F. Wagner of New York and into its House of Representatives by Edith Nourse Rogers of Massachusetts, calling for the admission over a period of two years of 20,000 German refugee children under the age of 14. Numerous charities are working in earnest to obtain support for the bill, against fierce opposition born of the fear that support for foreign-born children will come at the expense of needy Americans.

Loosening of immigration restrictions against Reich citizens is urgently needed in light of the vile treatment of those of Jewish descent in Germany, Austria, and the Sudetenland, which was ceded to Germany under the Munich Pact executed last September in exchange for peace. Despite the pact, Germany has recently renewed threats to destroy our city unless Czech borders are opened to its troops . . .

ANOTHER LETTER

Stephan curled up, his arms wrapped around Walter—too early for bed, but it was dark already and it was cold and, anyway, what did it matter what they did? He tried not to think about the letter, the sixth since his birthday, one letter continuing to arrive each week. His name and Walter's in Mutti's hand, and the letter inside beginning as it always did, saying how much Mutti missed them, but she wanted them to know she was fine. The rest of the letter reporting the doings of her neighbors in her little apartment in Leopoldstadt, in Vienna. But the envelope again was addressed in Herr Perger's hand, again postmarked Czechoslovakia, with Czech stamps pasted over the Austrian ones.

ON THE BEACH

Stephan, Walter, Žofie, and the baby sat on a blanket on the sand, Žofie working through a proof in the notebook in her lap, Stephan writing in his journal. Winter had broken, the sand now more golden and the ocean bluer with the bright sky. If it wasn't exactly warm, still it was pleasant enough to sit outside in their coats, with the sea lapping up toward them, just out of reach.

Walter threw his storybook onto the blanket, complaining, "I can't read this at all!"

Stephan closed his eyes, seeing still the sunshine through the thin skin of his eyelids, feeling the guilt of it all: of ignoring his brother for days as he wrote on the typewriter Mark Stevens, one of the students who taught the children English and a fellow Zweig fan, had brought him; of wanting last Sunday to hand Walter over to some parent, any parent; of the disappointment Mutti would feel in him.

He put his arm around his brother and opened the book. "Can Peter help us read it?" he asked. "He's very good at reading in English."

"He's better even than you," Walter said, cuddling up into Stephan's side, needing love. Of course he needed love. Of course Stephan couldn't turn him over to some stranger. Only sometimes Stephan imagined what he might do himself, unburdened of the care of his brother. Sometimes he imagined leaving this camp and getting a job somewhere, any job, where he could begin a life for himself, make money to buy books and paper of his own, have proper time to write.

Stephan said to Walter, "Remember all the books in Papa's library? I bet Peter could read them all now."

Hearing Mutti's voice: *Walter won't remember us. He's too young. He won't remember any of us, Stephan, except through you.*

Johanna took off crawling over the blanket, toward the sand, and Žofie tossed her notebook aside to scoop the baby up, saying, "Oh no you don't!"

"Mama," the baby replied.

"I'm not Mama, silly," Žofie said warmly. "Mama is for whatever lady takes us home."

Stephan, watching them, fingered the script in his satchel—the satchel also from Mark. "I wrote a new play," he said, gathering his nerve and pulling it out, handing it to her. "I thought you might read it and tell me what you think."

There, it was done. It was said. It had to be.

As she took the pages, Stephan scooped up Walter and stood, setting his brother to stand on the sand beside him.

"Race you!" he said, the way his father used to challenge Stephan himself on summer vacations in Italy.

Together they raced to the waterfront, Stephan resisting the urge to look back to Žofie-Helene until they were well down the beach, Walter chasing after a bird in the surprising sunshine. Žofie sat with the baby in her lap, her head bent over his pages, her hair falling toward the words he'd written just for her:

THE LIAR'S PARADOX
by Stephan Neuman
ACT I, SCENE I.

In the main room at the Warner's Holiday Camp, children sit more patiently than children should be expected to sit. Prospective parents browse the tables as if searching for a chop for dinner, an unbruised pear, an eggplant to set in a bowl on the table, just for show. Only older children are left, the toddlers all claimed in the weeks before.

Tall, elegant Lady Montague approaches a beautiful teenage girl, Hannah Berger, who holds a baby.

Lady Montague: Isn't this a dear baby. You aren't the child's mother, are you? I couldn't take a baby from its mother . . .

JUST A BABY ON A TRAIN

Stephan picked up Walter's blazer and Peter Rabbit from the ground, and called Walter out of a soccer game outside the main building.

"You weren't supposed to get dirty," he said.

"Adam said I could be goalie."

Stephan tucked in Walter's shirt and helped him put on his blazer, the sleeves already too short, but it was the best clothing Walter had. He handed Walter the Peter Rabbit. "All right," he said. "One more time, Wall-man. C'mon."

Walter said, "Good afternoon. It's very nice for you to visit us."

Inside the main building, Žofie was already seated at one of the long tables, with the baby on her lap and a notebook open. The baby was bathed and wearing a clean dress someone had donated to the camp. Žofie's hair was released from its usual braids and combed, long and wavy.

"Let's sit at a new table today, Wall," Stephan said.

Walter studied him for a long moment, as if he might be able to read his traitorous thoughts.

"Peter wants to sit with Johanna," Walter said, and he walked off to join Žofie and the baby, climbing up into the seat next to them.

"This is a proof I'm working on, Johanna," Žofie was saying to the baby as Stephan joined them. "See, the problem is—"

She looked up at Stephan.

Stephan reached across Walter to take her glasses from her face. "She's a baby," he said as he cleaned her smudged lenses on his shirt-tail. "She can't say three words."

"Papa used to say mathematics is like any language," she said. "The earlier you learn it, the more naturally it comes."

She eyed her equation through clear lenses, saying to the baby, "See, the problem is—we'll call it 'Stephan's Paradox'—is the set of all friends who have been inexcusably unkind to each other and refuse to apologize still friends? If they apologize, then they aren't quite so inexcusably unkind. If they don't, then they aren't friends."

Stephan said, "I'm sorry, Žofe, but I don't think friends help each other by letting the things that are holding us back from finding homes keep happening. It had to be said."

She slid the pages of Stephan's playscript across the table to him, with her edits:

THE LIAR'S PARADOX

by Stephan Neuman

ACT I, SCENE I.

In the main room at the Warner's Holiday Camp, children sit more patiently than children should be expected to sit. Prospective parents browse the tables as if searching for a chop for dinner, an unbruised pear, an eggplant to set in a bowl on the table, just for show. Only older children are left, the toddlers all claimed in the weeks before.

Tall, elegant Lady Montague approaches a beautiful teenaged ~~girl, Hannah Berger~~ *boy, Hans Nieberg*, who holds ~~a baby~~ *his younger brother.*

Lady Montague: Isn't this a dear ~~baby~~ *little boy*. You aren't the child's ~~mother~~ *brother*, are you? I couldn't take a ~~baby~~ *little boy* from ~~its mother~~ *his brother* . . .

Stephan sat, staring at the words.

"I'm sorry," Žofie-Helene said quietly, "but it had to be said."

"What had to be said?" Walter demanded.

Stephan folded the pages of the playscript and stuffed them in his satchel. He handed Walter a book to read, and opened his own journal. Sundays passed more quickly since they'd decided to do something rather than just sit there waiting for the parents to pass them over in favor of the newer arrivals.

"What had to be said?" Walter repeated.

"That even a damned stuffed rabbit could write a better play than I can. Now just read quietly, will you?"

Walter pulled his rabbit to him, of course he did.

"I'm sorry," Stephan said. "I'm sorry, Walter. I'm sorry, Peter." He patted the rabbit gently on the head. How low had he gone, having to apologize to a stuffed rabbit?

"I didn't mean to disparage your writing ability, little rabbit," he said.

Walter looked up at him from under his long eyelashes, which were moist now. Moist, but not wet. It left Stephan wanting to cry himself, not that his brother was tearing up, but that he wasn't crying, that in just a few weeks he had grown so much tougher.

"I'm sorry, Wall. I really didn't mean that the way it came out," he said. "I'm as cranky as old Rolf, aren't I?"

Walter said, "More cranky."

"More cranky," Stephan conceded.

Stephan said to Žofie, "Mark Stevens told me there's a rumor going around that the organizers are going to close the camp."

Žofie, still a bit disgruntled, said, "Your fellow Zweig fanatic?"

"Says the girl who has memorized every line of Sherlock Holmes."

Although that wasn't exactly fair either. Žofie didn't memorize the way most people did; she just read and remembered, recalled.

Žofie said, "They'll have to send us to families, then?"

"To hostels, I think. Or schools."

By the end of March, Mark had told him, which seemed pretty specific for a rumor. Today was March 12. Stephan didn't suppose he and Walter could go to the same school, so today might be their last chance to stay together.

"I'd like to go to school again, wouldn't you?" Žofie said. "Maybe I can go to Cambridge."

What Mark had said was that they would be sent to special Jewish schools, but Žofie wasn't Jewish, so he wasn't sure about her.

"I don't think they take girls with babies at Cambridge," he said.

It was mean. He knew it was mean and he oughtn't have said it, he saw that in the way Žofie quietly retraced a symbol in her notebook. But she refused to see what people thought; she refused to see that the prospective parents imagined the baby was hers and maybe his as well, that it was the baby who kept them all from finding families. So many parents wanted the baby until they got the idea that Johanna might be, as that woman the day they'd arrived at Dovercourt had suggested, the child of a "ruined" girl. Not just damaged but ruined, not capable of being restored. But Žofie's ruin was not what he now understood that woman had imagined. Žofie was ruined, as were he and Walter, by circumstance, parentage, the fact of a whole world sitting idle when someone, *someone*, needed to stand up.

Žofie set down her pencil and kissed the baby's head. "Her mama said my name," she whispered. "How will her mama find her if she isn't with me?"

Stephan stared down at his journal, the words blurring as he imagined Mutti searching for Walter and him. "I wonder if Peter is tired of reading so much," he managed to say, addressing the rabbit. "How about if I read to you both?"

Walter handed the book back and leaned toward him, impossibly forgiving.

"You are so like Mutti, Walter," Stephan said. He put his arm around his brother and pulled him close, and opened the book. "I'm sorry I was cranky. I really am."

The prospective parents began arriving, and an exquisite middle-aged lady and her husband approached them, the lady addressing the baby—"Well hello, little one, what's your name?"—as the husband eyed Žofie's notebook.

"May I look?" the man asked Žofie.

Stephan liked him already. Most of the prospective parents would just have assumed they could look at Žofie's work if they wanted to, or at Stephan's writing.

"It's just something I'm playing with," Žofie said, her English so much better now than when they'd first arrived.

The man, somewhat incredulously (*incredulous* was a word Stephan had just learned; he loved the sound of it), said, "You're 'just playing with' the axiom of choice?"

"Yes! You know it?" Žofie said. "It's quite controversial, of course, but I can't see another way for infinite collections, can you?"

The man said, "Well, it's not my area, precisely. How old did you say you are?"

"I didn't say," Žofie said. "I would, but you haven't asked. I'm almost seventeen."

The man said, "Look, darling. Look at this," indicating Žofie's notebook.

His wife hadn't heard him; she was across the room, speaking intently with a volunteer. She looked to her husband and smiled broadly, and hurried back.

Stephan watched Žofie watch the woman as all the while she snuggled Johanna. She would usually hand the baby to a prospective parent at this point. She knew how easy it was to fall in love with little Johanna once the child was in your arms, how much anyone who held her wanted to take her home, and they all knew that was the goal, to find parents who wanted to take you home. But Žofie only snuggled the child more closely. She wanted this family too much, this man who spoke her language when it came to mathematics even when it wasn't his area, precisely. Stephan wished he knew as much as the man did. He wished he could talk with Žofie about all those odd squiggles on the graph-paper pages. He wished he hadn't written the damned play, that he hadn't pushed her. What if this family took her? He wanted them to, of course he wanted them to. But he couldn't bear it.

"Lord Almighty," the woman said to her husband, her voice lowered as if for a secret. "The baby hasn't any papers." She turned to the baby, saying, "You haven't any papers, have you?" To her husband she continued, "It's complicated, I know, but . . . well, we could ask my brother Jeffrey to . . . to sort out a birth certificate, couldn't we? I mean if . . . in case no one ever comes to claim her? She must be an orphan. Who would send a baby from Germany with no one but strangers?"

Her husband looked to Žofie-Helene. The husband would take Žofie, Stephan was sure of it. The husband would rather take Žofie. Why didn't the man say so?

Žofie, clearly trying not to cry, handed the baby to the woman, like she did each week, except that she was usually dry-eyed.

The baby touched the woman's face and laughed.

"Oh, I could love you to death," the woman said.

The man said to Žofie, "Is she . . . Is she your sister?"

Žofie-Helene, unable to speak, only shook her head.

"What's her name, sweetheart?" the woman asked.

Žofie mumbled, "Johanna."

"Oh, I could love you to death, little Anna," the woman said. "I'm going to love you to death."

"The child's surname?" the man asked.

Žofie didn't answer. She peered at Stephan through her smudged lenses. If she tried to say a word, surely she would weep.

"We don't know," Stephan said to the man. "She was just a baby on the train. She was just there, in a basket, after the door had been closed and locked."

BROTHERS

Stephan waited in the main building with Walter, who held his suit-case and Peter Rabbit. Žofie waited with them, the three standing at the door, which was open to the spring afternoon, just as he and Walter had waited with her when the parents came to collect Johanna two days earlier, although that had been a cold, rainy day, and the door had been closed.

"You promised Mutti we would go to a family together," Walter said.

"I know, I did promise Mutti," Stephan agreed, and he again began the explanation. "The thing is, I'm eighteen now, so I have to work. I'm too old to go to a family, and I can't properly take care of you yet. But I'll think of you every day, and you'll be busy in your new school. I'll visit on weekends. The Smythes said I can visit every week-end. And after I've saved some money, I'll get an apartment and come get you, and we can live together again, okay?"

"And Mutti too?"

Stephan looked away, to the chalkboard, "Walter Neuman" now on the list of children going to homes. The radio was on, music with En-glish words and an English announcer, to help them all learn. He didn't know anything about Mutti, really. Not for certain. Her letters all came from Czechoslovakia, and told of life in Vienna; the only sense he could make of that was a sense he didn't want to know, a sense Mutti would not want him to tell Walter, certainly not today.

"I'll come visit you as soon as I can," he promised. "You and Peter."

"And Žofie will come too?" Walter turned his Peter Rabbit up to face Žofie. "You'll come visit us, Žofie?" he asked in his rabbit voice. "Mrs. Smythe says we can visit the Tower Bank Arms, from *Jemima Puddle-Duck*. Not the picture in the book. The real place."

It was a long way from Cambridge up to the English Lake District, where Walter's foster family lived. It was an even longer way from Chatham, where Stephan would be at the Royal School of Military Engineering—not as a student, but doing some job that needed doing. He hadn't yet been told what it was, but he would have two days off each week, just barely enough time to take the train to Windermere and back if he left right when his work was done.

Stephan said, "Žofie is going to be very busy." The foster father who had taken the baby had arranged for her to study mathematics at Cambridge, where he taught.

"I'll come visit you and Peter," Žofie promised, giving first Peter Rabbit and then Walter a fond kiss on the cheek. "And maybe Stephan will bring you both to visit me. Or we could even meet in London, at No. 221B Baker Street!"

The Smythes arrived then, in a black Standard Flying Nine four-door sedan, dirty from the drive. The car had barely stopped before Mr. Smythe was swinging his long legs out and hurrying around to open the door for Mrs. Smythe. As the two approached, Stephan wrapped Walter in a hug. He had not imagined how impossible this moment was going to be.

Mr. Smythe said, "Is Mr. Rabbit ready for a new adventure?"

Walter said, "You promise, Stephan?"

Stephan swallowed against the ache in his throat. What good was a promise? He'd promised Mutti so little, and disappointed her at every turn.

Walter pressed Peter's face to Stephan's cheek and made a kissing sound.

Stephan lifted Walter and held him tightly, one last time. "I promise," he said.

He set Walter down, then, and removed the tag, number 522, from around his little neck. "Now off you go, Wall. And remember, no looking back."

He turned his brother around then, to face the Smythes.

Mr. and Mrs. Smythe each took one of his little hands, Mr. Smythe with Peter Rabbit's hand in his too. They began chatting easily about the comfortable bedroom they had made for Walter and Peter to share at their new home in Ambleside, not far from a little house that was said to be the smallest in the world. Now that the weather was improving, they could take Peter out on the lake. They could take bicycles on the ferry down to the Mitchell Wyke Ferry Bay and bike over to Near Sawrey, to see the places in Mrs. Potter's picture books.

"Peter doesn't know how to bicycle," Walter said.

"We've put a basket on the front of your bicycle for him," Mr. Smythe assured him.

Walter said, "I'm going to have a bicycle?"

"We already have it for you," Mr. Smythe said. "You said your favorite color was blue, like Peter's coat, so we got you a blue one."

Walter said, "I don't know how to bicycle either."

Mr. Smythe scooped him up in his arms and, with a glance back at Stephan, stage-whispered so that Stephan would hear, "I'll teach you, so we can surprise Stephan when he comes to visit! Does Stephan know how to ride a bicycle?"

Walter said, "Stephan knows everything. He's even smarter than Žofie-Helene."

And then they were in the car, and Walter was looking out the window, and holding Peter Rabbit up to see. Stephan closed his fist around his brother's number as Žofie took his other hand in hers.

"You didn't tell him," Žofie said gently.

He didn't answer. He couldn't answer. He couldn't manage a word.

But he was keeping some sort of promise to Mutti, who hadn't wanted Walter to know, who hadn't wanted either of them to know. He was keeping some sort of promise to his mother as he watched the car pass under the Warner's Holiday Camp sign, and disappear down the road.

THE KOKOSCHKA PARADOX

There was no real line at the camp's little post office that morning, with most of the children now placed with families. Žofie didn't have to wait for the postmistress to hand over her day's haul: a letter from Mama and another, separate letter from Jojo. The postmistress asked Stephan to wait, though. As Žofie waited with him, she opened the letter from Jojo, not words but a drawing of all of them together inside a heart—Mama, Grandpapa, Grandmère Betta, and Žofie herself.

The postmistress returned with a letter for Stephan from his mother, which always made him sad. Žofie would have written Grandpapa to tell him to quit sending them, but she thought the only thing that might make Stephan sadder than getting his mother's letters from the grave would be when they stopped coming.

Today an intriguing package also arrived for him—a narrow box nearly as long as Žofie was tall.

"It's postmarked Shanghai," Žofie said. "It must be from your aunt Lisl. Well, go ahead, open it!"

Stephan set the package on the long, empty table where they all used to eat together and write in their notebooks—Žofie's maths and Stephan's plays—and wait while prospective parents passed them by. Stephan opened the package carefully. Inside, an envelope was loosely attached to a roll of something wrapped in butcher paper. He unsealed the envelope and read.

Žofie touched his arm gently as tears streamed down his cheeks. He handed the letter to her, and she read it herself:

Dearest Stephan,

I am so sorry to send you news of your mutti's passing. You must know how very much she loved you.

I hope you know how much I too love you—you and Walter both. I love you like I would love my own sons. I pray for the day this sorrow will be over and we can be together again.

I worry about you, Stephan. I know you are eighteen now, and are perhaps considered too old to be placed with a family? You are so talented. I know you will find work. But your mother would want you to continue your schooling. So I am sending the enclosed, which Michael arranged for me to have here in Shanghai. It is the only thing of real value I have to send you. Find the artist, Stephan. He lives in London now. He left Prague for London last year, but he is from Vienna. Tell him you are my nephew, tell him you are your mother's and your father's son, and he will help you find a reputable dealer.

I know you will not want to sell it, but I promise you I have the portrait of your mutti and I will arrange for you to have that someday. This one, Stephan, you *must* sell. I know you will want to keep it for my sake, but I will be glad for whomever owns it. It will mean that they will have allowed you to go to university, that they will have allowed you to thrive.

Much love,

Aunt Lisl

Žofie knew what the package contained even before Stephan gently lifted the canvas from the box and unrolled the portrait of his aunt Lisl with her scratched cheeks. Disturbing and elegant. Blush and wound.

THE PRAGUE GAZETTE

GERMAN TROOPS MARCH INTO CZECHOSLOVAKIA

Hitler proclaims from Prague Castle

BY KÄTHE PERGER

PRAGUE, CZECHOSLOVAKIA, March 16, 1939 — At 3:55 a.m. yesterday, following a meeting in Berlin with Adolf Hitler, President Hácha signed the fate of the Czech people over to the German Reich. Two hours later, the German army marched across our border amid a snowstorm, followed last night by a ten-vehicle convoy bringing Hitler himself to Prague.

Hitler was met not with cheering crowds, but rather deserted streets. He spent the night in Hradčany Castle, from which he spoke today . . .

AT THE PRAGUE TRAIN
STATION, SEPTEMBER 1, 1939

Käthe Perger watched Johanna's little face in the carriage window until she could no longer see her daughter. With the other parents, she watched the train disappear, then the empty space where it had been. She stood watching as the other parents trickled away, until she was nearly alone, before she went to the telephone booth.

She closed the glass door and dialed the long-distance operator and gave her the number for Žofie at Cambridge—a number Žofie had sent in her last letter. Žofie-Helene studying mathematics at Cambridge. Imagine that. She put in the number of coins the operator specified, and the telephone at the other end rang mercifully quickly.

A British girl answered, and when the operator asked for Žofie-Helene Perger, the girl said she would fetch her. Käthe listened to the clunk of the receiver being set down, and the faint sounds of Žofie's life in that other world.

Across the Prague station as Käthe waited for Žofie, two Gestapo with dogs on chains strode purposefully toward her.

"Please!" she called into the receiver. "Please! Tell Žofie her sister is coming! Tell Žofie Johanna is on a train from Prague!"

"Mama?" a voice said, Žofie's voice. It was all Käthe could do not to weep.

"Žofie-Helene," she said as calmly as she could manage.

"Johanna is coming to England?" Žofie-Helene said.

"Her transport just left," Käthe said quickly. "She has a sponsor, so she'll be sent directly on to London Liverpool Street station, where the family will collect her. She should arrive at eleven in the morning on September third. If you can get there, you can see her and meet her family. You can get there, can't you? Now I have to go, I have to let other parents use the telephone."

There were no other parents. There were only the Gestapo, one already opening the telephone booth door.

"I love you, Žofie-Helene," she said. "I will always love you. Remember that. Always remember that."

"You're getting a visa too, Mama?" Žofie asked. "And Grandpapa Otto?"

"I love you," Käthe said again, and she set the receiver back in place as gently as if it were the baby Žofie-Helene had once been, a baby set down in a cradle with a whole lovely life to come.

"Käthe Perger?" she heard, and she turned slowly from the telephone to the Gestapo standing just outside the booth. But her children were safe now. That was all that mattered. Žofie and Johanna were safe.

NEWNHAM COLLEGE, CAMBRIDGE

Žofie-Helene said into the receiver on a hallway telephone, "Yes, at Liverpool Street station the day after tomorrow—the third." She listened, then replied, "I know. Me too."

She hung up and returned to the crowded study room, some of the other girls glancing up as she retook her chair, a proof in her handwriting spread out on the table.

"Everything okay, Žofe?" her roommate, in the seat beside her, asked.

"My sister is coming," Žofie said. "They've found a sponsor for her, and Mama just put her on a train from Prague. She'll arrive in London the day after tomorrow, and I can see her at Liverpool Street station and meet her family before they take her to their home."

Her roommate threw her arms around her, saying, "That's wonderful, Žofie!"

"It is," Žofie said, and yet she didn't feel wonderful. Mama hadn't sounded wonderful about it. But of course it must have been hard for Mama to send Jojo off. She wished Mama and Grandpapa Otto were coming too, and Grandmère Betta. She wished her father were coming, but of course that was impossible.

"Would you like company?" her roommate asked. "I can go down on the train with you."

"I . . . Thank you, but a friend from Vienna who is studying literature at University College is going to meet me there."

Her friend raised an eyebrow. Žofie only smiled, and returned to her proof.

IT WAS AFTER dinner, and Žofie was back in the study room with just a few of the other girls when the matron entered and turned on a radio.

"Girls, I think you may want to set aside your studies to hear today's news," she said.

The voice was the BBC's Lionel Marson—Lionel, such a funny name, Žofie thought. She tried not to panic, not to imagine all the dreadful things she had been imagining ever since Mama hung up without even waiting for Žofie to say she loved her too.

". . . Germany has invaded Poland and has bombed many towns," Lionel Marson was saying. "General mobilization has been ordered in Britain and France. Parliament was summoned for six o'clock this evening. Orders completing the mobilization of the army, navy, and air force were signed by the King at a meeting of the Privy Council . . ."

"Is he saying England and France are at war with Germany?" Žofie asked her roommate.

"Not yet. But he's saying we're about to be at war."

LONDON LIVERPOOL STREET
STATION: SEPTEMBER 3, 1939

Žofie emerged from the train carriage amid steam and the sounds of metal on metal. In the chaos of Liverpool Street station, people everywhere, a clock tidily read 10:43. She was scanning the station for Stephan when he wrapped his arms around her from behind.

"Stephan! You're here!" She turned and threw her arms around his neck, and kissed him—surprising herself.

But he kissed her back, and kissed her again.

He removed her glasses, and he kissed her once again, a long kiss that drew disapproving looks. But Žofie didn't even notice the looks at first, and even when she did, when the kiss was over, she didn't mind. Žofie was used to disapproving looks. Even at Cambridge, people eyed her suspiciously whenever she spoke. And if she wasn't as dainty or well gloved as Dr. Watson's Mary Morstan, she understood now what had before been only story: how it felt when you could express feelings you'd kept buried inside yourself.

Stephan said, "I think if your train were any later, Žofe, I would have expired from the wait."

He cleaned her lenses on his shirttail, replaced them on her face, and smiled his crooked smile. "I've been watching for Johanna's train, but they haven't listed the track yet," he said. "It should be here any minute."

She slipped her hand in his as they crossed the platform into the station, his fingers still entwined with hers as they watched an overhead split-flap board roll to indicate an arrival from Harwich, Jojo's train. They waited at the end of the platform as passengers debarked: women and soldiers, and mothers with their children. Žofie felt happier even than when she'd learned she would be studying at Cambridge.

As the last passengers trickled out, Žofie said, "I must have the wrong train somehow?"

There was no Johanna. There were no unaccompanied children at all.

Stephan said lightly, "We all make mistakes. Even you, Žofie. We'll just call and get the right one."

Žofie said, "What if she's already arrived and left?"

"Then we'll figure out a way to get to her family's house."

He was so reassuring, Stephan.

"Even when you aren't with me in Cambridge," she said, "I take out your letters and reread them. It always makes me feel better."

"You know no one says stuff like that, Žofe," he said.

"Whyever not?" she asked.

He laughed his lovely, elliptical laugh. "I don't know," he said. "Anyway, I reread your letters too."

STEPHAN HESITATED. HE hated to let go of Žofie-Helene's infinity necklace, but he took it from his pocket and straightened the chain.

"My necklace!" Žofie exclaimed.

Stephan would have given up anything to see that joy in her face— even this cold little piece of gold he had fingered so many times for comfort since she'd given it to him at the train station in Vienna, since he'd retrieved it from the seam of the train seat at the first "Hurrah!"

"I meant to give it to you earlier," he said. "I ought to have given it to you already, but I . . . I wanted to keep a little piece of you for myself."

Žofie-Helene kissed him on the cheek and said, "You know, Stephan, no one says things like that."

"Whyever not?" he said.

She smiled as she said, "I have no idea."

Stephan took the necklace and looped it around her neck, and fastened the clasp so that it sat where it belonged, on her beautiful skin.

He said, "Most of us say what everyone else says, or we say nothing at all, so we won't look like fools."

"But you don't," Žofie said.

The Zweig line he'd read the night before came to him: *A thousand years will not recover something lost in a single hour.* He'd read half the night, unable to sleep for knowing he would see Žofie-Helene. He had tried to sort out what to say to her, how to tell her that he loved her. Then she had just kissed him, before he could say a word.

He hesitated, not wanting to break the spell of her affection, but needing to be truthful, to have her know everything there was to know.

"I do, though," he said quietly. "I saluted the German troops, Žofe, the day they entered Vienna."

He waited for her to be shocked, or appalled, or even simply disappointed. How could he have welcomed soldiers who came to murder his father? He hadn't known that was why they were coming, but he'd known they were not to be saluted, he'd known that no one in all of Austria ought to salute troops who invaded them. But Žofie only took his hand in hers again, and squeezed it.

He touched a finger to the pendant of her necklace, touching her skin with it. "Was he a mathematician, your father?" he asked.

"He was good at mathematics, but he was a writer, like you. He said he would be a better mathematician, but writers were more important now, because of Hitler."

They walked together to a red telephone booth. As they waited for a man to finish his call, a voice came over the station loudspeaker, Prime Minister Neville Chamberlain saying, "This morning, the British ambassador in Berlin handed the German government a final note stating that, unless we heard by eleven o'clock that they were prepared at once to withdraw their troops from Poland, a state of war would exist between us."

The entire station fell quiet. The man in the telephone booth emerged and stood with them. Stephan looked to the clock, a thousand stones in his stomach. Eleven o'clock was come and gone.

"I have to tell you now," Chamberlain continued, "that no such undertaking has been received, and that consequently this country is at war with Germany."

Stephan, still holding Žofie's hand, stepped into the telephone booth and dialed the operator. The telephone rang and rang as Chamberlain said, ". . . Now may God bless you all. May He defend the right. It is the evil things that we shall be fighting against—brute force, bad faith, injustice, oppression and persecution—and against them I am certain that right will prevail."

In the silence after the prime minister's words, a low murmur rose throughout the station. Only then did the ringing in the receiver stop and a voice, stifling a sob, say, "Operator. May I help you?"

"The Movement for the Care of Children from Germany, please," Stephan choked out. "I believe they're in Bloomsbury."

He pulled Žofie into the booth with him, closed the door, and put his free arm around her. He tilted the receiver so she too could hear.

"Yes, hello. I'm calling about the train bringing the children from Prague to London," he said.

PARIS: MAY 10, 1940

Truus sat on the balcony at Mies Boissevain-van Lennep's Paris flat, a map between them. The sounds of a radio trickled out, but the two didn't pay it much attention. They were absorbed in a discussion of where Germany's aggression might lead the world.

"But the Germans, with their wireless communication and their mobility, they can coordinate," Mies said. "They see a weakness, they can share the information and—"

They stopped talking as they registered what was being said on the radio: ". . . In view of the outrageous German attack on the Netherlands, an attack initiated without warning, it is the judgment of the Dutch government that presently a state of war has come to exist between the Kingdom and Germany."

Truus set down her cup and stood.

"It won't be safe to travel back, Truus," Mies said. "Joop will get out. Joop is probably—"

Truus said, "But, Mies, there are so many children still in the Netherlands."

IJMUIDEN, THE NETHERLANDS: MAY 14, 1940

The bus full of children came to a stop beside the *Bodegraven*. Truus turned back to see the second bus, Joop's bus, pulling to a stop behind them at the docks. Already, she was lifting little Elizabeth from the lap of her older sister, saying, "Hurry, children. Quickly."

The children spilled from the buses, hurried by the volunteers— seventy-four children with no identity cards to get them into Britain, but Truus would let the British worry about that.

"Look, Elizabeth," she said. "See that boat?"

The little girl said, "It's awfully dirty."

Truus removed the girl's smudged glasses and cleaned them, and replaced them on her adorable face. "Is it still?"

The girl laughed. "Yes! It's dirty!"

"Well, it is, isn't it?" Truus said to her, thinking that in this upside-down world, only the children could be trusted to tell the truth. "It tends to carry coal, but it will take you to England, where you can give my regards to their Princess Elizabeth."

"Like my name?" Elizabeth asked.

"And she has a sister Margaret, like your sister, except hers is younger and yours is older."

"Will the princesses be there to meet our ship, Tante Truus?" the girl's sister asked.

Truus gentled her hair. The girl looked up at her, worried eyes behind lenses as smudged as her little sister's had been, lenses that left Truus thinking of Žofie-Helene Perger. It was binary, the child had understood that. All of life was binary now. Right and wrong. Good and evil. Fight or surrender. War without the choice of neutrality this go-around.

"What if no one will take us?" little Elizabeth asked. "Can we stay with you, Tante Truus?"

"Oh, Elizabeth." Truus kissed the girl once, and again, and again, remembering Helen Bentwich at Harwich asking if Truus was sure she didn't want to take the baby back to Amsterdam with her. It hadn't ever been the baby Truus had wanted to keep.

"Even if the royal princesses aren't there to greet you," she told Elizabeth and her sister, "someone will arrange a very nice family to take care of you, a mother to give you love."

She quickly kissed these last seventy-four children goodbye, addressing each one by name as she sent them off to the ship.

She stood watching the last of them board, weeping now that the children couldn't see, trying not to worry that what she promised the two little sisters might not be true. The alternative, staying in the Netherlands, was now untenable. At The Hague the government were, even as Truus and Joop saw these last children off, giving the Dutch army the order to surrender to Germany.

Joop put an arm around her waist, and they watched the ship sail, the children waving from the deck rail, calling out, "We love you! We love you, Tante Truus!"

Part IV

AND THEN. . .

Some ten thousand children, three-quarters of whom were Jewish, found refuge in England thanks to the real-life heroes involved in the Kindertransport effort, including Geertruida Wijsmuller and her husband Joop of the Netherlands, Norman and Helen Bentwich of England, and Desider Friedmann of Austria, who died at Auschwitz in October of 1944. Rescued children grew up to be prominent artists, politicians, scientists, and even, like sixteen-year-old Walter Kohn, who was rescued from Vienna by Tante Truus, Nobel laureates.

The last ferry of seventy-four children left the Netherlands on May 14, 1940, the day the Dutch surrendered to Germany. Beginning that same spring, many of the older boys who had been brought to safety in England were interned by the British, sometimes with Nazi prisoners of war; many later joined the Allied forces.

Efforts to effect similar transports to the United States, through the Wagner-Rogers Bill introduced into Congress in February of 1939, met anti-immigrant and anti-Semitic opposition. A June 2, 1939, memo seeking President Roosevelt's support for the effort is marked in his handwriting "File no action. FDR."

The writer Stefan Zweig, among the most popular authors in the world in the 1930s and early 1940s, left exile in England for exile in the United States and, ultimately, exile in Petrópolis, in the mountains north of Rio de Janeiro. There, he completed a memoir, *The World of Yesterday,* and his final story, which he mailed to his publisher on February 22, 1942. The next day, despairing of the war, his exile, and the future of humanity, he and his second wife, holding hands, committed suicide.

Adolf Eichmann's system of stripping Vienna's Jews of assets and liberty became the model throughout the Reich. He oversaw large-scale deportations to death camps. After the war, he fled to Argentina, where he was captured in 1960, tried in Israel, and found guilty of war crimes. He was hanged in 1962.

The last Kindertransport from the German Reich—the ninth from Prague—boarded 250 children on September 1, 1939, the day Germany invaded Poland and World War II began. It never arrived in the Netherlands. The fate of those children is unknown.

Most of the children rescued in the Kindertransport effort never saw their parents again.

Geertruida Wijsmuller—Tante Truus—remained in the Netherlands during the whole of the Nazi occupation, smuggling Jewish children to Switzerland, Vichy France, and Spain. Arrested by the Gestapo a second time in 1942, she was, as she had been in Vienna, again released. An obituary described her as "Mother of 1001 children, who made rescuing Jewish children her life's work."

ACKNOWLEDGMENTS

My path to writing this novel began on an afternoon more than a decade ago, with my then-fifteen-year-old son arriving home from the Palo Alto Children's Theater; Michael Litfin, a director Nick worked with, had the idea that a small group of the theater kids he so loved might learn about the little-known Kindertransport effort and write a play about it. My son—generally so voluble—was troublingly silent when he came home from the first of four interviews he and his theater friends did with Ellen Fletcher, Helga Newman, Elizabeth Miller, and Margot Lobree. When Michael died only months later of stomach cancer, the head of the theater, Pat Briggs, made a deathbed promise to him to carry the story forward somehow. Pat, when she was near the end of her life, and with the children by then grown and scattered, allowed me to take it in hand in my own way. I held the silence of my son in my heart as I wrote this story, and beside it, the love of his directors for the children they nurtured.

This book was inspired by and is meant to honor Truus Wijsmuller-Meijer and the children she rescued, as well as the many people who made the Kindertransports possible. I have done my best to remain true in spirit to the facts of the Anschluss, Kristallnacht, and the shockingly rapid change in Vienna society in the few months between the two, including the role of the then-young and ambitious Adolf Eichmann, and the British and Truus's efforts to bring about the first Kindertransport from Austria. But as this is fiction rather than a history, I have taken smaller liberties in the interest of story. The pure historian will find for example that Helen Bentwich, while a real and important contributor to the Kindertransport effort, did not travel to Amsterdam with her husband, Norman, to appeal to Truus, and that it was Lola Hahn-Warburg rather than Joop who arranged the ferries from Hook of Holland to Harwich. I read and reread Truus's *Geen Tijd Voor Tranen*, yet much of the character of Truus presented in this novel is the product of my imagination drawn forward from that spare account of her life.

As Melissa Hacker of the Kindertransport Association suggested to me, "some details of the Kindertransport operation are still a bit unclear." Accounts vary even regarding the timing of the first Kindertransport from Vienna. Both the *Times of London* and the *New York Times* report in very short pieces that the first transport left Vienna on December 5, 1938—the same day on which Truus herself writes that she first met with Eichmann. Truus's own more detailed account states that she left for Vienna on December 2, met with Eichmann that Monday (which would have been December 5), then made arrangements for the children to leave Vienna on the Sabbath, arrive in Cologne at 3:30 on Sunday (December 11), and ferry overnight from Hook of Holland that same day. The United States Holocaust Memorial Museum puts the first Kindertransport from Vienna arriving in Harwich on December 12, 1938, which is consistent with Truus's account—and the timeline I ultimately determined to use.

Sources I turned to in addition to Truus's autobiography and the Children's Theater interviews included online materials and on-site information at the United States Holocaust Memorial Museum; interviews from the Tauber Holocaust Library at San Francisco's Jewish Family and Children's Services Holocaust Center; "Interview with Geertruida (Truus) Wijsmuller-Meijer, 1951, Netherlands Institute for War Documentation NIOD, Amsterdam"; *Into the Arms of Strangers* by Mark Harris and Jonathan and Deborah Oppenheimer; *My Broth-*

er's *Keeper* by Rod Gragg; *Never Look Back* by Judith Tydor Baumel-Schwartz; *Nightmare's Fairy Tale* by Gerd Korman; *Rescuing the Children* by Deborah Hodge; *Children's Exodus* by Vera K. Fast; *The Children of Willesden Lane* by Mona Golabek and Lee Cohen; *Ten Thousand Children* by Anne L. Fox and Eva Abraham-Podietz; "Touched by Kindertransport Journey" by Colin Dabrowski; "The Children of Tante Truus" by Miriam Keesing; and "The Kindertransport: History and Memory" by Jennifer A. Norton, her thesis for the master of arts in History at California State University at Sacramento. Also enormously helpful were Norman Bentwich's *The Found Refuge*; and *Men of Vision: Anglo-Jewry's Aid to Victims of the Nazi Regime 1933–1945* by Amy Zahl Gottlieb; as well as films including Ken Burns's *Defying the Nazis: The Sharps' War*; *The Children Who Cheated the Nazis*; *Nicky's Family*; and Melissa Hacker's film about her mother, *My Knees Were Jumping*.

Other sources included Stefan Zweig's *The World of Yesterday* as well as his fiction; the extraordinarily moving *The Hare with Amber Eyes* by Edmund de Waal; *The Lady in Gold* by Anne-Marie O'Connor; *The Burgtheater and Austrian Identity* by Robert Pyrah; *Becoming Eichmann* by David Cesarani; *If It's Not Impossible: The Life of Sir Nicholas Winton* by Barbara Winton; *Whitehall and the Jews, 1933–1948* by Louise London; *Eichmann Before Jerusalem* by Bettina Stangneth; *50 Children* by Steven Pressman; *Incompleteness: The Proof and Paradox of Kurt Gödel* by Rebecca Goldstein; and *Jewish Vienna: Heritage and Mission*, published by the Jewish Museum of Vienna.

I am indebted to the United States Holocaust Memorial Museum senior research historian Patricia Heberer-Rice, who answered my queries, and Sandra Kaiser, who facilitated that, as well as to the JFCS Holocaust Center's Yedida Kanfer, who helped me with research there. The Kindertransport Association, of which I am a quietly lurking member, has provided me much information and inspiration; thanks especially to Melissa Hacker. The Jewish Museum of Vienna and the "Between the Museums" app were helpful in grounding me in Vienna. And visiting the Vienna Kindertransport museum collection of suitcase contents is an experience I will never forget; my gratitude to Milli Segal for opening the collection to me, and for the quiet place to weep afterward.

More thanks than I can properly put into words to the editors who expressed early love for this novel, especially the HarperCollins trio of Lucia Macro, Laura Brown, and my amazing editor, Sara Nelson. Sara's thoughtful insights, careful attention, and boundless enthusiasm are a writer's dream. Thanks to everyone at Harper, including Jonathan Burnham, Doug Jones, Leah Wasielewski, Katie O'Callaghan, Katherine Beitner, Robin Bilardello, Andrea Guinn, Juliette Shapland, Bonni Leon-Berman, Carolyn Bodkin, and Mary Gaule.

I am, as ever, grateful for the amazing support I draw from friends and family. I am particularly grateful this time to my son Chris, for getting me the first pages I saw of Truus's autobiography (and to the Harvard Library for being one of a very few places in the United States to have a copy), and to Murielle Sark for getting me the rest of it and helping me translate passages Google Translate left in doubt. Also to Brian George for digging through the theater locker with me and cheering me on along the way; Nitza Wilon for the early enthusiasm for the story, and Elizabeth Kaiden for her thoughtful read of an early screenplay version; David Waite for help with the German, and for coming down from Berlin to greet me in Austria; Claire Wachtel, for so generously reading, and suggesting the opening author's note; Mihai Radulescu; Hannah Knowles; Bev Delidow; Tip Meckel; Kristin Hannah; Karen Joy Fowler; the many booksellers who do so much good for all of us, especially Margie Scott Tucker; and my enormously talented photographer friend, Adrienne Defendi.

Brenda Rickman Vantrease, for being Brenda, my best writer pal. Jenn DuChene and Darby Bayliss, without whose friendship I would be a much poorer me. The Four Brothers Waite and the sisters I have the good fortune to have collected by marriage. And Don and Anna Tyler Waite, who have always been there for me. (Mom, as always, thanks for reading.)

Marly Rusoff, for being, always, Marly, agent and friend, whose belief in my ability to write this one from the moment I first began to consider it allowed me to believe too. Thank you, Marly, for helping me in so many ways over these dozen years, and for giving this novel such a lovely introduction into the wider world.

And Mac for reading. And reading. And reading again. For convincing me to stay in Vienna. For your amazing spirit and humor on long walks through Vienna, Amsterdam, and London, and your quiet company in that berth on the night train from Vienna. For keeping me sane, more or less. For everything.

ABOUT THE AUTHOR

MEG WAITE CLAYTON is a *New York Times* bestselling author of seven novels, most recently *Beautiful Exiles*. Her prior novels include the Langum Prize–honored *The Race for Paris*; *The Language of Light*, a finalist for the Bellwether Prize for Socially Engaged Fiction (now the PEN/Bellwether); and *The Wednesday Sisters*, one of *Entertainment Weekly*'s 25 Essential Best Friend Novels of all time. A graduate of the University of Michigan and its law school, Meg has also written for the *San Francisco Chronicle*, the *Los Angeles Times*, the *New York Times*, the *Washington Post*, *Forbes*, and public radio, often on the subject of the particular challenges women face.